What others are saying about
AMONG THE ASHES

Among the Ashes is a novel a reader won't soon forget. It is a deeply moving and enthralling story whose characters will linger long in one's memory.

~ Zibby Oneal, Author of *The Language of Goldfish*

Cheryl Denton weaves characters and plotlines so that readers are immediately involved. *Among the Ashes* keeps the surprises coming.

~ Deborah G. Freitag, Communications Specialist

Among the Ashes is a compelling story full of rich characters, most of whom you either feel like you already know or would like to someday meet. A few of them make you glad you don't know them!

~ Carol Glenzer, High School Principal

From the moment you start reading, *Among the Ashes* captivates you and draws you in with memorable characters and surprising plot twists.

~ Rhonda Day, Women's Ministry Leader

Very few books live long in one's memory, but I won't soon forget the characters that I met in *Among the Ashes*. If I were looking for an excellent, well-crafted mystery to read more than once, I would certainly pick this one.

~ Margaret Moran Holter, Librarian

Out of her own experiences, Cheryl Denton is able to communicate how it feels to survive PTSD and to develop healthy coping mechanisms through her character, Kit Blume. Kit gives us a stellar picture of hope, showing us that survivors with PTSD can lead fulfilling lives, brimming over with great potential and happiness.

~ Gail Rizzo, Licensed Professional Clinical Counselor and Professor

Coming next from Cheryl Denton

WHEN HOPE WAS GONE

Darkfire Series Book Two

*Read a sneak preview and
reserve your future copy today
by visiting* **www.cheryldenton.com**

AMONG THE ASHES

Darkfire Series
Book One

Copyright © 2011 by Cheryl Denton.

Legacy 78 Press, Ltd.
P.O. Box 234
Fayetteville, OH 45118
www.legacy78press.com

All rights reserved. No part of this publication may be reproduced, stored in a retrieval system, or transmitted, in any form or by any means, electronic, mechanical, photocopying, recording, or otherwise, without the prior written permission of the author.

This is a work of fiction. Names, characters, places, and incidents are the products of the author's imagination or are used fictitiously. Any resemblance to actual events, locales, or persons, living or dead, is entirely coincidental.

Cheryl Denton can appear at your live event.
For more information or to book
an event, contact the author at:
www.cheryldenton.com

ISBN-13: 978-0-984674-70-1
Library of Congress Control Number: 2011917671

Cover design and typeset by Catalin Macarie
Author's photo by Spring Olmsted

Printed in the United States of America

AMONG THE ASHES

Darkfire Series
Book One

CHERYL DENTON

LEGACY 78 PRESS, LTD.

I can do all things through Christ who strengthens me.
Philippians 4:13

To my beloved husband, Joe Denton,
whose unconditional love, boundless energy,
and sense of humor brought me
back from despair to a life full of hope.

Acknowledgements

My heartfelt thanks to:

Zibby Oneal, whose encouragement and teaching inspired me to pursue a writing career; Harvey Whitney, whose great faith in God gave me the courage to write this story; Harry Moser, whose detective experiences helped me to understand cops and killers; Tim Pride, whose firefighting knowledge helped me to portray an arson scene; Lauren Olmsted, Maggie Holter, Deb Freitag, Carol Glenzer, Gail Rizzo, and Rhonda Day, whose reading and editing of the manuscript improved my story; Catalin and Valerie Macarie of Cat Creatives, whose imaginative designs and marketing expertise created the momentum this project deserved; and my friends from Mt. Carmel Christian Church, whose prayers gave me strength and peace along the way.

CHERYL DENTON

PROLOGUE
Twenty-Four Years Ago

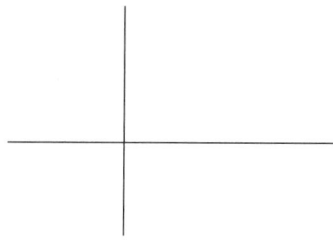

THE LITTLE GIRL TUMBLED OVERBOARD INTO THE WATER. With broad strokes, she kicked frantically downward. Above her, she heard the muffled pop of the gun again. With lungs burning, she opened her eyes and pulled her arms hard through the murky green water. She kicked towards what she thought was the nearby shore.

Again, the gun exploded overhead.

There was no air left in her lungs. She broke the water's surface and gasped.

Bang! Something sizzled past her head.

She ducked underwater and swam harder than ever. Her fingers grazed the sand beneath her, and she realized that she was nearing the shore. She swam more cautiously, hoping to remain hidden in the tall grasses that grew in the shallower water. Breaking the surface as quietly as she knew how, she drew a deep breath. With one last pull of her arms, she drifted until there was no more water to conceal her. Leaping to her feet, she charged up the bank towards the woods.

Something hissed past her ear, and she darted behind a tree. Standing rigid, she tried to control the heaving of her chest.

From behind her came a shrill laugh, followed by a threat: "You'd better keep on running!"

A second voice called out, "If you ever come back here, I'll kill you!"

Even greater fear seized the little girl, and she shot off through the woods. Her bare feet pounded over sharp rocks and broken hickory nuts, cutting into flesh. After a while, her legs grew so weary that all she wanted to do was sit down and rest. Her tongue stuck to the roof of her mouth, but she didn't dare stop to find water. No matter what it took, she would make sure that those two never found her.

The little girl glanced over her shoulder through the dim light of the dense forest time and again. Were they following her? Fear drove her onward as dusk gave way to dark. Carefully planting one foot ahead of the other, she repeated softly to herself, "Slow and sure…slow and sure…slow and sure…"

PART ONE
Cincinnati

1

KIT BLUME PEERED OUT THE KITCHEN WINDOW OF HER parents' east-side Cincinnati home. The early morning sun barely penetrated the heavy canopy of trees that hung over the murky water of the Little Miami River. In the distance, she could hear the bells pealing at the Catholic church. She thought that if her mother were there, she would insist that Kit go to mass.

With a yawn, she stretched and raised her arms over her head. She was glad for the opportunity to spend a Sunday outdoors, not in the dimly lit interior of the foreboding stone sanctuary where her mother spent so much time either praying or talking in hushed tones with the priest.

The espresso finished brewing, and Kit poured the thick, black liquid into a large mug, which she topped off with cream and sweetened with a teaspoon of sugar. She took a sip and sighed. There was nothing like sleeping in and waking up to a cup of Mom's Ethiopian coffee.

With her mug in hand, she hauled open the heavy glass door that led out onto the covered porch. Even though it was still early, Cincinnati's summer humidity enveloped her. Immediately, her tank top felt as if it were shrink-wrapping itself to her skin. She sat down on the old wooden swing and looked across the lawn.

For the past two weeks, she had been staying at her parents' house while they took a medical mission trip to Haiti. She had promised her mother that she would keep the weeds in check and cut the grass. So far, all she had managed to do was cut the grass.

When she had finished her coffee, she pushed up out of the swing. Grabbing a three-pronged hand rake from a bin on the porch, she made her way down the wide wooden steps and across the expansive lawn to the rose garden. She began scratching at the rich topsoil which her mother had created from composting vegetable peelings, eggshells, and coffee grounds. The earth felt warm in her fingers, and she thought about how much she loved the smell of the garden soil. It always reminded her of time spent in the yard with her mother.

Her thoughts turned to the first day of school. It was only a week and a half away, and she was worried about the stress. Sleeping in her old room, even without her parents at home, made her feel as if she were a little kid again on summer vacation. She didn't want to go back to her grown-up life of teaching and trying to prevent the flashbacks from intruding.

Kit firmly grasped the stem of a prickly nettle to avoid getting stuck with the annoying barbs when a voice from behind her asked, "So…how's it going?"

Kit gasped, dropped her hand rake, and whirled around.

Grant Osgood, her parents' next-door-neighbor and her former school mate, stood there in the freshly mown grass with his hands thrust into the pockets of his well-fitted jeans.

She grumbled, "You scared the snot out of me!"

"That's not hard to do," Grant said with a grin. The dimples in his cheeks appeared, and the cleft in his chin grew deeper when he smiled.

"Oh, shut up!" she said. She whirled away from him, crouched down, and wrenched on the nettle. The barbs pricked her skin and left her fingers smarting.

"So, what are you doing here?" Grant asked.

So much for feeling like a kid on summer vacation. There was nothing like the sight of Grant Osgood to wipe out any warm, fuzzy feelings she might have had about being at home again. He was the primary reason why she felt secure in knowing that she had her own house on the west side of Cincinnati. It was just far enough to keep him out of her hair, and yet close enough to stay connected to her parents. "I'm doing absolutely nothing," she snapped, tossing the nettle into the wheelbarrow that stood nearby.

Grant said, "Looks like you're working awfully hard for someone who's doing absolutely nothing."

She remembered her therapist telling her that when Grant annoyed her, she shouldn't allow herself to get upset. "I'm not working," she said, bending over and ripping open a heavy bag of mulch that she had hauled from the garage the day before. "I'm having fun."

Grant whistled. "Man, I don't know if I'll be able to keep a lid on things here. You're out of control already. I might even have to call the cops."

Kit felt her grip tightening on the bag and the muscles in her jaw tensing. He had had the nerve to send his friends—who also happened to be cops—over to her house on a number of occasions. The first time he pulled that stunt, her parents had actually believed the cop who told them she had been involved in a convenience store heist. When Grant's police force friend finally busted out laughing and admitted that Grant was pulling a practical joke on her, her parents had actually joined in the laughter.

After the sixth or seventh cop prank, her dad had said, 'Grant's got to get your attention one way or another. Haven't you noticed that he's sweet on you?'

Sweet on me? she had thought. Sweet was something delicious, like honey licked off a fingertip or the frosting from a cupcake. Grant Osgood was a sour dill pickle who delighted in playing sophomoric pranks on her. She glared at him and said, "You wouldn't dare do that to me again."

A smile played at the corner of his mouth. He said, "But it's so much fun to watch you get mad."

"Drop dead."

"Ouch."

For some reason, the mere sight of Grant Osgood had always annoyed her. The way he looked at her with that twinkle in his sky blue eyes made her angry. For whatever reason, he made her feel...abnormal. The last thing she wanted to do was spend the rest of the day trying to get rid of him. She decided it would be best to be blunt with him. She stood and said, "Look, I've got a lot to do here. So why don't you run back over to your house and leave me alone."

Grant shrugged. "Sure. It'll be fun watching you. I've already got my binoculars set up in my bedroom window."

Oh, he always said such infuriating things! She resisted the urge to slap him. Instead, she bent over and wrenched the bag of mulch off the ground, splitting it wide open and spewing the contents all over the grass. "Oh, for Pete's sake!" she muttered, thrusting the empty plastic bag down on the grass. She glanced back at Grant, who smiled smugly at her, then turned and ambled slowly away towards his house with his hands still in his pockets.

As she watched him walking away, Kit couldn't help admiring Grant's broad shoulders straining the seams of his faded green t-shirt and his well-sculpted backside wrapped so beautifully in his jeans. Even though he infuriated her at times, there was something about Grant Osgood that Kit found…well…unsettling.

With a shake of her head, Kit said under her breath, "Get a grip." He might be good-looking, but he was a pain. She decided to pull weeds on the other side of her house where Grant couldn't spy on her with his binoculars.

While Kit was refilling the hummingbird feeders outside the dining room window, her cell phone rang. She fished it out of her shorts pocket and glanced down at the caller ID: *Alice Blume*. She punched the SEND button and said, "Hi, Mom."

"Hello, honey. How are you?"

"Annoyed," she said.

"Grant bothering you again?"

"Yeah." She didn't want to keep thinking about pesky Grant Osgood, so she added with a forced smile, "I'm taking good care of your garden."

"I love my garden," her mother said with a sigh. "I can't wait to get home."

"How was your trip?"

"Tiring," her mother said, "But wonderful, as always. I'll tell you all about it when we get there."

A movement along the river bank caught Kit's eye. She stood on tiptoe to peer over the rose bushes and caught sight of Grant Osgood dragging his kayak down to the river. She noticed that he had changed into a swim suit, and when he bent over at the water's edge, she saw the pair of binoculars dangling against his bare chest. She couldn't stand the thought of Grant Osgood watching her with binoculars the rest of the day and into the evening.

She said to her mother, "Since you're so tired, why don't you stop at my house on the way home from the airport? I'll make dinner."

"That sounds so good," Mrs. Blume said. "We've been living on peanut butter and jelly for the past two weeks."

"I'll go to Country Fresh to pick up the stuff for a salad. I'll even make you that honey-mustard dressing that you like."

"Sounds good," her mother said.

Kit watched Grant Osgood paddling hard against the current. His efforts were getting him nowhere. What kind of a fool paddled upstream on the Little Miami River in a dinky little kayak? She hoped he drowned out there. She told her mother, "I'll get a movie, too."

"I don't want you to go to any bother," her mother said.

Kit said, "If I know you, the minute you set foot back in your own house, you'll find a hundred things that need to be done."

Her mother laughed. "You know me too well."

"Yep," Kit said with a smile. "Tonight's my treat. You can ease yourself back into reality and tell me all about your trip."

"Sounds great. See you at about eight." Her mother hung up.

Kit stood there in the yard, watching as Grant Osgood slid quickly downriver. "Good riddance," she muttered. "Now, maybe I can get something done around here without wondering what you're up to."

It was just before eight o'clock that evening when Kit drove back towards her west-side Cincinnati home with two LaRosa's pizzas, a movie, and the ingredients for her mother's favorite salad. After working most of the day in the yard, she felt tired, but satisfied. The lawn looked well-groomed, and she had freed the rose garden of weeds.

When she neared her street, she noticed that there was a City of Cincinnati police car blocking the way with its lights flashing. Kit frowned and rolled down her window. She called out to the policeman standing beside his car, "Excuse me, I need to get down this street."

"I'm sorry, ma'am," he said, "but the street's been closed."

"Why?"

"There's a gas leak."

"How long before I can get back to my house?"

The policeman said, "It's hard to say. Could be quite a while."

"Great," Kit muttered. She called her mother's cell phone and got the Verizon voice mail. She said into the phone, "Don't bother coming to my house. They've got the road closed because of a gas leak. I'll just meet you back at your place."

She was about to drive away when she had the idea that her parents might already be at her house. She dialed her own number and waited. In the distance, she heard a low rumble. Glancing up at the western sky tinged with shades of pink and orange, she thought it odd that it would be thundering on such a clear evening.

Her phone rang at her house, but the answering machine never picked up. She clicked off her cell phone and thought that she'd better check the machine later.

When she got back to her parents' eastside home nearly an hour later, she found it dark. "Oh, come on!" Kit said to the vacant driveway. "Where are you?"

She speed-dialed her mother's cell phone again, but there was still no answer, other than the voice mail. Kit decided that the best thing to do was to just sit tight and hope that her parents returned soon. She let herself into their house with her key, shoved the two pizza boxes into the oven, and tossed the greens for the salad.

Kit had nibbled most of the sausage off the supreme pizza and was completely engrossed in watching a movie when the doorbell rang. She glanced at the clock. 10:30? What had happened to the time? She pulled back the sheers and looked out the front window. Two Hamilton County sheriff's deputies were standing on the front porch in their grey pants and black shirts. She clenched her teeth, shook her head, and muttered, "Grant Osgood, you're a dead man."

At the front entry, she snapped on the outdoor light and yanked open the door. Of course, Grant Osgood had something to do with her parents' delay. He was up to his usual tricks. With a broad smile, she said, "So, what's Grant giving you guys tonight to come out and harass me? If I remember right, the last time, it was four tickets to see the Bengals."

The trim cops in their wide-brimmed black felt hats looked at each other, then back at Kit. The older of the two said, "Are you Kit Blume?"

"Yes," Kit said. She put one hand on her hip and waited for whatever stupid prank Grant had come up with this time.

The man cleared his throat, looked down at his shoes, then up at Kit. "Do you mind if we come inside?"

"Yes, I do," Kit said. "Now run along and tell Grant that I'm tired of his practical jokes." She began closing the door, and the older cop stuck his patent leather shoe out to stop it.

"Ma'am, we don't know who Grant is. The dispatcher sent us out here tonight."

Kit realized then that Grant's friends were all cops with the city, not the sheriff's department. Maybe these two really weren't in on one of his pranks. "I'm sorry," she said, stepping back and opening the door.

"Is there someplace where we could sit down?"

"Sure," Kit said, gesturing towards the living room.

The two men stepped inside, took off their black hats, and followed her.

She picked up the remote and turned off the TV. She sat down on the sofa, and the two men settled across from her in the wine-colored leather armchairs where her parents always relaxed at night to read the paper. She looked at the men's somber faces and wondered what on earth they wanted.

The older policeman said, "I'm sorry to have to tell you this, Miss Blume, but your house is on fire."

Kit felt her stomach lurch, and an image of her house in flames flashed through her mind. "What?" she gasped.

The younger cop said, "There was a gas leak, and the firemen are still working to put out the fire."

Kit stared at the two men. Suddenly, it occurred to her that, even though Grant's friends worked for the city, these two might be in on one of his pranks. "How did you know I was here?"

"We found you through the emergency contact information you left with the BMV."

The older policeman cleared his throat, and then looked her straight in the eye. "Have you been in contact with Norman and Alice Blume this evening?"

"No," she said, "They were supposed to meet me at my house for dinner. When I got to my neighborhood, my street was blocked off. I've been waiting here for them for hours."

The older cop asked, "Is there any chance your parents might have been at your house earlier?"

"I guess," Kit said. Her annoyance with Grant burned like the nettle stings on her fingers. She waited for the punch line, which she was certain was coming.

With a serious expression, the older cop said, "We ran a check on their plates when we evacuated your street. They're the only people who were still unaccounted for after your house exploded."

Kit tried to remember that this was a prank, but an image of her house exploding, with a mushroom cloud rising ominously skyward, took over her mind. She jumped up off the sofa, walked into the kitchen, and began pacing up and down on the cool ceramic tile. Her heart was pounding, and her hands began to shake. The impulse to scream became so urgent that she clamped her hands over her mouth. When she turned back to look into the living room, the two cops were still sitting there. She rubbed her eyes, took a deep breath, and looked again, hoping to see her mom and dad sitting in the leather chairs. When the cops failed to disappear, she leaned against the kitchen island and slid to the tile floor. "This isn't happening," she told herself. "It's just another nightmare."

The younger policeman walked from the living room into the kitchen and squatted down next to her. "Are you okay?" he asked.

Suddenly, it occurred to her that her parents might not have been inside the house. She leaped to her feet and said, "I think you're wrong about my parents. They probably weren't actually *in* the house. My mother loves the flower garden. Can you have somebody go over and check the patio?"

The man stood up and said quietly, "No one would have survived the blast if they'd been that close to the house."

Kit looked at the policeman who was watching her closely. And then it dawned on her: this *was* one of Grant Osgood's practical jokes. From the cop standing guard at the end of her street to these two hanging out in her living room, it was all a big hoax. Boy, Grant really went out of his way this time, she thought. And she had nearly believed it.

She exhaled a huge sigh of relief and smiled at the cop. She said, "I've got something for your trouble." She opened the oven and pulled out both of the pizza boxes. She thrust them into the man's hands and said, "My parents are going to come home any minute. It's so late, I'm sure they've already eaten. But I've got a little salad for my mother. She's been living on nothing but peanut butter and jelly for weeks."

The policeman asked, "Is there anyone we can call for you?"

Call? *Yeah, the loony bin so that they can take Grant Osgood away,* she wanted to say. Instead, she said, "No, but thanks for coming out." On her way to the front door, she said under her breath, "Grant Osgood, I'm going to kill you."

The policemen followed her to the front hallway and the older one said, "Did you say something?"

"No," Kit said, opening the door with a smile. "Now, if you'll excuse me, I've got to put together some salad dressing. My parents will be home any minute."

Kit awoke to the sound of someone pounding on the front door. She looked around and realized that she had slept on her parents' sofa. She picked up her cell phone from the floor: the screen lit up and told her it was nearly noon on Monday. And then, the realization that her parents had never returned home came rushing back at her. The knocking sounded again, a little louder. Oh, she thought, they're finally home! She shoved herself up off the sofa and called, "Just a minute!"

When she pulled open the door, she was surprised to find Grant Osgood standing there with his hands jammed into his cargo pants pockets. The memory of last night's escapade came rushing back at her. She glared at him and asked, "What do you want?"

Grant said, "Kit, I'm so sorry."

Kit stood there staring at him. For the first time ever, he was not giving her that stupid grin, and his sky blue eyes held a look of...what was that? Regret? She said, "Well, you ought to be. That was some stunt you pulled."

"What are you talking about?" A little wrinkle appeared on his otherwise smooth forehead.

She threw her hands into the air and said, "You can't even pull off an apology without going back on it!" She began closing the door.

"Wait!" Grant said, throwing himself against the door.

"Go away," she said, shoving the door against him. "I'm sick of you and your practical jokes."

"I don't know what you're talking about," he said, "but your parents—"

For the first time, she felt more than slightly annoyed with her father. He actually encouraged Grant's games. He'd made it clear on more than one occasion that she ought to return this jerk's affection...if that's what you could call his lunacy. "Was Dad in on your little charade, too?" she asked.

Grant stood there looking down at her, and she couldn't believe it: a lone tear began to trickle down his cheek.

She crossed her arms over her chest and said, "I don't think I've ever seen you cry. This is something I ought to record for posterity. It's fake, but it's a first."

Grant looked as if she had slapped him. In the next instant, he grabbed her by the arm and shoved her inside.

"Hey!" she said, "Let go of me!"

He squeezed her upper arm a little harder and said, "For once in your life, Kit, listen to me!"

She glared at him and squirmed out of his grasp. "You can't push me around like that. I'm calling the cops." She stalked over to the telephone on the table beside the sofa. Picking up the handset, she added, "Hopefully, I won't get one of your chump friends who came out here last night with that line of bull about my house burning down."

Grant strode across the room and snatched the remote from the top of the TV. The screen lit up, and he began scanning through the channels.

She dialed 9-1-1 and said to Grant, "Don't think you're going to just waltz in here and make yourself at home, just because my parents aren't here. They're—"

Kit froze. A newscaster was standing in front of a gaping hole in the ground with a pile of rubble in front of it. The houses on either side were missing parts of their roofs, and the glass was broken out of their windows. Kit walked closer to the set and said, "That looks a lot like Jack and Renee's house."

Grant said, "That's because it is Jack and Renee's house."

A voice on the phone in Kit's hand said, "What's your emergency?"

Kit shook her head and said to Grant, "That's not possible. If that's Jack and Renee's house, my house should be right there." She pointed to the great void between the two little Cape Cods.

The voice came across the phone line, a bit louder, "9-1-1. What's your emergency?"

Grant turned up the sound on the TV, and Kit heard the Channel 9 reporter saying, "…last night on this quiet street on the west side of Cincinnati." The newscaster turned to point at the pile of rubble on the lawn and said, "This is all that's left of the home of Kit Blume, a special education teacher with the Cincinnati Public Schools. Two people are presumed dead…" The reporter continued talking, but Kit couldn't seem to understand the rest of the words. *Dead* was the only word that kept reverberating in her mind. Her head suddenly felt fuzzy, and a sensation of intense heat washed through her. In the next instant, she felt a heavy black velvet curtain slowly coming down on her, as if she were on stage in a great theater where the performance had just ended.

From a tremendous distance, Kit could hear a voice saying, "We're sending someone out to your address now. Help is on the way."

Sometime later, Kit opened her eyes to find a paramedic kneeling on the floor beside her. "Welcome back," he said with a smile.

Kit lifted her head and looked around. Why was she lying on the floor? Another paramedic was standing across the room talking to Grant Osgood. "What's going on?" she asked.

"You fainted," the paramedic said. He took off his stethoscope and dropped it into his case. "But I don't think it's anything serious. Must've been the shock."

"What?" Kit was trying to wrap her mind around what was going on. She closed her eyes and said, "The last thing I remember, Grant came barging in here and grabbed me by the arm."

She opened her eyes to find Grant approaching her. "Then what happened?" he asked.

"You turned on the TV, and the reporter said…" Kit felt that heat washing through her chest again. She took a deep breath and forced herself to think. "…said that two people were presumed…" She couldn't bring herself to finish the sentence.

Grant glanced from Kit, to the paramedic, and back to Kit.

She had a feeling that she knew the answer to her next question, but she asked it anyway. "Who's dead?"

Grant knelt down on the carpet and took her hand in his. It felt much warmer than hers. She began to shiver. He said, "Your mom and dad, Kit. They died in the fire."

Kit felt her throat burning, and tears stung her eyes. She shook her head and tried to sit up. "It's not true," she said. "They were at the airport, and I told them not to go to my house. I told them to come straight here."

"They must have already been at your house when you called," Grant said. He pressed gently on her shoulder, and Kit dropped her head back onto the carpet.

From a long way off, she heard someone say, "She's out again."

Then someone else said, "That call probably sparked the explosion."

Kit felt as if she might throw up. She had blown up her own house with a phone call? How was that possible? She opened her eyes to find Grant looking into hers.

He said to her, "I want you to know that I'm ready to do whatever you need to get through this. I'm going to call work and tell them I need some time off."

At that moment, Kit desperately needed her mother to put her arms around her and tell her that everything was going to be all right. The last person she wanted to see was Grant Osgood. She said, "I don't want your help."

Grant said, "Kit, who's going to help you?"

From behind Grant, Kit could hear the birds chirping outside the open window. The sheers billowed on the breeze, and she looked past him to watch a robin hopping up onto a branch. The bird stretched his neck and gave a loud chirrup. She thought it was strange that the robin was still chirping. How could he sing when the world was falling apart? The two paramedics and Grant stood over her with looks of concern on their faces.

Grant asked again, "So, who exactly is going to help you?"

Kit felt the black curtain slowly lowering down on her again. Her voice sounded far away when she asked, "What did you say?"

Grant said, "I'm staying here with you and helping you."

Kit realized that other than Grant, there was no one to help her, except for maybe a great-aunt who was nearly a hundred years old and lived in a nursing home somewhere in Tennessee. Kit had never been very good at making friends, and her parents had always been the center of her world. Of all the people on the planet, though, her obnoxious neighbor was the last person she wanted with her right then. She closed her eyes and said, "Grant Osgood, I hate you."

"I know," he said. "And that's okay. You can hate me all you want, but I'm not going anywhere. You need me, and there's no getting around it."

She hated to admit he was right. She had no idea which way was up, and there wasn't anyone else knocking on her door to help. "Do what you want," she said. She sat up, and then rose slowly to her feet. One of the paramedics steadied her, and then she walked away from all of them. She climbed the stairs, stumbled down the hallway, and crawled into her parents' bed. She was going to go back to sleep, and when she woke up, she felt certain that all of this would turn out to be just another one of her nightmares.

After a long, hot shower on Tuesday morning, Kit walked into her parents' kitchen, feeling a little better. She was surprised to find Grant sitting at the glass-topped table, flipping through her mother's red leather address book. Kit felt that it was an invasion of her mother's privacy and asked him, "What do you think you're doing?"

Grant looked up and said, "I was just thinking that somebody's got to call all of your parents' friends to let them know that they're—"

"That they're what?"

"Dead," he said.

The word pierced her like a knife. She refused to believe that her parents weren't okay. "Don't you think that's a little premature?"

Grant looked at her in surprise and asked, "Premature?"

"I mean, the cops aren't even sure my parents are dead. They haven't identified bodies yet or anything."

"Kit—"

She cut him off with, "Maybe Mom and Dad decided to take a walk, or they got a little burned and called an ambulance to take them to the hospital. They could call or come home any time now."

Grant stood up and touched her arm, "I know it's hard, Kit, but you've got to face it. They're dead."

Before she could tell him to stop saying that awful word, the doorbell rang. Kit went to answer it. Two policemen were standing on the porch, and one of them showed her a badge. "Miss Blume," said the taller of the two, "I'm one of the detectives from the sheriff's office. Can we talk to you?"

Kit felt a sense of déjà vu, and her heart skipped a beat in anticipation. Surely, they had come to tell her where she could find her parents. She said, "Come in."

The two cops followed her to the kitchen, and Grant shook hands with them. "You want something cold to drink?" he asked.

"No, thanks," the deputy said.

They all sat down at the table, and the tall detective said to Kit, "I'm sure you're anxious to know about your parents."

Kit nodded. She squeezed her hands together and held her breath. *Please let them be okay.*

The tall detective said, "The coroner verified this morning that the dental records provided by your family dentist matched the remains that we found at your house."

Kit felt her breath go in a whoosh. Her first thought was that her parents had to come home. Who would help her with the flashbacks? She felt her chin quivering, and she blinked back hot tears. With the back of her hand pressed hard against her lips, she tried to breathe. But it felt as if a boulder had just been rolled onto her chest. Kit said, "I want to see them."

The detective shook his head and said, "There's nothing to see. Their teeth and bones were about all that was left."

Grant patted her on the shoulder, and for once, she didn't have the strength to tell him to keep his hands to himself.

The deputy asked, "Where were you between seven and nine on Sunday?"

Kit swallowed hard and blinked back her tears. She shrugged and said, "I guess driving to my house and back again."

"Did you stop anywhere?"

She tried to remember where she had gone. "Blockbuster...and LaRosa's."

"You wouldn't happen to have receipts for the movie and food, would you?" the deputy asked,

Kit pushed herself to her feet and walked over to where her purse lay beside the sofa. Her eyes swam with tears, and she brushed them away. She fished out the receipts from her wallet and handed them to the tall detective. She said, "I should never have told them to meet me at my place. I should've let them come home, like they wanted to."

The tall detective looked at the receipts, and then handed them to his partner. "Don't blame yourself," the detective said.

"You should count yourself lucky," the deputy chimed in.

Kit stared at him in disbelief. "Lucky? That my parents are...dead... and I'm not?"

"I didn't mean that," the deputy said. "You could've died there with them. Nobody could have escaped this arsonist's fires."

"Arsonist?" Kit said. "Somebody *meant* to burn my house?"

The deputy nodded.

"Why?" Kit asked.

"That's what we'd like to know," the tall detective said.

Grant asked, "Do you have any idea who this arsonist is?"

"Not a clue," the deputy said.

Kit's head felt as if it were wrapped in cotton. How could any of this be real? An arsonist had set her house on fire, presumably to kill her? And inadvertently, he had killed her parents, instead? She swallowed hard. Why in the world would someone want to kill her?

The tall detective was saying, "...could put together a list of every person your family knows, we can start an investigation. We'll need addresses and phone numbers from you." He handed Kit his business card. "You can fax or email the list to our arson specialist."

Kit stared at the business card with the sheriff's logo on it. "That could take forever," she said. "My dad lectures at medical conventions all over the world."

"That's okay. Take your time, and send me what you can, bit by bit," the tall detective said.

"We'd rather have you be thorough than to rush and overlook something," the deputy added.

Kit didn't want to gather addresses for the cops. She just wanted her life back.

By lunch-time on Tuesday, a number of the women from her parents' church had stopped by to bring Kit casseroles and pies. She stood in the kitchen looking at all the dishes of food spread across the kitchen counter tops, wondering who on earth they thought was going to eat it all. The doorbell rang again, and she went to see who was there.

Father Quincy, the grey-haired priest in charge of missions at her parents' church, stood on the porch in black dress pants and a black short-sleeved shirt with a stiff white collar. He held a large brown envelope under his arm. "Hello, Kit. May I come in?"

She really didn't feel like talking to anyone, but Kit stood back and waited for him to step into the hallway. She shut the door behind him and said, "Let's go in the living room." She showed Father Quincy to one of the same leather chairs where one of the cops had sat the night before. She sat down across from him on the sofa. From the kitchen, she could hear Grant re-arranging casseroles in the fridge.

Father Quincy looked across at her with his expressive, dark eyes. He reminded her of a baboon she had once seen at the Cincinnati Zoo who sat staring at her without blinking. Father Quincy pulled a white handkerchief out of his pants pocket and mopped the sweat from his wrinkled forehead. "It certainly is warm today," he commented.

Kit nodded and folded her hands in her lap. Why didn't he just get on with the reason for his visit? Churches and priests had always made her nervous for some reason that she could not explain.

"Kit," he said, "I don't know you all that well, but I knew your parents even before you were born." He paused and smiled at her.

Kit forced herself to smile back and crossed her ankles, waiting for him to get to the point.

He continued, "Your parents were good people. I am so sorry about your loss."

Kit nodded. What was she supposed to say? Nothing came to mind, so she simply murmured, "Thanks."

He went on, "They left me with instructions for their estate, in the event of their simultaneous deaths. I never dreamed I would outlive them."

They left this old baboon in charge of their millions? She asked, "Why did they put you in charge?"

He said, "It was your mother and father's wish that all of their insurance money be given to you." He smiled at her and added, "Provided you are a good steward, the several million dollars will keep you very comfortable for the rest of your life."

Several million dollars should have left Kit feeling like a lottery winner. Instead, she said flatly, "If you can call living without your parents comfortable."

"Yes, well…" he said, clearing his throat, "…at any rate, the rest of their estate…their savings, your father's retirement funds, and the money from the sale of their house…have all been directed to be donated to the church's mission fund."

"What?" Kit leaped to her feet. "That's ridiculous! Do you know how much money you're talking about?"

The old baboon shook his head. "Not exactly, but I'm sure it is a considerable sum."

"I won't let that happen," Kit said, pacing up and down. "It doesn't belong to you."

"You're right," Father Quincy said softly. "It belongs to God."

Kit's heart was pounding. She whirled to face him from her place in front of the bay window, wondering how she could put a stop to this. She said, "You've got a lot of nerve coming here to tell me you expect me to sell my parents' house and give you the money from it." She bit her lower lip to keep herself from adding, *you crazy old baboon.*

"Kit," he said gently, "sit down."

Kit flopped down onto the sofa and glared at him.

He withdrew a letter from the large envelope he had brought with him and said, "Your father wanted me to give this to you."

Kit snatched the envelope from Father Quincy's hand and tore it open with shaking fingers. Inside was a letter that read:

Dear Kit,

We know that it may be difficult for you to understand our decision to give most of our money to the church. This does not mean that we do not love or care for you. We have made arrangements through our insurance company so that you will never want for anything. What you must try to understand is that we would have nothing if it weren't for God's grace.

We always gave to the church, because we were so thankful for all of the blessings God showered over us through the years. More than anything, we were particularly grateful for the opportunity to take care of you. You were always our greatest treasure on earth.

Listen to what Father Quincy has to say, and don't fight him for the money. It belongs to God now. There's no hurry to sell the house. The Lord will let you know when the time is right.

With love,

Dad

P.S. I have directed my attorney to mail an important letter to your birth family in Minnesota. If they are interested in having a relationship with you, I'm sure you will be hearing from them within the week.

Kit re-read the part following the *P.S.* Her dad knew about her birth family? Why hadn't he ever told her?

Kit sat back against the soft pillows behind her and looked up at Father Quincy. The image of the old baboon faded from her mind as she contemplated this new information.

"I only came today," Father Quincy said in a gentle voice, "to offer you my sympathy and to deliver this message. It was very important to your parents that it be given to you as soon as possible after their deaths, and I wanted to respect their wishes. A similar letter was mailed from your father's attorney's office to your birth family this morning."

Kit looked more closely into the old priest's eyes, and she realized that he felt some concern for her. She suddenly felt a little embarrassed and quickly asked, "Do you know who my birth parents are?"

Father Quincy shook his head. "No." He held her gaze, and his eyes seemed to be able to look straight into her heart. Could he see that it was breaking?

Kit said softly, "I'm sorry I yelled at you."

The old priest sat back in the chair and said with a smile, "I would probably be yelling if I were in your shoes."

The fight went out of Kit, and the letter slid from her fingers onto the carpet. Too much was happening too fast. She felt as if she were on a roller coaster that kept whisking her from one dark surprise to the next. She looked out the front window and stared at a monarch butterfly that had landed on a bush. She remembered teaching her students that monarchs migrate. How would that one out there know when he was home? After this house was sold, she'd have no home. Where would she migrate?

Father Quincy cleared his throat and asked, "Is there anything I can do for you?"

Kit shifted her focus from the butterfly to the old priest's gentle face. She shrugged.

"May I pray for you?"

Kit's gaze shifted once again to the world outside the living room window. For years, her parents had been telling her about God and how he had created everything. They had talked about feeling God's love and experiencing joy all the time. She knew that her parents loved her, but she had never been able to really understand God's love, especially at times like this. It was hard to believe in a God who let such terrible things happen. She looked up at the priest and said, "I don't believe in prayer." What she really meant to say was that she didn't believe in God.

Father Quincy said, "We all have moments when it is hard to believe."

Kit looked down at the pale pink polish chipping off her fingernails and said, "It always seems like good things happen to other people." She thought about the few times she had asked God for things, but she never got them. Maybe he didn't love her for some reason. She said to the priest, "And I've never felt God's love the way my mom and dad always talked about it."

The priest smiled. "His love is always there. You can feel it through the people at church."

Kit said, "I've never felt that I belonged in the church, either."

Father Quincy said, "When you decide that you want God near, that feeling of being on the outside looking in will change."

Kit stood up, and Father Quincy rose, too. Together, they walked towards the door. Father Quincy tucked the brown envelope back under his arm and asked, "Would you like me to do the memorial service?"

Kit said, "I guess that's what Mom and Dad would have wanted."

"Why don't you come over to the parish office tomorrow afternoon, and we'll talk about the details," he suggested.

"No," Kit said, opening the front door. "I wouldn't know anything about that. You take care of it."

"Even though you don't think it's important," he said, "I think you should come. It always seems to help families bring some closure to their loss."

"I'll think about it," Kit said.

After he left, Kit stood there staring at the letter written in her father's cramped scrawl. Someone from her birth family would be coming this week? It was more than Kit could absorb.

She took a deep breath and ambled into the kitchen, where Grant was spooning casserole onto two plates. Not since the Blumes had found her at the age of four curled up in a laundry basket out back had Kit felt so lost and alone. She asked Grant, "Where am I supposed to go?"

"For what?" he asked.

"Didn't you hear what he was saying?"

Grant shook his head.

She handed him the letter and said, "My parents left everything but their insurance to the church...even the house."

Grant took the letter from her, read it, and asked, "Your father was in contact with your birth family?"

"Apparently," Kit said.

"How do you feel about that?"

"Mad," Kit said.

Grant said, "I can understand that. I'd hate to lose my house on the same day that I found out I had a family that no one ever told me about." He took her by the elbow and led her over to a chair at the table, then set a plate in front of her. He laid the letter on the table beside her.

"Where am I supposed to go?" she asked again, sinking into the chair.

"You're always welcome to stay with me," he said. He sat across from her and reached out to put his hand over hers.

Kit looked at his fingers, and her heart began to pound. Something about men's hands had always frightened her. She jerked her hand out from under his and said, "No way."

Grant handed her a paper napkin and said, "Maybe you can move to Minnesota with your birth family."

"Like I'd want to move in with complete strangers," Kit said. She looked down at the letter beside her plate and asked, "What kind of parents would just let somebody adopt me like they did?"

"Maybe they were trying to give you a better life," Grant said. He looked intently into her eyes.

Kit broke off eye contact with him and stared down at the plate of chicken casserole in front of her. She didn't want to eat chicken casserole for lunch with Grant Osgood staring at her like that, and she really didn't want to meet her birth parents. All she wanted was for this nightmare to end, and to wake up to find her parents at the dinner table with her.

"How long before you think you'll sell?" Grant asked.

Kit looked up and said, "Dad wrote in the letter that God would tell me when the time was right…like that's going to happen."

Grant got up to pour them each a glass of lemonade and then sat down across from her. "Your dad had such great faith," he said.

"Yeah," Kit said. "He used to tell me that God talked to him all the time. I've never heard him."

"You know," Grant said, putting a napkin in his lap, "God doesn't necessarily talk to you out loud."

"Obviously," Kit said.

Grant said, "Sometimes I get answers to prayer just by talking to other people."

"I suppose you pray a lot," Kit said.

"I try to," Grant said. "You want me to pray now?"

"Do whatever you want," Kit said.

While Grant was praying, Kit looked down at her father's letter. The final words seemed so strange to her:

P.S. I have directed my attorney to mail an important letter to your birth family in Minnesota. If they are interested in having a relationship with you, I'm sure you will be hearing from them within the week.

Why should she knock herself out to meet with her birth family? They had never come looking for her. No, she decided, it was best to just forget about them for good. She had a memorial service to get through, not to mention an arson investigation. All she wanted to do was focus on getting ready for school next week. Maybe if she did that, life would go back to being somewhat normal again.

2

IT WAS NEARLY DINNER TIME ON TUESDAY WHEN GRANT found Kit huddled in her parents' bed with one of her mother's quilts pulled up over her head. He felt sorry for her, and he wished he could push a rewind button on her life to make things better. But he knew that wasn't possible, and it wasn't healthy for her to hide from the truth like this. He stood beside the bed and said, "I think we need to talk."

There was no response.

"Kit," he said again. He reached out and touched her shoulder.

Kit shot upright in the bed and let out a shrill scream. In the next instant, she began swinging at him.

Grant ducked and felt adrenaline coursing through his veins. He grabbed Kit's hands to keep her from hitting him. "Kit!" he said firmly. "It's all right. Stop screaming."

Kit was like a frantic rabbit with its feet in a trap. She wrestled to free herself from his grasp.

"Kit!" he said, a little louder. "Stop it!"

Kit blinked several times, collapsed back onto the pillow, and then looked up at him. He released his grip on her wrists.

"What are you doing in here?" she asked with a look of confusion.

"I came up to see if you were all right," he said.

Kit yanked the quilt up to her chin and said, "What makes you think I wouldn't be all right?"

He had never been able to understand why she always reacted with such fear. It reminded him of the day he'd found her out back, sleeping in Alice Blume's laundry basket. He sank down onto the edge of the bed, feeling a little drained. He could tell that it still hadn't sunken into Kit's head that her parents were never coming back. "We need to talk."

Kit glared at him and said, "I don't talk to strange men who walk into my bedroom."

Grant felt the familiar tension that always knotted his muscles whenever he tried to get close to Kit. What was she so afraid of? He stood up and looked around. From the corner, he pulled up a dressing table stool and sat down. "First of all," he said, "I'm not a stranger. You've known me most of your life."

"You may not be a stranger," she said, "but that doesn't mean you're not strange."

Grant felt a stab of hurt, but he chose to ignore her remark to say, "And second, you're not in your own bedroom. I believe this bed belonged to your parents."

Kit looked down at the quilt in her hands, and he saw tears spring to her eyes. Crying was good, he thought. It meant that the truth about their deaths was sinking in.

"It *belongs* to my parents," Kit said. "They'll be home any minute. I know they will."

He had to do something to help her to understand that denial was not a good way to cope right now. He reached out to touch her on the shoulder and say, "Kit…"

She looked at his outstretched hand, scuttled like a crab backwards to the other side of the bed, and sat huddled against the headboard with her arms wrapped tightly around her knees. "Stay away from me," she growled.

Grant sank back onto the stool and folded his arms over his chest. "I wish you'd stop being afraid of me, Kit. I would never hurt you."

Kit glared at him and said, "I'm not afraid of you. I just don't like you."

Grant let out a sigh. This was going to be harder than he had expected. He decided to try something different. If he was going to get Kit to start talking about her parents, he had to get her out of the bedroom and back downstairs. "Maybe you should get out of bed and take a shower. It's almost time for dinner, and I'm sure your mother would appreciate a nice, hot meal."

Kit sat up straighter and said, "Yes, she would. She's been living on peanut butter and jelly for weeks." She threw aside the quilt, and Grant noticed that she was still wearing the same Bermuda shorts and t-shirt she had been in the day before. But in spite of the fact that she hadn't showered or changed her clothes, he thought she looked incredibly beautiful. Her short, wispy blonde hair framed her heart-shaped face. He loved her wide, violet eyes with their unbelievably long, dark lashes. Her skin looked so soft…he shoved his hands into his pockets to keep himself from reaching out and caressing her cheek.

He stepped away from the bed. As Kit strode across the room towards the bathroom, Grant forced himself to remain rooted to the spot. It took every bit of will power to keep himself from rushing after her and pulling her into his arms. For as long as he could remember, he had wanted to comfort Kit…to hold her close until all of her fears vanished. But for another day, he would have to be patient. He decided that whatever it took, he was going to keep on loving Kit Blume until she relented. One day, she would be his.

In the meantime, the responsibility of convincing Kit that her parents were dead fell on his shoulders. On the way back downstairs, he tried to figure out what he could do to help Kit see the truth. What if they went over to her house? Seeing was believing. She hadn't been there since the fire. Maybe seeing it would snap her out of denial.

When Kit came down to the kitchen, he said, "I think we should take a drive over to your house."

"Fine," she said, "but I'm driving."

"Suit yourself," he said.

When they arrived at what remained of her house, Kit got out of her Mini Cooper and stood on the sidewalk outside of the yellow police tape that had been wrapped around the perimeter of the lawn. Grant walked up beside her and stared at what used to be a really cute little bungalow. He'd seen a lot of fires, but he knew this one had been really serious. He also knew that a loss like this left most people reeling. An acidic smell lingered in the air.

Kit whispered, "There's nothing left."

Grant couldn't agree more. There was absolutely nothing left of her house or garage, except for the cinder block basement foundation. It looked as if a meteor had fallen and shattered her house into a million pieces. There was debris strewn all over the lawn, the sidewalk, and along the curbs in the street. Plywood covered the windows of the houses on either side of Kit's. It was terrible to lose a home, but for Kit, it was far worse. She had lost the only family she had. He said, "I'm so sorry. This is awful."

Kit said softly, "My parents' remains are down there among the ashes."

Grant didn't know how to tell her that the coroner had already removed what little remained of their bodies. Norm and Alice Blume had been like a second set of parents to him. A lump rose in his throat, and he put his hand on Kit's bare shoulder. Her skin felt smooth and warm, and he found comfort in knowing that she was still there with him.

She shrugged off his hand and said, "I think we should take some of the ashes and put them in an urn or something."

Not having any bodies had made it difficult for Kit to accept her parents' deaths. At least she was thinking about their remains. That was a step in the right direction. "I think that's a nice idea," he said, "but it might not be safe to go crawling around in there."

She had that look on her face that told him it was best to let her do whatever she had in mind. She said, "I'll be right back."

Grant watched Kit hurrying towards the house two doors down, where she rang the doorbell. A woman opened the door, but he could not hear exactly what Kit was saying to her. Kit walked away from the house and circled around behind it. He knew that she would probably get mad at him for interfering, but he hurried after her to ask, "What are you planning on doing?"

"Getting my parents' ashes." She picked up a metal bucket from the edge of a vegetable garden, and then walked into the neighbor's garage and lifted an extension cord off the shelf. With a couple of quick movements, she had the extension cord tied to the handle of the bucket.

Grant followed her back to the shattered remains of her house. He didn't think it was wise for Kit to go into a crime scene. She could mess up important evidence. He said, "Kit, I don't think you should do this."

"I have to," she said with a stubborn set to her chin. "It's the least I can do for my parents."

He had a feeling this was going to end badly. "Let's get the police or somebody from the fire department out here who knows what they're doing."

She halted and turned to him. "Are you saying I don't know what I'm doing?"

He could see that she was angry, and for as long as he had known her, when she got like that, there wasn't much use in arguing with her. Still, he had to try. He didn't want her to destroy important evidence or, worse, get hurt. "Of course, you know what you're doing. I just don't want to see you get hurt."

"If you were half a man, you would have offered to do it yourself."

Grant felt his muscles tense and said, "Are you saying I'm not a man?"

"Maybe." She stalked away from him and stepped over the yellow plastic tape.

He took a deep breath and shook off her insult. "Kit," he called, "I'll do it."

"I can do it myself," she said.

Against his better judgment, he stepped over the tape and gingerly tiptoed around the rubble to where she stood on the edge of the cinder block basement foundation. Slowly, she lowered the bucket down, dragged it sideways to scoop up some ashes, and then carefully began raising it back upward. Grant stepped forward to help her pull it up, and when he did, the cinder block beneath him gave way. In the next instant, he landed hard in the rubble below.

After he was certain that nothing was broken, he slowly rose to his feet. Ashes wafted all around him. He coughed and wiped his face on his sleeve. He looked up at Kit, who was still standing on the edge of the foundation with the bucket in her hand.

Kit said, "I told you I didn't need your help. Now I'll have to call the fire department to get you out of there." She disappeared.

Was she really going to call the fire department? Or was she going to just leave him down here? He looked around. There was no way out. Grant shoved aside a sliver of panic and prayed for help. Then, he brushed the ashes off his clothes.

A short time later, a couple of the guys that he had worked with years ago at the fire department appeared above the rim of the cinder blocks. With a rope, they hoisted him up out of the basement. Grant continued brushing off ashes and spitting on the grass. "I'm a mess," he muttered.

His buddy laughed and said, "We ought to hose you down, man."

A woman suddenly appeared beside him, flipped open a badge, and said, "Hamilton County Sheriff's Department, Arson Investigation."

Grant stopped swiping at the ashes to look up at her. He blinked hard and tried to focus on her. His eyes began to burn. "I must look crazy," he said.

The detective asked, "What were you doing in there?"

The detective probably thought he was the arsonist. He knew that they frequently returned to the scene afterward. Grant said, "I was helping my friend get some of her parents' ashes out of the basement."

The detective reached up to tuck her medium-length dark hair behind one ear. "Your friend?"

"Kit Blume," he said, gesturing towards the street where they had parked. "This was her house."

The detective looked around and asked, "Where is this Kit Blume now?"

Grant looked up and realized that Kit's Mini was gone. He shrugged. "I guess she left."

"You fall nearly eight feet into a crime scene, and she leaves. Just like that?"

He could see that the detective was really wondering about him now. He nodded.

"Some friend," the detective said. She raised an eyebrow at him.

Nervousness gripped Grant, and he blurted out, "She hates me."

"Is that right?" She eyed him more closely.

He nodded and forced himself to smile. "We've got one of those love-hate relationships."

"How's that?"

He cleared his throat and said, "I love her. She hates me."

The detective's amber eyes narrowed. "Why does she hate you?"

He recalled all the times Kit had been angry with him and said, "She says I annoy her."

"Do you?"

He thought about the hundreds of pranks he had played on her and smiled. "Sometimes," he said.

"How long have you known Kit Blume?" the detective asked.

He remembered the day he'd found her naked in Alice Blume's laundry basket. He'd wondered if that's how little girls came into the world. "Since we were four."

"And your name is?"

"Grant Osgood."

"Do you live in the neighborhood?" the detective asked.

"No," Grant said, "I live next door to her parents."

"And where do they live?" the detective asked.

He gave the address, and the detective glanced back at a young Hispanic guy who had come with her. He was scribbling frantically in a little notepad. Grant accepted a towel from one of the fire fighters, and then he swiped at the ashes on his face.

She asked, "Any idea how this fire got started?"

He shrugged and said, "Gas leak, of course."

"Really?" She was really giving him an odd look now. "What do you think made it so hard to put out?"

He shrugged. "Beats me," he said, "but based on my experience, I'd say your arsonist tampered with the gas lines before he started the fire."

"Your experience?" the detective asked.

"I'm a paramedic, but I started out as a fire fighter."

The detective glanced back at her associate, who was still scribbling. She asked Grant, "Any idea why the fire couldn't be put out quickly enough to save the people inside?"

"Hard to say," Grant said. "I've been to fires like this one before. If they don't get the gas line shut down fast enough, there's not much we can do to save the structure...or the people. We can't send guys inside when it's burning that hot." He looked over at the houses on either side and added, "They're lucky they didn't lose both of those houses, too."

The detective nodded. "Any clue why someone would want to kill Miss Blume or her parents?" she asked.

Grant thought about Norm and Alice, and he felt tears sting his eyes. He had been so focused on helping Kit, he hadn't realized until that moment how much he was grieving. Norm had been like a father to him. At last, he shook his head and said, "Norm was a great guy. I'm really going to miss him."

"What about Alice Blume?"

Grant thought of Alice and her incredible kindness. She had helped him so much when his own mother was dying. He said, "I can't imagine anyone wanting to kill Alice Blume. She was the nicest person I've ever known."

"And what about Kit Blume?" the detective asked. "Any reason why someone would like to see her dead?"

Grant thought about Kit's life. From what he could see, all she ever did was work or hang out with her parents. He shook his head. "Not that I can think of."

"Mind if we get your address, Mr. Osgood?" the detective asked.

He rattled off his address and telephone number, and then he said, "Is it okay if I go now? These ashes are really burning my eyes."

"Sure," the detective said.

Grant walked towards the paramedics' truck, and a short time later, they dropped him off at home. He went inside to take a shower, and then walked back over to Kit's house. He could hear her running water in the upstairs bath, so he sat down to start working his way through her mother's address book again.

The memorial service was scheduled for Saturday, and he had only called half of the names in the book. He didn't relish going back to this task. Calling people and listening to their shocked reactions had been draining.

The doorbell rang, and Grant got up to open the front door. The Hamilton County arson investigator and her assistant were standing on the front porch. She said, "Mr. Osgood, you look a little different without the ashes."

Grant said with a grin, "Black's not my best color, is it?"

The detective gave him a long hard look, smiled, and said, "No, but the blue's working for you."

Her partner cleared his throat loudly.

The detective said quickly, "We were wondering if Miss Blume was available to talk with us."

"Actually," Grant said, "She just went upstairs to take a shower."

"We can wait," the detective said.

Grant couldn't imagine Kit having the strength to deal with the cop's questions right then. "I doubt that you're going to get very far with her," he said. "She's having a hard time right now."

"I understand," the detective said. "Maybe we should come back tomorrow."

"That would be better," Grant said. "She's had quite a shock."

The arson investigator and her sidekick walked down the driveway, and Grant stood at the window watching them. As the cruiser pulled away from the curb, he realized that Kit was going to be dealing with the aftermath of her parents' deaths for a lot longer than most people would. Death was one thing to cope with…murder was another. Whatever happened, he promised himself that he'd be there for her.

3

On Wednesday morning before dawn, Kit drove to Midway School to work on setting up her classroom. While she was stapling butcher paper to a bulletin board, a loud bang reverberated down the hallway.

In the next instant, her legs were propelling her down the hallway towards the exit door.

"Stop!" someone shouted after her.

That was the last thing Kit intended to do. She shot out the door and pounded across the parking lot in the direction of a row of pine trees. When she was certain that no one was following her, she huddled under the branches of a fallen tree, trying to catch her breath.

She didn't think very much time had passed, but the next thing she knew, she heard someone saying, "Kit, wake up."

She opened her eyes to find Grant sitting on the ground beside her. Looking around, she realized that she must have had another flashback. How long had she been out there? She sat up and tried to brush the dirt from her arm. "What are you doing here?"

"The principal called to tell me that you took off when the custodian knocked over a ladder outside your room."

Kit groaned. She didn't want her boss to know about the flashbacks. "Did you tell her anything about me?"

"No," Grant said, brushing pine needles from her shoulder. "But I think she's probably wondering what's going on."

"I don't want her to know," Kit said. "I'll lose my job."

"How about telling me?" Grant asked.

His voice sounded gentle, just like her dad's did whenever she came back to reality like this. Suddenly, she remembered that her dad was gone. How was she going to make it without him? Tears threatened to give away how terrible she felt. Without answering Grant, she stood up and brushed at a muddy spot on her pants.

"Kit," Grant stood and said softly. "You're going to have to let me help you now."

She shook her head and started towards the edge of the stand of pines.

"Kit," Grant said, "you've been out here for nearly two hours. What are you going to do if this happens while you're with your students?"

Kit froze. She looked down at her watch and realized that Grant was right. She stood there with her back to him without saying a word. What was she going to do? She didn't have a clue, but the last thing she wanted to do was discuss her flashbacks with Grant Osgood. She took off running across the open field that lay between her and the school.

From behind her, Grant shouted, "How long are you going to keep on running?"

Keep on running! Kit's feet pounded over the uneven grass. She stumbled and caught herself to avert a fall. With a deep breath, she slowed to a walk and began saying softly, "Slow and sure...slow and sure...slow and sure."

In that instant, she realized that there was a very distinct memory from somewhere in the deep recesses of her mind...someone yelling at her, *You'd better keep on running!* She came to an abrupt halt and blinked several times in an effort to clear her head.

Grant caught up with her and asked, "Do you see a doctor for this sort of thing?"

She thought of Dr. Irene and nodded.

"Can I drive you there?"

She didn't want him coming with her to her psychiatrist's office. She shook her head and said, "I don't want to talk to her right now."

Grant reached up to touch her sleeve and said, "I know you hate me, but I'm a pretty good listener. Maybe I can help."

She stood there staring at her shoelaces. For years, she'd been taking medication to control the flashbacks. Suddenly, she felt strongly that if she didn't figure out what the flashbacks were about, someone would kill her. They had already killed her parents and burned her house to the ground.

Kit looked up at Grant and said, "For the record, I have always felt like strangling you. But if you can actually help me figure out why I keep on running, I might be able to just hate you."

Grant grinned at her and said, "Well, that's more than I had hoped for." He held out his hand and said, "Let's go home."

She looked at his outstretched hand and said, "Don't push your luck." She marched off in the direction of the school, hoping that she wouldn't regret this decision later.

Grant suggested picking up breakfast burritos and taking them to Ault Park. She liked that idea. It would be easier to talk to him about the flashbacks if she didn't have to face him over her parents' kitchen table.

They were walking along the sidewalk in one of the gardens when Grant asked, "What was the trigger for the flashback today?"

Kit said, "I don't know. A noise that sounded like a gunshot, I think."

"Does it happen often?" he asked.

Kit watched a boy trying to walk a boisterous young Lab down the middle of the grassy space between the gardens. She shrugged and said, "It depends on a lot of things."

"Like what?"

"Whether I'm tired, or stressed, or somewhere out of my own comfort zone."

"Do you remember anything about someone actually firing a gun at you?"

Thinking about her memories made her uneasy. Sometimes a memory could trigger a flashback. She nodded and said, "After the gunshot, I took off running through the woods."

"Anything else?"

Kit glanced over at him and said, "Yeah. Today, I realized that someone was yelling at me to keep on running."

Grant asked, "When was the last time this happened?"

"Yesterday."

"What happened?"

"I was just walking down the stairs at Mom and Dad's house, and the next thing I knew, I was laying on the floor in the kitchen."

Grant frowned and asked, "Did you hurt yourself?"

"Just a couple of bruises," Kit said. She sat down on a cement bench under a tree, and then she pulled up one of her pant legs to reveal the spot on her knee that had turned frighteningly purple overnight.

Grant shook his head and sat down next to her. He asked, "Any idea why someone would want to kill you?"

"I don't know," Kit said, looking away from Grant's penetrating gaze and turning her attention to the people dotting the park's lawn. When she was younger, she had had the same flashbacks. Dr. Irene had helped them to go away with medication and therapy. Kit thought they were under control, but, apparently, they were not.

Grant handed her a burrito and said, "Losing your parents is hard. I could hardly function after my mom died."

The knot in Kit's throat did not allow her to respond. Tears streamed down her cheeks, and she brushed them away with the back of her hand.

Grant handed her an extra napkin.

He always seemed to know what she needed, even before she did. Kit felt the knot in her throat relax a little, and she blew her nose on the napkin. At length, she said, "I've got to remember what happened. It's the only way to stop the flashbacks."

"Sounds reasonable," Grant said, "but how are you going to do it?"

Kit laid aside her burrito and bent down to pull a familiar drawing out of her well-organized purse. She unfolded the dog-eared piece of lined notebook paper that she had laminated and handed it to Grant.

Grant looked at the paper, frowned, and asked, "Did one of your students draw this?"

Kit looked at the drawing she had made years ago of an A-frame house. "No, I did."

"It looks like a Swiss chalet," Grant said.

Kit pointed to the exterior walls of the house and said, "I remember that these were covered with wooden shingles."

"What color were they?"

Kit shrugged. "They were weathered. Grey, I guess."

"It's good that you can remember that much," Grant said.

Kit moved her finger to the roofline. "These pieces of trim were painted yellow."

Grant asked, "What else do you remember?"

Kit closed her eyes and tried as hard as she could to imagine the house, but she couldn't bring up any other details. She opened her eyes and shook her head.

"What was the weather like outside?" he asked.

Kit stared across the way at a squirrel raiding a bird feeder. "It was warm."

"What time of year do you think it was?"

The squirrel hopped down and scampered away to his home in a nearby tree. She wondered what was to become of her when she no longer had a place to call home. She turned her attention back to Grant and asked, "What did you say?"

"What time of year do you think it was?"

"Definitely summer. The woods were really green."

"How were you feeling when the flashback started today?"

"Scared, like always."

"Why?"

"Someone was shooting at me."

"Any idea why?"

Kit shook her head. "I can't remember anything else."

"Well, you'll just have to keep working on the parts that you can remember," Grant said. "Maybe your mind will fill in the details."

The word *work* made Kit feel overwhelmed and depressed. "I'm tired of working," she said.

"I'm sure you must be," Grant said. "But my guess is that until you face your fears, they'll keep interrupting your thoughts."

"That's what Mom always told me." Kit's eyes filled with tears, and Grant handed her another napkin.

They sat there munching on their burritos in silence. After a while, Grant asked, "Any particular reason why you always wear the same necklace?"

Kit shrugged.

"Mind if I get a closer look at it?" Grant asked.

Kit reached up and unclasped the twisted gold chain that had been hanging around her neck since Grant had discovered her at the age of four sleeping in the Blumes' laundry basket. She held it out, and Grant took it from her. "I've just always had it on."

"Yeah," he said with a grin. "It's all you were wearing when I found you in Alice's laundry."

Kit felt her face growing warm and quickly took a bite of her burrito.

He peered closely at the front of the medallion and asked, "Any ideas about where this might have come from, or who gave it to you?"

Kit glanced at the light blue enamel on the orb. A beautiful young woman stood in front of a fountain and held onto a huge sword. A feeling of tremendous sadness washed over her. She said softly, "That's Saint Guinevere. The man who assaulted her cut off her head."

"How do you know that?"

Kit said, "My father told me the legend."

Grant turned the medallion over to read the inscription. "Any idea who *Von Will* is?"

Kit looked at the cursive script. Trying to remember someone named Von Will always made her head hurt. "No idea," she said. For nearly ten years, she had been going to Dr. Irene for treatment, and she had made so little progress in remembering her past. Frustration drove Kit to blurt out, "The harder I try, the worse it gets."

"Maybe you're trying too hard," Grant said. "Maybe that's why the flashbacks come to you when you're tired…or distracted."

Kit rubbed her temples and said, "I want to start living like a normal person. I feel like I checked my brain at the door."

"Maybe that's why you're so good with your students," Grant said. "They must feel the same frustration."

Kit shrugged.

Grant said, "I've heard that when a person gets traumatized, they can get kind of stuck. But if they can deal with it, they usually get better."

Kit had felt stuck for years, and she was tired of it. In fact, at times like this, she felt rather angry. She asked, "Why can't I remember anything? I'll bet you have all kinds of happy childhood memories."

Grant said gently, "Most blocked memories are probably left in the dark to protect us. If you knew all the details, you probably couldn't handle whatever happened to you. When you're stronger, you'll remember." He reached out and wrapped his fingers around her hand.

That movement started Kit's heart hammering in her chest. The urge to run became so intense that she jumped to her feet. "I've got to get back to the school," she said.

"Don't you want to finish eating?"

"No," she said. She quickly began walking in the direction of his car.

"Kit!" he called after her.

She hurried towards the parking area.

"Did I say something wrong?" he asked, jogging alongside her.

"No," she said. She forced herself to slow down. *Slow and sure...slow and sure... slow and sure...*

Back at her parents' house, Kit stood at the kitchen window, watching Grant washing his car. It suddenly dawned on her that the increase in flashbacks might have something to do with spending so much time with pesky Grant Osgood. She decided that whatever happened, Saturday would be the last day she'd be spending with him.

PART TWO
Moose Creek

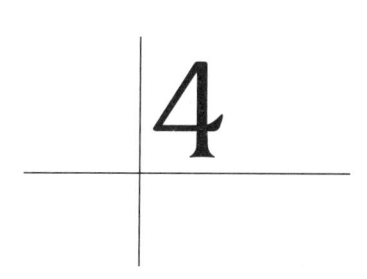

4

HARVEY TRENT HATED THE WAY HIS LIFE WAS TURNING OUT. With a deep sigh, he cast his fishing line once again towards the ramshackle dock that had once received guests for the Lakeshore Inn. From the bow of his father's blistered Chris Craft, he watched the lure hit the water and send rings of motion across the surface of Heron Lake.

He sat there gripping his fishing rod, with his shoulders hunched halfway to his ears. He shivered against the damp chill that was seeping over northern Minnesota. While a light drizzle dripped from his hat brim, to his nose, to his chest; he thought that his father's illness was a lot like his lure hitting the water. The ripple effect over the past five years had crossed every area of his life.

First, he'd postponed the doctorate research at Berkeley. His sister, Oona, had said she would only need his help for a few weeks…a month at the most.

After a while, he'd given up his apartment in Vallejo, with a promise to himself that he'd find a better place closer to campus when Oona no longer needed his help. Four springs had slipped past. Fat chance he'd be leaving anytime soon.

Harvey listened to the blue jays screeching in the pines along the north shore. He wasn't a man prone to fits of depression, but lately, a dark melancholy had settled over him. His dream of returning to sunny California grew fainter recently after he received notice that his architecture license had expired. He felt that life had left him adrift on a watery, directionless path, like a fishing boat without moorings.

There just seemed to be some things that held him as fast to Moose Creek as an anchor secures a boat…things that he should have shaken off long ago. He knew he had to make a change soon, or he'd be trapped in his God-forsaken hometown forever.

From the western shore, he heard a shout. Harvey's black Labrador, Jet, leaped to his feet and trotted to the back of the boat. Harvey lifted his chin to peer at the shoreline from beneath his hat brim. He spotted his sister, Oona, standing alongside the road that followed the west side of the lake.

"What's up?" he shouted.

"The nursing home called. I need you to go out there with me."

Harvey looked down at his watch. It was only 9:30. He hadn't caught a thing all morning.

Harvey shouted to his sister, "I'll meet you at the house in thirty minutes!"

Oona waved, got back into her blue Subaru Outback, and drove away.

Harvey knew there'd be a price to pay when he got back home. He was certain that his older sister would chew him out, because she had had to go out to the lake to fetch him again. She'd nag him for the millionth time about getting a cell phone. He hated cell phones, and he had decided long ago that he would never be caught dead with one.

As he was putting away the rest of the fishing gear, the hum of a trolling motor interrupted his thoughts. He looked towards the eastern shoreline, where a bass boat made its way slowly along near the tall reeds. He waved at old Doc Daggert, who lifted his arm in response.

Back in town, Harvey pulled up to the house on Second Street, where he and Oona had grown up. She stuck her head out the upstairs dormer window, waved at him, and called out, "I'll be down in a minute!"

Oona appeared on the porch, and Harvey watched her turn back to lock the door. For years, she had done a wonderful job of taking care of their father after teaching all day. Together, they had made the unhappy decision to place their father in a nursing home. Somehow, the years had passed without much notice, and now, Oona was pushing forty-five. Harvey often wondered if she felt as displaced as he did.

Oona skipped down the front steps, and Harvey watched her hurrying towards the truck. He smiled, because she reminded him of one of the junior high girls that came into the grocery store after school. Oona was about the girl's same height, and they both walked like they were going to a fire.

She pulled open the door and asked, "What are you grinning at?"

"Was I grinning?" Harvey asked.

"Yes, you were," Oona said, dragging her over-sized purse in behind her and slamming the door shut. "At least one of us is in a good mood today. I'm certainly not." She yanked on the seatbelt and fastened it around her middle.

Harvey frowned and asked, "What's going on?"

"You'll see when we get there," she said, crossing her boney arms over her flat chest. "Just drive."

Harvey glanced over at Oona's short-cropped hair and wondered what had gone wrong with the dye this time. When he left the house, it had been blonde. At the moment, it was pea green. He wanted to tell her that she ought to just start going to the salon to get her grey covered, but he bit his tongue. Instead, he said, "Not a good day for Dad, huh?"

She shook her head. She flipped open the visor mirror and sighed deeply.

Harvey turned to back out and felt one of his contacts slip off-center. He opened the console, but his glasses and contact case weren't there. He scratched his head. Where had he left them? Then he remembered that they were on the kitchen counter in the old house he had been renovating. He said, "I'm going to have to stop at the old house. I left my glasses there."

"The longer you take," she said, "the longer the nurses have to deal with Dad." She scrunched her fingers through her spiky, damp hair. "A cell phone sure would make your life a lot easier. You could call the nursing home to let them know you're on the way."

Harvey felt his jaw tighten. "Call them on your cell," he said.

"It's inside, charging," she said.

"You know how I feel about cell phones. Don't start in on me again."

"But you could save everyone so many headaches if you'd just give in," Oona said. She pulled a little can of hair wax out of her purse and rubbed some into her palms. The interior of the truck began to smell like a coconut cream pie.

"The reception out here is terrible," Harvey said. "It would be different if I lived someplace civilized. I'd have a normal job, and I'd actually need a cell."

Oona tossed the can of hair wax back into her purse and pulled her sweater together at the front. "One of these days," she said, "you're really going to regret not having a cell phone."

"Hm," Harvey said, which is what he always said when he didn't want to discuss something further. He turned on the radio and drove two blocks down to the old LeClerc mansion and pulled to a stop at the curb.

Oona looked up at the old Victorian with the peeling paint and dead front lawn. She said, "I don't know why you bought this old place. It's a money pit."

Sometimes, Harvey wondered himself about the wisdom of his purchase. "I'll be right back," he said.

Inside the vacant old house, he went directly to the kitchen, where he found his glasses and contact case lying on the counter. As he was removing his contacts, he thought about what Oona had said. He knew exactly why he had bought the old house. He and his high school sweetheart, Annabelle Vernon, had always dreamed of fixing it up and filling the six upstairs rooms with kids. Even though she was no longer a part of the picture, he had never been able to give up his dream.

A noise from the floor above made Harvey look up from the contact he was trying to drop into the case. What was that? He snapped the lid on the case and dropped it into his pocket. Again, a thumping from upstairs made him pause. There was definitely something up there. He slipped on his glasses and went to the bottom of the sweeping circular staircase to listen.

Thump, thump, thump.

Harvey held the smooth old walnut banister and silently climbed the steps. When he got to the top and turned to the right, he nearly bumped into Ralph Rivers, the new maintenance man he had hired to work nights at Paul Bunyan's General Store. "Judas Priest!" Harvey exclaimed. "What are you doing up here?"

Ralph towered over Harvey in his tie-dyed t-shirt and jeans. He stared through his over-sized silver rimmed glasses at Harvey with his piercing, pale blue eyes. Ralph carried several pieces of broken glass in one hand and a rubber mallet in the other. He gestured with the mallet towards one of the front bedrooms. "I noticed this morning that you've got a window busted out up here," he said. "I put in new glass."

"Broken window?" Harvey asked. He headed down the hall. "Where?" He walked into the first bedroom on the left and noticed a clean piece of glass in the lower left pane. Harvey didn't recall that it had been broken.

Ralph stood in the doorway and said, "I see kids throwing rocks at the house late at night."

Harvey looked back at Ralph in surprise. "Really?"

Ralph nodded.

Harvey noticed then that Ralph was wearing a headband with peace signs on it. Was it to keep the sweat out of his eyes or to hold his long, grey hair in place? He walked back across the room and said to Ralph, "Well, thanks."

Ralph nodded and turned away without another word.

Harvey watched as Ralph slipped soundlessly down the steps on his white canvas sneakers. He heard the front door click shut.

Harvey quickly glanced into the other rooms to find out if any of the other windows were broken. He discovered nothing more than the crack in one that had been there all along. Satisfied that the house was as secure as it was going to get for the time being, he hurried back downstairs and paused to lock the front door. As he held the key in front of the lock, he wondered how Ralph had gotten inside. He was certain he had locked the door when he left for the lake earlier.

From the truck, Oona called, "Are you coming?"

Harvey locked the front door and hurried back to the truck.

"What was Ralph doing in there?" she asked.

"Fixing a broken window," he said. He started the engine.

"I didn't know you hired him to work on the house, too."

"I didn't," Harvey said. He pulled away from the curb. "He said kids have been throwing rocks at the house late at night."

"How'd he get in there?" Oona asked.

"That's what I was just wondering," Harvey said. Concerns about Ralph surfaced in his mind, and he added, "I hope I don't regret hiring him."

Thirty minutes later, they walked into the Golden Acres Nursing Home lobby, and Harvey wrinkled his nose at the smell of urine mixed with pine cleaner and chicken soup. Harvey followed Oona down the threadbare aqua-blue carpet towards the Old Man's room. Midway down the hall, Oona stopped and knocked on a partially open door.

"Come in," a woman called.

Oona pushed open the door, and they found a nurse sitting beside their father. His thin white hair stood out from his head in wisps, and his enormous black glasses made his face appear almost skeletal. The nurse left, and Old Man Trent pointed a blue-veined hand with knobby knuckles at the corner and shrieked, "There's that man again."

"What man?" Harvey asked.

"That guy who stole my shoe polish. Took every last can…even the cordovan."

Harvey walked close to the bed and said to his father in a conspiratorial tone, "I'll shoo him out of here." He went to the corner, waved his arms at the air, and then said loudly, "Give me that can of cordovan!" He pretended that he was watching someone exit the room, and then he shouted into the hallway, "And we'd better not see you in here again!" With that, he slammed the door shut.

Old Man Trent collapsed back onto the stack of pillows propped up behind his liver-spotted head and laughed. "That's the last we'll see of him…and that filthy dog. He's been pissing all over the hydrangeas."

Harvey looked at Oona, and he began to laugh, but then he quickly contained it. The Alzheimer's was getting worse by the day…it was no laughing matter.

Oona sat down on the edge of the bed, took her father's hand, and asked, "How are you feeling?"

Harvey saw a flicker of recognition in his father's eyes. "Gracie," he said. "You've come back to me."

Harvey's shoulders sagged. Gracie was their mother's name, and Old Man Trent frequently mistook Oona for his wife.

Oona smiled and went along with him. "Can I get you anything, Dolly?"

Hearing his wife's pet name for him made Old Man Trent smile, revealing his three remaining teeth. He said, "Not a thing. Just having you here with me is all I need." He sighed and closed his eyes.

Oona patted her father's hand and glanced up at Harvey. She gave him a wink and held up her hand to cross her fingers.

In the next instant, Old Man Trent reared up in the bed and shouted, "Gracie! Did you see that?"

"See what, Dolly?"

"That car that just went by," he said, following an imaginary car with his gaze. "I could've sworn that was Annabelle Vernon driving."

"Who?"

"Annabelle Vernon."

"Oh, you mean Paul and Mimi's oldest girl?"

"Yes," he said with impatience. "How many Annabelle Vernons do we know?"

"Just one," Oona said.

Old Man Trent turned to Harvey and said, "Don't just stand there! We've got to call the police."

Oona indicated with a hand signal behind her father's back that Harvey should go on with the charade.

He asked his father, "What do you want me to tell them?"

"Why, that we've seen Annabelle Vernon!" Old Man Trent said. "It's not too often that you see people who are supposedly dead."

The thought of his beloved Annabelle and her death stabbed Harvey through with a pang of grief, which hadn't eased in over twenty years. He swallowed hard and tried to go along with the chain of events in his father's mind. "Annabelle's dead?" Harvey asked.

"Don't you read the paper or listen to the news?" his father asked.

"I guess I missed something," Harvey said.

"Missed the biggest news this two-bit town has ever heard," Old Man Trent said. "The Lakeshore Inn burnt to the ground last night, and Ron Frank told the reporters that every single member of the family had been killed...all but Benny, that is. He was at Wildred's place yesterday." Old Man Trent folded his shriveled arms across his chest.

"So..." Harvey prompted his father.

"So if the rest of them were all killed, how come Annabelle Vernon's out burning up the highway this morning?"

Harvey looked across at Oona and shrugged. He wasn't as good at this game as she was.

Oona said, "Now, Dolly, don't excite yourself too much over this. If there's been some mistake, I'm sure the police will figure it out."

Old Man Trent turned to Oona and asked, "Is Ron Frank still chief of police?"

Oona said, "I'm afraid so."

"Christ," Old Man Trent muttered. He looked up at Harvey and asked, "Why don't you run against him?"

"Me?" Harvey asked. "I don't have the training for that sort of work."

"Neither does Ron," his father said, "but that hasn't stopped him from getting re-elected year after year." He yanked his hand away from Oona's and asked, "Aren't you getting a little too old to be hanging on me like that?"

Harvey noted that his father was back to present day. He wondered if it might be a good time to ask him about his plans for renovating the old house he'd recently bought. He sat down on the edge of his father's bed and resisted the urge to cover his nose. His father smelled like a wet diaper. Harvey said, "Dad, I could use some advice about fixing up the old LeClerc place."

Old Man Trent squinted at Harvey and asked, "Why are you calling me Dad?" He shied away from Harvey, and with his voice rising, he demanded, "Who are you?"

Harvey's shoulders sagged. This definitely was not a good day. He stood up and asked his father, "Are you comfortable?"

Old Man Trent groaned and said, "My hip's killing me. Feels like I'm sitting on a nail."

Harvey leaned over and shifted his father, who felt as light as a child, into a different position. "How's that?" he asked.

Old Man Trent smiled and said, "Ah, much better." He closed his eyes, and within seconds, he began to snore.

Harvey sighed and whispered to Oona, "You think we should stay a while?"

She shrugged and looked at her watch. "He's had his morning meds. He'll probably sleep until noon. I'll go tell the nurse to check on him in a while."

Oona hurried away, and Harvey paused to watch his father's chest rising and falling. Old Man Trent was growing noticeably weaker, and Harvey wondered how much longer he'd last. With a sigh, he bent to kiss his father on the forehead, and then he went in search of Oona.

Harvey found her near the front entrance, where she had encountered Eric Larsen. Eric's Ojibwa mother had given him his high cheekbones, heavy brow and prominent nose, while his Danish father had contributed his blonde hair and steely grey eyes. Harvey looked at the stubble on Eric's cheeks and wondered again if the guy was trying to grow a beard, or if he just detested shaving. Eric was toting his banjo, as he did every Wednesday morning when he visited the nursing home. When Harvey had seen him perform, he wondered how Eric could have ever learned to play so well. Eric had the thickest fingers Harvey had ever seen. They looked like bratwurst sausages attached to his broad palms.

Harvey shook Eric's beefy hand and asked him, "How's the hunting and fishing guide business?"

Eric grinned and said, "Never better. I'm scheduled to take the governor fishing over the weekend."

Harvey had always admired Eric's skills in the great outdoors. The man, who was in his mid-forties, never seemed to want for dinners made from elk, bear, moose, or the wide variety of fish that swam in the nearby lakes. "The governor's coming here?" Harvey asked.

Eric smiled and said, "No, he wants me to fly him up to a lake in Canada. The walleye have really been hitting there this week." He shifted his banjo case from one hand to the other and asked, "How's your dad?"

"Okay, I guess," Harvey said.

"You don't sound too sure about that," Eric said in the deep baritone that made him a hit with the old ladies. He looked directly at Harvey and then at Oona with his steely grey eyes.

Oona said, "Our dad's seeing things, and he has no clue who we are."

"That's tough," Eric said.

"Yeah," Harvey said, "and when he is in his right mind, you can't have a decent conversation with him."

Oona said, "It's as if his brain is jumping from moments in the past to present day and back."

"I've heard him tell some wild tales," Eric said with a laugh. "Last Sunday night, he was telling one of the other residents that he knocked up the school nurse after he married your mama."

Harvey couldn't believe his father had said something that crude. He cleared his throat and looked down at an unraveling seam in the carpet.

Oona said, "As a matter of fact, that's true."

Eric's ruddy cheeks turned a shade redder, and he ran his fingers through his short-cropped hair. "You don't say."

Harvey wasn't accustomed to talking to other people about family matters. But he felt compelled to do something to cover over his father's indiscretion. He said, "The nurse was Oona's mother, Nettie Kelly. She died shortly after Oona was born, and my parents took her in."

Eric nodded and said, "I always wondered why the two of you had different last names."

Unlike Harvey, Oona could be as open as an all-night convenience store. She told Eric, "Mom forgave Dad for what he did, but she never wanted him to forget it, either. She'd call him at the store just before dinner every night and say, 'Dolly, Oona Kelly and Harvey Trent, Jr. are waiting here for you to come home. Don't you be stopping by anywhere else on your way.'"

Eric laughed and said, "I can just hear your mama saying that, too. She was a pistol."

"Lately," Oona said, "Dad's been going on and on about seeing Annabelle Vernon the day after the Lakeshore Inn burned down."

"Who's Annabelle Vernon?" Eric asked.

Harvey said, "She was one of the kids who died in the fire."

Oona added, "That was nearly twenty-five years ago. I don't think you lived here then."

Eric scratched one of his long sideburns and said, "You know, maybe your dad's beginning to see people who have gone on ahead of us. The Ojibwa elders say that happens when a man's time is almost up."

Oona glanced up at Harvey and said, "That's what I've been thinking."

Harvey didn't want to talk about his father's death. He pulled his keys out of his pocket and said to his sister, "Time we headed back, Oona. I've got to get over to the store."

On the way home, Oona said to Harvey, "I think Eric's right. Dad is knocking on death's door."

"Hm," Harvey said. He fiddled with the radio and found the sports station. The Twins were beating the Royals. After a little while, he realized that the subject of the Lakeshore Inn had come up twice in one day. He asked, "Do you think it could be possible that Annabelle escaped that fire?"

"Highly unlikely," Oona said. "You've seen what's left of the Lakeshore Inn."

An image of an old brick foundation and a crumbling fieldstone fireplace in the woods flashed through Harvey's mind. He turned onto the highway and said, "But if she did escape, where would she have gone?"

"Maybe Paris," Oona said.

"Why Paris?"

"I heard her talking once about her dad. He lived in Paris."

"Paul Vernon wasn't her dad?"

"No," Oona said, "not everyone's parents are really who people think they are."

How could he not have known something so important about the girl he loved? If Annabelle had survived the fire, would she have gone to live in Paris?

At times, the memory of her seemed so clear. She used to call him H.T., but only when they were alone. He remembered that she hated the fact that she was overweight, but he had loved the fullness of her hips and the soft contours of her ample bosom. And then there were other times, he could barely recall the curve of her cheek or the color of her eyes. He asked Oona, "Why do you think Dad's so hung up on talking about her?"

"I don't know," Oona said. "If I were you, I'd put a lot more thought into fixing up that piece of crap house you bought. Forget about Annabelle Vernon. She's just a figment of Dad's imagination."

Harvey drove on, with his hand stroking Jet's silky head, reflecting on his father's memories of the Lakeshore Inn fire and Annabelle Vernon. He decided he would talk to some other people in town. Maybe there was an outside chance that someone else besides Old Man Trent had seen Annabelle the morning after the Lakeshore Inn burned down.

At lunch time, Harvey parked his brown Toyota Tundra in front of Paul Bunyan's General Store on Main Street. He grabbed his newspaper from the seat beside him and walked across the street to Swenson's Bakery and Delicatessen. He spotted the town's police chief, Ron Frank, in his usual spot on the bench between Pauly's Pizza and the bakery. Harvey watched Ron winking at a couple of the junior high girls as they came out of the bakery.

Harvey noticed that Ron's comb-over wasn't covering his ever-broadening bald spot. And he'd gained so much weight over the years that Harvey wondered how on earth the man could possibly respond in an emergency. If he ever did have to chase down a criminal, Harvey figured Ron would be completely winded within half a block.

He walked up to Ron, and the junior high girls hurried away, whispering to one another and clutching small boxes of doughnuts tightly to their chests. He asked Ron, "Don't you think those two are a little young for you?"

"I'm not doing anything wrong," Ron said.

"Sure you are," Harvey said. "You're going to get yourself into trouble with the law."

"I'm not going to get into trouble with the law," Ron said, standing up and shoving his shirt tail over his rotund belly and down into the front of his too-tight tan polyester pants. "I *am* the law."

Harvey looked at Ron and said, "Your daughter's about the same age as those two. Would you like it if I were flirting like that with Lily?"

"It's all harmless," Ron said flatly.

"No, it's not," Harvey said. "If you don't believe me, ask one of them how they feel when you do that."

"You should mind your own business," Ron said.

Harvey shook his head. The man had the sense of a toadstool. Maybe it was time to bring this up to the town council. He said to Ron, "I've got my eye on you." He walked away and pulled open the front door of the bakery.

Inside, the warm, sweet smell of doughnuts and the aroma of fresh coffee gave Harvey a sense of calm. He had been coming into the bakery for as long as he could remember. As a child, his father had brought him and Oona there every day before school. It was still the place where everyone in town kept up with what was going on.

Wildred Swenson bustled about behind the counter, sending a loaf of pumpernickel bread through the electric slicer for the librarian, and then turning to box up a dozen glazed doughnuts for the mayor. She paused to adjust the nearly invisible hairnet that she always wore over her wavy, snow-white hair.

When Harvey approached the counter, Wildred walked over to him and said with a smile that creased her heavily wrinkled face, "What's distracting you today, Harvey?" Her heavy German accent made the *w* sound like *v*, and the way she said his name made it sound like *Harfee*.

Harvey sat down on a stool at the counter. Wildred knew him well. He was constantly getting himself sidetracked with little distractions. He glanced out the plate glass window and said, "Kids are throwing rocks through the windows at the old LeClerc place, my dad can't remember my name, and Ron's out there flirting with twelve-year-olds."

Wildred poured Harvey a mug of steaming coffee and slid it across the counter. "Ron is going to wink at the wrong girl one of these days," she said.

Harvey watched Wildred hurrying along behind the counter in her black orthopedic shoes. He noticed that the hem of her dark blue cotton dress was unraveling along the back. A thread dangled to the point where her knee-high stockings didn't quite meet the lower edge of her dress. He saw her whisk a wax tissue from a dispenser, lean into the glass case, and pick up his usual: a custard-filled long John. She placed the doughnut, along with a pastrami sandwich, on a white plate and set it in front of him, adding, "I'll go over and sit with your dad this afternoon."

Harvey heaved a heavy sigh, smiled at her, and said, "Wildred, the world needs more people like you."

She dismissed him with a wave of her hand and said, "You would do the same thing for me."

Harvey shrugged and reached for a packet of sugar. In the next instant, Oona burst through the front door and flung herself onto the stool beside him. His pixie-like sister turned to him with her green eyes flashing and said, "That SOB was winking at me again."

Harvey sighed and said, "I tried to tell him to knock it off when I came in."

Oona turned to watch Ron Frank through the plate glass window and then said to Harvey, "Look. Now he's chatting up Jacqueline Corbett."

Jacqueline Corbett, a woman who had made a fortune in northern Minnesota real estate over the past fifteen years, was standing on the sidewalk next to Ron Frank. While Harvey didn't approve of Ron eyeing the young girls in town, he could understand why their police chief was ogling Jacqueline. She had turned heads the first time she set foot in Moose Creek on a crisp fall day, wearing a full-length mink and four-inch spike heels. Today, her long, chestnut brown hair was swept up into a stylish twist, and sparkly silver earrings brushed against her neck as she laughed at something Ron was saying. Jacqueline's low-cut sundress plunged to a deep V and revealed so much that there was little left for a man to imagine.

Harvey turned back to Oona. He noted that her short-cropped hair had been dyed a frightening shade of red. It just about matched her new red and purple striped reading glasses that were perched on the end of her nose. A second pair of green glasses was nestled in her hair, and a third black pair dangled from a beaded chain hanging around her neck.

As she sat there beside him with her legs dangling from the stool, Harvey noticed again the resemblance between his sister and the junior high girls that Ron kept eyeing. They were about the same height, and Oona had the same figure: all bones and no curves.

Oona was saying, "Ron Frank gives me the heebie-jeebies." She slid down off the stool and hurried towards the ladies' room.

Benny Vernon appeared behind the counter and reached into the doughnut case.

Wildred called sternly, "*Ach, nein!* Benny!"

Benny jerked his hand back and stood up. Harvey noticed that Benny's ball cap nearly brushed the hanging lamps that lit the space behind the counter. The thirty-two-year-old man with Down's syndrome wore jeans hiked up high on his belly, and a thick, black belt cinched them tightly around his broad girth. White socks shone too brightly in the gap between the navy blue of his jeans and his black tennis shoes. His enormous form blocked the area.

"You hungry?" Benny asked Wildred.

"No, I am not," Wildred said, pushing past him to place a cake into a box. "And it is not raspberry doughnut day."

"Ron Frank's an SOB," Benny said.

"If you can't say something nice," Wildred said, "don't say anything at all."

Benny loped slowly away towards the back of the bakery. As he walked out, Harvey looked up at the wall behind the counter. Old black and white photographs of people from Moose Creek were intermingled with Dirk Swenson's fishing trophy plaques. Harvey noticed a fading picture of the Lakeshore Inn. It reminded him that he wanted to ask someone about Annabelle Vernon and the Lakeshore Inn fire.

Wildred lowered a cake into a box on the counter near Harvey. She began taping the box shut.

Harvey asked her, "Why was Benny with you the night the Lakeshore Inn burned down?"

Without looking up from her work, Wildred said, "His mother hired me to take care of him while she worked in the restaurant. Most nights, he slept at my place. I took him home in the morning."

"Oona said you were the one who called the fire department the night of the fire," Harvey said.

"That is right," Wildred said. "But Benny, he was the one who noticed the fire. He woke me up to show me a strange, orange light glowing on the north shore."

"My dad swears he saw Annabelle Vernon the day after the fire. Do you think there's any truth in that?"

A man called from the other end of the counter, "Wildred! How about some more coffee?"

Wildred looked up at Harvey and said, "Don't you have better things to worry about?" She turned to pick up a pot of coffee, and then she hurried away.

Oona returned from the restroom. She paused to look up at the television set that was suspended from the ceiling. Harvey glanced up at the set and heard the announcer saying, "The Fishing Lure Killer seems to have struck again, this time at a small lake just north of Brainerd."

Oona said, "Jesus, Mary, and Joseph."

The announcer continued, "The victim was found in a boat that drifted ashore near Jack's Marina. As was the case in each of the past seven killings, this victim was also wearing a fishing lure in his lower lip."

"Judas Priest," Harvey muttered. "Who would do such a thing?"

Oona shook her head and said, "Some sociopath."

The announcer continued. "Each lure found on the victims' bodies was similar." A close-up of several lures flashed onto the screen.

Harvey recognized a couple of the neon-colored Minnesota Minnies with feathers; he carried them at Paul Bunyan's General Store. He said to Oona, "I sell those all the time."

Oona said, "You think the Fishing Lure Killer might have bought one of those lures from you?"

Could it be possible that someone he knew was out there killing innocent people? He said, "I sure hope not."

Oona said, "God help us if we ever have a murder here in Moose Creek." She lifted her chin in the direction of Police Chief Ron Frank, who was sitting with his arm draped over the booth behind Jacqueline Corbett's shoulders. "The law around here isn't worth much." Oona slid off her stool, picked up her coffee, and hurried out the front door.

Harvey sat there staring into his mug. Something about Annabelle Vernon kept nagging at the back of his mind. After picking up a second cup of coffee from Wildred, he found Fred Ianelli in the kitchen, decorating tea cookies with little blobs of yellow frosting.

As always, Fred wore his white baker's pants and shirt, and a slender paper hat perched at a jaunty angle on his short-cropped salt and pepper hair. Harvey noticed that Fred's goatee had taken on a bit more silver lately, too.

"Those cookies look good," Harvey commented.

Fred handed Harvey one of the tiny treats and smiled. "How's your day going?" he asked.

Harvey shoved the cookie into his mouth and said, "Fine." He took a sip of his coffee and pulled up a stool beside the table to watch Fred's hands flying over the tops of the cookies with the precision of a machine. He asked Fred, "Have you ever heard about anybody seeing Annabelle Vernon the morning after the Lakeshore Inn burned down?"

Fred wiped his hand on his white apron and continued decorating a second tray of cookies, this time with pink frosting. "No," he said. "Where'd you hear something like that?"

"My dad's been talking about it for weeks," Harvey said.

Fred arched one of his very thick, dark eyebrows at Harvey and said, "I guess I'd consider the source on that one."

Harvey wondered at what point people should stop believing things that Alzheimer's patients said.

At that moment, the back door opened, and Fred's son, Mike, walked inside. Harvey smiled at the teen, who was wearing his green scout shorts with a red polo shirt. He asked Mike, "You want to shoot some clay pigeons next Saturday?"

"Sure!" Mike said.

Harvey noticed then that Mike was carrying a big tube of rolled-up paper. "You working on your art merit badge today?"

"No," Mike said, "wilderness survival."

Harvey pointed at the tube of paper and asked, "What you got there?"

Mike said, "A topographical map."

"Let's see it."

Mike pulled the rubber band off of his tube and unrolled it on the stainless steel countertop beside Fred. Harvey walked over and peered at the pale green and tan map that was marked with hundreds of looping lines. "What are all these lines?" he asked.

Mike said, "Each line shows a change in elevation." He pointed to an area where a number of the lines appeared in concentric circles. "When they're closer together like this, it tells you that there's a hill there."

Harvey peered at a large, pale blue area in the upper right-hand corner and a second one in the lower left-hand corner. "What lakes are these?" he asked.

Mike pointed to the right-hand corner and said, "That's Upper Red Lake." He pointed to the lower left-hand corner, and said, "And that's Lower Red Lake."

"This map's mostly Indian reservation, then," Harvey said.

"Native American," Mike corrected him. "One of the guys from the reservation council is coming to talk to us today about the trip up there in the spring."

Harvey asked Fred, "The scouts are going to the Red Lake Reservation?"

Fred said, "You sound as surprised as I was when I first heard about it."

Harvey said, "I didn't think they allowed anybody in there, since it's a members-only reservation."

Mike said, "Eric Larsen's been trying to help us understand the importance of respecting the Ojibwa land."

Fred shoved a tray of cookies onto a shelf and said, "A friendly little hike gives the boys some fun and keeps them from going onto the reservation without an invite." He winked a black-brown eye at Harvey.

Harvey asked Mike, "Is Eric Larsen going to lead the hike?"

Mike said, "I don't think so. The council guy said it has to be led by a member."

Harvey looked across at Fred and said, "I thought Eric was a member at the Red Lake Reservation."

Fred shrugged.

Fred's wife, Sophie, came in the back door of the bakery. As soon as she saw Harvey, she flashed her even, white teeth at him and said cheerily, "Hello, sunshine."

Harvey noted that Sophie Ianelli stood in stark contrast to Jacqueline Corbett. While Jacqueline wore dresses that left little to a man's imagination, Sophie chose pretty skirts and blouses that didn't reveal too much of her curves. Her low heels were sensible, but attractive, whereas Jacqueline's footwear bordered on being dangerously high. Sophie kept her shoulder-length light brown hair twisted up on the back of her head. It curled in childlike wisps around the nape of her neck. No matter what modest outfit she chose, she always wore a smile with it.

Harvey watched Sophie walk over to Fred, pick up a cookie, and pop it into his mouth. She looped her arms around his neck and leaned into him to give him a kiss. "Hi, cupcake," she said.

Fred's hand slid down to give Sophie's rear end a little squeeze.

Unlike Jacqueline Corbett, who flirted with every guy in town, Harvey knew that Sophie only had eyes for one man: her husband. Not only was Sophie beautiful, Harvey thought, she was also brilliant. On top of taking care of Mike, helping Fred in the bakery, and keeping an eye on Benny sometimes; she also worked part-time for the city clerk and took night classes in criminal justice. Harvey asked her, "How are your classes going?"

"Really well," she said. "I'm on my last semester."

"What'll you do when you're finished?"

Fred looked up and said with a grin, "Run for police chief, of course."

Harvey chuckled and said to Sophie, "You've got my vote."

Mike rolled up his map and headed for the front of the store. Sophie caught up with him in the doorway. "Hey!" his mother said to him. "No kiss for your mama?"

Fred made kissing noises and said, "He's saving them for Lily Frank."

Harvey saw the color rising in Mike's cheeks and wished that Fred had not teased the boy like that. Still, it was probably true. He had noticed that Mike seemed sweet on their police chief's daughter, Lily. Mike ducked out of Sophie's grasp, and she followed him to the front.

After Mike and Sophie left, Harvey said to Fred, "So, you don't think there's any truth in what my dad's saying about Annabelle Vernon?"

"Absolutely not," Fred said. "There's no way anyone could've survived that fire. It took them nearly two days to put it out."

"Then why does my dad keep going on about it?" Harvey asked.

"Who knows?" Fred said. "Alzheimer's makes people say and do strange things."

Harvey shrugged. "I guess you're right."

"Forget about the Lakeshore Inn," said Fred. "One of these days, those guys from North Shore Development will have bought everything out there at the lake, including your dad's lot and boathouse. You'll be so busy designing condos for them, you won't have time to worry about how the old inn burned down."

The words *North Shore Development* sounded like fingernails screeching across a blackboard to Harvey's ears. For years, Jacqueline Corbett had been hounding him to sell out his dad's property at Heron Lake so that developers could build condos around the entire place. It would spoil everything he loved about it.

No, he had told Jacqueline repeatedly, he wouldn't sell to them. Not in a million years. He and Doc Daggert were the last two land owners who refused to sell out…and Wildred, of course. Since Benny Vernon was not competent, and he was the sole surviving heir, Wildred managed the old Lakeshore Inn property for him. Harvey smiled at Fred and said, "Thanks for the advice. See you later."

As he walked back across the street to Paul Bunyan's General Store, Harvey thought about what Oona, Wildred, and Fred had said to him about the questions regarding the Lakeshore Inn and Annabelle Vernon. He decided that they were probably right. Annabelle's survival of the fire was nothing more than a figment of his dad's imagination. The quicker he forgot about it, the better.

It was later on Wednesday afternoon when Harvey was reading the directions on how to set up the new cardboard diaper display that he overheard a familiar voice at the register asking, "Do you know if you got any tofu in yet?"

The clerk said, "I'll ask the manager."

Harvey looked up to see Jacqueline Corbett standing at the check-out. He didn't want to have to tell her that he'd forgotten to order the tofu again. So, he ducked through the swinging doors that led to the loading dock.

From where he stood, he could see Jacqueline through the round, Plexiglas window, but she couldn't see him. Her long, chestnut hair was now tied loosely at the back. Dramatic eye shadow and black liner rimmed her dark brown eyes that were accented by carefully penciled brows. Her slender nose and high cheekbones looked like she'd been out in the sun. Harvey felt desire pulsing through his veins, and he fought to push the feelings aside as he stood there between the cases of lettuce and boxes of prunes.

Seeing Jacqueline never failed to bring out two of his worst emotions: lust and grief. He watched her moving as she always did…languidly…from the check-out stand towards the produce aisle. As she drew closer, he could see the afternoon sun slanting right straight through the front windows and the thin sundress she was wearing. Why did she have to torment him every day with her forays into his store? She leaned over the peaches to pull down a paper bag. The movement hiked her dress several inches upward to reveal even more of her long, tanned leg. Harvey wanted to tear himself from the sight, but he was under a spell; it had been cast over him fifteen years ago, and he didn't know how to break it. His heart would always belong to Annabelle, but the rest of him demanded Jacqueline.

And then, as usual, Harvey's lustful feelings for Jacqueline reminded him of the pain that had been seared into his heart twenty-four years ago.

Harvey had loved Annabelle all his life, but he had only dated her for a few months that summer before he left for Berkeley. After a year away at college, he had realized that he never wanted to live without his high school sweetheart again. He had bought a diamond ring in Minneapolis and driven straight home to propose to Annabelle. He arrived on the afternoon following the fire at the Lakeshore Inn just in time to hear Ron Frank announcing on TV that the entire Vernon family had died...all but Benny.

Harvey had dragged himself home and asked Oona, "Why did God let this happen?"

Oona had said. "I don't know."

"I loved her," Harvey had said, showing Oona the ring in the black silk box.

"She was a lucky girl," Oona had said. "I'm sorry."

Miserable and heartbroken, Harvey had returned to the university and buried himself in work. Each time a memory of Annabelle came to his mind, he worked harder and buried himself deeper. In time, he hoped to forget her.

When his father had become ill, Harvey was forced to move back home. In Moose Creek, it was impossible to forget Annabelle. He encountered her brother, Benny, at least once a day at Swenson's Bakery, in Paul Bunyan's General Store, or on the street. And day by day, Harvey's bitterness over the situation grew. He was angry at God for taking her from him, but he was even angrier at himself for leaving her behind when he went to college.

Overhead, the sound of the intercom jolted Harvey back from his memories. He heard the clerk repeating, "Manager, lane two. Manager, lane two." He stayed where he was and waited for Jacqueline to leave the store.

Harvey tried to forget about Annabelle. He busied himself as best he could, but memories of her kept distracting him. He tried to focus on his work, but eventually, he began stewing about the Lakeshore Inn again.

Later that afternoon, Harvey walked across the street to Swenson's Bakery and Deli. He approached Wildred, who stood behind the counter slicing turkey for sandwiches. He said to her, "Could I talk to you...in private?"

Wildred held up a finger and walked to the curtain that divided the front half of the bakery from the kitchen. She pulled the black and white checkered fabric aside and said, "Sophie, I must go out. Could you look after the front counter, dear?"

Sophie came out with her beautiful smile and waved them away.

Wildred said to Harvey, "Let's take a walk."

Outside, the two of them turned left and walked along the sidewalk on Main Street. They turned the corner at Third Street, where the businesses quickly gave way to old Craftsman houses with picket fences around the little front yards. Harvey said, "I don't know what's the matter with me. I think I must be having a mid-life crisis or something."

"You are a little young for that," Wildred observed.

Harvey said, "Lately, everything that used to seem important to me doesn't anymore. And things that shouldn't matter are really worrying me."

"Like what?" Wildred asked.

Harvey said, "Well, for one thing, I seem to be losing focus on fixing up the old LeClerc place."

"Maybe you bit off more than you could chew," she said.

"Maybe," he said. "And my dad's really making me wonder about something."

"About what?" Wildred asked.

Harvey stopped and turned to look squarely at Wildred. He said, "I can't stop thinking about what Dad said…about seeing Annabelle the day after the Lakeshore Inn burned."

Wildred raised an eyebrow, turned to resume walking, and said, "And this is coming from an old man in a nursing home who can't remember who you are?"

Harvey nodded and said, "I know it sounds crazy, but Oona says he keeps telling her the same thing, over and over."

Wildred patted him on the shoulder and said, "*Schatzie*, that is what people do when they have Alzheimer's."

Harvey pressed on and asked, "But don't you think it's possible Annabelle could have survived?"

Wildred said, "If she did, then why didn't she come to me? Or the police? Or you?"

Harvey said, "Oona told me that Annabelle might have gone to Paris to see her father."

Wildred shook her head and said, "Poor Annabelle. She was such an unhappy girl."

Harvey drew his brows together. Of all the words he could have used to describe Annabelle, unhappy would never have come to mind.

He remembered happy moments with her when they were laughing over something funny. There were times when she was antsy, just as most teens could be. And like most, she had fits of the blues that came and went. But he had never gotten the sense that she was generally unhappy. "Unhappy?" he asked.

Wildred said, "She was...angry."

Now Harvey was really taken aback. Annabelle didn't seem to have an angry bone in her body, as far as he could remember. "Are you sure we're talking about Annabelle Vernon?" Harvey asked.

Wildred nodded. "I could never figure it out. The Vernon children had a beautiful home and wonderful parents. I think Annabelle ate to cover up her anger."

On that count, Wildred was correct. Annabelle had had a penchant for Dirk Swenson's doughnuts and cookies that had made her...he hated to admit it...considerably overweight. And while it had bothered Annabelle that she wasn't as thin as other girls, he had never found her size unattractive. In fact, he had always liked the fact that she was rather portly. It made hugging her so...

Wildred was walking on ahead without saying anything. He hurried to catch up with her. At length, she said, "I am going to tell you something that I have never told anyone else in this town."

Harvey said, "Whatever you have to say will stay between the two of us."

Wildred nodded and said, "After the fire, I kept having dreams about the children. Nightmares, really." She continued walking and then added, "And I could not get past the feeling that they needed help."

Harvey thought of the countless nights when he had dreamed that Annabelle was calling out to him. Through endless fires, floods, and disasters in his imagination, he had rushed to her aid, only to have her snatched away from him before awakening. "I've had dreams that seemed so real, I wondered if they were," Harvey said.

The mayor walked past with his fat little yellow dog and gave them a nod of his head. Wildred clasped her lips tightly shut, as if words might slip out if she weren't careful...words that no one should hear.

When the mayor was out of earshot, Harvey asked Wildred, "Is that all you wanted me to know?"

Wildred shook her head. "I had a lot of pictures of the children, since they spent so much time with me. So, about five years after the fire, I sent some of them in to a missing children's group."

"What happened?"

Wildred shrugged. "I prayed, and I waited." They paused at the driveway leading into the school parking lot so that a car could pull out. "And I waited some more. And then, about ten years after all this happened, I got a letter from a man who would not give his name."

"What kind of a letter?"

"A rather disturbing one."

They resumed walking.

Wildred said, "He wrote that he had adopted a girl who looked exactly like the picture I had sent in of Catherine Vernon."

"Really?"

Wildred nodded. "He sent me a picture of the girl he had adopted. She *did* look like Catherine." Wildred grew silent, and Harvey noticed that her eyes misted over with tears. She continued, "He said his daughter had traveled an incredible distance, judging by her condition when his wife found her."

"How old was Catherine when the house burned?"

"Four."

"Do you think that girl really was Catherine?"

"It is hard to say," Wildred said, "because I never responded to his letter."

Harvey felt taken aback. "Why not?"

"Because he wrote that it had taken the little girl nearly two years before she trusted anyone enough to speak. When she did, she never said a word about where she had come from. He said he thought she was so terrified of the people who had hurt her, she could not even talk about her past."

"Where did you say this guy lived?"

"Ohio," Wildred said. "He would not say exactly where."

"And you never heard from him again?"

"No," Wildred said. "He told me that he would not contact me again unless I wrote back to him."

"Why did he wait so long to try to contact you?" Harvey asked.

"Maybe he felt guilty for not trying harder to find out where this girl had come from before he adopted her," Wildred said. "But can you blame him? I probably would have done the same thing."

Harvey looked at the kids lining up on the playground at the school where Oona taught art. During the summer, his sister ran a day camp there.

"I don't think it could have been Catherine," he said. "There's no way a four-year-old could've gotten herself from northern Minnesota all the way to someplace in Ohio."

"That is what I thought," Wildred said. "And no one here in Moose Creek would have hurt Catherine like that girl must have been. So I never gave it another thought. From that point on, I decided to focus on doing the best I could to raise Benny."

Wildred stood still as a couple of little boys on bikes wobbled around them on the sidewalk. She slipped her hand in Harvey's arm and said, "Sometimes, you just have to move on."

They approached the school, and Harvey said, "I'm going to forget all about this nonsense over Annabelle and the Lakeshore Inn fire. It's time I got back to working on my house."

Suddenly, the children on the playground began screaming. Harvey looked across the parking lot and asked, "What in the world?"

Harvey and Wildred hurried over to where the children were clustered around something under a maple tree. Oona was standing there, saying calmly, "Just move back over to the steps now."

When the children backed away, Harvey could see that there was a possum staggering around in front of Oona. "That thing's sick," he said.

Wildred said, "I will go back to the bakery and call the animal control people." She hurried away.

Oona did her best to lure the kids around to the other side of the building with a game of Simon Says. Harvey stood near the possum to make sure none of the kids got close to it. A few minutes later, Ron Frank roared up in his cruiser with the lights flashing and the siren blaring.

What an idiot, Harvey thought. All he managed to do was get the kids more excited than ever.

The kids rushed at the police chief.

A girl pointed in Harvey's direction and said, "There's a wild animal over there!"

A little boy told Ron, "It's got big, ugly teeth!"

Harvey walked up to Ron and said quietly, "Come with me." He led Ron back to where the possum was standing under the tree. Oona and some of the children followed them. The possum turned and began hissing at them. Ron reached for his gun.

Harvey put his hand on Ron's arm. He said, "Not in front of the kids." He turned to Oona and motioned for the kids to move.

Oona said to the kids, "I want every one of you to walk back around to the other side of the building and stand in line at the front door." She pointed to a tall boy near the edge of the group. "You," she said, "are the leader for the boys." She chose an older girl and said, "And you lead the girls." The children moved slowly, and Oona called after them, "Walk quickly now."

When all of the kids had moved to the other side of the building, Harvey said to Ron, "Okay, now take care of it."

Ron pulled his gun and slowly approached the creature. "Possum," he said in an undertone. "Nasty things." He motioned for Harvey to step back. When he got closer, the ugly rodent hissed at Ron and showed its teeth. Ron pulled the trigger and missed. The possum reeled to the right. Ron shot a second time and missed again. The possum lurched around and began stumbling towards the underbrush at the edge of the school yard. Ron fired another shot, and the possum dropped. Ron fired three more shots and shoved his pistol back into his holster.

Harvey's ears were ringing. He asked, "Don't you think that was a bit excessive?"

"What?" the chief asked.

He said, "You shot that poor thing four times."

"I only shot him twice."

"No," Harvey said, "I counted. You fired six shots, and you missed on the first two."

Ron bent over and picked up what was left of the possum by its tail. He held the bloody carcass out away from his side and began walking back around the building.

Harvey hurried after the chief and said, "I don't think the children should see that."

Ron switched the possum to his other hand and attempted to hide it from the children's view as he rounded the corner.

The children came rushing at the chief, shouting, "We want to see it! Show it to us!"

"No, you can't see it," he said. He held the possum partially behind his back.

Harvey stepped between the children and Ron. He glared at the chief and said, "They've already seen it. Might as well give them the full view now." Harvey stepped aside.

Ron held the possum out in front of himself, and a glob of guts oozed from its mouth onto the grass.

Some of the children shrieked and ran back to another teacher who was now standing on the steps.

Oona stalked up to Ron and asked him, "Are you through now?"

Ron glanced down at her and shrugged. He walked over to his cruiser, popped open the trunk, and slung the dead possum into it before slamming the trunk shut. Ron opened the driver's door, and Harvey watched him drive off with the blue lights still flashing.

Oona said to Harvey, "Any time you want to run for police chief, I'll head up your campaign."

Later on, Harvey was assembling the new diaper display and trying to keep his mind off Annabelle Vernon and the Lakeshore Inn fire. But the escapade at the school with the possum and the way Ron Frank had handled the situation made him feel more and more uncertain. Wildred's letter about an adopted girl who looked like one of the Vernon kids, combined with Old Man Trent's claims that he saw Annabelle Vernon the morning after the fire, made Harvey wonder again what really happened the night the Lakeshore Inn burned. He might not be police chief of Moose Creek or a qualified detective, but it sure sounded to him like Ron Frank had bungled the whole investigation. Harvey wondered if he should call somebody…like the FBI.

In the next instant, Harvey froze with a package of diapers held mid-air. He realized once again that he had allowed himself to get distracted over something that was none of his business…something that had happened nearly twenty-five years ago. If he called the FBI, they would think he was nuts! He shoved the package of diapers onto the shelf and told himself it was high time he started focusing on more important things.

He strode back to the office and picked up the phone. If he didn't take care of his own problems, winter would be upon him, and the roof on the old LeClerc place would collapse under the weight of the snow. He decided once and for all that it was time to forget about whatever happened at the Lakeshore Inn. He had better things to do with his time.

5

ON WEDNESDAY EVENING, HARVEY WALKED FROM THE store down to the old house at the end of Second Street. He stood on the sidewalk out front, wondering again why he had taken on such a daunting project. When he had bought the place, it had all fallen together so easily. A design firm in Minneapolis had just sent him a huge project to work on. In no time at all, he had been able to save up enough to buy the old place… not that it was worth much in its present condition. He had easily won the bid at the sheriff's auction, and the closing had been relatively uneventful. That's when things had stopped falling together with ease, though. The fact of the matter was, things had simply begun falling apart.

Harvey went back to the store and got Tommy Anderson on the phone. Tommy was Moose Creek's only handyman. Harvey said, "I could use your help."

"From what I hear, you could use a few sticks of dynamite," Tommy said.

Harvey said, "Do you want to help me, or should I call somebody else?"

Tommy said, "I never said I didn't want to help, but I'm not sure there's much I can do with the old LeClerc place…assuming that's why you're calling me."

"That's why I'm calling," Harvey said. "Can you meet me out there tonight?"

"Sure," Tommy said. "I'll be there around six."

It was well past seven when Harvey heard Tommy coming. Harvey walked over to the grimy living room window just as the handyman's old red work truck came roaring up Second Street. When Tommy pulled up in front, the truck backfired loudly. A curl of blue smoke rose from the tailpipe, and the rusted piece of junk shuddered to a stop. The door squealed on its hinges when Tommy shoved it open and stepped out. Harvey braced himself for the second grating screech when Tommy closed the door.

Tommy stopped at the front of his truck to pull out a pack of cigarettes from the pocket of his red t-shirt. He lit up and continued walking towards the house. He hadn't changed much since Harvey had called him last spring to work on the plumbing at the store. Today, Tommy wore a short-sleeve green plaid shirt over his t-shirt. The buttons were undone, and it fluttered around his lanky frame as he walked. His thick red hair was cropped close on the top of his head, and the sides of it cascaded in waves well past his shoulders. Tommy paused near the front porch to take a drag on his cigarette and then spit out a stream of tobacco juice onto the ground. He wiped his mouth on his sleeve, and then clomped up the front porch steps in his heavy work boots.

Harvey opened the front door for him.

Tommy stepped inside. He held a cigarette in one hand and an empty carry-out cup in the other. Craning his neck to look upward, his mouth hung open as he looked up the open staircase to the second story ceiling. Harvey could see that Tommy's lower teeth were dark brown from the cud of chewing tobacco he always held in his lip.

A bird fluttered through a hole in the roof and disappeared.

"This is some place you bought yourself," Tommy Anderson said. He laughed, and then he broke into a fit of coughing that turned his face beet red.

Harvey wondered how long it would take Tommy to figure out that he was killing himself with tobacco. He said, "How about leaving your cigarette outside?"

"Yeah," Tommy said, walking over to the door and flicking his cigarette onto the dirt that had once been a lawn. "This place is a tinder box." He walked back to stand in the middle of the entry. "One little spark, and whoosh..." He flashed his fingers and added, "...that's all she wrote."

"Should I take you around and let you see what needs to be done?" Harvey asked.

"Everything," Tommy said.

"You haven't even looked yet," Harvey said.

"Don't need to," Tommy said, spitting tobacco juice into his paper cup. "After twenty-five years of sitting empty, it needs everything."

"Maybe," Harvey said, "but at least take a look so that you can give me a price."

"You sure you want to pour money down a rat hole?" Tommy asked. He wiped some brown dribble from his scruffy beard onto his sleeve.

"It's going to be really great when I get finished with it," Harvey said. "Come and look at the kitchen."

Tommy followed Harvey into the kitchen at the rear of the old house that he and Annabelle used to sneak into at night. She had loved the mint green vintage stove and the original oak cabinets. He said, "Have you ever seen anything like this?"

Tommy shook his head. "Does that stove even work?"

"I'm not sure," Harvey said. "The gas is turned off."

Tommy asked, "What do you want me to do in here?"

Harvey said, "I want to do all of the cabinet repairs and painting myself."

"You going to keep them old cabinets?"

"Of course," Harvey said. "They're what give the kitchen character."

Tommy opened one of the drawers, and a mouse leaped from its interior. It scurried across the floor and ran under the stove. "There's your first character," he said with a laugh.

Harvey said, "All I want you to do in here is replace the sink and the counter top."

Tommy peered at an electrical outlet and said, "You're going to need GFI outlets."

"Are you licensed to do that sort of thing?" Harvey asked.

"Don't need one, unless you're planning to pull a permit from the county." Tommy winked at him. "And what they don't know don't hurt."

Harvey decided he would definitely not be hiring Tommy to do any wiring.

Tommy said, "It's going to take me a while to look over the place. No sense tagging after me if you've got something you'd rather do."

Harvey went out onto the front porch of what would one day be his own home. He put one hand up on the porch post and leaned against it. The post gave a mighty crack, and the lower half of it toppled onto the ground. Harvey lurched forward and nearly fell onto the dead lawn. He righted himself and looked up at the top half of the post, hanging there like a lone tooth in an old man's mouth. He hoped he wouldn't regret buying the place. More importantly, he hoped he wouldn't regret calling in Tommy Anderson to do the repairs. He got the feeling that Tommy was the sort of guy who wasn't much into details, but there weren't any other handymen in the area. He wondered if he should call a few other guys from Big Bear to give him estimates before he had Tommy do any work. Maybe Oona could give him some insights about what to do.

While Tommy was checking out the house, Harvey walked two blocks back to his father's house. Inside, he found a note on the counter that read:

Dinner will be a little late. I'm getting my hair colored. –Oona

Harvey felt so agitated by his meeting with Tommy Anderson that he couldn't stand the thought of waiting to talk to Oona. So, he walked down Main Street, pushed open the door of Mandy's Day Spa, and stepped inside. Several women were huddled under the hair dryers. He found Oona sitting under one of them with some sort of plastic cap tied under her chin. Strands of her hair had been pulled through the cap. Harvey walked up to her and said, "That looks painful."

Oona lifted the dryer dome from over her head and shouted, "What?"

"When are you going to be done?" he asked.

Jacqueline Corbett appeared at his elbow and said, "She's got just a couple of minutes."

Harvey turned to find Jacqueline standing just inches from him. She was so close, he could smell her perfume. There was something strangely familiar about it. Was it the same one his mother had worn?

Oona stood up and glared at Harvey. "What are you doing in here?"

He looked from Oona to the three other women staring up at him from their seats under the dryers. What had possessed him to walk into a beauty salon? Suddenly, he felt awkward and realized that his visit must look ridiculous. He blurted out, "I wanted to ask you for your opinion about some repairs on the old house." He followed his sister over to the bank of sinks. The beautician began tugging the cap off of Oona's head.

Oona asked him, "What kind of repairs?"

Jacqueline reached for a bottle from the shelf beside Harvey. He glanced up just in time to see the curve of her breast where her dress didn't quite cover things. The view made Harvey drop his gaze to the floor for a moment. He said to Oona, "Tommy Anderson said it needs everything, but I'm thinking of just starting with a new roof."

Before Oona could respond, Jacqueline said, "A new roof is a good place to start. With winter coming, you'll want to make sure you keep out the snow."

Oona looked up at Harvey and lifted a brow.

He hated to agree with Jacqueline. Every conversation always ended with her harassing him about selling the property at the lake. But she was right in this instance, and he said to her, "That's exactly what I was thinking."

Jacqueline set the bottle back on the shelf and smiled at him.

Harvey felt his pulse pounding in places it shouldn't be, and he quickly backed towards the door. "I'll see you at home later," he said to Oona. "I want to get the old kitchen floor torn up tonight."

Oona called out, "I'll come over and help you as soon as I get finished here."

Less than thirty minutes later, while Harvey was chipping away at the old green linoleum, Oona appeared in the kitchen. He looked at his sister's head. Her hair was now a subtle mix of henna and caramel. He said, "Your hair looks really nice."

"Thanks," Oona said, peering at her reflection in a mirror near the back door. "Jacqueline's coming over here to help us as soon as she finishes up at the salon."

Harvey froze. "Jacqueline's coming here?"

"Yeah," Oona said. "She feels sorry for you. You're in over your head, you know."

He didn't want Jacqueline there. Between harassing him about his dad's place at the lake and tantalizing him with her skimpy get-ups, he didn't know how much of her he could tolerate. Without responding to Oona's observation, Harvey strode out the front door and banged it shut. He paced up and down the old planks on the front porch, wondering if he should just get in his truck and drive somewhere to avoid Jacqueline.

Suddenly, she appeared on the front walk, wearing a pair of old jeans and a t-shirt. "Where would you like me to start?" she asked with a smile.

Harvey didn't want anyone's help just because they felt sorry for him. "I can fix the place myself," he said to her.

Jacqueline looked up at the old house and then back at him. She said, "You're kidding, right?"

Thunder rumbled in the distance, and the sky began to grow so dark that it seemed more like twilight than early evening. The storm gave him a good excuse to tell her he'd decided to knock off the work for the evening. "Looks like it's going to storm," he said. "Maybe—"

Jacqueline cut him off with, "All the more reason to let me come inside before I get soaked."

Jet trotted up the sidewalk and licked Jacqueline's hand. The wind gusted suddenly, and a heavy branch crashed to the ground right next to the old house. The black Lab ran across the dead grass and began barking furiously at the fallen limb.

"Jet!" Harvey shouted, "Come!"

The dog trotted back to Harvey's side and looked up at him.

"Sit," Harvey said.

The dog tucked his hind end under his haunches and sidled up to Harvey before sitting. Harvey rubbed the smooth hair on the top of Jet's head. Harvey suddenly felt protective of his dog…the offspring of another dog that he and Annabelle had chosen together before the Lakeshore Inn had burned down.

"That was close," Jacqueline said.

Oona appeared on the porch and said, "At least it didn't fall on the roof."

A streak of lightning burst from the sky, and a loud boom sounded from down the street.

"That was even closer," Jacqueline said. She hurried up the steps and pushed past Harvey. Inside the front door, she began flipping the light switches on and off. "Power's out," she said.

Harvey bustled inside and walked through the darkened entry. He found his flashlight on the kitchen counter. He opened the cover on the fuse box that was in the walk-in pantry. He flipped the top switch, but nothing happened. "Crap," he muttered.

Jacqueline appeared at the doorway and said, "We can't work without any lights or power, unless you've got a generator."

Harvey was about to open his mouth to say they should all go home for the night.

Oona said to Jacqueline, "There's a generator out back in that old shed. Let's go start it."

Harvey felt the situation spiraling out of control. All he had wanted to do was get as far from Jacqueline as he could. The last thing he wanted was for her to start nosing through the house and the shed. "Hold on," he said, "I'll go start the generator."

Harvey aimed the flashlight at the scabby floor and walked out the back door to the rickety wooden shed that stood behind the house. He pulled out his keys and unlocked the rusty padlock on the old metal clasp that held the door shut. He stepped inside the dirt-floored shed and shone the flashlight around. He spotted an old generator behind a faded red push mower and a stack of empty boxes. He shoved everything aside and bent over to get a grip on the handle of the generator.

Suddenly, the door banged shut behind him. Startled, he dropped the flashlight, and it went out. "Judas Priest!" he exclaimed. He bent over to feel around in the dark for the flashlight, and he felt something furry scurry past his hand. He found the flashlight, flipped it back on, and hauled the generator outside into the grey light. He lumbered across the grass between the shed and the house towards the back door.

Oona and Jacqueline appeared on the back stoop. Jacqueline said, "You'll never get that old thing started."

It was bad enough having Jacqueline in his house. He didn't need her telling him what he couldn't do. It was obvious that she wasn't going to leave him alone, so he decided he'd send Oona and her down into the basement to work. He checked the gas in the generator. There wasn't much in it, but he figured it would run long enough to at least get some of the junk hauled out of the basement. As soon as that was finished, he'd get rid of Jacqueline. He primed the gas engine, and then yanked on the tattered pull cord. Nothing.

"Might as well give it up," Jacqueline said.

Harvey glared at her. "Why don't you go back inside and let me handle this?"

Jacqueline disappeared, and Harvey gave the pull cord another mighty tug. Nothing.

Oona called out, "Try again."

He yanked on the cord and said, "Come on!" The generator roared to life, and he looked up at Oona. She gave him a smile and a thumbs-up. Harvey stepped away, satisfied that he had proven Jacqueline wrong.

He connected an auxiliary power cord to the generator and then went back inside to attach the cord to the fuse box. The lights came back on. A few minutes later, Jacqueline turned on the radio on the kitchen counter. The oldies station began playing, and she turned up the volume, flashing a smile at Harvey. She snapped her fingers and began swaying with the beat.

Harvey felt like groaning out loud. They were playing the song that he and Annabelle had danced to the night of his senior prom. He had to get Jacqueline out of his sight. He said to the women, "You two can go downstairs and start bagging up the junk in the basement." He grabbed a broom and hurried out to the front porch.

Harvey was surprised to find Doc Daggert standing on the front walk. The retired dentist, who was wearing a yellow ball cap and a blue plaid shirt, was the kind of guy who mostly kept to himself. Harvey could understand why. Rumor had it that mercury poisoning had made the old guy a little off. He walked funny, and his hands shook like a drunk in detox. The old dentist's right shoulder drooped, and his left arm hung stiffly at his side.

Doc Daggert said, "This place is a dump."

Harvey leaned the broom against the blistering paint on the clapboard and said, "It's a mess now, but it's going to be great when it's all finished."

Doc walked in, made his way to the kitchen, and peered out the back door at the rumbling generator, "Your power went out?"

"Yeah," Harvey said.

"Lightning hit a transformer on Main," Doc said, making his way across the room. "Power went out at Skeeter's. Too dark to finish eating, so I left." He shuffled over to the old refrigerator and pulled open the door. He peered into its dark, moldy interior and then closed it. He turned to Harvey to say, "I'm going fishing. You got any minnows?"

Thunder rumbled overhead, and Harvey asked, "You're going out there in this weather?"

Doc said, "Nah. I'm headed out early in the morning. I'm hoping to catch some walleye."

"With this storm, you may not catch much."

"Maybe not. I'm going to Upper Red Lake this weekend, though, and I always luck out there."

Harvey said. "Did you hear about that guy who tried launching his boat on *Lower* Red Lake last week? He got his boat confiscated."

"He was an idiot," Doc said. "The Indians haven't ever allowed outsiders on the lower lake."

Harvey said, "I've got some minnows downstairs." As soon as the words were out of his mouth, he wanted to kick himself. Jacqueline was down there.

Harvey followed Doc down to the cellar with its uneven flagstone floor and past the side room where Jacqueline and Oona were chattering and shoving old junk into big black garbage bags. Harvey hurried over to the cavernous laundry sink, where he had recently dumped several dozen minnows. The aquarium pump he had bought to keep the water oxygenated hummed, and a bare bulb gave off thin light. While he was chasing the fish around with a little net, he asked, "How do you like fishing Upper Red Lake?"

Doc said, "It's great. A guy from the reservation takes me onto a part of the lake that's off-limits to the rest of the world."

"How'd you manage that?" Harvey asked.

"I ran a free dental clinic for the folks on the reservation for nearly forty years," Doc said. "I guess it's their way of saying thanks."

"Not a bad deal," Harvey said. He scooped up a net full of wriggling minnows. Suddenly, it struck him that Doc Daggert had been around back when the Lakeshore Inn had burned. He said, "Doc, can I ask you a question?"

Doc Daggert shrugged and stood there swaying, holding himself up on the edge of the laundry sink.

Harvey said, "My dad's been talking about seeing Annabelle Vernon the morning after the Lakeshore Inn burned. Do you think it might be true?"

A far-away look came across Doc Daggert's face, and he said, "I never thought about it before, but I suppose it's a possibility."

Harvey felt his stomach flip-flop with a mixture of excitement and foreboding. "Why do you think that?"

Doc shifted his weight and swayed slightly before answering. He said, "The fire burned so hot for so long, it was impossible to identify the bodies." He shook his head and added, "I told Ron Frank that if he would let me take a look at the remains, I could identify them by their dental work."

"Of course," Harvey said.

Doc said, "But Ron never let anyone else see the bodies."

"Why not?" Harvey picked up a quart jar from a shelf over the sink.

"He said he wanted to spare people...claimed he was having nightmares afterward."

"That seems like sloppy police work to me," Harvey said. "If no one ever identified them, how did Ron know who was dead?" He shook some minnows into the jar.

"That's what I thought at the time," Doc said, "but back then, we didn't question what Ron was doing. The mayor had brought him in from some big police force outside of Chicago, and he came across as really knowing what he was doing."

"I can't imagine that," Harvey said. He added a little water to the jar.

Doc nodded and said, "If Ron let that sort of thing happen today, I'd be the first one to demand an external investigation."

"I'd be the second," Harvey said. He screwed the lid on.

Doc Daggert paused to look at Harvey's lure collection in an open tackle box. He picked up a Minnesota Minnie lure and asked, "Mind if I take one of these?"

"Go ahead," Harvey said, hanging up the little minnow net behind the sink. "Mike Ianelli caught the biggest northern Pike I've ever seen with one of those." He dried his hands on the front of his shirt. "You had any luck with them, Doc?"

Doc Daggert said, "Haven't you heard? They're great for landing men. Snagged seven so far this month."

Harvey looked at Doc in surprise, and then handed the old dentist the jar of minnows.

The old man winked and shoved the lure into his shirt pocket.

Doc's comment reminded Harvey that there was a killer on the loose in their county. He wondered if he ought to keep track of everyone who purchased Minnesota Minnie lures at Paul Bunyan's General Store. That way, he could help the police catch the guy. In the next instant, he realized it would be a complete waste of time if Ron Frank were on the case.

Glancing up at the old man standing before him with his hands shaking made Harvey's idea seem doubly ludicrous. Doc Daggert didn't strike him as the type of guy who would go around snagging people in the lip with those lures. With those shaky hands, Harvey was amazed he could even hang onto a lure without snagging himself. He pushed the Fishing Lure Killer from his mind.

Doc turned and began making his way slowly up the steps. He said, "I'll see you later."

Harvey called after Doc, "If you land anything besides men with that lure, bring it back to the house. We'll have a fish fry."

Doc Daggert disappeared, and Jacqueline came out of the furnace room. She said, "That old guy is weird."

"No, he's not," Harvey said.

"I heard what he said about snagging men. That's creepy," Jacqueline said.

"He was joking," Harvey said.

"It didn't sound like a joke to me," Jacqueline said. "I wouldn't go fishing with him if I were you."

Having to contain his agitation toward Jacqueline was getting to Harvey. In the next instant, he snapped, "Why don't *you* go fishing?"

Jacqueline lifted an eyebrow.

Harvey instantly regretted his words. Jacqueline might be annoying, but it didn't give him license to be rude to her.

Jacqueline hurried up the stairs.

He turned to ask Oona, "Did you call the power company?"

"Nope." She dragged a bag full of junk over to the bottom of the stairs.

"Why not?"

"Phone's out."

Harvey sighed deeply. "That's great," he said. "Just great."

She hoisted up a bag of trash into her arms and started up the stairs. Over her shoulder, she said, "If you had a cell phone, you wouldn't need to worry about the land line going out in a storm."

"You know how I feel about cell phones," Harvey called after her. He gripped the railing and thought that if he didn't get away from his problems, he'd explode. He hurried up the stairs and stopped in the kitchen to say to Oona, "I'm going over to the store to call the power company. Turn off the generator and lock up when you get finished."

On his way through the kitchen, he heard someone yell from downstairs, "You have this place inspected before you bought it?"

That's when he remembered that Tommy Anderson was still there. "No," Harvey called out. "I bought it *as is* in the sheriff's sale."

Tommy shouted from his position near the basement stairwell, "*As is* is code for you're screwed."

Harvey felt his heart sinking as he waited for Tommy to climb up the stairs. "What do you mean?"

They went back into the living room, and Tommy began counting off the repairs on his fingers. "First off, your chimney's cracked. Can't start a fire until you put in a flue liner. Second, you've got two layers of roof up there that need to come down before you can fix the rotted plywood under it. You've got water rot in the rafters, so some of them'll have to be replaced. Third, you've got old knob and tube wiring that's shorting out.

The whole place has to be rewired, unless, of course, you want to burn it down and collect on the insurance. Fourth, some fool came through here after the fact—probably sometime in the forties—and put in a bunch of galvanized pipe. It's all junk. Fifth, unless you want to heat the entire state of Minnesota, you'll probably want to put in replacement windows, doors, and insulation." He paused and asked, "You want to hear the rest, or have you come to your senses?"

Harvey had to admit that things were a lot worse than he had originally thought. Maybe it had been foolish to buy the old place, but when he looked around at the twelve-inch solid walnut baseboards, the curving banister and open staircase that led to the second floor, the original wainscoting in the library, and the stained glass peacock in the window next to the living room fireplace, he couldn't possibly give up on it. It was a work of art, and he was determined to restore it…even if Annabelle wasn't ever going to live there with him.

He said to Tommy, "Let's just start with the roof. I know I can't get those old scalloped shingles anymore. How about you get me a price for replacing the rafters, tearing off both layers of roofing, repairing the plywood, and replacing the old shingles with some dimensional ones?"

Tommy shrugged. "Okay," he said. He opened the front door and began walking down the steps. He said, "There is one thing you got going for you."

"What's that?" Harvey asked.

"Somebody knew what they were doing when they laid that brick. Most old houses around here have rock foundations. They're all crap."

Harvey nodded and smiled. "If the foundation's solid, anything's possible. Right?"

Tommy looked back at him and busted out laughing. Then, in another fit of coughing, he staggered back to his truck and drove away with a roar.

Harvey had come to the old house to get his mind off the Lakeshore Inn and Annabelle Vernon. But no matter how hard he tried, thoughts of both kept surfacing. He decided to go back to the store. Work had always been the only way he knew to maintain his sanity.

6

THE POWER WAS BACK ON, AND HARVEY WAS SITTING IN HIS father's office at Paul Bunyan's General Store, going over the clerks' time schedules for the following week. From the doorway, he heard someone say his name. He looked up to find Wildred Swenson standing there with a FedEx packet in her hand. He was surprised that she was still awake at that time of night. It was close to nine.

"You need me to send that for you?" he asked her.

Wildred shook her head and stepped forward to lay the package on the desk. Harvey realized then that she was not sending something out; she had received something and had already opened it. He looked down at the label and noted that the return address was from a company in Cincinnati. He looked up at Wildred and asked, "What's this about?"

Wildred sank into the chair opposite the desk and said, "Read it."

He noticed then that Wildred looked unusually pale. "You okay?" he asked.

Wildred shrugged and pointed at the letter. She repeated, "Read it."

Harvey nodded and sat down at the desk. From the package, he withdrew a sheet of paper. Judging by the letterhead, it was from an attorney's office. He read:

Dear Mrs. Swenson:

My office has been directed to contact you in the event that two of my clients predeceased their adopted daughter. Based on some information that you provided to our client approximately fifteen years ago, we believe that our client's daughter may be the missing child you identified as Catherine Vernon of Moose Creek, Minnesota.

Our client's daughter has been notified that you, or your personal representative, will be contacting her within the week. If you should decide that you wish to pursue this matter, please contact this office immediately for further information. Time is of the essence.

Attached to the letter were two old photographs of a little girl. In the first, she glared into the camera from her seat on a tricycle. On the back, someone had scrawled, *Six months with us and still not talking.* The second photo seemed to be the same little girl beaming at an enormous birthday cake. He turned it over and read, *Catherine, on her fourth birthday.* He looked up at Wildred, held up the second picture, and asked, "Is this the picture you sent them?"

Wildred nodded. "Do you realize what else this means?"

Harvey's mind was racing. He could see that the girls in the photos looked like the same person. If Catherine Vernon had survived the Lakeshore Inn fire, maybe Annabelle had, too. Logic told him that no one could have survived the fire. But a tiny flame of hope flickered inside him, nevertheless. At length, he said, "It means that my dad might not be as confused as everyone thinks."

"Do you think Ron Frank made a mistake all those years ago?"

Harvey stood up and said, "Maybe. And if someone can prove it, he's going to be in a lot of hot water."

Wildred leaned forward in her chair and said, "Do you think there is a chance that Peter might be alive, too?"

Harvey stood there thinking about the four Vernon children. If Annabelle had driven out of town the day after the fire, and Catherine had wound up in Cincinnati, anything seemed possible in Peter's case. "Maybe," he said.

"What should I do?" Wildred asked.

"Ask Ron to reopen the case," Harvey said.

"Well, yes, eventually," Wildred said, "But what I meant is, what should I do about this young lady in Cincinnati?"

Harvey walked around to the front of the desk and sat down on it. Wildred had such a hopeful look in her eyes; he hated to tell her that it could all be a mistake. How could these people in Ohio possibly believe that their adopted daughter was a missing child from northern Minnesota? Wildred was getting old. He didn't want her running off to Cincinnati just to have her hopes dashed. It might be her undoing.

But on the other hand, who was he to say that this young woman wasn't Catherine Vernon? If she were, she had a right to know where she had come from. And if Peter were still alive, wasn't it just as important to try to find him, too? The mere chance that Annabelle might still be alive set his heart racing. He decided there was too much at stake to just do nothing. At last, he said, "The letter says that you or your personal representative can initiate a meeting with her. You could send someone to meet her."

Wildred sat there for a moment, staring at the floor. At last, she looked up and said, "I think that would be best." She pointed at the letter on Harvey's desk and said, "Hand me the letter."

Harvey handed her the letter.

Wildred said, "Do you mind if I use your phone?"

Harvey said, "I doubt that you'll get an attorney on the phone at this time of night." He handed her the phone and waited while she dialed the number.

A moment later, Wildred said into the phone, "Yes, my name is Wildred Swenson. I am calling about a letter that you sent me about Catherine Vernon."

After a moment, she said, "Yes. Now I would like you to speak to my personal representative, Harvey Trent." She held out the phone to Harvey. "He wants to speak to you."

Personal representative? Harvey hadn't meant that he should take on that role. He took the phone from Wildred and said, "Hello?"

"Harvey Trent?" a man asked.

"Yes," he said.

"I'm going to need some information from you before we can continue."

"Okay," Harvey said. He walked around behind the desk and sat down. "Go ahead."

The man said, "In order to protect our client's identity, you are going to need to provide some proof that this girl is actually Catherine Vernon."

"How am I supposed to do that?" Harvey asked.

The man said, "Catherine Vernon arrived at my client's house wearing something that would immediately identify her. In all likelihood, only her birth family could explain. Can you describe it?"

"Hold on," Harvey said. He covered the mouthpiece and said to Wildred, "He's saying that Catherine arrived there wearing something that would immediately identify her. He wants me to describe it."

Wildred frowned. She rose and picked up the picture of Catherine Vernon on her tricycle.

Harvey waited, but Wildred didn't say anything. Into the phone, he said, "Just a minute."

The wrinkles between Wildred's eyebrows grew deeper as she studied the picture. She laid it down and picked up the other photograph of the girl on her birthday. Suddenly, Wildred let out a little gasp. With a trembling hand, she handed the pictures to Harvey and said, "Give me the phone."

Harvey said to the man on the other end, "Wildred wants to talk to you again."

Wildred took the phone and said, "If this girl is Catherine Vernon, she was wearing a gold chain with a medallion on it."

Harvey watched Wildred's expression. Her lips were pressed tightly together as she listened to something the man was saying.

At last, Wildred said, "Yes, the front of it was light blue." She nodded. "It had St. Guinevere holding a sword. Around her neck was a red ring."

There was a pause.

Wildred added, "And on the back were the words, *Von Will*."

There was another pause, and Wildred said, "No. It means Von Willebrand. All of the Vernon children had Von Willebrand…it is a bleeding disorder."

Wildred stood there listening, and suddenly, a broad smile spread across her face and deepened every wrinkle. She motioned to Harvey that she needed something to write with. He fished a sheet of paper out of the drawer and handed it to her, along with a pen. Wildred bent forward and began frantically scribbling down information. While holding the phone, she straightened up and said to Harvey, "Can you go to Cincinnati for me before next Tuesday?"

Go to Cincinnati? Before next Tuesday? Harvey shrugged.

Before he could answer, Wildred said, "Someone will be there before Tuesday. Yes. Oh, thank you. Thank you!" Wildred handed Harvey the phone and sank into the chair.

Harvey put down the phone and asked, "What did he say?"

Wildred clasped her hands to her chest and said, "Oh, Harvey! It *is* Catherine!" She leaped to her feet and shouted, "I cannot believe it! Oh, I just cannot believe it!"

From the doorway, Eric Larsen asked, "Believe what?"

Wildred whirled around and stood there staring at their town's favorite banjo player. In the next instant, she said, "The price of milk. It has doubled in the past five years."

Eric said, "I'll bet Benny drinks a lot of it, too."

Wildred nodded and swiftly closed the door. She turned back to Harvey, and her eyes shimmered with tears.

Harvey asked, "So, what do we do next?"

Wildred said, "They want someone to go to Cincinnati for a meeting with Catherine." She bent over the paper on the desk and said, "Her adopted name is...oh, where is it...Kit Blume."

Harvey's concern about this adoption thing being a hoax or a mistake had vanished with Wildred's description of the Vernon children's medallions. "So you're going there this week?" Harvey asked.

Wildred picked up the photo of Catherine and said, "No, I have something very important that I must do here."

"What?" Harvey asked.

"I want to throw a huge party," Wildred said, "a surprise party."

"For Catherine?" Harvey asked.

"For everyone," Wildred said. In an undertone, she added, "Promise me you will not tell a soul what is going on. I want the whole town to be in a state of shock when you bring Catherine home from Cincinnati."

Harvey felt as if a rug had been yanked out from under him. He didn't want to go running off to Cincinnati to drag some girl back to Moose Creek. How did Wildred think he was going to convince her that any of this was true? He said, "Wildred, what if she doesn't want to come back here?"

"Of course, she will!" Wildred exclaimed. "This is her home."

Harvey didn't want Wildred to get her feelings hurt. He said, "It was her home, but you have to consider that she has had a much different home since she left here."

"Of course, she will want to meet all of us."

"Maybe not," Harvey said. "It says in that letter that her parents just died. She might not want to leave Cincinnati to come up here right now."

Wildred handed Harvey the letter and shoved Catherine's photos into her purse. She said, "I am not going to let you spoil my happiness right now. When can you leave?"

"Did I hear you say someone would be there by Tuesday?" Harvey asked.

"Yes," Wildred said. "The lawyer said that if someone is not there by Tuesday, no further information will be given to us. He said that Catherine's father made it clear that he did not want this dragged out. If we are interested in meeting her, it has to be within one week of the date on that letter."

Harvey looked at the date and then down at the schedule he'd been working on. If he increased some hours for his two part-time clerks, they could manage the store for a few days without him. And then something hit him. "Suppose Catherine doesn't want to get into a truck with a strange man all by herself?"

Wildred said, "You have a point." She pressed her index finger to her pursed lips for a moment and then said, "We will tell Oona. She can go with you."

The thought of telling Oona that the two of them were going to leave town on very short notice to travel to Cincinnati didn't strike Harvey as a very good idea. She would remind him that he was once again letting himself get sidetracked from his duties at the store and his projects at the old house. "I don't know," Harvey said. "It's going to be pretty hard to keep all of this quiet if Oona and I just suddenly take off like that. She's got to think about school again on Tuesday, and I've got to take care of things here at the store."

"Oh, I see," Wildred said. She slumped into the chair.

"Why don't I drive you to the airport in Minneapolis? You can fly to Cincinnati to meet Catherine yourself."

"Me?" Wildred looked frantic. "I have never been on a plane in my life."

"How did you get here from Germany?"

"On a ship, of course," Wildred said.

"Flying's no big deal," Harvey said. "People do it all the time."

"What about terrorists?" Wildred asked.

"I'm sure you can get from here to Cincinnati and back without worrying about a terrorist attack," Harvey said. "It's not like you're flying to the Middle East."

"Oh, dear," Wildred said. "Are you sure you will not go for me?"

Harvey's resolve wavered. Wildred looked so…old. At that moment, someone knocked on the door. "Come in!" Harvey called out.

One of the clerks said, "There's water all over the floor under the frozen food section. I think something's wrong with the freezer."

"I'll be right there," Harvey told the clerk. He stood up and closed the door. "Do you see what I'm talking about?" he asked Wildred. "If I leave here, the whole place will go down the drain. There's no one else besides me to handle these kinds of problems."

He picked up the phone and dialed Tommy Anderson. "Can you come over to the store? The freezer's leaking again."

After he got Tommy to come over right away, he hung up and looked at Wildred.

She sighed and said, "You are right. I suppose Fred and Sophie could manage the bakery without me for a few days."

"It's going to be pretty hard to keep this a secret," Harvey said.

"Well, I might have to tell Fred and Sophie, but I am sure they will not tell anyone," Wildred said.

"Then it's all settled," Harvey said. "Do you want me to call the airlines for you?"

"That would be fine," Wildred said. "Get me a flight after the town council dinner on Friday night. If I am not there, people will suspect something."

"Good idea," Harvey said.

Wildred pulled a credit card out of her purse, handed it to him, and said, "Charge it. I don't care how much it costs." She stood and went to the door. She reached out, put her hand on the knob, and then turned back to say with a smile, "Just imagine, after all these years, Catherine is coming home."

He was imagining how he would feel if this missing person coming to town were Annabelle. He said to Wildred, "I'll come over to your house later tonight with your ticket."

Wildred disappeared, and Harvey went to check out the frozen food section. Tommy Anderson was sprawled on his back near the broken freezer, wrestling with something beneath it.

From the opposite end of the aisle, Harvey saw Ron Frank approaching. Their police chief sauntered up to Tommy Anderson and said with a chuckle, "You look like part of a crime scene, Anderson."

"This dang bolt's going to kill me," Tommy Anderson muttered. He wiped his forehead on his sleeve and threw his weight into an enormous crescent wrench.

Harvey asked Tommy, "What do you think is wrong with it?"

The wrench clattered to the floor, and Tommy Anderson sat up. "Compressor's gone bad," he said.

"Can you fix it?"

"Nope. Needs a new one."

"How much will that cost?"

Tommy told him the price, and Harvey felt as if he'd been socked in the gut. Surely, there had to be some other way.

Ron Frank gave Harvey a little punch in the shoulder and said, "Time to let Jacqueline Corbett sell this place for you. It's a money pit."

Harvey didn't like running the old store, but he really disliked hearing Ron Frank bashing it. He didn't respond to him, but said to Tommy, "I'll give you a call back first thing in the morning."

Tommy stood up and said, "I'll send you a bill for the service call."

"Hoo-hoo, glad I'm not you today," Ron Frank said to Harvey. He reached into one of the freezers, picked up a bucket of ice cream, and sauntered back towards the front.

After closing up the store for the night, Harvey left Paul Bunyan's with Wildred's ticket information printed out on a sheet of paper. He tucked the paper into his shirt pocket and drove the few blocks to Wildred's little bungalow to knock on the front door. To his surprise, Oona opened it.

"What are you doing here?" he asked.

"Wildred's sick," she said.

Harvey followed Oona inside and found Wildred lying on the sofa. "What's the matter?" he asked her.

She looked up at him and said, "All this excitement has my heart all out of whack."

Harvey looked back at Oona. She said, "Wildred told me all about Catherine."

Harvey nodded.

Oona pulled him into the kitchen and said in a low tone, "I can't believe you told Wildred that she'd have to fly to Cincinnati all by herself."

Harvey figured Oona would have been glad to know that he hadn't allowed this recent event to sidetrack him from his own issues. He said, "You're always telling me not to get sidetracked. I figured a trip to Cincinnati would be a major detour."

Oona crossed her arms and said, "Harvey Trent, there is no way that we're going to send Wildred all by herself to Cincinnati. You'll have to go with her."

Wildred called out from the living room, "I am not going to Cincinnati at all."

Harvey looked up at Oona, wondering what to say next.

Oona approached the sofa and said, "Surely, you want to be the first one Catherine meets."

"Yes," Wildred said, "but I cannot risk going on a plane right now. I remember the doctor telling me a long time ago that flying could be bad for my heart."

Harvey walked into the living room. "I can't go to Cincinnati to bring this girl back here all by myself," he said to Wildred. "She'll never agree to it."

"Then I'll just have to go with you," Oona said.

"Why don't you go by yourself?" Harvey asked.

"Because I think it's going to take two of us to get this girl to come back here," Oona said.

"And what am I supposed to do about the store?" Harvey asked. "One of the freezers broke today."

"Fred can fill in for you," Wildred said. "Sophie and I can manage by ourselves."

"I just don't know…" Harvey said.

Suddenly, Wildred pressed her fist to her chest and said, "Oh, dear, here we go again."

Oona hurried out to the kitchen and came back with a prescription bottle. She shook out a tiny white pill and said, "Here, put this under your tongue."

Wildred put the pill into her mouth and closed her eyes. Harvey stood there watching as the old woman's face took on a pained expression. Oona sat beside her and stroked Wildred's snow-white hair. She said, "Just try to take a few deep breaths. You're going to be fine."

After a minute, Wildred's face relaxed, and she sighed deeply. Opening her eyes, she said, "I am sorry to have to ask you to do this, Harvey, but there is no one else that I trust. Will you please go to Cincinnati for me?"

Harvey looked from Wildred to Oona and back again.

Wildred said, "I must see Catherine again at least once before I die."

Harvey couldn't see any way out of it. "Fine," he said at last. "Oona and I will fly out on Friday night as soon as the town council dinner ends, and we'll come back on Sunday." He added, "Just don't get your heart set on having Catherine come back with us."

"Then it is all settled," Wildred said. "We will have a grand party at the bakery on Monday morning. It will be a wonderful surprise for everybody."

"If she agrees to come," Harvey pointed out.

Oona stood up and said to Wildred, "Let me help you get into bed."

Wildred shooed her away and said, "I will sleep here. You two run along. You must pack your bags."

Benny came loping into the room and asked, "You hungry?"

Harvey turned to look at Benny and said, "I'll bet you are."

"Uh-huh," Benny said, rubbing his belly. "Real hungry."

Oona said to Harvey, "I'll get him something to eat. You go on home. I'll be there in a little while."

Harvey turned back to Wildred and said, "Try to get some rest."

Wildred reached up and took Harvey's hand. She said, "Benny has at least one sister who is still alive. Maybe his brother is, too. We are both counting on you to bring Catherine home so that we can figure out what happened the night of the fire."

Harvey realized at that moment that worrying about his house renovations, or his broken freezer, or even Jacqueline Corbett harassing him about his dad's property could not take precedence over this. Somebody had to do something, and Wildred needed him to deal with it. He said, "Don't worry about a thing. I'll do everything I can to get Catherine to come back with me. One way or another, we'll figure out what happened the night the Lakeshore Inn burned down."

7

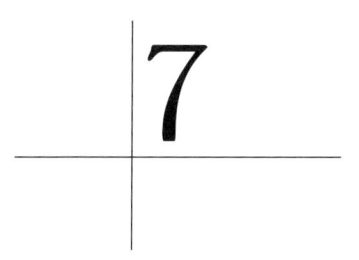

AFTER OONA HAD FIXED BENNY SOME DINNER AND PUT him to bed, she tucked a blanket around Wildred. She stepped out onto the front porch to breathe in the balmy night air that had moved in after the storm. She glanced back into the living room. Wildred lay with her feet propped up on the sofa. For the past hour, the old woman had been snoring softly. Oona sighed and hoped the two of them would be okay by themselves. She walked down the porch steps and turned right on Maple Street.

As she walked, Oona contemplated all that was happening. Life in Moose Creek was unraveling like a cheap piece of fabric, and she didn't know how to keep it from falling apart. Her father's revelation about Annabelle Vernon had been like a tiny, dangling thread. But the news of Catherine Vernon's adoption was like a giant tear clean through the middle of that fabric.

Oona crossed Fourth Street, and a cat scurried away from a trash can standing at the curb. She wondered what things would be like in Moose Creek if the Lakeshore Inn had never burned down. She had a feeling that things might have turned out differently. As she turned at the corner of Second and Maple, she glanced up at the old LeClerc mansion. The wind lifted the leaves on the trees overhead, whispering something softly into the night.

She thought of the young woman from Cincinnati who would arrive in Moose Creek on Sunday…provided she agreed to return with them. How would she see Harvey's house, their father's bungalow, and their little town after having spent most of her life in a big city?

Oona looked around and tried to imagine what it would be like to look at Moose Creek through different eyes. Overall, she decided, it looked pretty shabby. A lot of the historic homes on Maple Street were in need of an overhaul, but most of the residents didn't have the money to make the repairs. Oona had to admit that Harvey's newly purchased house was at the top of the list of the town's biggest eyesores. If she had the resources to help everyone, she would see to it that they painted, repaired their fences, overhauled their lawns, and towed away the mounds of junk piled up on porches.

It was too bad that Catherine Vernon had to come home to such a run-down place. It had not always been this way. When Oona was a girl, people had taken greater pride in their little town. With the Lakeshore Inn attracting tourists, they had all had more money in their pockets, too.

Oona thought of a letter that lay folded in the top drawer of her desk. It was from the University of Chicago, and they had offered her a position in the art department. It was hers for the taking. All she had to do was send in an acceptance letter and make the move. She had not been able to make up her mind about whether to take the job or to stay in Moose Creek. On the one hand, she loved living in the same town where she had grown up. She had a good job teaching art at the Moose Creek Local School. And yet, on the other hand, it was beginning to feel as if it were time to move on to something fresh…to a place where a new set of people needed her skills… to a place that didn't feel as if it were on the verge of a painful death.

She walked across the grass in the city park, towards a bench where she could see Harvey sitting by himself. She came to stand in front of him. He had leaned over with his elbows resting on his knees. Obviously, he was deep in thought. And then, he sighed deeply and sat back. When he looked up and saw Oona standing there, he started and said, "Judas Priest, you scared me!"

"Sorry," Oona said. "You looked so deep in thought, I didn't want to interrupt."

Harvey slid over to one end of the bench and said, "You can't sleep either?"

Oona sat down and stretched her legs out, crossing them at the ankles. She said, "I can't stop thinking about what it's going to be like for Catherine to come back here."

Harvey said, "I was thinking about the same thing."

Oona asked, "Are you sure we're doing the right thing?"

"You mean, going to get her?"

"Yeah, I mean, maybe we should let sleeping dogs lie."

"That would certainly be a lot easier," Harvey said, "but I'm not sure that it's the right thing to do."

While they sat there under the light of the street lamp, Harvey told Oona about his broken freezer at the grocery store, the overwhelming list of repairs at the old LeClerc place, his frustration with their aging father, and the nagging sense that something went very wrong with the investigation of the Lakeshore Inn fire. When he finished, he said, "I'm so stressed out, I just want to crawl into bed and pull the covers over my head."

Oona noted that her brother did have a lot on his plate. If their father hadn't gotten sick, Harvey's life would have turned out so differently. He would probably be happily married to someone from the city and be successfully designing buildings in California. He wouldn't be worrying about mundane things, like broken freezers at the store. She said, "You've let your problems just pile up until you're like a truck stuck in mud with a two-ton load in the back."

Harvey nodded and said, "That's exactly how I feel."

Oona wanted to tell him to just pack up and move back to the West Coast, but she hated giving people advice that could prove to be wrong. So, she said, "You're going to either have to unload some of the junk or wait until your engine gives out and you have to get towed to a repair station."

"What should I unload?" Harvey asked.

Oona wanted Harvey to come to his own conclusions. She raised an eyebrow and said, "That's only a question you can answer. What do you want to unload?"

Harvey asked softly, "Truthfully?"

Oona nodded.

"I'd love to sell Paul Bunyan's and the money pit and just get in my truck and drive back out West."

So, they were both thinking of leaving their little town. "What's stopping you?" she asked.

Harvey shrugged and said, "A sense of duty to the family, I guess."

Oona could relate to that same sense, but she also understood how duty could hold a person back. She crossed her arms and said, "There's no joy in living a life that is based on nothing more than duty."

Harvey sat there staring across the park at the empty benches scattered under the trees. He looked really miserable.

Oona wished she could wave a magic wand and make life easier for her brother. But, she knew that he had to learn how to adapt to both the valleys and the mountain top experiences that life had to offer. She said softly, "Did you know that I was married once?"

Harvey looked up at her in surprise. "When?"

"Right after high school."

"To who?"

Oona thought about the first man she had ever loved. He had taken her through some pretty deep valleys. She said, "I married a guy I met during college orientation. We were too young, and it only lasted six months. While I was with him, I felt a sense of duty to stick it out, just like you. But after a while, I felt like a robot, just going through the motions."

Harvey nodded. "I know that feeling."

Oona recalled the unbearable pain that came with the divorce. She hoped Harvey never had to experience that. "When I left him, I felt guilty. I guess that's what drove me to join the convent at St. Anne's." Oona sighed and said, "I never told the Reverend Mother I had been married before. In fact, you're the only person now in Moose Creek who knows."

Harvey said, "I feel ashamed of myself for just thinking about leaving Moose Creek or selling dad's store."

Oona remembered feeling completely broken and lost after giving up on her service to the church. For a long time afterward, she couldn't even pray. "How hard do you think it was to break my vows to the church?" Oona asked.

"Now that would be tough," Harvey said. "Why did you do it?"

Oona had sunken to such a deep valley back then, she had to do something. She said, "I was looking at my paintings one day, and I realized that they had all become the same…lifeless, colorless, dark images. While I may have been helping a lot of people…like when I went to Africa to work with the Red Cross…I wasn't being true to myself. My paintings reflected how I felt on the inside." She leaned back and draped her arm over the back of the bench. "I realized then that my spirit was dying, and I had to do something different."

"Weren't you worried about what people would say?" Harvey asked.

She had come to realize that what other people thought about her was the least of her worries. "At first," Oona said. "But eventually I understood that we aren't supposed to live just to make other people happy. We have to live to please the spirit that God has placed in us." She looked over at him and smiled.

Harvey said, "I think you're the craziest, wisest, bravest person I have ever known."

Oona laughed, and her heart swelled with love for her brother. He was getting the point. She leaned her head on his shoulder.

Harvey put his arm around her and asked, "Are you happy now?"

Closing her eyes, she sat there thinking about his question. From across the park, the sound of footsteps made her look up. Ron Frank was walking his night-time beat, his cigarette tip glowing red in the shadows. She watched him turn up Main Street in the direction of his own house. Within minutes, she knew he would be watching TV from his recliner that everyone could see from the street. The man never bothered closing his blinds.

Her thoughts turned back to Harvey's question. Was she happy? Feeling the warmth of her brother's body beside her, the cool evening breeze on her face, and the comfort of knowing that their childhood home stood waiting just blocks away made her feel safe. And yet, at the same time, there was a restlessness that refused to go away. She opened her eyes and said, "I thought I was, but there's something bothering me."

"The Lakeshore Inn fire?" Harvey asked.

Oona didn't want to burden Harvey with her own troubles, but she had no one else to talk to that she could trust. She turned to look up at him and said "There's something I've been keeping to myself."

"Other than the fact that you've been married before?" Harvey asked with a lift of one eyebrow.

Oona grinned and elbowed him in the ribs. "Yes."

"Don't tell me you've been robbing banks or knocking over convenience stores."

Oona chuckled and said, "No, nothing like that." She took a deep breath and said, "I've been thinking of moving to Chicago."

He looked at her in surprise. "Really?"

She nodded. "I got an offer from the University of Chicago. It's a position with the art department."

"You going to take it?"

Was she? It was such a great job, but there was something holding her back. "I can't make up my mind."

"Why not?"

She really wanted to leave Moose Creek and experience life more fully in Chicago. There were so many more things to do there…so many more available men. Soon, she would be too old to have a child of her own. Oona felt her life slipping through her fingers, but, at the same time, she was reluctant to leave her father or Harvey or her students. "One part of me wants to go, and another part of me wants to stay."

"It sounds like you and I are in the same boat."

Oona nodded. There did seem to be a common undercurrent of dissatisfaction between them, combined with this sense of duty that kept them rooted to Moose Creek.

Harvey said, "Maybe this trip to Cincinnati is just what you and I need."

Oona thought he had a good point. She said, "A little adventure into the real world couldn't hurt."

He sat there staring at the ground for a moment and then said, "Maybe we want to leave Moose Creek to escape this new problem with the Lakeshore Inn fire."

Oona had wondered about that, too. She said, "It's not going to be easy to convince somebody to re-open an investigation into a case that's been closed for nearly twenty-five years."

"Ron Frank sure as heck won't," Harvey said.

Oona thought about how badly Ron had handled the possum incident at the school. Surely, everyone else in town could see that he was useless as a cop. "How do we get rid of him?" Oona asked.

"I'm not sure," Harvey said. "I guess we'd have to start with the town council. They have the ultimate say in whether or not we keep him on. If it can be proven that he is incompetent, the council could vote to replace him."

Just thinking about all of the red tape and bureaucracy involved made Oona feel impatient. "That could take a really long time," she said.

"Yeah, and I'm not sure I want to be living in the same town with Ron Frank while that type of thing is going on."

Leaving town would be so much easier than dealing with these problems. But then, she thought of the way Ron irritated her and made the young girls feel creepy. She knew that somebody had to do something. "But if we don't initiate it, nothing will ever change," Oona said.

Harvey said, "You're right. It's time to blow the whistle on Ron Frank."

"We could try to prove that he messed up the investigation after the Lakeshore Inn fire," Oona said.

Harvey said, "I guess that going to Cincinnati to bring Catherine back would be proof positive that he screwed up big time."

That seemed like an easy enough way to go about it, but there was just one problem. Catherine might not just jump on a plane with them. Oona said. "What if she won't come with us?"

Harvey said, "We'll have to convince her somehow that a lot hinges on her coming back."

Oona wondered how she would react if she were in Catherine's shoes. Making it short and simple would sway her into making a long trip. "Maybe she'll do it if we tell her she just needs to make a quick appearance."

"Maybe," Harvey said. He leaned forward and put his head in his hands.

Oona began thinking more about the fire at the Lakeshore Inn. If Annabelle were still alive, how had she just disappeared? How had Catherine gotten from Moose Creek all the way to Cincinnati by herself? She asked, "What do you think really happened the night of the fire?"

"Who knows," Harvey said.

Oona's mind began clicking, and she felt her interest in the case growing. "Let's look at the possibilities," she said. "First, we have to consider whether the fire was an accident or something intentional."

"If it had been an accident," Harvey said, "I don't think Ron would have glossed over the details and missed a couple of live kids in the process."

Oona felt certain that Ron had something to do with the fire. "I think you're right," she said. "So, let's assume that the fire was purposely set."

"How do you think the fire was started?" Harvey asked.

Her mind was humming too fast to get bogged down in the details yet. She had to get her thoughts out before she lost them. "I don't know," Oona said, "Second, we have to think about who would set a fire at the inn and why."

"There's always the obvious…that the owner set it himself to collect on the insurance money."

"Maybe," Oona said. "But from the way tourists flocked to the Lakeshore Inn, it seems unlikely that the Vernons were desperate for money. Besides, Paul and Mimi died...remember?"

"You sure about that?" Harvey asked.

Oona realized then if the children were alive, the parents could be, too.

"You never know," Harvey said. "Maybe one of them was a compulsive gambler. Maybe debt collectors were after them, and they burned the place for the insurance money."

Insurance money didn't seem like the right angle. "Maybe," Oona said, "but another obvious reason that people start fires is to cover up something."

"You mean like stolen property?"

Oona suddenly began to feel that something really sinister had happened the night of the fire. She said, "I have a gut feeling that somebody used the fire as a smoke screen."

"A smoke screen for what?" Harvey asked.

Goose bumps suddenly rose up on Oona's arms, and she said, "Murder."

"Are you serious?" Harvey asked.

"I don't know," she said. "Let's try to think about who might have gotten killed and who tried to cover it up."

Harvey looked at her expectantly.

There were too many thoughts tumbling through Oona's head. They needed to be organized before she forgot them. She asked, "Do you have a piece of paper and a pen?"

Harvey took a folded-up sheet of paper out of his shirt pocket and fished a pen out of his pants pocket. "Don't lose that," he said. "It's got the flight information on it, and I've got to call for another ticket for you."

Oona nodded and quickly scribbled down the names of the people involved in the Lakeshore Inn fire:

Paul
Mimi
Annabelle
Peter
Catherine

She said, "These are all of the people who were involved."

"Maybe not," said Harvey. "You don't have Ron Frank, or Benny

Vernon, or Wildred Swenson on there. Benny saw the fire, Wildred called the fire department that night, and Ron handled the investigation."

Oona quickly scribbled their names at the bottom of the list.

"And don't forget Doc Daggert," Harvey said.

"Doc Daggert?"

Harvey said, "He told me the other day that he offered to match dental records to the victims, but Ron never let him."

"That's seems suspicious," Oona said.

Harvey said, "That's what I thought."

Oona sat there tapping the pen on the paper. The most likely person on the list who had done something wrong was Ron Frank. She said, "It's obvious that we have to suspect Ron Frank of trying to cover up something."

Harvey nodded and said, "Without a doubt."

What had Ron done, and why had he worked so hard to cover it up? Oona asked, "If you were a cop, and you covered up a crime, what would be your motivation?"

Harvey shrugged. "Money…sex…power…What else is there?"

Oona thought of Ron's penchant for young girls and his insistence that not only did he uphold the law, he *was* the law. He also seemed to enjoy the company of wealthy people, like the mayor and Jacqueline Corbett. She said, "Maybe all of the above." She had a nagging sense that there was more. She added, "And I don't think he was in on this alone."

Harvey nodded. "So, if Ron Frank was involved, and if there was someone else in the picture, then that person must have known him at the time."

None of the other people on the list seemed like the type to commit a murder. Oona said, "Unless Ron is covering up a murder *he* committed."

Harvey looked at her and said, "You really think Ron Frank is smart enough to murder someone *and* cover it up?"

At the same instant, both of them shook their heads and said, "No."

Harvey said, "Whoever was in on this with Ron had to have known him at the time of the fire."

Oona thought about the two thousand plus residents who lived in their town. She said, "One way of figuring it out would be to make a list of people who *weren't* living in Moose Creek at the time of the fire."

"How do we find that out?" Harvey asked.

"Well, some of them we know about…like Jacqueline Corbett. She moved here fifteen years ago," Oona said.

Harvey asked, "Do you think Sophie could help us look up something on the computers at City Hall to help us figure out when people moved here?"

Oona nodded and said, "I'll ask Sophie to get a list of all the Moose Creek homeowners who bought property here in the past thirty years."

"Some people rent," Harvey said. "They may not be on the tax records."

He had a good point. School records could tell them a lot, too, but family privacy laws didn't make them publicly accessible. As a teacher, though, all she had to do was look through their old files. Oona said, "I'll look back through all of my old students' records. That will give us a pretty good idea of when their families moved to town."

"It's settled, then," said Harvey. "We'll go after this systematically, and we'll come up with a list of people who couldn't have been involved in the fire."

"And another list of people who could have been," Oona added.

Harvey stretched his arms overhead and said with a yawn, "Man, am I tired."

Oona felt her own mind slowing. Talking things out always helped. She smiled at him and said, "Let's go home and get some sleep."

Harvey stood up and said, "We've got a lot to do before we leave here on Friday."

On the way out of the park, they encountered Eric Larsen, who was leaving Skeeter's Pub. Eric looked down at Oona and said, "You're up late." He shifted his banjo case from one hand to another.

Oona said, "We're headed home now."

"Me, too," Eric said. "I've played one too many songs and drunk one too many beers."

Oona smiled, thinking about how much fun that sounded. She couldn't remember the last time she'd been out at night to listen to music or have a couple of drinks with friends. Maybe that was part of why she wanted to go someplace new. She spent all of her time working and very little time relaxing. She looked up at Eric and wondered why he had never settled down and married. He was reasonably good looking, knew how to have fun, and seemed to make a decent living. Maybe she should take up the harmonica. She smiled at Eric and said, "See you later."

Eric crossed the street and disappeared down an alley.

Harvey and Oona continued walking towards home, and Harvey said, "We can put Eric Larsen on the list of people who couldn't have helped Ron. He's only lived here about ten or fifteen years."

Oona nodded and thought about the task ahead of them. With only about two thousand residents in town, it shouldn't be that hard to come up with a short list. But when she thought about trying to talk to them about what happened the night the Lakeshore Inn burned down, she felt a little overwhelmed. She said, "I'm glad we're tackling this together."

Harvey said, "It should make the job a lot easier."

Oona walked quickly towards their house, and her mind turned back to their trip to Cincinnati on Friday. "Convincing Catherine Vernon to come back to Moose Creek with us is going to be a lot harder than coming up with a list of residents."

Harvey added, "And getting someone to re-open the case is going to take a miracle."

He had that right. This was going to take a lot more than just the two of them snooping around through old records. "I'll be praying for one," Oona said.

On Thursday morning, Oona pulled Sophie into the alley behind Swenson's Bakery to tell her about Catherine Vernon and the need to research the dates when residents had moved to Moose Creek.

Sophie asked, "What if the person responsible for the fire wasn't a resident?"

Oona hadn't considered that possibility. She frowned and said, "We think it's someone Ron Frank knows."

"I have a feeling you might be right, but what if that someone lives in another town, or even in another state?"

"Then we'll have to try something else," Oona said. "But for now, I think we should focus on the people who lived here at the time of the fire."

"It's a good enough place to start," Sophie said. "Ruling out possibilities is a technique I learned during my first year in criminal justice classes."

Oona nodded.

Sophie said, "Maybe you should run for chief of police."

"Me?" Oona asked. "Can you imagine my campaign posters?" She held out an imaginary poster and read, "Elect Shorty Kelly, the smallest cop in the north."

Sophie said, "Don't underestimate yourself. You may be small, but you've got some pretty big ideas."

Oona appreciated Sophie's confidence in her. She smiled at her friend and said, "Thanks."

Sophie looked down at her watch and said, "I've got to get going if I'm going to check those records before Ron comes into work."

Oona laid her hand on Sophie's arm and said, "Remember, don't breathe a word of this to anyone. Wildred wants to be sure that everyone is surprised on Monday morning."

Sophie nodded and said, "And it probably wouldn't be too smart to alert people to the fact that I'm digging around like this on the city's computer system. It could get me into some hot water."

Oona knew they were both taking some risks. She said, "I'll talk to you later."

Long before school began, Oona went down to the boiler room, where the old student files were stored. In a notebook, she began making a list of each family name and when their oldest child had first enrolled in school. It wasn't too difficult, since there were never more than a couple hundred children in the little school each year. Within a few hours, she had made her way through half of the student files. She decided to save the rest for later on, and she ascended the stairs to hurry towards the supply closet where she prepared materials for the students.

One of the other teachers approached her and said, "You missed the staff meeting this morning. Where were you?"

Oona froze. Staff meeting? She looked at the date on her watch and realized that it was Thursday. How could she have been so careless? She blurted out, "I haven't been feeling well, and I slept through my alarm this morning."

The teacher said with a concerned look, "I'm sorry to hear that. When you feel better, check back with me, and I'll go over the plans for the art work at Open House."

"Okay," Oona said. She waited for the teacher to walk away, and then she hurried into the supply closet and shoved the notebook with the list of names into her purse. She'd better not let this issue with the Lakeshore Inn get in the way of work. She decided that after everyone left that night, she'd go back and finish the list. She also didn't want to risk getting caught, especially if the person responsible for the fire just happened to be the one who found her copying names out of file folders.

The phone rang at about nine o'clock Thursday night, just as Oona was gathering up her notebook to go back to the school. Sophie was on the line, and she said, "I've got a print-out of all the tax payers' names who lived here when the Lakeshore Inn burned. You want me to bring it over to your house?"

"No," Oona said. "I'm on my way to the school. Come to the back door of the building."

A few minutes later, Sophie appeared at the back door of the school. Oona said, "Come with me."

Together, they hurried down the dark stairway to the boiler room. A single bulb cast an eerie light over a collection of brooms and mops standing in a barrel.

Oona asked, "What have you got?"

Sophie handed Oona a sheaf of papers and said, "Those are the names of everybody who has bought a house here."

"Did you go back twenty-five years on this?" Oona asked.

"Thirty," Sophie said.

"This certainly narrows down the list of names," Oona said. "Thanks."

"No problem," Sophie said. "If I can do anything else to help you get rid of Ron Frank, just let me know."

"I will," Oona said.

Sophie added, "But don't tell anybody where you got that list, or I could lose my job."

"And your chances at a better one," Oona said.

Sophie nodded. "Now I'd better get out of here before somebody finds us."

Sophie left, and Oona pulled up a chair in front of the records file cabinets. She was on the ninth drawer when she heard the back door open and bang shut. Who would be coming in at this hour? Swiftly, she shoved the notebook into her purse and stepped into a gap between the filing cabinets and the wall. For once, she was glad that she was so small. She held her breath and listened. Her ear drums felt as if they were swelling with the effort. She heard footsteps on the stairs, and then someone closed the filing cabinet drawer she had left open. From where she stood, it was impossible to see who was there, without giving herself away. She waited, praying for invisibility. And then, the footsteps retreated up the stairway, and the lights went off. She blinked in an effort to see in the dark.

Oona stood there with her heart pounding in her ears, wondering who had come in. Must have been the janitor, she finally decided. He lived next door, and he probably saw the light on in the basement. She heaved a sigh of relief. "Nothing to worry about," she said to herself.

The light switch was at the top of the stairs, and there was no way she could continue working on the list without going back up and turning on the lights. The lights would alert the janitor again that someone was down there, and she preferred to let him think that he had simply forgotten to turn off the lights when he left. She decided it was best to just go home and resume in the morning.

She walked forward and bumped into something. She gasped and then reached forward with both hands. When she realized that it was just the janitor's broom collection, she let her breath out in a whoosh. Slowly, she shuffled to the bottom of the stairs. When she had a firm grip on the handrail, she hurried up the steps and pushed open the back door.

In the next instant, a hand came over her mouth. A strong arm dragged her back inside. Oona struggled to free herself. The door banged shut.

A voice in her ear whispered, "You know, Oona, it's best to let sleeping dogs lie."

Oona stomped down hard on her captor's instep. The hand released its hold on her. She flung herself out the back door of the school building and fled the two blocks to her house. Once inside, she slammed the door shut and locked it behind her.

Harvey came out of the kitchen and said, "Oona, what's the matter? You look like you've seen a ghost."

Oona leaned against the door and tried to catch her breath. At last, she said, "Actually, I didn't see him. It was too dark."

"What are you talking about?" Harvey asked.

Harvey approached her, and Oona felt her entire body beginning to tremble. She said, "Somebody knows."

"Knows what?"

"That we're onto them," Oona said. She put a shaking hand over her mouth.

Harvey said, "Sit down and tell me what happened."

Oona wobbled into the living room and fell onto the sofa. She looked up at Harvey and said, "Somebody put their hand over my mouth and told me that I should let sleeping dogs lie."

"Who?"

That's what she was wondering. It had all happened so quickly, she had no idea who it could've been. "I don't know," she said. "It was too dark to see."

The color drained from Harvey's face. He asked, "Where were you?"

"At the school," Oona said. "In the boiler room."

"At this time of night?" Harvey asked.

"When else was I supposed to get that list?" she snapped. "I can't very well just waltz in there in broad daylight and announce to the staff that I'm snooping through a lot of old files. There are family privacy laws. I could get fired."

"Or maybe killed," Harvey said with a very serious look on his face.

The enormity of what they had taken on suddenly came over Oona. She said, "Are you sure we shouldn't be calling somebody…like the FBI?"

"I'm not sure of anything," Harvey said. "But I do know one thing."

"What?"

"From now on, we stick together as much as possible. When we aren't together, we stay in public places and in plain sight of plenty of other people."

"Good plan," Oona said. She took a deep breath and began to feel her strength returning. She opened her purse and pulled out the notebook and Sophie's list. She stood up, handed them to Harvey, and said, "Go put these in Dad's safe in the basement. I don't want anybody catching us with them."

Harvey took the papers from her, set them on an end table, and then pulled her into his arms. He said, "We'll go over everything after we're on the plane to Cincinnati." Oona wrapped her arms around Harvey's waist and buried her face in his sweater. He smelled familiar, and with him, she felt safe. "I'm scared," she said.

Harvey patted her back and said, "Whoever this guy is, if he thinks that picking on a weak little woman will get him anywhere, he hasn't met me yet."

Oona hated it when people suggested that her height made her an automatic weakling. "Weak?" she said, drawing away. "Who are you calling weak?"

Harvey grinned at her and said, "Reverse that. You're not weak, you're just small."

"Darn right," she said. "I may be little, but I've got some big ideas."

"And a well-developed kick-butt attitude," Harvey added with a grin. "The only person who has anything to worry about is the guy who's behind all of this. God help him if he ever tangles with you again."

Oona's fear disappeared, and in its place, she began to feel outraged. Who did this bully think he was? She drew herself up to her full four feet six inches and said, "As soon as the town council dinner ends tomorrow night, I'll be ready to head for the airport."

Harvey said, "I'm going to make sure that Catherine Vernon comes back here with us…even if I have to tie her up and put her in my suitcase."

"I'm with you all the way," Oona said. "I'll go pack my rope."

8

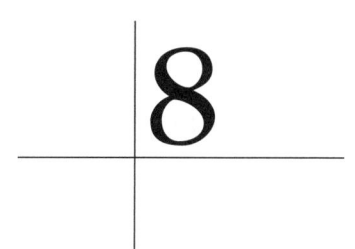

IT WAS LATE ON FRIDAY AFTERNOON WHEN HARVEY SAT down behind his father's desk in the back of Paul Bunyan's General Store. He pulled out the estimate for repairing the freezer condenser and peered at the figures. Tommy Anderson's price was really high, but he didn't know who else to call. While he was sitting there, Mike Ianelli and Lily Frank appeared in the doorway.

"Hi, Mr. Trent," Mike said. "Do you have a minute?"

Harvey set the estimate aside and said, "Sure, what's up?"

Mike said, "My dad got me another topographical map, and we went out this morning."

Lily added, "Mike's working on his wilderness survival badge."

Harvey wished he were outside tramping around in the woods, instead of worrying about problems like the LeClerc place, his broken freezer, and his upcoming trip to Cincinnati. "That sounds like fun," Harvey said, shoving the papers into his top desk drawer. "How'd it go?"

Mike and Lily looked at each other.

"Not so hot, huh?" Harvey said.

Mike said, "We were wondering if you could help us find something."

"What are you looking for?"

Mike slid his backpack off his shoulder and pulled out one of his maps. He unfolded it on Harvey's desk and pointed to something in the center of the map. "Do you know where this bridge might be?"

Harvey looked at the pale green map with the squiggly thin lines. "What's this map of?" he asked.

"The area north of Heron Lake," Mike said.

"That's the old Vernon place," Harvey said.

Mike shrugged. "I guess."

Harvey used his index finger to trace along the north edge of Heron Lake. He paused when he came upon some light brown print. "What's that say?" he asked.

Mike bent down and read, "Lakeshore Inn dock."

"That's what I thought," he said.

"We found that this morning," Mike said. He slid his finger up the map. He stopped at some more fine print in brown type. "Have you ever seen this bridge?"

Harvey looked at the spot where the dock was and the place where the map said they would find a bridge. He asked, "How far is it from the dock to the bridge?"

Mike explained the legend on the map, and Harvey said, "So, we're talking about a distance of maybe a mile?"

"Probably," Mike said.

"I've been out there hunting quite a bit," Harvey said. "I've never seen a bridge."

"Maybe somebody made a mistake on the map," Lily said.

"No," Mike said, "I read that they're pretty accurate."

Harvey said, "Maybe a lot of brush has grown up over it."

"I guess," Mike said. "I'd really like to find it."

Harvey looked over Mike's head. The clerk at the check-out was reading a magazine, and there was only one customer in the produce aisle. He needed to get out and do some thinking about how he was going to convince Catherine Vernon to come back to Moose Creek with them. If he had to stay inside and worry about his problems, he thought he might just go crazy. He said, "We could take your map out and see if we can find that bridge."

"Now?" Mike asked.

"I've got a little time," Harvey said.

"I promised Dad I'd mow the lawn this afternoon," he said.

Harvey suddenly felt desperate to get out of the store. "Well, I could go out there by myself and leave something on the bridge so that you could find it later."

Mike beamed. "That'd be great."

Harvey asked, "You got a compass I could borrow?"

Mike slid his backpack off his shoulder and said, "Take my backpack. Then you'll have everything you need."

Harvey folded up the map and said, "I'll be back in a couple of hours. I'll let you know what I find." He looked up just in time to see his maintenance man, Ralph, ducking through the swinging doors at the back of the store. What was he doing at work? He wasn't due in until later in the evening.

Mike and Lily left, and Harvey went into the back to find Ralph at the work bench. "What are you up to?" he asked.

Ralph looked up at Harvey and said, "Just making a few repairs."

"To what?" Harvey asked.

"Your freezer."

"The condenser's shot," Harvey said.

"Who told you that?"

"Tommy Anderson," Harvey said.

Ralph continued tinkering with the condenser. Then, he picked it up and walked back out to the frozen foods section.

Harvey followed him and watched as Ralph set the condenser back in place and bolted it in. He flipped a switch, and the freezer began humming quietly.

"It's working?" Harvey asked.

Ralph bent over to pick up his tools and then straightened up. "Yep."

"How'd you know how to fix it?" Harvey asked.

Ralph shrugged. "Experience," he said. He began walking towards the back of the store.

"Wait!" Harvey said. "I want to give you something."

Ralph stopped and turned around to stare at him with that odd, faraway look in his pale blue eyes.

Harvey went to his office and took several large bills out of the safe. He hurried back to where Ralph was cleaning off the workbench and held out the money to him. "I want to pay you for making the repair."

Ralph stood there staring at Harvey with his sinewy arms dangling at his sides. "I don't need that," he said.

"You did me a big favor," Harvey said, thrusting the money at Ralph.

Ralph shook his head and said, "Too much money gets a man into trouble." He turned and disappeared out the back door.

Harvey was dumbstruck. He stood there staring at the bills in his hand. Ralph had saved him a ton of money. On top of that, he had spared him a lot of headaches. Why would he go out of his way like that…and then accept nothing for his efforts? The man certainly was odd.

Fifteen minutes later, Harvey pulled up into a gravel drive on the north side of Heron Lake. He opened the door, and Jet leaped out. Harvey slid his arms into the straps on Mike's red backpack and picked up the map from the front seat of the truck. Jet ran along the shoreline and began barking at something. Harvey hurried after the dog and found Doc Daggert sitting in his bass boat near the Lakeshore Inn's old dock.

"Jet, quiet!" Harvey said.

The dog stopped barking and ran along the length of the dock. He stood still, sniffing at the air.

"Any luck?" Harvey called to Doc.

"Only a couple of fishermen," Doc said. He smiled and winked at Harvey. "Where you headed?"

Harvey said, "Mike came out here this morning to work on his orienteering skills. He couldn't find a bridge on the old Vernon property."

Doc Daggert said, "That's because it's covered in brambles."

"You've seen it?" Harvey asked.

"I used to cross it years ago to get over Moose Creek," Doc said. "There's not much left of it now."

Harvey looked at his watch and wondered how long it might take him to find the bridge. "You think I'll be able to find it with this map?"

Doc said, "If you've got all day."

Harvey didn't have all day. He wondered if Doc had the strength to walk that far into the woods. He said, "I don't suppose you'd want to walk out there with me and show me."

Doc said, "Sure." He reeled in his line and set his pole aside.

The sound of a trolling motor made Harvey glance across the water. A couple of guys were fishing along the west shore in a bass boat.

Half an hour later, Harvey was following Doc along the east side of Heron Creek. From time to time, Jet trotted off into the ferns that grew alongside the trail, and then rejoined them. Harvey kept checking the map and Mike's compass. The squiggly lines were beginning to make sense to him, but it wasn't easy. He was glad Doc had come with him.

Doc stopped abruptly and said, "Here it is."

Harvey looked at the map and then at the tangle of brush on the side of the creek. "Are you sure?" he asked. "I don't see anything that looks like a bridge."

"You could see what's left if you cut away some of this brush."

That would take a machete or small hatchet, which he didn't have. Then, Harvey remembered what Mike had said about the backpack. He lowered it to the ground and knelt down to open it up. Jet stuck his nose into the backpack, and Harvey pushed him aside. In the backpack, he found a small hatchet with a leather cover snapped over the blade. He stood up and said, "Mike's a good scout…always prepared."

Doc nodded and stepped aside while Harvey began hacking away at the underbrush. Sweat was beginning to make Harvey's shirt stick to his back. He was about to give up when the hatchet hit something with a ping.

"Sounds like you hit something metal," Doc said.

Harvey bent down and discovered an old piece of wood with some big rusty bolts in it. He said, "I guess this is all that's left of the bridge."

Doc handed Harvey the red bandana from his rear pants pocket. "Here," he said. "Tie this to what's left so Mike can find it later."

Harvey took the bandana from Doc and bent down to tie it to the old plank. Jet was digging frantically at something in the dirt. Suddenly, the dog stepped back and let out a growl.

"What's the matter, boy?" Harvey asked. Something in the dirt caught Harvey's eye. He bent closer and scraped the ground with the hatchet.

Jet growled again.

Harvey thought he must be imagining things. He straightened up and asked Doc, "Does that look like some kind of bones to you?"

Doc shuffled over to where Harvey was kneeling and asked, "You got a spade in that backpack?"

Harvey hurried over and found a folding spade in the outer compartment of Mike's pack. With the spade, he quickly scraped the dirt away from what appeared to be the skeletal remains of a hand. "Judas Priest," he muttered. He turned and asked Doc, "Am I seeing what I think I am?"

Doc said, "If you're seeing a human hand."

Harvey couldn't believe it. There was a body buried here, and it shouldn't be. He said, "We should call the police."

"Ron Frank?" Doc asked.

Harvey looked up at Doc and said, "I guess we'd better think of something else." He sat back on his heels and thought about what was happening. If they didn't go to the police, he and Doc could later be accused of tampering with evidence…or worse, burying somebody themselves.

Doc said, "If that's somebody from Moose Creek, I can identify them."

"How?" Harvey asked.

"Keep digging," Doc said. "If you find a skull, I can check the teeth and compare them to my old records."

For the next half hour, Harvey dug carefully until he had unearthed the head. Doc bent down and held out his hand. "Give it here," he said.

Slowly, Harvey lifted the dirt-filled skull from the earth and handed it to Doc.

Doc brushed away some of the dirt and said, "This was a kid."

"How do you know that?" Harvey asked.

"He didn't even have his twelve-year molars yet." Doc turned over the skull and whistled.

"What?" Harvey asked.

"He's got a perfectly round hole in the back of his skull."

"Is that normal?"

"Only if you've been shot," Doc said. He peered more closely at the hole and said, "Looks like the size of a .22 bullet."

Harvey couldn't believe his ears. "How'd he end up out here?" he asked.

"Think about it," Doc said. "Whose land are you on?"

"The Vernons' old place," Harvey said. And then it hit him: this was one of the Vernon kid's remains. He looked up at Doc and said, "There's something I need to tell you, but you need to keep it quiet."

Doc nodded.

"Wildred got a letter the other day from a lawyer in Cincinnati. Catherine Vernon didn't die in the fire at the old Lakeshore Inn. She was adopted."

"What the hell?" Doc muttered. He looked down at the skull in his hands.

Harvey said, "If you look up Peter Vernon's old dental records, you'll probably find that they match the ones in that skull."

Doc's hands shook so much, that Harvey was afraid he might drop the skull. He took it from him and wrapped it up in Doc's bandana. Then, he slid it into Mike's backpack. "We're going to put everything back out here the way we found it," Harvey said, "other than the skull."

"Why?" Doc asked. "I think we should go to the state police…or the FBI."

"Not yet," Harvey said. "I want to make sure we've got enough proof to hang Ron Frank."

"How much proof do you need?"

Harvey said, "Listen, Oona and I are going to Cincinnati tonight to bring back Catherine Vernon. Oona and Sophie have been helping me figure out who lived in Moose Creek when the inn burned. We already know that somebody in town is on to what we're doing. They tried to scare off Oona last night."

"You'd better be careful," Doc said.

Harvey said, "Somehow, we've got to pull together enough of the puzzle pieces to convince someone to re-open the case."

"Ron Frank's got a lot of friends down there at the state police post in Big Bear," Doc said. "You sure you want to tell them?"

"We'll go to a bigger post…one where he doesn't know anybody."

"When you thinking about blowing the whistle on Ron Frank?"

"As soon as we can get Catherine here." Then Harvey had a thought. "Say, could you identify her by her dental records, too?"

"As long as she's got teeth," Doc said.

Harvey noticed that Doc's hands were shaking worse than ever. He said, "It's settled then. You take Mike's backpack and the skull to your place. I'll meet you there as soon as I put all this brush back. I don't want Mike and Lily finding this." Harvey bent over to pick up a branch he had cut away with the hatchet.

"You sure you want me to leave you out here alone?" Doc said. "That somebody who tried to scare Oona could've followed you."

Harvey glanced around. He hoped they were alone, but could he be sure? He didn't want to worry Doc, so he said, "I don't think anybody followed me. You go ahead. I'll be right behind you."

Half an hour later, Harvey stood with Doc Daggert in the basement of his weather-beaten house on the east side of Heron Lake. Doc's hands shook as he slid an x-ray into the clip on the light box that hung on the wall. He flipped the switch, and the light flickered on. He reached over and picked up the skull.

"What do you think?" Harvey asked.

With shaking fingers, Doc tugged on one of the front teeth. He swore. Then, he handed the skull to Harvey and said, "Give that front tooth a good yank."

"Why?" Harvey asked.

Doc pointed at the x-ray and said, "See that little peg in the right front tooth?"

Harvey looked at the x-ray and nodded.

Doc said, "Peter fell off his bike and broke that tooth off at the gum. I put a peg in the root and re-attached the tooth."

Harvey got a firm grip on the tooth and jerked downward on it. The tooth came free, and in its place, he found a small, metal peg protruding from the root.

"Bingo," Doc said.

Harvey stood there holding the tooth. "You got something we can put this in?" he asked.

Doc opened a drawer and took out a small plastic bag.

Harvey took the bag from Doc's trembling hand and dropped the tooth into it. He wondered what to do next. He looked at his watch and said, "I've got to get going. The council dinner is in less than an hour."

Doc said, "I'll clean up Mike's backpack and get everything else put in a box."

"Fine," Harvey said. "I'll pick it up after the dinner and drop it off at the state police post in Minneapolis before we fly out tonight."

On his way out, Harvey thought about how someone had tried to silence Oona. He remembered the report on the TV about the Fishing Lure Killer. He paused at the door and said, "Maybe you shouldn't go back out on the lake by yourself for a while."

Doc nodded. "You'd better watch your back, too."

Jet had been waiting for Harvey on the front porch. Harvey suddenly realized that he hadn't made arrangements for anyone to look after the dog while he was away. He said, "Would you mind keeping Jet with you for a couple of days?"

"No problem," Doc said.

Harvey directed the dog inside and walked away to his truck. He looked back at the old man swaying behind the screen door and felt good that Jet was going to be with Doc. If anybody came nosing around, Jet would alert Doc and scare them off.

A short while later, the members of the town council, their spouses, and most of the area business people were beginning to gather in the conference room at City Hall. Patriotic music was playing a little too loudly in the background.

Harvey had just walked in the door when Jacqueline Corbett hurried over to him and said with a smile, "Just the man I've been looking for."

He had so much on his mind; he really wished he could've skipped the whole affair. But, as a member of the council, it was important for him to attend the annual meeting. What he really needed to do was focus in on how he was going to garner the support of the other members next week to get rid of Ron Frank. There were eleven members on the council, and he needed at least a two-thirds majority vote to fire their police chief. For tonight, Harvey decided, he would just observe who he thought was in Ron Frank's pocket. It didn't take much thought to figure out that Jacqueline Corbett was on Ron's side. "Hello, Jacqueline," he said.

She was wearing a grey skirt and jacket with a soft blue silk blouse. Of course, the blouse was so low-cut that it was probably causing lustful thoughts in the minds of at least half the men in the room. "How are you?" she asked.

"Fine," Harvey said. He shoved his hands into his pockets and tried to keep his mind focused on votes and his eyes off of Jacqueline's bust line.

Jacqueline said, "I wanted to talk to you about your dad's property out at Heron Lake."

Harvey looked across the room at the mayor, who was stuffing an enormous shrimp into his mouth. The short, rotund civic leader looked as if his button was going to pop off the front of his suit jacket, which was straining across his belly. The mayor was Ron's cousin and most ardent supporter. He was definitely on Ron's side, too. That made two votes in favor of Ron. Harvey looked back at Jacqueline and said, "I've told you, I'm not interested in selling."

She said, "I know, and I can understand your hesitation. You're worried that a condo development would spoil the lake."

Harvey watched the librarian out of the corner of his eye. She had once threatened to keep Ron out of the library for bothering the junior high girls when they came in after school. He would be sure to get her vote next week. Two votes for Ron Frank, one against. He said to Jacqueline, "Overbuilding the lakeshore would destroy all kinds of wildlife."

"What if you had some say in the way it was developed?"

Harvey trained his eyes on hers and asked, "What are you talking about?"

"What if I could get you a seat on North Shore's board?" she asked. "We could stipulate in a sales agreement that you wouldn't sell unless they agreed to let you have some say in the way the lake was developed."

Harvey thought of another lake that North Shore had gotten a hold of. They had ruined some really great hunting land that he used to enjoy. He said, "I've seen the way they've developed other lakes."

"That's because they didn't have someone like you to keep them from spoiling the landscape." Jacqueline smiled at him.

Was it his imagination, or was she shoving back her shoulders to reveal even more cleavage? Harvey didn't know how much more of Jacqueline he could take. He said, "If I've told you once, I've told you a thousand times, Jacqueline. I'm not interested."

With that said, he strode across the room to where Wildred Swenson was ordering something from the bartender. He knew Wildred could be counted on to help him get rid of Ron Frank. That made two votes for Ron and two against.

"How are you feeling?" he asked Wildred.

"Much better," Wildred said with a broad smile. "And you?"

"Fine," Harvey said. He ordered an iced tea. While he stood there waiting for the drink, he thought that *fine* was such a stupid response to that question. Nothing was fine. In fact, he had a feeling that in a few days, the whole town would be in an uproar.

Wildred whispered, "Have you got your tickets?"

Harvey took his iced tea from the bartender and pulled Wildred aside. He said, "I don't think we should talk about things here. The walls might have ears."

"Oh," Wildred said with a nod. She smiled at him again before drifting away to talk to the local accountant. Harvey stood there watching Wildred talking to him. The accountant was wearing a ridiculously outdated plum-colored sports coat and a black and white checked bowtie. The man was so closed-mouthed, it was hard to say whether he would be on Ron's side or not. Knowing how the accountant had made council decisions in the past, he'd probably abstain if there were a vote to oust Ron. That made two for, two against, and one abstaining.

Harvey sat beside Oona while the council members were eating dinner. With her vote, he counted up two for Ron, three against, and one abstaining. "What time do we need to leave?" she whispered.

Harvey said. "As soon as the mayor stops talking, you go to the ladies room, and I'll go to the men's room. I'll meet you in the hallway by the bathrooms, and we'll slip out the back."

The mayor stood up behind the wooden podium near the head table and said, "Welcome to the annual meeting of the Moose Creek Town Council. Isn't this some dinner?"

Everyone clapped.

The mayor put on silver-rimmed reading glasses and read about the faltering financial position of Moose Creek. Then, he began to talk about the drop in attendance at the area churches. The mayor called the minister from the First Methodist Church to the head table, and the black-garbed council member began speaking to the group about the need for a revival in their little town. His voice rose, and he thumped the podium from time to time. The microphone squealed.

Harvey thought about the minister's vote. Like the accountant, it was hard to tell whose side he would fall on when it came to a decision. He figured that made his count two for Ron, three against, and two abstaining.

Harvey could hardly stand to sit there. Doc Daggert was holding an important piece of evidence that would hang Ron Frank, and he was eager to get back out to the lake to pick up the skull. He could feel Oona's leg jiggling up and down. Obviously, she was anxious to get going, too. Harvey leaned over and said, "The minute the minister quits talking, let's go."

Oona nodded.

The minister ended his speech, and Harvey shoved back his chair. Eric Larsen was called to the podium. The mayor said, "Now, don't anybody try to leave just yet. We've got a special award to give out tonight."

Harvey looked at Oona, who raised an eyebrow at him. He heaved a sigh and sat back in his chair.

Eric said into the microphone, "As Director of Tourism and Economic Development, I'd like to present a special award to someone who has been very instrumental in getting funding for improvements to our town through the Community Development Block Grant Program." He announced the sum that would be forthcoming from the federal government, and a cheer went up.

Oona poked Harvey in the leg, and he looked over to find her jerking her head in the direction of the restrooms. He shook his head and looked back up at Eric Larsen.

Eric said, "...and in honor of this accomplishment, we'd like to present two awards tonight for Council Member of the Year: Miss Jacqueline Corbett and Mr. Harvey Trent!"

Disappointed by the delay from the party, and yet pleased with the award, Harvey strode to the front of the room. He took the plaque from Eric, shook hands with the mayor, and turned to the microphone. All eyes were on him, and a hush fell over the room. He had a bizarre feeling that he would soon be standing in this same spot within a few days to announce that Ron Frank was being booted from his position, and an extensive investigation into the fire at the Lakeshore Inn would soon be underway. Someone coughed, and Harvey realized he had been standing there without speaking for some time. He cleared his throat and said with a smile, "I guess I'll be first in line to apply for some of those funds to fix up the old LeClerc place."

A ripple of laughter floated across the room.

Harvey looked at the plaque and realized that he was making an impact in his little town. With the funding he had been able to win through a grant he had written at Jacqueline's suggestion, a lot of people in town would now have the money to repair their homes and businesses. It would mean a lot to them. For the first time in years, he realized that he felt some pride in his work. He looked over at Jacqueline and realized that, over the years, he had come to admire her business savvy. He leaned into the microphone and said, "Thank you."

Jacqueline stepped up to slip her arm around Harvey's waist. She said, "I came up with this brainstorm, but it was Harvey who really made it happen for us." She gave him a squeeze.

Everyone clapped, and Harvey hurried back to his seat as the town's legal advisor took the podium. "Now!" Harvey whispered to Oona. They retreated to the hallway near the restrooms, and Harvey shoved his sister out the back door.

As they were getting into Harvey's truck, Wildred Swenson appeared at Harvey's elbow. "Take this with you," she said. "It might help you convince Catherine to come home." She pressed something into Harvey's hand and hurried back inside. Harvey got into the truck, closed the door, and looked down at the gold chain and medallion Wildred had given him.

"That must be Benny's," Oona said.

Harvey handed his sister the necklace, started the engine, and sped away from the curb.

"I hate those dinners," Oona said. "I'd rather have a root canal than go to another one."

Harvey felt the same way. He wanted to see a lot of things change for the better in his little town. "I have a feeling that things are going to be much different at next year's annual dinner," Harvey said.

"Hey, you're going the wrong way," Oona said.

Harvey was anxious to get to Doc's as quickly as possible. "We're making a stop on the way out of town," Harvey said.

"Where?"

"Doc Daggert's."

Oona said, "I didn't mean I really wanted to have a root canal done. Turn around."

Harvey gripped the steering wheel and pressed the accelerator down farther. He said, "Listen to me. Doc and I found Peter Vernon's remains today."

Oona gasped, "Where?"

"It's a long story," Harvey said. "I'll tell you later. For now, we've got to pick up the evidence and take it to the state police in Minneapolis."

"Okay," Oona said. "I got the lists out of Dad's safe, and I made copies of everything."

Harvey appreciated his sister's thoroughness. "Good," he said. "We'll give those to the cops, too."

At Doc Daggert's, Harvey took the box from the old man, directed Jet to stay inside, and said to the retired dentist, "I meant what I said earlier about staying off the lake this weekend."

Doc nodded. "I won't go out alone."

When they got near Minneapolis, it was after two o'clock in the morning. Oona asked, "Do you have any idea where the state police post is?"

"No," Harvey said. "I figured we'd ask somebody."

"You know," Oona said, "if you'd buy a new cell phone, you could look up the directions online."

Harvey felt his muscles tensing. He was tired, and the last thing he wanted to do right then was argue with Oona about cell phones. "Use yours," he said.

"I don't have internet service on mine," she said, "but with a new contract, you could get it."

"Hm," Harvey said.

After stopping twice for directions, they found out that the Minnesota State Patrol's office wasn't in Minneapolis; it was in St. Paul. They made their way to the office on Cedar Street. Harvey looked at his watch. It was nearly three o'clock, and their flight left at 6:05. He said, "We're really going to have to keep this short if we're going to make our flight." He picked up the box from the seat and walked around the car.

"Watch your step," Oona said. She pointed at the ground.

Harvey stepped over a dead squirrel that had been flattened on the pavement. When they got to the front door, they discovered it was locked. "Now what?" Harvey asked.

Oona pointed to a sign on the wall that read, *For service after 8 pm, please use this phone.*

Harvey lifted the phone, and a moment later, a voice came on the other end.

A man said, "Minnesota State Patrol."

Harvey said, "I need to talk to someone about something that's going on up in Moose Creek."

The man said, "What kind of a problem are you having?"

Harvey said, "We think several people have been murdered."

The man asked, "What makes you think someone's been murdered?"

Plenty, Harvey thought. He looked down at the box in his hand and said, "We've got some things here that you should take a look at."

The man said, "I'll be right over."

Ten minutes later, an older patrolman in a grey uniform with maroon trim pulled into the parking lot. He said, "We'll go into the conference room." He unlocked the front door, and Harvey and Oona followed him into a small room and sat down at a table.

The older state trooper had pock-marked skin and greasy black hair. He introduced himself as Sergeant So-and-So, but Harvey couldn't understand his name.

The Sergeant asked, "What have you got there?"

Harvey said, "Take a look."

The Sergeant pulled open the lid on the box and said, "Well, this is interesting. Where'd you find it?"

Harvey said, "On a piece of property north of Heron Lake."

"Where's that?" the Sergeant asked.

Harvey said, "Just east of Upper Red Lake, about 80 miles from the Canadian border."

Oona handed the Sergeant the copies of their lists and said, "We've pulled together a list of people who lived in Moose Creek twenty-five years ago."

The Sergeant took the papers and asked, "Why twenty-five years?"

"That's about the time when we think this boy was killed."

"What makes you think that?" the Sergeant asked.

Harvey said, "There was a restaurant called the Lakeshore Inn on the north side of the lake. It burned down, and the police chief said that everyone in the Vernon family, including the children had died."

"Who's the chief up there?" the Sergeant asked.

"Ron Frank," Harvey said.

The Sergeant shook his head. "Don't know him."

Harvey breathed a sigh of relief. He said, "Doc Daggert—he was a dentist for years up there—he gave me these x-rays." He handed the Sergeant the x-rays from Doc's files. He added, "If you look where the right front tooth was, there's a peg in it." He fished the little plastic bag with the tooth in it from the bottom of the box. "Here's the tooth."

The Sergeant took the tooth and said, "It certainly looks like a match." He peered at the x-ray and said, "What's the name on this x-ray?"

"Peter Vernon," Harvey said. "He was one of the children who supposedly died in the fire."

"Where did you say you found this?" the Sergeant asked.

"Under an old bridge about a mile north of the where the Lakeshore Inn used to be."

The Sergeant turned the skull over.

Harvey pointed to the hole and said, "Doc Daggert says that's a bullet hole."

"Looks like it," the Sergeant said.

"We want someone to re-open this case," Harvey said.

The Sergeant set the skull, x-ray, and tooth back down in the box. "That's up to your chief," he said.

"That's where the trouble is," Oona said. "We think our chief is involved somehow. He said everyone died inside the restaurant, but Harvey found Peter's body in the woods."

"And we've just gotten news that it looks like one of the other children was adopted by a couple in Cincinnati," Harvey put in.

"Cincinnati?" The Sergeant looked at Harvey, across to Oona, and back at Harvey.

Harvey could see that the Sergeant was beginning to wonder about them. "I know it sounds crazy," Harvey said, "but we're on our way now to Cincinnati to bring her back here."

"Let me get this straight," the Sergeant said. "This fire at the…"

"Lakeshore Inn on Heron Lake," Oona said.

"This fire supposedly killed an entire family, and you're telling me that you've found one kid alive and this one buried in the woods?"

"That's right," Harvey said.

The Sergeant said, "I'll have to get with your chief before I can make a decision about re-opening this case."

Harvey's hopes flagged. If Ron Frank got involved, nothing would be resolved. He said, "Isn't there any other way?"

"No," the Sergeant said. "That's how the chain of command works here in Minnesota."

"But if you alert Ron Frank to what's happening," Oona said, "a lot of people could be in danger."

"Why do you think that?"

Oona said, "Because we really believe he was involved somehow. And lately, someone's been trying to stop us from figuring this out."

"Ron Frank?"

"I don't know," said Oona. "Some man attacked me in the dark last night."

"Did you file a report?" the Sergeant asked.

Oona shook her head. "If I did, it would alert Ron Frank to what we were doing."

"What were you doing?"

Oona glanced over at Harvey and said, "Gathering the information on those lists."

The Sergeant shuffled through the lists. "Who else knows about this?" he asked.

Harvey was beginning to sense that the red tape involved in all of this could prove to be problematic. Maybe they shouldn't have come here. On the other hand, he didn't know where else to turn. He said, "Our town clerk's assistant, Sophie Ianelli, and Doc Daggert, the dentist who identified the body."

"I'll tell you what," the Sergeant said. "I'll check into this for you without involving Ron Frank for the moment. If what you say is true, you'll have to come back in to file a report about all of this."

"Why not write a report now?" Oona asked.

The Sergeant smiled and said, "Because I'm bending the rules for you, and I don't want to get my butt in a sling over a report with the wrong date on it. You get my drift?"

Harvey stood up and said, "Yes. Thank you."

The Sergeant slid a pad of paper across the table and said, "Write down your names, addresses, and telephone numbers. Include your cells."

Harvey glanced at Oona and then said, "I don't have a cell phone."

"How do you function without a cell in this day and age?"

"Not very well," Oona said, rising to her feet.

Harvey glared at her and wrote down the information on the paper. "We'll be back through here on Sunday. Can we check back with you then?"

The Sergeant said, "I'll be off at seven tomorrow morning, and I won't be back in until Tuesday. I'm spending Labor Day weekend fishing with my brother-in-law."

"That's nice," Harvey said. "Do you have a business card?"

The Sergeant handed him a business card, and Harvey gave it to Oona. She shoved it into her purse without looking at it.

Harvey said, "We'll call you Tuesday."

They stood to leave, and Oona pointed down at the box. "Will you need to keep all of this, or should we take it with us?"

"I think you'd better leave it," the Sergeant said.

Harvey said to her, "They'll need to start working on that list and getting another opinion on the dental records." He looked up at the Sergeant. "Isn't that right?"

"That's right," the Sergeant said. He smiled and asked, "You flying or driving to Cincinnati?"

"Flying," Harvey said. He glanced down at his watch. "And we'd better get out of here, or we're going to miss our flight."

"What time does it leave?" he asked.

"6:05," Harvey said.

"Oh, you've got plenty of time," the Sergeant said. "You're not that far from the airport."

After they were settled into their seats, and their commuter jet was on its way to Chicago for the connecting flight, Oona asked Harvey, "You want to go over the list of names now?"

Harvey said, "My head's swimming from everything that's been happening."

"Mine, too," said Oona. "At least the state police are involved now."

"Yeah, that's a plus." Harvey leaned his head back against the seat and said, "Let's try to get some shut-eye. As soon as we get to Cincinnati, we've got to head straight to the lawyer's office. He can only wait for us until noon, and then he's leaving for the weekend."

"Why does everything always happen on holiday weekends?" Oona asked.

"I don't know," Harvey said. "It sure makes things more difficult, doesn't it?"

It was nearly noon on Saturday when Harvey pulled into a gas station.

Oona asked, "Why are you stopping now? If we don't hurry up, we may not catch Catherine before she leaves the funeral reception that the lawyer told us about."

Harvey said, "If I don't stop now, we may not make it to the funeral reception. We're driving on fumes." He turned off the engine and shoved the paper with the directions to the reception in his pocket.

While he was pumping the gas, Oona went inside to use the restroom. Harvey went into the gas station a few minutes later to pay, and he met his sister near the cash register. "You want anything?" he asked.

Oona said, "I'm getting a headache from not sleeping. Get me some bottled water, and I'll take one of the aspirins I have in my purse."

She walked ahead of him to the car and opened the door. Harvey got in behind the wheel and started the engine. Oona continued to stand there.

"Are you getting in?" he asked.

Oona said, "I'm pretty sure I left my purse on the back seat."

Harvey turned around to look, but there was nothing there but his jacket. "You must have left it in the bathroom."

Oona hurried away.

Harvey got out and looked in the trunk and under the seats. It would be pretty hard to lose one of Oona's purses. They were all the size of small battleships.

Oona reappeared and said, "It's not there."

"Think," Harvey said. "Are you sure you didn't lay it down while I was paying for the gas?"

"Positive," said Oona. "I distinctly remember laying it on the back seat after we came out of the lawyer's office."

"Maybe you just think you did," Harvey said.

Oona glared at him. "I'm not that daft," she said. "We went to the lawyer's office, and he gave us those introduction papers to show Catherine. You gave them to me, and I put them in my purse." She pointed at the back seat. "I put it right there."

In that instant, Harvey knew she was right. He punched the top of the car and said, "Crap."

Oona looked around at the people pumping gas and said, "Somebody stole it while we were inside."

Harvey realized then that they had lost far more than Oona's aspirin and the lawyer's letters. "You know what else we've lost?" he asked.

"What?"

"Benny's medallion."

The color drained from Oona's face, and she sank into the passenger seat. "And that state cop's card," she said.

Harvey got back in the car and closed the door. He said, "Somebody's been following us."

Oona looked around and asked, "How hard do you think it will be to convince Catherine to come back with us now?"

"I don't know," Harvey said. "But it's going to be awfully hard without the papers."

"Or the medallion," Oona said.

"We'll just have to do what we can when we meet her," Harvey said. "…and pray that nobody kills us before then."

CHERYL DENTON

PART THREE
The Road Home

9

ON SATURDAY BEFORE LUNCH TIME, KIT STEPPED OUT OF the shower. Just as she was reaching for a towel, a voice from the other side of the bathroom door asked, "You hungry?"

Kit gasped and snatched the towel off the bar to wrap it around herself. She yanked open the door an inch and discovered Grant Osgood in the hallway. She asked, "How'd you get in here?"

Grant said, "I let myself in with one of the keys I found yesterday in the kitchen drawer."

He had a lot of nerve, she thought. "Well, put it back!"

"No problem," Grant said with a grin, "I got a copy made this morning at the hardware."

Great. Now she'd have to get the locks changed. "Grant Osgood, I hate you," she muttered under her breath.

"What'd you say?"

"Nothing," she said, slamming the door shut and turning the lock. She called out, "I'll be down in half an hour."

A lot of things were uncertain about Kit Blume's future, but there was one thing she knew: whatever it took, she was going to make sure that Grant Osgood was not a part of her life after today.

The memorial service began at two o'clock, and Kit moved as if in a trance down the long aisle of her parents' church. At the front, Father

Quincy waited with his censer in hand. Enormous pictures of her father and mother flanked the altar. Kit had actually taken the photo of her mother one afternoon when they visited Krohn Conservatory for the spring butterfly and flower show. Her father's portrait had been taken the year prior to his trip to San Francisco, where he taught seminars on open heart surgery.

Grant Osgood moved beside her, holding her elbow gently. For some strange reason, the entire scene made her feel like a bride walking down the aisle to get married. She glanced over at Grant Osgood. What a nightmare that would be!

At the front pew, he leaned over to whisper, "Here we are."

In spite of Kit's resolve to get rid of Grant Osgood that morning, he was still there. She glanced over at him and took note of the suit he was wearing. It was a fine, summer weight black wool that had obviously been custom fitted. A crisply starched white shirt accented by a red tie completed his outfit. With him sitting so close to her, she could smell his aftershave. The scent reminded her of her father, and she instantly found that tears were falling onto her cheeks.

Grant put his arm around her shoulder and gave it a gentle squeeze.

When the service ended, Grant Osgood was still there beside her, tucking her arm into his and leading her up to a seat between the two large silver urns that held her parents' remains. She wanted to turn to him to say that she could handle this by herself. But before she could, the sea of people began passing by in waves to offer their sympathy. With Grant standing behind her, she shook hand after hand, accepting the whispered words and gentle hugs.

After most of the crowd had left, Grant Osgood was still there. He led her away from the church and stepped into a limo with her. Where were they going? Kit couldn't recall where the meal was supposed to be that had been arranged. Everything seemed to be fuzzy and in slow-motion.

Throughout the meal that was served at one of the big hotels overlooking the Ohio River in Covington, Grant Osgood kept reappearing beside her to bring her a plate of food…a glass of water…a box of tissues…a more comfortable chair. He was the most supportive person in the room, and no one else seemed inclined to take his place.

Kit decided as the day wore on, that as soon as she gave Grant a sincere thank you, she would make it clear that she did not want to have anything more to do with him. He might appear to be the most gracious guy in the restaurant, but she knew the real Grant Osgood, and she wanted nothing to do with him. In fact, she decided, it would be best if she simply went back home to spend a quiet evening alone. With him out of the picture, she could relax.

The last of the memorial service guests were leaving the restaurant, and Father Quincy came to Kit's table to ask, "Do you have somebody to take you home, Kit?"

Before she could answer, Grant said, "I am."

"Fine," the priest said. "Thanks for taking such good care of her, son." He shook Grant's hand.

One of the nuns gave Kit a hug. "Are you going to be okay on your own?" she asked.

Kit asked, "Do I have any other choice?"

"Sure," the sister said. "You can bawl your eyes out and sleep 'til noon every day if you feel like it."

Kit didn't respond. If she started crying, she was afraid she'd never be able to stop.

The nun turned to Grant and said, "I'm sure you'll take good care of her. She's so blessed to have you."

Grant reached out to place his hand on Kit's shoulder. He said, "I'll be there for her for as long as she needs me."

After they left, Kit shrugged off Grant's hand and said, "That was quite a performance you put on today."

"What are you talking about?" Grant asked.

"Acting all lovey-dovey with me so that no one would suspect."

"Suspect what?"

"That you're a jerk."

Grant said, "I'll pretend I didn't hear that, since you're in mourning."

"All my life, you've been following me around like some blood hound. I'm sick of it," Kit said. "Leave me alone, or I swear…I'll kill you."

Grant ran his hand through his hair, loosened his tie, and leaned closer to Kit. He pressed his cheek to hers and said, "Don't say such awful things. You'll regret it later."

Feeling his rough beard against her cheek made Kit shudder. She shoved him away, stood up, and slapped him hard across the face.

Grant's hand shot up, and he grabbed onto Kit's wrist. She tried to free herself, but he held firm. He said, "You may not think so right now, but you're going to need me. Maybe not this minute, and maybe not an hour from now. But eventually, you'll realize that you've always needed me and always will."

"I'll never need you, Grant Osgood." Kit said through gritted teeth. "Not an hour from now. Not a century from now. I hate you!"

At her elbow, a voice said, "Excuse me, are you Kit Blume?"

Kit whirled around to find a man standing beside the table. His copper hair matched the color of his beard and eyebrows, which arched over penetrating blue eyes. Beside him stood a child…no, a woman who was incredibly short. She had red hair that stood out like a dandelion puff. Who were these people? She couldn't remember ever seeing them. They must have been more of her parents' friends, or maybe her father's co-workers from the hospital. "Yes," she said. "I'm Kit Blume."

The bearded man said, "My name is Harvey Trent." He turned to the little woman with the Technicolor hair and said, "This is my sister, Oona Kelly."

Mechanically, Kit extended her hand and said, "Thanks for coming today."

The two of them shook Kit's hand and nodded their heads. "Do you mind if we talk to you for a moment?" Harvey Trent asked.

Kit wanted to scream. Couldn't these two understand that she was exhausted? The last thing she wanted to do was make small talk. She just wanted to ditch Grant Osgood, get out of her too-small shoes, and crawl into bed.

Grant stood up and said, "Kit's had an awfully long day…"

"Please," Harvey Trent said. "This will only take a few minutes."

Oona Kelly added, "There's something really important we have to tell you."

Kit sighed deeply and motioned to the chairs across from them. Harvey Trent pulled out a chair for his sister and then sat down beside her. Kit and Grant sat back down. What on earth could they have to say to her that couldn't wait? She looked at her watch. It was going on five o'clock.

Harvey Trent said, "We're from Moose Creek, Minnesota. We're here as personal representatives for Mrs. Wildred Swenson. Your attorney contacted Wildred when your father and mother died to tell her that they had adopted you."

Kit felt as if the room were beginning to tilt sideways. She pressed her palms to the table and closed her eyes.

"Are you okay?" Oona Kelly asked.

If somebody from her birth family was interested in a relationship with her, she highly doubted that they would send 'personal representatives.' She surveyed the two sitting in front of her and decided that they must be scam artists. They were obviously after the several million dollars she had just inherited. She said, "Yes, I'm fine." The room settled, and she asked, "Why didn't Wildred Swenson come herself?"

"She's very old and not in good health," Harvey Trent said.

"She really wanted to," Oona Kelly added, "but she just couldn't. She's back home making preparations for your return."

"My return to what?" Kit asked.

"Why, your home, of course," Harvey Trent said.

Kit said, "Cincinnati is my home." In the next instant, she thought, *at least it used to be*. Now that she didn't have a house, and her parents' house would soon be for sale, she wasn't sure where home would be.

"Of course, it is," Oona Kelly said. She gave her brother a stern look, and she sat back with her lips pressed in a thin line.

After a moment, Harvey Trent said, "What I meant to say is that we'd like you to come with us to Moose Creek for a little visit. A lot of people can't wait to see you."

"I couldn't possibly go to Minnesota with you," Kit said. "I've got to go back to work on Tuesday."

Grant said, "Kit, I'm sure the school district would give you some family leave time."

Kit glared at Grant, who was obviously falling for their ridiculous tale—hook, line and sinker. She turned to the two in front of her to say, "Besides, I don't even know you. You could be a couple of scam artists trying to kidnap me and hold me for ransom or something."

Oona Kelly looked across at her brother. "Those papers sure would be handy right now."

Harvey Trent nodded and said to Kit, "We went to your father's attorney's office this morning. He gave us some papers to prove that we are Wildred Swenson's personal representatives."

Oona Kelly said, "But someone stole my purse when we stopped for gas."

Kit looked at Grant and asked, "Are you buying this story?"

Grant shrugged.

Harvey Trent said, "We had something to show you that would have proven beyond all doubt that you have a living relative in Moose Creek—"

Oona Kelly added, "—but it was in my purse, too."

"I don't know how on earth you could possibly have anything that could prove that," Kit said. She stood up and said, "Grant, I'm ready to go home now."

"Wait!" Harvey Trent said. "Unless I'm mistaken, that chain you're wearing around your neck has a medallion on it. It's got a picture of St. Guinevere on the front of it."

"A lot of people have seen my medallion," Kit said. "That doesn't prove anything." She picked up her purse from the table and said to Grant, "Let's get out of here."

Harvey Trent asked, "But do many people know that the inscription on the back of the medallion reads *Von Will?*"

Kit froze. Then, she slowly sank back down onto her chair. "How did you know that?" she asked.

"Because all of the children in your family wore them," Oona Kelly said.

Kit blinked. She had always assumed that somewhere in the world, she had a mother and a father at birth. But she had really not given much thought to the possibility of having siblings. Could these two be telling her the truth? "There were other children in my birth family?"

"Yes," Harvey Trent said. "Four of them. Annabelle, Peter, Benny, and you."

Kit looked more closely at Harvey Trent and asked, "What does *Von Will* mean?"

Harvey Trent said, "It's an abbreviation for Von Willebrand. It's like a medic alert bracelet."

"I don't understand," Kit said.

"You've never heard of Von Willebrand's disorder?"

Kit shook her head.

"I have," Grant said. "It's a bleeding disorder."

Kit reached under the neckline of her dress and lifted out her own medallion. She looked at the back of it and peered at the cursive script that read, *Von Will.* "You mean I have a bleeding disorder?"

Harvey Trent nodded.

"And so do the rest of the children in the family?"

Again, Harvey Trent nodded. "It's inherited."

Kit couldn't believe it. After all this time of trying so hard to figure out why she had this medallion with the cryptic inscription on the back, these two strangers just walk up and tell her all about it. What else did they know about her? And how had they found out? Part of her wanted to believe them, but another side of her kept screaming that they were just great actors. She asked, "Why didn't my parents come looking for me?"

Harvey Trent looked over at his sister and raised an eyebrow. She nodded at him, and he said, "They couldn't."

"Oh, yeah," Kit said. "You said my mother was too sick to come."

"Oh, no," Harvey Trent said, "Wildred Swenson isn't your mother. She's the one who adopted your brother."

"I'm confused," Kit said.

"I can understand that," Harvey Trent said. "Your parents couldn't come, because they died when you were four years old."

Kit closed her eyes and remembered that her parents had just died, but she was twenty-eight years old.

"Oh, this must be so overwhelming for you," Oona Kelly said

"You can say that again," Kit muttered. Her head was swimming, and she needed to lie down. She stood and said, "Can we talk about this later?"

Oona Kelly stood up and said, "I'm afraid there's not time to do it later."

"Why not?" Kit asked. "Is this Wildred Swenson dying or something?"

"No," Oona Kelly said. She glanced over at her brother, and he laid a hand on her arm and shook his head. She said, "We're pretty sure your parents didn't just die. We think they were murdered."

Kit blinked. Were they trying to confuse her? She asked them about Wildred Swenson, and then the elf woman changed the subject. What was going on? She said, "You're not telling me anything new. The story about my parents' murder has been in the papers all week."

Harvey Trent stood up and said, "Are you telling me that your parents—the ones who just died—were murdered?"

"That's how it looks," Kit said. "They were in my house when it burned down, and the cops are telling me that an arsonist set the fire to kill me."

Both Harvey Trent and Oona Kelly sank into their chairs.

"Judas Priest!" Harvey Trent muttered.

Oona Kelly said, "Jesus, Mary, and Joseph!"

Kit thought their reactions seemed a little theatrical for people who had never even met her parents. She said, "You don't have to act so shocked on my account. It's sinking in that my parents were murdered."

Harvey Trent looked up at her and said, "There's something you don't understand."

"Clue me in," Kit said, "but do it fast. I'm really tired."

Harvey Trent swallowed hard, and Kit saw his Adam's apple bob. He said, "Your parents…died in a fire at their house."

Now she was getting more than tired. These two clowns were making her ticked off. "No," Kit said, "They died in a fire at *my* house. It's on the west side of town. They lived on the east side, on the Little Miami River."

Oona Kelly stood and approached Kit. She put her hand on Kit's arm and said, "Honey, what we're telling you is that your *birth* parents were killed by an arsonist. We're shocked, because we didn't know your *adoptive* parents died the same way."

Grant tugged on Kit's arm and said, "Sit down."

Kit glared at him and jerked her arm out of his grasp. Their story was beginning to sound ludicrous. They were obviously scam artists. "Do you realize how far-fetched all of this sounds? I think I should call the cops." She reached into her purse for her cell phone.

Harvey Trent said, "Wait! There's one other thing."

"Please don't tell me that the two of you are related to me, too," Kit said. She pulled her cell phone out of its cover.

Before she could dial 9-1-1, Oona Kelly snatched the phone out of Kit's hand. "Listen to us," she said fiercely. "Harvey found your brother's remains in the woods last week. He'd been shot through the back of the head when he was a boy."

Now Kit was really getting fed up.

Oona Kelly's green eyes flashed at her.

Kit decided to play along with her and then yank the phone back out of the pipsqueak's hand. She said, "Someone shot my brother?"

"Yes," Oona Kelly said, adding, "There were four children in your family. Your oldest sister disappeared the day after the fire, and one of your brothers was shot. There are two of you left alive, and we'd like to keep it that way."

Her words were beginning to sound like something out of a TV drama. "Are you suggesting that the arsonist who killed my birth family is trying to kill me?" Kit asked.

Harvey Trent said, "Yes. Someone's trying to stop us from uncovering the truth about what happened to your family."

"How?"

Oona Kelly said, "A man attacked me the other night and told me it was better to let sleeping dogs lie."

Kit said, "Well maybe you should."

Harvey Trent added, "And then someone stole Oona's purse and took with it the things that might help us convince you to come back with us."

"Too bad you lost them," Kit said, "because I'm not buying any of this."

Harvey Trent said, "You're our best hope. If you don't come back to Moose Creek with us, we may never have enough evidence to re-open the case. We've got to prove that your birth parents were murdered."

They were becoming so adamant about taking Kit with them, she was certain it was some kind of a scam. She said, "I don't have to do anything. Now, would you mind giving me back my phone? I've had a really long day."

Reluctantly, Oona Kelly handed Kit her phone. She turned to her brother and said, "Forget it, Harvey. She's not going to do it. Let's go."

Harvey Trent stood and slowly pushed in his chair. Oona Kelly began to walk away, and he reached out to touch her sleeve. She turned back to look up at him. To Kit, he said, "If you change your mind, we'll be staying at the Best Western on Beechmont Avenue until tomorrow afternoon." They left, and Kit put her cell phone back into her purse.

Grant said, "What did you think of all that?"

Kit waved her hand in the air and said, "Cockroaches, coming out of the woodwork because somebody got wind of my inheritance."

Grant said, "Doesn't it seem odd that they knew about the inscription on the back of your medallion?"

"Spies," Kit said. "Haven't you heard about what happens to people who win the lottery? Money mongers make up all kinds of scams about being long-lost relatives."

"But what about your father's letter? He told you someone would be coming within the week."

Kit began walking towards the exit and said, "You really think those two actually went to the lawyer's office today? He doesn't work on Saturdays."

Grant held the door for her and said, "They sounded pretty believable to me."

Outside, the humidity immediately wilted Kit's hair. She would be glad when autumn came and brought some relief from the heat. She said,

"They sounded like actors from a low-budget movie." She got into Grant's green and grey Honda Element and said, "Now, if you don't mind, I'd like to forget about them and go home. My feet are killing me."

10

GRANT DROVE AWAY FROM THE RECEPTION CENTER IN Covington and crossed the Roebling Bridge, which connected northern Kentucky with downtown Cincinnati. The evening sun glinted across the muddy water of the Ohio River. Scores of small boats dotted the river, and he wondered why there were so many of them. Then he remembered that it was Labor Day weekend, and they were positioning themselves on the river for the fireworks display on Sunday night. He glanced over at Kit, who was dozing in the passenger seat. She looked unbelievably tired. He had to admit that he was really worn out, too. It had been a draining day for both of them.

A short time later, he dropped down onto Riverside Drive, where the boats on the Ohio River were almost as numerous as they were near downtown. A horn blared behind him, and he looked up into the rearview mirror. A delivery truck was just inches away from his back bumper. "Geez Louise," he muttered, "back off."

Kit lifted her head and asked, "What?"

Grant's muscles tensed, and he sped up. He said, "Some jerk's trying to park in my trunk."

Kit looked back and said, "Just pull over and let him pass."

Grant wouldn't ordinarily let some loser get away with something like that. But, since Kit was in the car with him, he put on his blinker, slowed down, and turned into a marina parking lot. The truck roared past, and Grant pulled back out onto the road. "He's going to get a ticket driving like that," he muttered. He stomped on the accelerator. "I should get his plate number and report him."

Kit said, "The cops will catch up to him eventually. Let him go."

He realized she was right. The road curved, and Grant shifted downward. He slowed, and the truck disappeared around the bend. Relax, he told himself. He consciously took a deep breath and dropped his shoulders. Kit didn't need to be worrying about some guy with road rage today. Grant wanted to get her back home so that she could rest.

He rounded the bend just in time to see the delivery truck rear-end a small blue sedan. The little car swerved into the oncoming lane of traffic and then back into its own lane. It sped ahead of the truck and zipped around a curve. Grant gripped the wheel more tightly. "Did you see that?" he asked.

Kit lifted her head and asked, "See what?"

Grant watched the little blue car disappearing over a rise in the road. "That truck just hit a car!"

Kit sat up straighter in her seat. "I don't see a thing," she said. "The truck's still moving."

"I know it is," Grant said, "but I'm telling you, he just hit the back end of a blue car. I don't understand why it didn't stop."

"I think you're seeing things," Kit said. "You're tired."

Grant watched the truck closely as it disappeared over the hill. He was certain the truck had hit the car. He stomped on the accelerator and came up over the crest. The road curved hard to the left, and the truck sped forward and closed the gap between it and the blue car. He could see what was coming. "Look out!" Grant shouted.

The blue car slowed for the curve, and the truck rammed it hard from behind. The little car missed the curve and shot off the road.

"Oh, no!" Kit cried. "That car's headed for the river!"

Grant ground to a stop at the curve. The blue car hurtled down the embankment towards the water. He jumped from the car and shouted at Kit, "Call 9-1-1!"

The small sedan slammed into a tree just a few feet from the water's edge. Grant grabbed his first aid kit out of the back of his SUV. He charged down the hill. Loose gravel rolled away from under his feet.

Branches scraped his face. He lost his footing and slid on his backside the final twenty feet. When he reached the car, he yanked open the passenger door.

To his surprise, he found himself looking at the little woman with the red hair who had just left the memorial service reception. She was frantically beating back the air bag that had burst open. Her skin was the color of Elmer's glue.

"Are you okay?" he asked.

She said, "I…I think so."

"Just sit still," Grant said. "Kit's calling 9-1-1."

Harvey Trent said from the driver's seat, "I smell gas."

Grant froze. He sniffed. The smell was strong. He glanced at the hood and noticed that small flames were licking out from under it. They had to move quickly. He asked, "Are you hurt?"

Harvey Trent shook his head.

Grant said, "We've got to get you out of here as quickly as possible."

Harvey nodded and shoved open the driver's side door. He stepped out, and Grant held Oona's hand as she emerged. Her knees buckled, and Grant bent forward so that she crumpled onto his shoulder. He picked up his first aid kit and walked to the back of the car. Harvey went ahead of him, and they climbed as quickly as possible up the bank.

A blast from behind them knocked Grant to his knees. Oona cinched her arms more tightly around his waist. He looked back to see a huge fireball erupting skyward. "Keep going!" he shouted at Harvey.

He and Harvey hung onto tree limbs and the undergrowth to haul themselves up the hill.

At the top, Grant carried Oona to his Honda Element. He opened the rear door and set her down gently on the seat. Harvey slid in from the other side.

Harvey asked his sister, "Are you okay?"

She nodded and said, "That truck driver just tried to kill us."

Harvey said, "I know."

Kit came to stand beside Grant and said, "I called 9-1-1."

In the distance, Grant could hear the wail of a siren. He turned to look back at the car. A plume of black smoke rose skyward. A cluster of small boats circled nearby. He said to Kit, "Looks like the tourists are getting a two-for-one deal."

The paramedics arrived, along with a fire truck. While they were checking over Harvey and Oona, Grant gave a report to the Hamilton County sheriff's deputy who arrived on the scene.

Kit asked the deputy, "Why would a truck driver just slam into a car like that?"

"You wouldn't believe what road rage will make some people do," he said.

Grant said, "I don't think this was a case of road rage."

"Why not?" the deputy asked.

"Because I think someone's trying to kill those two," he said, nodding his head in the direction of the red-headed pair.

"What makes you think that?" the deputy asked.

Grant told the deputy the details of the conversation they had had with the two of them after the memorial service.

When he finished, Kit asked, "Do you think someone wants them dead?"

"Maybe," the deputy said. "We'll use the information you two gave us on the truck to see if we can identify the driver."

Grant nodded.

The deputy walked to the side of the road and began directing traffic around the fire trucks. Grant and Kit got into the Honda and closed the doors. "Do you want me to take you to the hospital?" he asked.

"No, the airport," Harvey said. "I need to get to the state police in St. Paul as soon as possible."

"Uh, Harvey," Oona said, "I don't think we're going to get very far at the airport."

"Why not?" Harvey asked.

"Because the plane tickets and my driver's license were in my purse," Oona said.

Harvey groaned and said, "There's no way you'll make it past security without ID."

"You're right," Grant said. He sat there thinking. Whoever was after them was tracking their movement. He had attacked Oona in Moose Creek, followed them to Cincinnati, stolen her purse, and tried to drown them in the Ohio River. He said, "Whoever is after you isn't going to give up easily. We've got to talk to the police before one of you winds up dead."

"That may not be such a great idea," Harvey said.

"Why not?" Kit asked.

"We think our police chief is involved in some kind of a cover-up," Oona said.

"And we wouldn't be surprised if other cops were helping him," Harvey said.

Grant considered the possibility of cops being crooked. It wasn't inconceivable. He'd seen a few go bad over the years in the Cincinnati department. There was obviously some connection between Harvey and Oona and Kit's birth family. He thought about her flashbacks and how someone was firing a gun at her. Were they flashbacks or premonitions of things to come? "You think the same people who are trying to stop you are after Kit?"

Harvey said, "Why do you think they set fire to her house?"

Grant thought back over the events of the week. The arsonist who had burned Kit's house obviously had more in mind that just destroying a home. But why? He said. "The cops already told us that this arsonist was bent on killing someone. We just can't figure out his motive."

"He's trying to cover up something, and he thinks Kit might remember what that something is," Oona said.

Harvey added, "And he's willing to do anything to stop us from figuring out what happened when Kit was little."

Grant felt as if he were having a bad dream. This was the sort of thing that only happened in movies, not in real life. He heard himself saying, "We'd better do whatever it takes to stop this guy."

Oona said, "Then you'd better take us back to Minnesota so we can get someone we can trust to help us."

Grant looked over at Kit and saw a terrified look in her eyes that had not been there before. He was beginning to understand that something terrible had happened to her birth family. Why else would someone be trying so hard to keep people quiet about what had happened all those years ago? He also knew that he had to help Kit. He had to make her see that she could no longer pretend that her parents weren't dead. She couldn't bury herself in her work anymore. She had to face the facts that she had been adopted under very unusual circumstances, some of which Norm Blume had known. He realized, perhaps for the first time, that her flashbacks stemmed from more than just an overactive imagination. He had to help Harvey and Oona figure out what had happened. If they didn't, all of them could wind up dead. He said to Kit, "We have to go to Minnesota."

She asked him, "What are you sitting here for? Let's go!"

Grant roared away towards the interstate. No matter what, he vowed to protect Kit from the dangers that lay ahead of them.

11

AFTER TAKING TURNS DRIVING ALL NIGHT, HARVEY, OONA, Grant, and Kit arrived in St. Paul just after noon on Sunday. Harvey found his way back to the state police post on Cedar Street where he and Oona had left Peter Vernon's skull, along with Doc Daggert's x-ray and Oona's lists of Moose Creek residents. The four of them went into the station, and Harvey approached the grey and maroon uniformed man behind the glass partition. He was surprised to find the same Sergeant there that they had talked to previously. He walked up to the glass wall and asked, "Didn't you say you were going fishing until Tuesday?"

"Excuse me?" the Sergeant said.

"We were in here on Friday night," Harvey said. "You told us you weren't working again until Tuesday."

The Sergeant stared at Harvey blankly and then asked, "Is there something I can help you with?"

Harvey said, "Someone's been following us."

Oona piped up with, "They're trying to kill us."

The Sergeant surveyed Harvey and Oona from behind his glass wall.

Harvey realized how they must appear to the state trooper. His clothes were torn and covered in dried mud. Oona had a large bruise on her forehead where the airbag had hit her.

The Sergeant said, "I'll be out in a minute. Have a seat."

The four of them sat down.

Harvey said to Grant and Kit, "I'm certain he's going to be able to help us. That skull with the bullet hole through it and Doc Daggert's x-rays are proof positive that there was a murder at the Lakeshore Inn."

Harvey watched the state trooper emerging from a door beside the front counter. It was definitely the same guy with the pock-marked face. His curly, dark hair still looked like it needed washing.

The Sergeant walked up to Harvey and asked, "How can I help you folks?"

Harvey stood up and said, "We were here on Friday night. Remember, we talked to you about the fire at the Lakeshore Inn."

The Sergeant stared at Harvey without commenting.

Harvey added, "We gave you some evidence to prove that there were several murders in our town."

"Which town is that?"

"Moose Creek," Harvey said.

"That's Ron Frank's jurisdiction then," the Sergeant said, "not ours."

"We realize that," Harvey said, "but we think he's involved in some sort of cover-up."

"What kind of cover-up?"

"Ron Frank called a fire at the Lakeshore Inn an accident. We think it was set intentionally."

"What makes you think that?"

"Ron said the whole family who lived there died in the fire." Harvey turned and pointed to Kit. "But this girl, as you can see, is very much alive."

"Let me guess..." the Sergeant said, "...she supposedly died in this accidental fire?"

"That's right," Harvey said.

"I don't remember hearing about any big fire up that way," the Sergeant said.

"That's because it was twenty-five years ago," Harvey said.

The Sergeant's eyebrows shot up. "You want the police to look into a fire that happened twenty-five years ago?"

"You have to," said Harvey, "before somebody gets hurt."

The Sergeant put his hands on his hips and said, "What kind of proof do you have—other than this live specimen here—that the case was mismanaged?"

"We brought you a skull," Harvey said, "with x-rays that proved his identity." He pointed to his own front teeth and said, "Peter Vernon had knocked out his front tooth, and Doc Daggert pegged it. I saw that peg in the tooth and on the x-ray."

"Where did you say you took this evidence?" the man asked.

Harvey was so aggravated, he felt like slugging the guy. "Here!" he said. "We gave it all to you."

"I think you must be mistaken," the Sergeant said. "I've never seen you in here before."

What was going on? "I tell you," said Harvey, "we left it all in a cardboard box. You took us into a room back there, and I gave you a big box with everything in it."

"Where's your receipt for the evidence?" the Sergeant asked.

Harvey felt a mounting sense of frustration. Overwhelming fatigue was making him light-headed. "You didn't give us one."

"That's impossible," the Sergeant said. "No police station ever takes in evidence without giving a receipt."

Harvey clenched his fists and said, "You told us that you didn't want to write one out until Tuesday, after you'd gone fishing with your brother-in-law." He took a deep breath and said, "You said you'd wait to date the receipt on Tuesday so that you could have a quiet look at things without telling our chief what you were doing."

The Sergeant shook his head. "Are you sure you've got the right station?" he asked.

Harvey looked around and then back at the Sergeant. "Positive," he said.

The Sergeant surveyed both Harvey and Oona, smiled, and said, "I sure wouldn't forget you two if I'd seen you before…especially this young lady. She's a pretty memorable character."

Harvey got the sense that the Sergeant was making fun of Oona.

Oona took Harvey by the arm and whispered, "Let's get out of here."

"Not until I get back what we left here," Harvey said.

Oona whispered, "He's not going to give it to you. Let's go." She tugged on his arm.

Reluctantly, Harvey followed Oona outside to Grant's green and grey SUV. He stopped and stood there staring at the station. Yes, he was certain this was the same place. There, in the parking lot, was the same dead squirrel he had nearly stepped on the last time. He grabbed Oona by the arm and pointed at the squirrel. "We *were* here the other night."

"I know," she said. "Get in the car."

All four of them got into the car.

Harvey said, "I don't get it."

"I do," said Oona. "Did you hear what he said about Moose Creek?"

"What?" asked Harvey.

Oona said, "He knew right off the bat that Ron Frank is chief there. I told you we shouldn't go to the state police. Ron knows that guy."

Harvey knew then that Oona was probably right. Without realizing it, they had tipped off Ron Frank about what they were doing. He rubbed the back of his neck and sighed. "If he told Ron about what we've been doing, that would explain why somebody's been trying to stop us."

"Now what?" Oona asked. "We've lost every shred of evidence we had."

"Except me," said Kit.

Harvey looked at Kit Blume. He said, "If we could get you to Doc Daggert and get him to take some x-rays of your teeth, we'd be in luck."

"That's right!" Oona said. "He's got her old dental records. He can compare the old ones to the new ones. It'll at least prove that Catherine didn't die in the fire, and we can go after Ron Frank."

Harvey said to Grant, "I have to get my truck from the airport. You can follow me from there to Moose Creek."

It was late Sunday afternoon when Harvey pulled up in front of his father's house. Oona said, "I've never been so glad to be home in my life."

Harvey said, "Don't get too excited about it. I think we'd better all go together to Doc Daggert's before something else happens."

"I guess you're right," Oona said.

Grant and Kit got into the back of Harvey's king cab, and the four of them drove directly to Doc Daggert's old cabin on Heron Lake. Harvey and Oona got out and went to the door. He knocked, waiting expectantly for Jet to come to the door. There was no movement or sound from inside. "That's strange," he said.

"What is?" Oona asked.

"If Jet were inside, he'd have been barking long before we got out of the car."

Oona scowled. "You're right." She tried the door, and it was unlocked. "I'm going to check inside. You look around out back."

Harvey nodded. "Be careful," he said. He turned and followed the wrap-around porch to the rear of the house. When he got close to the back door, he froze. Jet lay in a pool of blood on the wooden planks. Harvey rushed to his dog's side and shouted, "Jet!" The dog didn't move. His eyes stared, unseeing, at the woods beyond the house. Rage welled up in Harvey's chest, and he swore.

Oona opened the back door and let out a gasp. "Oh, Harvey!" she said, "Poor Jet."

Harvey stood up and asked, "What did you find inside?"

"Doc's not here," Oona said, "And somebody trashed his house. It looks like they've taken all of his old files."

Fear for the old dentist's safety gripped him. Harvey said, "We've got to find him."

Oona stepped out onto the porch. "Where do you think he is?"

Harvey walked around to the front of the house and looked out at the lake. He could see Doc Daggert's bass boat in the middle of the lake. Why hadn't Doc stayed close to the house? He pointed across the lake and said, "There."

They got back into the truck, and Kit asked, "Wasn't he home?"

"No," Harvey said.

Oona added, "And it looks as if someone broke in."

"How could you tell?" Grant asked.

Oona said, "The door was open, and the place was trashed. All of his old dental files were gone."

Grant said, "Someone really is trying to stop you, aren't they?"

Harvey said, "Yes, they are." He drove around to the other side of the lake. When they neared Doc's boat, he said, "I'm going to pull over here." He got out and shouted across the water, "Doc!"

There was no response.

Harvey frowned. Again, he called out, "Doc!"

Nothing.

Harvey said to Oona, "Something's wrong. I'm going to take Dad's boat out there."

At his father's boat house, Harvey lowered the old Chris Craft into the water and untied it. He felt the boat jiggling, and he looked up to find

Oona standing in the back. "I'm coming with you," she said. "We need to stick together."

Harvey nodded and put the key in the ignition.

Within minutes, they were pulling up close to Doc's boat. It began bobbing on their small wake. Harvey cut the motor and said, "Hand me a paddle."

Oona pulled out a paddle from the storage compartment, and Harvey maneuvered the boat closer to Doc's. When they got near, Harvey could see that a man lay face down in the bottom of the boat. An oversized orange life vest obscured his head.

Oona gave a little gasp.

Harvey grabbed onto the side of Doc's boat and hopped into it. Swiftly, he bent down to turn the man over. He was surprised to discover a stranger staring up at him...a middle-aged man whose eyes were as unseeing as Jet's were. He had a bullet hole through his life jacket, and a hot pink Minnesota Minnie lure dangled from his lower lip. "Judas Priest!" Harvey muttered.

"Is he dead?" Oona asked.

Harvey checked the man's neck for a pulse. "Yeah," he said, releasing his hold on the dead man. Harvey straightened up and looked around. There was no other boat on the lake. He scanned the shoreline, but nothing stood out, other than his own truck. On the floor of the boat, he noticed a cigarette butt.

"Someone's watching us," Oona said. "I can feel it."

"Me, too," said Harvey, "And I don't mean Kit and Grant."

Harvey got back into his own boat and sat there thinking. Why was this guy in Doc Daggert's boat? Had they been fishing together? If they were, how did Doc get back to shore? Harvey got the feeling that Doc was too unbalanced to swim so far.

"Do you think Doc's the Fishing Lure Killer?" Oona asked.

Was he? Harvey thought back over the conversations that he and Doc had had over the past week. The little jokes about frying up men and the old man's wobbly grin accompanied by a wink led Harvey to believe that Doc was *not* a killer. He had seemed so helpful when they found Peter's body. "I don't think so," Harvey said.

"Me neither," said Oona. "But why is that guy in Doc's boat? And why did the Fishing Lure Killer do that to him?"

Harvey felt so confused. There was so much happening. Did the Fishing Lure Killer have something to do with the Lakeshore Inn fire? He couldn't figure it out, but he didn't feel that Doc had anything to do with this murder. And yet, it didn't answer the question of why there was a dead body in Doc's boat. "I don't know what's going on," Harvey said, "but if we can find Doc, maybe he can answer some of our questions."

"In the meantime, I think we'd better report this," Oona said.

"If we tell Ron, he might try to convince someone that we did it," Harvey said, "considering that he's been interfering with everything else we've been trying to do."

"But I don't want to spend the rest of my life in jail. Your fingerprints and mine are all over Doc's house and boat now," Oona said.

"You're right," Harvey said. "But isn't there someone besides Ron that we can trust?"

"Like who?" Oona asked.

Harvey shrugged. "Maybe the county sheriff."

"You mean the guy who meets Ron for doughnuts at Swenson's every week?" Oona asked. "Like they aren't thick as thieves!"

"What do you suggest?" he asked.

Oona said, "I think we should talk to Sophie. She'd know."

"Good idea," Harvey said.

"Too bad you don't have a cell phone," Oona said. "You could call her from here."

Harvey glared at his sister and then fired up the Chris Craft. Back at the truck, they found Kit and Grant waiting in the back seat.

"Did you find Doc?" Kit asked.

"No," Harvey said, pulling the door shut. "He wasn't the one in the boat."

"Who was?" Kit asked.

"Hard to say," Harvey said. "Dead men don't usually introduce themselves."

"What?" Kit exclaimed.

Oona said, "There's a serial killer leaving fishermen dead with lures stuck in their lower lips."

"Oh, that's awful!" Kit said.

"Why's there a dead guy in Doc's boat?" Grant asked.

"That's exactly what we'd like to know," Harvey said.

"Don't you think we should tell the police there's a dead man out on the lake?" Kit asked.

"Yeah," Harvey said. He reached down to start the engine and stopped when he noticed something near the north shore. He peered through the windshield and said, "Is that a truck parked under the trees near the old Vernon dock?"

Oona looked where Harvey was and said, "Yeah."

"Maybe we should check this out."

"Maybe we should just get out of here," Kit said.

Harvey opened his door, and Grant said, "I'll go with you."

Kit said, "I don't like this one bit."

Oona said to her, "You and I can wait here and let the men go."

Kit nodded and said, "I never expected that my past would be anything like this."

Harvey turned back to Oona and said, "Hand me your phone."

"You mean the one that was in my purse?" Oona asked.

"Yeah," Harvey said. That's when he realized again that Oona's purse had been stolen. He turned and kicked a rock across the road. When was just one thing going to go right for them?

Grant said, "I've got a phone. We can call Kit's if we run into trouble."

"You may not have reception out here," Oona said.

Grant nodded and closed the back door of the truck.

Harvey turned back to his sister and said, "Remember, stay in the truck and keep the doors locked. Don't unlock them for anyone but us."

Oona nodded and then said, "How long do you think you'll be gone?"

Harvey shrugged and said, "Give us an hour."

"What if you don't come back?" Oona asked.

Harvey hadn't considered that possibility. He reached out and squeezed Oona's hand. "We'll be back," he said.

Oona said, "If you're not back here in an hour, I'm going to town to get Sophie to help us."

"Okay," Harvey said.

They began to walk away, and Kit called after them, "Be careful!"

12

OONA SLIPPED INTO THE DRIVER'S SEAT OF HARVEY'S TRUCK and pulled the door shut. She watched the men threading their way along the lakeshore. When they disappeared into the woods, she looked at the clock. It was 7:05. She would give them until 8:00. If they weren't back by then, she would drive to town to find Sophie. She turned to Kit and said, "They'll be back soon."

Kit nodded and reached up to brush away a tear. Her chin wobbled, and Oona reached back to squeeze her hand.

Oona said, "We're going to get through this. Everything's going to be okay."

Kit looked down at Oona's hand and pulled hers away. She said, "I don't know how you can say that. Nothing has ever been okay for me."

"You've had a really rough time for the past few days, haven't you?" Oona said.

Kit looked away out the passenger side of the car and said, "I've had a rough time my whole life."

Oona thought that it might make Kit feel better to talk a little bit about her parents. Their deaths were so fresh; she doubted that Kit had even had a chance to catch her breath with all that was going on. She asked, "What were your mom and dad like?"

Kit's eyes lit up, and she looked up at Oona to say, "They were pretty amazing." She paused and smiled slightly. "My mom grew the most beautiful roses you've ever seen. You should see her garden."

Oona was glad that Kit was talking. She asked her, "What else do you remember about her?"

Kit said, "She was the most selfless person on the planet. Whenever someone needed something, they called Mom. She helped start orphanages in Bangladesh, Ethiopia, and Ecuador."

"Wow," Oona said. "That's really something. You must be proud of her."

Kit nodded and said, "Wherever she went, she always brought back something for me." Her face darkened then, and she said, "But it's all gone now."

Oona couldn't imagine how she would feel if her family's home burned down. So many memories would be lost without the photographs, the knick-knacks, and the familiarity of it all. She said, "I'm so sorry about your house, too."

Two tears slid down Kit's cheeks, and she said, "And now, I'm going to have to sell my parents' house."

"Surely, you can keep it if you want to," Oona said.

Kit shook her head. "My dad left me a letter that said I had to sell it and give the money to the church."

Oona knew then that Kit's parents must have been very dedicated to the work of the church. She had encountered a few parishioners over the years who had left their entire estates to the church. They had blessed so many people with their gifts, but often, their families complained…families who didn't understand the importance of God's work in comparison to man's accumulation of wealth. "How do you feel about that?" Oona asked.

Kit said, "At first, I was really mad. But, if that's what they want, who am I to argue?"

Oona said, "Your parents must have been very special people."

Kit nodded and said, "My dad was my hero. Even though he worked like a dog at the hospital, he always had time for me."

"They must have loved you a lot."

Kit nodded again, but she didn't say anything.

Oona sat there in silence, staring ahead at the dense pines that grew along the shoreline. She thought about the family that had lived at the Lakeshore Inn all those years ago. She asked Kit, "Would you like to know about your birth family?"

Kit looked up and asked, "You knew them?"

Oona smiled and nodded. "Harvey was two years older than your sister, Annabelle. They were high school sweethearts."

"What was she like?" Kit asked.

Oona knew that it wouldn't serve any purpose to tell Kit about Annabelle's surly moods or her weight problem. Kit needed something positive to cling to right now. Oona said, "I was always envious of her. She had the most beautiful clothes. And her hair! I would kill for long, smooth hair like she had."

Kit glanced up at Oona's hair, but she made no comment about it. She asked, "What were my birth parents like?"

Oona tried to recall some details about Paul and Mimi Vernon, but they were sketchy, at best. She had never been to the Inn all that often, and she certainly hadn't hung out with Annabelle. She said, "Your mother was French."

"She was?" Kit said.

"Mm-hm," Oona said. "I didn't know her very well, but she seemed like a really class act. Whenever I saw her, she was always wearing these slim skirts, pretty blouses, and heels." Oona recalled how plain her own mother had appeared in her polyester pants, rayon tops, and plastic shoes that she bought at a thrift store in Big Bear. She added, "I'm sure Mimi must have bought all of her clothes in Paris. We didn't have anything like it in our stores."

"What did she look like?" Kit asked.

Oona considered Kit's features and said, "You have her nose."

Kit asked, "Did you know my dad?"

Oona didn't know much at all about the man, but there was one thing she did recall. She said, "Everybody loved your dad. He was a great big, loveable teddy bear."

Kit asked, "Was he French, too?"

"No," Oona said. "I think he was an Ojibwa from Canada."

"Oh," Kit said. She added, "Harvey said that I had two brothers. Can you tell me anything about them?"

A flash of the skull they had recently delivered to the state trooper's office in St. Paul flashed through Oona's mind. Thinking about it reminded her that Harvey and Grant were out there where a killer had hidden Peter Vernon's body. She wished they would hurry. Oona said, "I didn't know Peter well at all, but I know Benny better than most people do."

"Why?"

Oona said, "He was one of my students for years, and I still see him every day."

"Does he remember me?"

"It's hard to say," Oona said. "He was so young when the Inn burned down." She wondered how much Kit knew about people with special needs. Sometimes, they weren't very receptive to them, but she certainly didn't want to give her false expectations about Benny. She added, "There are a lot of things Benny can't remember…he's got Down's syndrome."

Kit said, "That's weird."

"Not really," Oona said. "It's more common than most people realize."

"I don't mean weird like that," Kit said. "What I meant was, it's weird, because I teach kids with special needs."

Oona felt surprised, and yet, at the same time, it made sense. She said, "When you and Benny were little, I used to watch you playing at the beach near my dad's boathouse. You were always really patient with him."

Kit asked, "I was?"

Oona nodded and said, "You had a gift back then, and I'm sure your students are benefiting from it today."

Kit smiled slightly and said, "I wish I could remember Benny."

Oona said, "Is there anything you remember about Moose Creek?"

Kit's smile became a frown. "Not much."

"But you remember some things?"

"Only a couple."

"Like what?"

Kit drew a deep breath and stared out the window. After a minute, she said, "I have flashbacks about my life here…nightmares really."

"Nightmares?" Oona said. "What are they about?"

"Running through the woods…with someone shooting at me."

Oona frowned. Why would someone have been shooting at a four-year-old? She asked, "Any idea who was behind the gun?"

Kit shook her head. "No. That's really why I came up here. I thought that if I could figure out who wanted me dead, I'd sleep better."

Oona said to Kit, "As long as they're not still out there with a gun."

The color drained from Kit's face, and she said, "Oh, I wish the guys would come back."

They both fell silent, and Oona watched the lengthening shadows made by the enormous pines along the western side of the highway. She glanced down at her watch. The men had been gone now for nearly forty minutes. She hoped the pick-up on the north shore wasn't the killer's. And she prayed that whoever was trying to stop them from finding out the truth about the Lakeshore Inn fire was not out there with a gun.

CHERYL DENTON

13

HARVEY WALKED UP TO THE BACK OF THE OLD BLACK pick-up truck parked on the north side of the lake. In the bed, he noted that there were a number of wooden posts. Was someone working on the old Lakeshore Inn dock? He glanced toward the old dock and noticed that it looked the same.

"What do you make of this?" Grant asked.

"I don't know," Harvey said, "but I have a feeling that this is somehow related to finding Peter Vernon's remains on Friday."

"Any idea who this truck belongs to?" Grant asked.

Harvey walked around the battered old vehicle and stopped to look at the license plate. It was a Minnesota plate with their local county tag on it, but Harvey couldn't remember ever having seen it. "Not a clue," he said.

"What now?" Grant asked.

"I think we should take a walk. I have a sneaking suspicion that whoever is behind all this may be snooping around what's left of Peter's body."

"Is that safe?" Grant asked.

"Probably not," Harvey said, "but if we leave without checking, we may regret it later."

"We may regret it if the person driving this truck wants us dead," Grant pointed out.

"True, but I've got to know," Harvey said. "If you want to go back to wait with the women, you can."

Grant shook his head. "I'll go with you."

As they walked along, Harvey began to hear a noise in the distance. He stopped on the path between the ferns and asked, "Did you hear something?"

"Yeah," Grant said. "Sounds like a hammer."

Harvey stood there listening. "I think you're right. Who would be building something out here?"

They walked on, and the pounding grew louder. At length, the site of the old bridge came into view, and Harvey stopped abruptly.

"What's wrong?" Grant asked.

Harvey couldn't believe his eyes. Up ahead, his maintenance man, Ralph Rivers, was nailing down the last of the boards on a new bridge that spanned the few inches of water in Heron Creek. He hurried forward and asked Ralph, "What are you doing out here?"

Ralph slowly rose to his feet, with his sinewy arms dangling at his sides. A hammer hung in one ropey hand. "Just finishing up," he said.

Harvey looked down at the spot where he had last seen Peter's body. A heavy post was now buried deep in the ground in the exact same spot, and the dirt was covered with a fresh layer of crushed rock. "Who gave you permission to come out here?" Harvey demanded. "Don't you know this is private land?"

"Yes, sir," Ralph said. "It belongs to Wildred Swenson. She told me to come out here and fix up this old bridge."

"What?" Harvey's head was swirling. "Did she tell you why?"

"Sure," Ralph said, pulling a nail from his carpenter's apron. "She wanted it nice for when a certain somebody came home."

"Did she tell you who that was?" Harvey asked.

"Nope," Ralph said. He bent down and began hammering in a nail.

"Wait!" Harvey said. He ran halfway across the bridge and looked down at the gulley below. "Did you find anything…unusual…out here?"

"Like what?" Ralph asked.

Harvey shrugged. He felt like saying, *a dead body… the Fishing Lure Killer…or Doc Daggert*. "I don't know," he said. "Anything other than dirt and rocks?"

"Nope," Ralph said. He bent down and resumed hammering.

Harvey looked back at Grant and raised an eyebrow.

Grant shrugged and indicated with a nod of his head that they should leave.

Harvey began walking towards the truck, with Grant on his heels. After a while, he said to Grant, "I don't understand why Wildred would send Ralph out here to rebuild that bridge. Why not the dock? Or the old shed near the place where the inn burned down?"

Grant said, "If what you're telling me about the skeleton you found is true, I don't understand how that guy could've dug those post holes without digging up bones."

"That's exactly what I was thinking," Harvey said. "Either Ralph's in on the cover-up, or somebody else removed the body before he got there."

"Either Ralph's Superman, or he had help," Grant said.

"What makes you say that?"

"I've built decking before, and what he did out there over the past couple of days was no small task. Surely, he had help."

As it grew dark, Harvey prayed that he and Grant would find their way back out of the woods without getting lost. The way to the bridge had been easy, with all the hammering guiding them. He thought of the Fishing Lure Killer or someone else out there watching them. He hoped they made it back to his pick-up truck and the women without incident. "Pick up the pace," he said to Grant. "It's getting dark."

14

WHILE KIT AND OONA WERE WAITING IN THE TRUCK, something hit the back of it with a thud. The sturdy vehicle shuddered. Kit gasped and whirled around in her seat. It was growing so dark, she couldn't see anything other than the silhouettes of the trees around them. She whispered to Oona, "What was that?"

"I don't know," Oona said.

Kit's heart pounded in her throat as she sat there staring rearward. Her mind flashed back to a moment years ago when someone had shouted at her, "You'd better keep on running…" Kit kept her eyes wide open and told herself to stay alert.

In the next instant, something thumped against the window beside Kit's head. She whirled back around to find a bloody hand sliding down the glass. She screamed.

Oona said, "Jesus, Mary and Joseph!"

Peering beyond the blood-streaked glass, Kit made out the face of an enormous man wearing a baseball cap. Please, God, she prayed, if you're out there, help us.

The man groaned and slumped to the ground.

In the next instant, Oona punched the unlock button.

Kit punched the lock button, and the locks went back down. "Harvey said not to unlock the doors!"

"He's bleeding," Oona said. She unlocked the truck again and shoved open the door.

Had Oona lost her mind? "Please, don't get out!" Kit begged her.

Oona slid out of the truck and hurried around it. Kit heard her asking the man, "Are you okay?"

Kit held her breath. Oona was going to get them both killed. She peered through the windshield at the northern shoreline. Where was Grant Osgood when she really needed him?

The big man followed Oona to the rear of the truck, where she was bending over. The man raised his hands over his head.

He's going to kill her! Kit thought. "Oona!" she shouted, "Look out!"

Oona straightened up and turned to the man to say, "You broke your front wheel when you ran into the truck."

The man began to wave his hands over his head and shout, "Blood is bad! Blood is bad!"

"Hush," Kit heard Oona say. "You're okay."

The enormous man shook his head vehemently and said, "Gotta show Mrs. Swenson right away. Right away." He hurried off down the road.

Oona called after him, "Benny! Come back here!"

Suddenly, Kit realized that the man was not a killer. He was her brother. She watched him lope away until he disappeared around a bend in the road. Kit called out to Oona, "Is he going to be safe out there by himself?"

Oona opened the tailgate and lifted Benny's bike into the truck bed. She came back to the open driver's side door and said, "Your brother may have special needs, but when he gets it in his mind that he has to do something, there's no stopping him."

A movement from the northern shoreline caught Kit's eye. She turned to see Harvey and Grant hurrying towards the truck. She said to Oona, "Look, they're back."

Never in her life had Kit been so happy to see Grant Osgood. When everyone was back in the truck, she asked, "What did you find?"

"Not what we expected," Grant said.

Harvey started up the engine and said to Oona, "Ralph's out there building a new bridge over Heron Creek."

"Why?"

"That's exactly what I was wondering," Harvey said. "He claims Wildred sent him out there."

AMONG THE ASHES

"Wildred could care less about that old bridge," Oona said.

"That's what I thought, too," Harvey said.

"Who's Ralph?" Kit asked.

"A guy I hired to do night maintenance at my store," Harvey said.

"You think he's part of the cover-up?" Kit asked.

"Hard to say," Harvey said, "but it does seem odd that he never noticed Peter's body while he was digging holes for the new bridge."

"At least that's what he claims," Grant said.

"Sounds fishy to me," Kit said.

"We had an unexpected visitor while you were gone," Oona said.

"Who?" asked Harvey.

"Benny," Oona said. "He ran right smack into the back of your truck with his bike."

"Poor guy," Harvey said. "Is he okay?"

"He cut his forehead," Oona said. "He went running off to tell Wildred that he was bleeding."

"What was he doing out here all by himself?" Kit asked. "A guy with Down's syndrome shouldn't be alone like that."

"Benny knows how to take care of himself better than you'd think," Oona said.

Grant said, "You don't think he's responsible for killing the dog or the guy in the boat, do you?"

Harvey and Oona both looked into the back seat of the truck and said in unison, "No."

Kit leaned her head against the glass and closed her eyes. She knew that Oona had been trying to distract her while the men were away. Oona had been wrong...nothing was going to be okay. Kit said, "Maybe we should have let sleeping dogs lie."

"Sophie can help us," Oona said.

"Are you sure we can trust her?" Kit asked.

"Absolutely," Harvey said.

Grant asked, "Are you sure we should get another person involved? It might put her in danger."

Oona said, "She's already in on it. And I think we should definitely report that fisherman's death right away. But I don't think we should tell any cops that we're snooping around the Lakeshore Inn case."

"You've forgotten one small detail," Harvey said.

"What?" Oona asked.

"Without Peter's body, we're fresh out of proof that something terrible happened at the Lakeshore Inn," Harvey said.

"You're right," Oona said. "At this point, I don't know what we're going to do. We seem to have hit a wall."

Kit sat there in the back seat, staring at the sinister-looking pine trees in the fading light. She realized all of a sudden that these were the kind of trees she had been running through as a child. She wondered if continuing to dig deeper might help her to remember why someone had been shooting at her with a gun. A quiet voice within told her that they needed to press on. But she was tired and scared.

On the other hand, Harvey was right about having very little proof that someone had intentionally burned down the Lakeshore Inn and killed her family. They had lost Peter's head, not to mention his body. Doc Daggert's x-rays were gone, and so was Doc. She could have made an excellent witness, but she couldn't remember anything. And without her old family dentist or his records, they didn't have anyone to identify her properly.

"I guess we should just go to Sophie and try to figure out what to do after that," Oona said.

Suddenly, Kit realized that she held their one last hope for finding whoever was trying to cover up the events that led up to and followed the Lakeshore Inn fire. She dug through her purse and retrieved her drawing of the A-frame house with the yellow trim. She held it out to Oona and asked, "Do you think this might help?"

Oona took the laminated piece of paper from Kit's hand and turned on the dome light. She looked at the paper and asked, "Where did you get this?"

Kit said, "I drew it."

Oona said, "Where'd you see it?"

"I don't know," Kit said. "I just remember it."

Harvey said, "There are hundreds of places like that all over Minnesota, not to mention Wisconsin and Michigan. Where would we even begin looking?"

Oona sat straighter and said in an excited tone, "I'll tell you where we start. If anybody has a clue where that place is, it's Jacqueline Corbett. Find her, and you find that house."

"Who's Jacqueline Corbett?" Kit asked.

Harvey said, "Only the best realtor in the state. If she can't point us in the direction of that house, nobody can."

"Where do we find her?" Grant asked.

Harvey looked at his watch and said, "The same place you'd find her on any Sunday evening…at the Girl Scout meeting at the Methodist Church."

On the way back to town, Kit stared at her drawing, trying to make sense of everything. Harvey and Oona believed that someone had intentionally burned down the Lakeshore Inn and killed her family. Someone had threatened Oona and stolen her purse. They had stolen Doc Daggert's files, and he had disappeared. Someone had removed Peter's body from the woods and built a bridge in the same spot. Who was the Fishing Lure Killer? And what, if anything, did he have to do with the Lakeshore Inn fire?

They pulled up in front of Fred and Sophie's house on Maple Street. Harvey went to the door and knocked. There was no answer. He returned to the truck and said, "They're not home."

"What now?" Oona asked.

Harvey said, "We'll report this to the county sheriff as just another one of the Fishing Lure Killer's victims. We can figure out after that how to get someone to help us with the Lakeshore Inn problem."

Oona said, "Let's go straight to Bemidji after we talk to Jacqueline. Surely, the sheriff will pour on the steam to find the Fishing Lure Killer. If the Lakeshore Inn murderer and the Fishing Lure Killer are the same person, we'll have answered the question about who was involved."

Kit said, "Is there any place where we could take a shower first?"

Grant piped up with, "And eat a real meal?"

Oona said, "We're sorry. We've been so focused on figuring out what happened that we didn't even think about eating or resting. You two must be exhausted."

Harvey said, "We'll stop at our house, take showers, and change."

Grant said, "The sheriff might actually take us seriously if we aren't covered in mud."

Oona said, "After we talk to Jacqueline and make the report to the sheriff, we can get something to eat."

"Sounds good to me," said Grant. "I'm starving."

"I just want to get a good night's sleep," Kit said. She yawned and looked out the window at the pine trees slipping by. If she were completely honest, a good night's sleep wasn't the only thing she wanted. She wanted the truth, and she wasn't going to be able to rest until she found it.

CHERYL DENTON

15

AFTER EVERYONE HAD GOTTEN CLEANED UP AT THE house, Harvey drove them in his pick-up down to the Methodist Church. The Girl Scout meeting was just letting out, and he spotted Jacqueline Corbett on the front steps, chatting with several women. He turned to Kit to say, "Wildred didn't want anyone in town to know you were here until tomorrow morning. She's planning a big surprise for everybody at the bakery, so how about if I just take your drawing up to Jacqueline and see what I can find out?"

"Okay," Kit said. She took the drawing of the house from her purse and handed it to Harvey.

Harvey got out and walked up the steps towards Jacqueline. Two girls looked up as he approached and quickly said their goodbyes to Jacqueline.

Jacqueline smiled at Harvey and asked, "You want to be a Brownie, too?"

Harvey smiled and said, "No, but I would like to talk to you."

Jacqueline said, "I have to make sure all of the girls have been picked up. Let me check inside real quick."

Harvey waited while Jacqueline went inside. He glanced back at his truck. Jacqueline couldn't possibly see Kit through the truck's tinted windows. Besides, it was nearly dark. When she reappeared at the doorway, he said, "Let's talk inside."

Jacqueline followed him inside the dimly lit tiled foyer and asked, "What's up?"

Harvey held out Kit's drawing and said, "Do you have any idea where we might find this house?"

Jacqueline took the laminated sheet from him and said, "Not unless I have some clue as to where it might be. There are hundreds of houses like this all over northern Minnesota."

Harvey nodded. "That's what I thought," he said.

Jacqueline peered more closely at the picture and asked, "Where'd you get this?"

Harvey hated to spoil Wildred's surprise for everyone, including Jacqueline, but he also knew that if he didn't tell her where he had gotten the drawing, she wouldn't be able to help them. He said, "Can you keep something quiet?"

Jacqueline shrugged. "Sure," she said.

Harvey told her, "Wildred got a letter this week from a man in Cincinnati. It seems he adopted Catherine Vernon after the Lakeshore Inn burned down."

"Didn't that entire family die in a fire?" Jacqueline asked.

"That's what Ron Frank always claimed, but some people never quite believed it."

"And you're one of those people?" Jacqueline asked.

"Yes," Harvey said.

Jacqueline said, "I'm assuming that you got this picture from Catherine Vernon."

"That's right," Harvey said. "It's about the only thing she can remember from her childhood here in Moose Creek."

Jacqueline said, "I find it hard to believe that the girl could've survived the fire or that she got adopted by a man in Cincinnati. How does a kid get from here to there?"

"I know it seems hard to swallow," Harvey said, "but you've got to believe me that Catherine Vernon is alive and well." He didn't add that she was sitting in the back seat of his king cab. He wanted something of Kit's appearance in town to be a surprise to Jacqueline.

"Assuming that she is alive," Jacqueline said, "then that makes it pretty easy to identify this place."

"Really?" Harvey couldn't believe it, and yet he could. Jacqueline was a whiz at Minnesota real estate, even little cottages like this in remote places.

She nodded and said, "The Vernon estate includes a piece of property on the southern shore of Upper Red Lake. There's an A-frame on it that looks exactly like this."

"The southern shore of the lake?" Harvey asked, "Isn't that part of the Red Lake Reservation?"

"No," Jacqueline said, "only the western half of the lake belongs to the reservation. It's right on the border. And, it's almost impossible to get to it unless you cross through the peninsula that runs between Lower Red Lake and Upper Red Lake."

"You've been there?" Harvey asked.

"Yes," Jacqueline said with a smile. "Didn't you know? I've been to every piece of property in northern Minnesota at least once." She winked at him.

Harvey was dumbstruck. Leave it to Jacqueline to have the answers. After the way she had managed to help him get the Community Development Block Grant money, Harvey had thought she was worthy of the award the town council had given her. But this revelation made him really respect her.

He appraised her from her silky, chestnut hair that brushed her shoulders, all the way down to her polished toenails in her summer sandals. He realized that he had been misjudging her all these years. She was far more than some sex-crazed siren who was after everybody's property. And so what if she got along with Ron Frank? She got along with everybody. No, he realized that she was, perhaps, the smartest woman he had ever met. For the first time, he was glad that she had chosen to settle in Moose Creek. He asked, "Can you take us there?"

Jacqueline handed him the laminated paper and said, "If I had a lot of time and energy, I could. I'm short on both, and that place takes some hard work to hike to. It's surrounded by marshes, and it's miles from any paved roads."

"Catherine really wants to see the place as soon as possible," Harvey said. He didn't say that it could be a matter of life and death. He didn't want to upset Jacqueline.

"Well," she said, "you do know somebody who could take her there."

"Who?" Harvey asked.

"Eric Larsen," Jacqueline said. "He's the one who took me out there the first time I saw it. We spent two days hiking there and two days coming back. I had blisters on both feet, and I swore it was the biggest waste of time investigating a piece of real estate. No one would ever buy it today, unless they wanted to live like a hermit."

"Didn't you say you have to cross part of the reservation to get to it?"

"Yes," she said.

"How'd he pull that off? It's closed to everyone but members."

Jacqueline said, "Eric's got a connection with somebody on the reservation council. Without that, you'd never get permission to cross over Native American land."

"Do you think he'd take Catherine and me out there?"

She shrugged. "Ask him."

"Isn't he fishing with the governor this weekend?"

"I think so," Jacqueline said, "but he'll probably be back in town on Tuesday morning. With Labor Day behind us, things should be a lot quieter for him then."

Harvey felt encouraged by this turn of events. He didn't say anything to Jacqueline about finding Peter Vernon's body or Doc Daggert's disappearance, but he had renewed hope that they could figure out what had happened at the Lakeshore Inn if he could just get Catherine out to the A-frame on the southern shore of Upper Red Lake. He simply said, "Thanks for your help."

"No problem," Jacqueline said. She started down the steps, and then turned back to Harvey to smile and say, "Just remember, my offer still stands to list your dad's property out at Heron Lake. I could make your family very wealthy if I could ever convince you and Doc Daggert to sell to North Shore."

Hearing her say Doc Daggert's name reminded Harvey that he was on a mission. "I'll pass," he said to Jacqueline. He glanced down at his pick-up truck where Oona waited with Kit Blume and Grant Osgood. He said goodbye and hurried down the steps, filled with hope.

As soon as Eric Larsen got back from his fishing trip with the governor, Harvey would make arrangements to have him take Catherine out to the Vernon family's cottage. In the meantime, he had to report the fisherman's death to the sheriff and take everybody out to eat. He would be glad when Tuesday morning arrived, because he felt instinctively that the lakeside A-frame held the answers they were all looking for.

When they arrived in Bemidji a short time later, Harvey said to Grant and Kit, "There's no need for the two of you to sit at the sheriff's office, waiting for us. How about if I drop you off somewhere to get a table?"

"I think we should stick together," Kit said. "That way, none of us gets killed."

"I'm sure you'll be fine," Harvey said. "We won't be gone all that long, and I'm assuming no one's going to murder you while you're sitting in the middle of a crowded restaurant."

"Okay," Grant said. Then he handed Oona his cell phone and said, "Call if you need us."

After dropping Grant and Kit off at a busy restaurant that was famous for its local fish dishes, Harvey and Oona headed for the sheriff's office. "I'm not exactly sure where it is," he said.

Oona pulled out Grant's phone and began punching buttons. After a moment, she said, "It's on Minnesota Avenue. Turn right up here."

Harvey said, "That thing gives directions, too?"

Oona said, "Yeah, I told you...you can use cell phones to tap into the GPS mapping system."

"Hm..."

When they got to the sheriff's office, they walked into the lobby and found it empty. Harvey looked around. "Now what?" he asked.

Oona walked over to a phone on the wall and punched a few buttons. Within minutes, she was talking to someone. She finished, hung up the phone, and said, "They're sending a deputy over to take our report."

A few minutes later, a deputy walked in the front door.

"You're here to make a report?" the deputy asked.

"Yes," Harvey said.

The deputy said, "Come with me."

Harvey and Oona followed the deputy down a series of hallways. He finally directed them to a room on the left and said, "Have a seat. I'll be right back."

They went into the room and sat down. As the deputy's footsteps faded away, Harvey leaned over and whispered to Oona, "Remember, we're only here to tell him about the dead fisherman so that they'll look for the Fishing Lure Killer. Don't mention the Lakeshore Inn or Kit or anything else."

Oona nodded and said, "We find the Fishing Lure Killer, and we might figure out who's behind the Lakeshore Inn fire."

Harvey nodded. He prayed that their plan would work.

When the deputy came back, he had a couple of clipboards with forms on them. He sat down and asked, "What type of report are you making tonight?"

Harvey said, "A murder."

The deputy looked surprised, and he asked Harvey for his name and personal information. He wrote down everything carefully on his form. "Do you have a driver's license, Mr. Trent?"

Harvey slid his license across the table, and the deputy continued writing.

The deputy said, "Mr. Trent, I want you to come with me. Miss Kelly, I want you to stay here." He handed Oona several sheets of paper and said, "Write down everything you can remember about what happened." He stood up and said, "If you need to use the restroom or get a snack, the bathrooms and the break room are right down the hall here."

Harvey followed the deputy down a maze of corridors to a small room. They sat across from each other at a table, and the deputy said, "Tell me what happened."

Harvey said, "My sister and I went to see our friend, Doc Daggert. He wasn't at home, but we noticed his boat in the middle of the lake."

"What lake?" the deputy asked.

"Heron Lake," Harvey said.

"Go on," the deputy said.

"I shouted at him from the shore, but he didn't answer. So Oona and I took our boat out to Doc Daggert's."

The deputy wrote on the form and said, "What did you find?"

Harvey said, "It wasn't Doc in the boat. Some fisherman had been shot in the chest, and he had a Minnesota Minnie lure in his lower lip."

The deputy glanced up and asked, "You've heard about the Fishing Lure Killer?"

"Yes," Harvey said. "It looks like he did this."

The deputy continued writing and asked, "What else can you tell me?"

"The Minnesota Minnie was hot pink."

The deputy wrote some more and then said, "So, you took your boat out onto the lake, found this dead guy, and then came straight here?"

Harvey hesitated.

The deputy stared hard at him and asked, "You didn't go anywhere else?"

Harvey said, "We went back to the house to clean up. We were all covered in mud."

"How'd you get all covered in mud?"

Before he realized it, he was saying, "We had a car accident in Cincinnati yesterday afternoon, and we got all muddy trying to climb back up the banks of the Ohio River. We hadn't had a chance to clean up yet."

The deputy looked closely at Harvey and said, "Let me get this straight. You had what sounds like a pretty serious car accident yesterday that left you muddy, you drove all the way from Cincinnati to northern Minnesota, found a dead body in a boat, and *then* you went home to get cleaned up?"

Harvey could see that it did look suspicious that they had not slept or changed clothes following their accident. And it looked even more suspicious that they went home to shower after finding a dead body. He merely said, "Yes."

The deputy asked, "Why didn't you call in to make a report, instead of driving all the way here?"

Harvey blinked. That would have made a lot of sense. What he didn't dare say was that they were afraid a phone call might tip off Ron Frank, who seemed to be working fast and furious to cover up something that went very wrong the night of the Lakeshore Inn fire. "I don't know," he said. "I guess I figured we'd have to make a formal report and sign papers."

The deputy wrote some more on his form and then took Harvey back to the room where Oona was waiting. He handed Harvey some forms and said, "I want you to write down exactly what you just told me on this paper. Sign and date the bottom." To Oona, he said, "Come with me."

Harvey watched Oona following the deputy out of the room. He hoped Oona would tell the deputy the same story he had. Otherwise, they could be in a lot of hot water. He could tell that the deputy was wondering if he and Oona had killed the fisherman. Harvey bent over the form and began writing. Shortly after he finished, Oona returned with the deputy.

The deputy said, "I'll be turning this in tomorrow morning to our investigative team. I doubt that they'll be doing much with it."

"Why not?" Harvey asked.

"Because with a case this complicated, we'll probably be calling in the BCA."

"The BCA?" Harvey asked.

The deputy said, "The Bureau of Criminal Apprehension. They're kind of like the state of Minnesota's version of the FBI."

Harvey had no idea that such a bureau even existed. He asked, "The state troopers don't do that sort of thing for you?"

The deputy said, "No. They're only equipped to patrol traffic."

In that instant, Harvey was certain that the state trooper in St. Paul was involved with Ron Frank. He had told them that the state troopers were up the chain of command from the local police. He worried that something might happen to Doc if the cops didn't find the Fishing Lure Killer. He asked, "Is somebody going to go out there soon to bring in the body?"

"The county coroner will go out there tonight."

Harvey said, "You're going to need a boat."

"The sheriff's department has several," the deputy said. "Can our team call you if they have any questions?"

"Sure," Harvey said. He gave his phone number.

The deputy asked, "Is that your home or cell number?"

"Home," Harvey said.

The deputy asked, "You don't have a cell?"

"No," Harvey said, with a glance at Oona. "Not everyone does, you know."

When they were finished, Harvey and Oona got into the truck and pulled away from the station. "How'd it go in there?" Harvey asked.

"Fine," Oona said.

"Did you tell him about going home to take a shower?" Harvey asked.

"No," Oona said, "I figured that would tip him off about our trip to Cincinnati for Kit and everything else about the Lakeshore Inn fire."

"Crap," Harvey muttered.

"What's the matter?" Oona asked.

"I slipped up and told him we were all muddy and stopped by the house for a shower."

Oona said, "Well, don't be surprised if the two of us get questioned as suspects in the case."

"I'm sorry," Harvey said. "I guess we should've just told him everything."

"I saw what happened when you told that state trooper everything in St. Paul," Oona said. "I think we did the right thing. We'll just have to hope that we come up with some answers about the Lakeshore Inn before they decide to arrest us for a string of murders we didn't commit."

Harvey envisioned what it would be like to have the cops arrest him. What if Ron Frank came to the door to put him in handcuffs? And what if he couldn't get a decent attorney, and he and Oona spent the rest of their lives in prison? He shook off the thought, and they went into the restaurant where they had left Grant and Kit.

"How did it go?" Grant asked him as they sat down.

Harvey shrugged and said, "I think I blew it."

"Why?" Kit asked.

"I told them that we stopped to take a shower on the way to the police station, because we were all muddy from the accident."

"So, you told the truth," Grant said.

"Yeah," Harvey said, "but you should've seen the look on the cop's face. I think he would've locked me up on the spot if he'd had the chance."

"Especially since I told the cops we didn't stop anywhere," Oona said.

"You lied?" Kit asked.

Oona looked over at her and said, "That was the agreement...we wouldn't say anything about the Lakeshore Inn so that the sheriff would start searching for the Fishing Lure Killer right away."

"Well, I don't think you should've lied," Kit said. "You both look guilty now."

Harvey's palms began to sweat as he considered how dangerous all of this had become. "We need help from someone we can trust," he said.

"It doesn't sound like you can trust your police chief," said Grant, "and it's clear that the state police were covering up the evidence you gave them."

Harvey was beginning to feel panicky. He said, "We're up to our hind ends in alligators, and all I wanted to do was pull the drain on the swamp."

Oona said calmly, "So, quit focusing on the alligators and get your sights back on the drain."

At that point, Harvey realized he was worrying again about something that hadn't even happened, and he had to stop. It wouldn't help him figure out why somebody was trying to stop them from uncovering the truth about the Lakeshore Inn fire. He said, "You're right. I've got to stop worrying about what could go wrong and focus on what is."

Oona said, "The truth is, someone out there killed Peter Vernon and tried to kill Catherine. They probably killed Paul and Mimi and set the inn on fire. They know that we're uncovering the evidence of those crimes, and it looks like they'll do whatever it takes to stop us."

"Oh," said Kit, "I wish I could remember what happened, but it's all so unclear."

Harvey leaned forward and said, "Jacqueline Corbett knows exactly where that A-frame with the yellow trim is."

"Really?" Kit asked. She sat up straighter. "Where?"

"It's on the south shore of Upper Red Lake."

"That's part of the Ojibwa reservation," Oona said.

"No," Harvey said, "it's on the edge of it. You just can't get to it without passing over land owned by the Ojibwa."

"Well, that's a dead end," said Oona. "No one's allowed there other than the people from the tribe."

"And their guests," Harvey pointed out.

"Like they're going to invite us for dinner," Oona said.

"No, but apparently, they don't mind having Eric Larsen over for tea," Harvey said.

"How do you know that?" Oona asked.

"Jacqueline told me that Eric has a friend on the tribal council who lets him through there. He's taken Jacqueline out there before."

Grant asked, "Would he be willing to take Kit out there?"

"I don't see why not," Harvey said. "When he gets back to town tomorrow night from taking the governor fishing, we'll ask him."

Kit said, "I'm not going anywhere by myself with some strange guy I've never met."

Harvey said, "Grant and I can go with you."

"What about me?" Oona asked.

"It's really rough terrain," Harvey said. "Jacqueline told me the place is surrounded by marshes."

"So," Oona said, "I'm not afraid of getting my feet wet."

Harvey said, "I think one of us should go to the Bureau of Criminal Apprehension and get them to start working on this case. You'd be a lot better than me at helping them put together all the facts. You're more detail-oriented."

"What's the Bureau of Criminal Apprehension?" Kit asked.

Harvey said, "The guy at the sheriff's office told us that every state has its own FBI-type bureau. The BCA investigates complicated cases like the Fishing Lure Killer."

"You mean the state cops don't have anything to do with cases like this?" Kit asked.

"Nope," Harvey said. "All they pretty much do is hand out traffic tickets."

Kit said, "That guy in St. Paul lied to you!"

"Yep," Harvey said. "And he probably destroyed our evidence."

"What about sticking together so that nobody gets killed?" Kit asked. "I don't think Oona should be left to do things by herself."

Harvey scratched his chin. She did have a good point. He looked across at Grant and asked, "Do you have much experience with hunting or hiking?"

Grant smiled and said, "I've hauled my kayak over plenty of wet ground, and I've camped out more than I've slept at home. I'm your man."

"Well," Harvey said, "It's settled then. First thing Tuesday morning, Grant and Kit will talk to Eric about going to the house on Upper Red Lake, and Oona and I will work on the BCA to get the case re-opened."

"Why wait until Tuesday?" Kit asked.

Harvey smiled at her and said, "Because, I promised Wildred I'd bring you to the bakery at seven tomorrow morning. She has a surprise for you, and if I know Wildred, it'll be something spectacular."

When Harvey's wind-up alarm went off on his night stand on Monday morning, he reached over to turn it off. He had been awake for hours, too nervous to sleep. Today, Catherine Vernon's life would pick up where it had left off. Never before had he felt such apprehension about the future. As he took a quick shower, he thought about all of the possibilities ahead of them. As soon as they introduced Kit, Ron Frank would realize that they were digging up evidence from the Lakeshore Inn fire. Harvey worried about how Ron might respond.

Outside, it had grown unusually cold for early September, and Harvey noticed that there was a thin layer of ice on the top of Jet's water bowl. He took it to the outdoor spigot, where he rinsed it out and filled it with fresh water. And then he remembered that Jet would never again wag his tail and woof at him when Harvey set out fresh food and water.

When he went back inside, Oona was standing at the kitchen counter in her over-sized night shirt that read, *I Don't Do Mornings*. She turned to him and asked, "You want me to make Kit and Grant something to eat?"

"No," he said, "I'm sure Wildred's got a feast laid out over at the bakery."

"You're probably right," she said.

"Are they awake yet?" he asked.

"Grant's in the shower, and Kit's still asleep," she said.

"Better wake her up," Harvey said. "We're supposed to be over there by seven."

"I'm going to get dressed first," Oona said. She hurried up the stairs.

There was a knock at the front door, and Harvey opened it to find Jacqueline Corbett standing there. Her tight black knit jogging pants clung to her hips and made Harvey want to run in the opposite direction.

She said, "I came over to find out if you have any idea what's going on at Swenson's this morning. The place is packed, and I couldn't even sit down to get a cup of coffee."

Harvey pulled on his jacket and zipped it. "That's because Wildred has a surprise planned for everybody in town."

Jacqueline said, "So, you know what's going on?"

Harvey knew that Jacqueline would be upset with him if she found out that he was in the loop, and she wasn't. Nevertheless, he had made a promise to Wildred, and he intended to keep it. He said, "You'll have to wait and see." He looked at his watch and added, "Surely, you can wait another thirty minutes."

"Where's Oona?"

"Getting dressed," Harvey said. He picked up his truck keys from a hook beside the door and said, "Why don't you run back over to Swenson's and get us a table?"

Jacqueline put her hands on her hips and said, "Didn't you hear me? There aren't any left."

"Surely you can find someone to let you pull up a chair or two," he said.

"Obviously, you're deaf this morning," she said. "I told you, it's standing room only."

She certainly was testy. "What side of the bed did you wake up on this morning?" he asked.

She grumbled something incoherent, and Harvey tried to think of a snappy comeback. He squeezed his keys so tightly that they bit into his palm, and he asked, "Can't you make yourself a cup of coffee at your place?"

Jacqueline rolled her eyes and stomped into the kitchen to pick up the coffee pot. She slammed the glass pot down so hard on the counter that Harvey was afraid she might smash it.

Harvey stared at Jacqueline and wondered why they never seemed to be able to hit it off. It was as if there was a wall between them that deflected their conversations. Without another word, he went outside and bent over to pick up the newspaper from the walk. When he straightened up,

Fred Ianelli appeared on the lawn. Harvey said to him with a grin, "I can't believe Wildred let you out of the bakery this morning. I hear it's jammed."

"It is," Fred said. "I came over here to tell Wildred she's got to come and help us. Is she inside?"

"Wildred?" Harvey said, feeling confused. "She's not here."

Fred frowned and said, "She didn't come in this morning. I figured she was over here visiting with Catherine."

Harvey said, "I haven't seen Wildred since Friday."

"You think she's at home?"

"Maybe Benny's giving her some trouble," Harvey said, remembering that Oona had told him about Benny running into the back of the truck and cutting himself.

Fred ran his hand through his hair and said, "I don't know how we're going to keep up. Sophie's about ready to drop. We've never had so many people in the bakery at one time."

"As soon as we get there," Harvey said, "Oona and I will help you."

Fred heaved a sigh of relief and grinned at Harvey. "Thanks. I owe you one."

Harvey said. "Don't worry about a thing. I'm sure Wildred will be there by seven."

He sat in the living room and watched Jacqueline making coffee until the sound of running water upstairs reminded him that he had house guests. He went up the steps and tapped lightly on the guest room door. Kit appeared with a white sweater on her arm. She was wearing a sky blue and white dress that must have belonged to his mother. It was a little baggy on her, but she looked far better than she had for the past two days. Harvey asked, "You ready to go?"

She nodded, and Harvey went to give Grant some clean clothes. A few minutes later, the three of them went downstairs together. When they got to the bottom of the steps, he saw Jacqueline standing near the kitchen sink, pouring coffee into Styrofoam cups. He said, "Jacqueline, there are a couple of people I'd like you to meet."

He couldn't give away Wildred's secret, so he introduced his house guests as Grant Osgood and Kit Blume.

Jacqueline said, "We might want to take our own coffee to the bakery. It's a zoo over there." She handed a cup to each of them.

Harvey noted that Jacqueline seemed a little less aggravated. It was amazing what a cup of coffee could do. On the way over to Swenson's, he asked Kit, "Does anything look familiar to you?"

Kit looked around and said, "Not really."

Harvey smiled at her and said, "Maybe something will jog your memory today."

Kit shrugged and said, "I have a feeling that going to the house at that lake will give me some answers."

"Me, too," said Harvey.

When they arrived at Swenson's Bakery and Deli a short time later, Harvey was shocked. There were so many people inside, there wasn't a seat remaining. He said to Jacqueline, "You were right."

She gave him a smug look and waited while he held the door for her.

Harvey turned to Kit, who was hanging back on the sidewalk. He asked, "Are you ready for this?"

"As ready as I'll ever be," Kit said.

Grant put his arm around her shoulder and said to Kit, "I'll be right beside you the whole time."

Sophie appeared at the front door with a smile. She beckoned them inside and said, "Thank God, you're here."

Kit looked at Harvey, and he smiled at her. "Go ahead."

Kit stepped through the front door, and Sophie led them to a large, round table in the center of the room. "For our guest of honor," she said to Kit.

"Where's Mike this morning?" Harvey asked Sophie.

"Making Kit a surprise," Sophie said. "He'll be here soon."

Jacqueline peered more closely at Kit and asked Harvey, "Guest of honor?"

Harvey motioned for Jacqueline to sit down next to Oona. "You'll see in a minute."

Fred appeared at Harvey's elbow and said, "Wildred's still not here. You think we should wait?"

A hush fell over the room, and Harvey said in an undertone to Fred, "It's obvious to everyone that somebody at this table is the guest of honor. I don't think we should keep them waiting any longer. They may riot."

Fred grinned at him and straightened up to say loudly to the crowd, "Thank you all for coming in to help us celebrate one of the biggest events this town has ever witnessed."

Harvey looked around the room. Everyone from the town council was there, all of the bakery regulars, and a few people Harvey had never even seen. They all stared at Kit and Grant with open curiosity.

Fred turned to Harvey and said, "Why don't you introduce them?"

Harvey really wished that Wildred were there. She should be saying a few words, not him. But the people sat staring at him, and he knew it was time. He slid out of his chair and stood up to say, "Twenty-four years ago, Moose Creek experienced a great loss. The Lakeshore Inn burned to the ground, and the newspapers announced that everyone in the family had died."

Ron Frank glared at Harvey.

Now, Harvey was certain that their chief knew he was up to something. But it was too late now to go back to the way things had been. In a few seconds, everyone in Moose Creek would realize that Ron Frank was a failure as the chief of police. Harvey continued, "I wish Wildred were here to tell you about some recent turn of events, but suffice it to say, that we got news last week that at least one of the Vernon children survived that fire."

A gasp went up from the crowd, and a murmur of voices rippled through the room.

Harvey held up his hand for them to be quiet, and then he said, "It is my great pleasure to introduce to you a young woman who has traveled all the way from Cincinnati, Ohio, where she is known as Kit Blume. For those of you who were around here twenty-four years ago, you already know her as Catherine Vernon."

"Oh!" the crowd breathed.

Harvey turned to Kit and held out his hand. She took it and stood up. Harvey could feel her shaking. He leaned over and whispered, "Just say a few words."

Kit nodded and cleared her throat. In a small voice, she said, "I want to thank everyone who helped to make this possible, especially Wildred Swenson. Without her determination to find me, I doubt that I would be here today."

At that moment, Ron Frank stood up and said, "Don't you all think it's strange that Wildred's not here today?"

A murmur went up from the crowd.

Ron shouted, "I, for one, think this woman is a fraud."

Everyone gasped.

Kit gripped Harvey's hand tightly.

Harvey said, "Ron, you're out of line."

"No," Ron said, "I think you are. I was at that fire, and I'm telling you, nobody survived."

Harvey opened his mouth to tell Ron what he thought of him, but before he could, Oona stood up and said, "It looks as if Wildred has left something special here for Catherine this morning. Why don't you all have a seat and let her open it?"

Harvey noticed then a large cake box on the table with Catherine's name printed neatly on the top. "Go ahead and open it," he said.

Kit began peeling away the tape that held the box shut. The crowd quieted, and chairs scraped as people sat back down.

Sophie appeared beside the table, and Harvey asked her, "Were you and Fred in on this?"

Sophie shook her head. "No, but it's just like Wildred to make up something special for Catherine's first day back home."

Harvey asked, "Any idea where Wildred could be?"

Sophie said, "I can't imagine why she's not here."

"Maybe Benny gave her a little trouble this morning," Harvey said.

"Maybe," Sophie said, "He was pretty upset about his scrapes yesterday."

Kit slowly lifted the lid. When he saw what was inside, Harvey gasped. Wildred's head lay inside the box, with her eyes bulging and looking straight up at them. Blood dribbled from a hole in her forehead, and a moss green fishing lure dangled from her lower lip.

Kit screamed and sagged against Harvey.

"Judas Priest!" Harvey groaned. He turned Kit away from the dreadful sight and shoved the lid down on the box. Who would do such a thing?

From the other side of the room, a voice came to Harvey, sounding hollow and far-away. "What's wrong?"

Harvey gripped Kit tightly around the waist. He could feel her trembling, and her heart thudded against his chest. He lowered her quickly into her seat and sat down in the chair beside her. He asked, "Are you okay?"

Kit looked over at him with eyes wide with fear and shook her head. She covered her face, and great sobs racked her body. She began gasping for air.

Grant moved swiftly to Kit's side and said, "Take a deep breath."

People began shouting and jostling into one another. A crowd pressed in around the table. From the other side of the cluster of people, Ron shouted, "What's going on here?"

Kit leaned against Grant. The gasping grew worse.

Ron pushed his way through the crowd, and Harvey tried to help Grant hold Kit upright. Harvey heard Grant saying, "Try to slow down your breathing."

Ron appeared beside Harvey and repeated loudly, "What's going on?"

Harvey looked up at Ron, took a deep breath, and said, "Wildred Swenson…is…is *dead*."

Sophie said, "Oh, my God." She collapsed on the floor beside the table.

Harvey looked across the table at Oona. Her face lost all color, and he worried that she might faint, too. Thank God she hadn't seen what was in the cake box.

Ron asked, "How do you know that?"

Harvey said, "Her head's been cut off."

Oona said, "Jesus, Mary, and Joseph!"

Ron asked, "Where is it?"

Harvey said, "In the cake box."

Ron squinted at Harvey and asked, "Did you say in the cake box?"

Harvey nodded.

Kit shouted something incoherent. She hugged herself tightly and began rocking back and forth. When her hands began to shake and the color drained from her face, Harvey could see that something was clearly wrong with her.

Grant said to Ron, "I think you'd better get her an ambulance."

Ron used his radio to call the dispatcher at City Hall. He said, "Get an ambulance over to Swenson's. Then call the coroner."

Kit suddenly lurched sideways and nearly fell off her chair. Harvey reached out to steady her, and she vomited on Ron's shoes.

Ron leaped back from the table and swore. Then he shouted into his radio, "Get the paramedics over here *now!*"

Grant gently eased Kit down onto the floor. He took off his jacket and laid it over her. The crowd pressed in more tightly, and the din in the bakery became deafening.

Just then, Benny burst through the front door and shouted, "You hungry?" He stopped abruptly when he saw Kit and Sophie lying on the floor. "They sleeping?" he asked.

Harvey stood up and steered Benny towards the back of the bakery. "They're not feeling well," he said. "Why don't you go wait in the back?"

Benny yanked his arm away from Harvey and roared, "Benny hungry! Raspberry doughnut! Now!"

"There isn't going to be any raspberry doughnut right now," Harvey said.

"Benny hungry!" the behemoth shouted more loudly.

Oona stood up and took Benny by the arm. "Come on, Benny," she said in a soothing voice. "I'll get you something to eat."

Benny hesitated. He looked at Oona, and then he spotted the cake box on the table. In the next instant, he reached across and yanked open the lid. When he saw Wildred's head, he reeled back and roared, "Blood is bad! Blood is bad!"

Oona said, "Shush now, Benny. Come in the back with me."

"Gotta tell Mrs. Swenson right away," Benny said. And then he paused to peer at Wildred's head in the cake box. He leaned in close to it and shouted, "Mrs. Swenson, blood is bad!"

Oona said, "Okay, Benny. You told her. Now come with me."

Benny allowed Oona to lead him through the noisy throng and into the back room.

Fred helped Sophie up off the floor and led her to a nearby chair. Then, he stood on top of one of the tables and gave a piercing whistle. The crowd quieted, and he said, "Please, everyone, go home."

Harvey pushed the lid back down on the box, and the crowd slowly filed out the front door. When everyone but the Ianelli's, Ron Frank, Benny, and the four of them had left, Sophie said to Fred, "I need to go home and check on Mike."

Harvey watched Fred leading his wife towards the back of the bakery. Ron called out to them, "You two stay put at your place. I'll need to come and ask you some questions later."

Harvey glared at Ron and said, "This isn't Hawaii Five-O. Leave them alone."

Ron went from one window to the next closing the blinds, and one of Ron's police officers arrived at the back entrance a few minutes later. "What's the matter?" he asked. "There's a huge crowd out front."

Harvey said, "Take a look in the cake box on the table."

When the officer saw Wildred's severed head, he stepped backward and said, "I've seen some gruesome things in my day, but this takes the cake."

"No pun intended," Harvey said. He walked over to stand beside the officer. He looked down at Wildred's head and wondered again who could do such a thing.

The officer bent down to look more closely at Wildred's head. "I'd say this happened last night. Looks like she's been here a while."

Harvey squinted at the lure dangling from Wildred's blue lip. He asked the cop, "Does that look like dust on that lure?"

The officer leaned over and looked carefully. "Yeah."

How would a lure get so dusty? Harvey wondered. He stood there thinking about where people might put lures…inside tackle boxes, attached to a fishing hat, or maybe…on a fishing trophy. He looked up then at Dirk Swenson's fishing trophies that lined the wall behind the counter. The third one from the right was missing the green lure that had always hung there.

Ron shoved Harvey aside and looked down at Wildred's head. "What are you two talking about?" he asked.

Harvey said, "I think that lure came from Dirk's old fishing trophy." He pointed to the plaque on the wall and said, "That one there."

Ron Frank walked around the counter to lift the trophy off the wall.

"You think you should be touching things like that?" Harvey asked.

Ron glared at him and asked, "Who's the law around here, you or me?"

"You are," Harvey said, "but I've watched enough detective shows on TV to know that you might be messing with fingerprints or something."

Ron barked at his assistant, "As soon as the ambulance gets here, I want this place cleared."

Harvey went back to sit with Kit and Grant. While they waited for the ambulance, he wondered again who could have done such an awful thing. If Wildred had fallen victim to the killer, could one of the four of them be next? Oona came to stand beside him.

"We've got to get the BCA involved *now*," whispered Oona.

Harvey nodded. "As soon as we get Kit taken care of, we'll get the ball rolling."

He stood up and went over to where Ron and another cop were discussing the matter of the fishing lure in Wildred's lip. He asked, "How long's it going to take for that ambulance to get here?"

From outside, the wail of a siren announced the arrival of the ambulance. Ron said, "They're here now."

"Thank God," Harvey said. He hurried back to Grant and said, "Help is on the way." He knelt down and took Kit's hand. Her eyes fluttered open, and he said, "I want you to promise me something."

Kit focused on him with difficulty and asked, "What?"

"No matter what," Harvey said, "I want you to promise me that you'll stay with Grant until Oona and I come back from reporting all of this to the BCA."

Kit closed her eyes and sighed.

Harvey gave her shoulder a little shake and said, "Promise me."

Kit opened her eyes and said, "I promise."

Just then, the paramedics burst into the room and pushed Harvey aside. They bent over Kit, checking her pulse and respiration. One of them said, "BP's way too low. We'd better transport her right away."

Harvey followed the paramedics outside, and one of them stopped Grant. He said, "You'll probably want to use your own car to get to the hospital. That way, you can take her home later."

The second paramedic said, "And you might as well take your time. With all of the tourists in town, the hospital is like Grand Central Station. It's going to be a while before she gets seen."

Harvey stepped forward and said to Grant, "You go with her now, and I'll pick you up later. Remember, you two stay together."

Grant nodded and stood there for a moment on the sidewalk, waiting for the paramedics to lift the gurney into it. As soon as Grant climbed inside and the ambulance door closed, Harvey tapped on the window and signaled to Grant. He mouthed the words, "Stay together."

Grant nodded again, and the ambulance pulled away.

Harvey pushed his way back through the crowd and knocked on the locked front door of the bakery. Ron Frank opened the door and said, "The show's over. Go on home."

"Where's Oona?" Harvey asked.

"I told her to get Benny out of here," he said.

Harvey nodded and hurried the two blocks back to his house. He found Oona in the living room with Benny, who was sitting on the sofa and rocking from side to side.

"How's he doing?" he asked.

"Not very well," Oona said. "I gave him some Benadryl. It usually knocks him out."

The phone rang, and Harvey walked into the kitchen to answer it.

"Harvey," came a voice on the other end. "I can answer some questions for you about the Lakeshore Inn."

"Who is this?" Harvey demanded.

"It's Jacqueline."

Harvey wondered what Jacqueline could possibly know about the place. It had burned down ten years before she had moved to Moose Creek.

Jacqueline asked, "Can you meet me in thirty minutes out at the old Lakeshore Inn dock…you know, the one on the north side of the lake?"

Harvey knew exactly where she was talking about. Benny bellowed something, and he turned to see him take a swing at Oona's head. She ducked and stepped out of his reach. "I don't think this is a very good time," he said. What he didn't add was that the four of them had agreed to stick together for safety's sake.

Jacqueline said, "I can't believe what happened to Wildred."

Neither could Harvey.

Jacqueline said, "The sheriff just showed up at Swenson's. I heard him saying that it looks like the Fishing Lure Killer did her in."

She wasn't telling Harvey anything he didn't already know. "Can't you tell me whatever it is you know about the Lakeshore Inn over the phone?" he asked.

"No," she said. "I have to show you something."

From the living room, Harvey heard shattering glass. "It'll have to wait, Jacqueline," he said. "I'll call you later."

He hung up the phone and rushed back to the living room. Oona was picking up the pieces of a vase that Benny must have slung against the wall. He hurried over to help her and asked, "You want me to call the doctor to give him something stronger?"

"No," Oona said. "Just give it a few more minutes. Benadryl usually works like a charm."

Harvey carried some of the larger pieces of the vase outdoors to the trash. By the time he came back inside, Benny was out cold on the sofa.

Oona was sweeping up the last of the glass. She asked, "Who was that on the phone?"

"Jacqueline Corbett."

"What did she want?"

"She said she could answer some questions about the Lakeshore Inn fire," Harvey said. He followed Oona into the kitchen.

Oona dumped the contents of the dust pan into the trash can under the sink and asked, "How would she know anything about it? She moved here ten years after the fact."

"That's what I thought," Harvey said, "but she insisted on showing me something out there."

"When?"

"Right now," Harvey said.

"What did you tell her?" Oona asked.

"I told her this wasn't a good time," Harvey said.

"You shouldn't have told her that," Oona said. "We need all the help we can get."

"I didn't want to leave you alone, with Benny trashing the place." He noticed then that she had a bright red handprint on her upper arm. "I saw him take a swing at you."

"He does that all the time," Oona said.

"You're lucky you're not the one who's out cold on the sofa," Harvey said.

"I can handle Benny," Oona said. She drew herself up to her full height and folded her arms across her chest.

Harvey smiled and walked across the kitchen to give her a hug. "I know you can," he said. "I think I'd rather tangle with Benny than you any day." He chuckled, and Oona ducked out from under his arm.

She said, "I think you should meet Jacqueline now, before things get more complicated with the sheriff here in town."

Harvey wondered how long it would take for the sheriff to incorrectly conclude that he and Oona had killed the fisherman in Doc's boat. And then it hit him that the sheriff might also think they had killed Wildred. He said, "Are you thinking that we could be hauled in for questioning about Wildred?"

"Absolutely," Oona said. "I expect the sheriff will be over here shortly."

"Then I guess I'd better get going," Harvey said. "Jacqueline may be our only hope for staying out of jail."

"I agree," she said.

Harvey reached for the phone and then stopped. "But what about our plan to stick together?" he asked. "I don't want anything to happen to you while I'm gone."

"I can take care of myself," Oona said.

Harvey glanced back into the living room at Benny. Oona certainly did have skills when it came to defending herself. At last, he said, "Okay, I'll go." He dialed Jacqueline's number. While the phone was ringing, he said to Oona, "But if I'm not back in an hour, you come out to—"

Jacqueline answered, and Harvey said into the phone, "I guess I can meet you out at the old dock after all."

"Good," she said.

"Give me fifteen minutes," he said.

"Okay," she said, "and Harvey?"

"What?"

"Don't tell anyone else where you're going. We wouldn't want the wrong person following you."

"Got it," he said. He hung up the phone and turned to Oona. "I'm meeting her at the old Lakeshore Inn dock in fifteen minutes. If I'm not back in an hour, go straight to the BCA office in Bemidji."

"They wouldn't be open today," Oona said. "It's a holiday, remember?"

"Oh, yeah," Harvey said. "I'm beginning to hate holidays." Then he had an idea. He hurried up the steps to his father's bedroom and felt along the top closet shelf. His fingers curled around something cold, and he pulled out his father's old Walther pistol. He found some bullets in a box on the shelf and loaded the gun. Back downstairs, he laid the handgun on the counter. "If I'm not back here in an hour, bring this out to the lake with you."

Oona opened the kitchen drawer and shoved the gun into it. "I wouldn't want Benny getting a hold of that," she said.

Harvey looked at the enormous man splayed out on their sofa. He asked, "How long do you think he'll sleep?"

"At least a couple of hours," Oona said.

"Are you sure he's going to be okay?"

"Benny is the last person I'm worried about right now," Oona said. "Be careful out there."

Harvey nodded and hurried out the front door.

16

WITHIN TEN MINUTES, HARVEY WAS AT HIS FATHER'S BOAT house on the east side of the lake. It would be a lot quicker and easier for him to take the boat across the water than it would be to drive the curving road around the perimeter of the lake. He untied the Chris Craft and shoved away from the dock. He sat down behind the steering wheel and turned the key. The engine gurgled to life, and he felt a sense of satisfaction. Replacing the old engine had been a good decision. The new one never failed him, and it made the old boat fly.

Harvey pushed the throttle forward and made his way quickly across the mirror-smooth water towards the north shore. It was so cold that a light fog was rising up from the surface of the lake.

When Harvey got close to the ramshackle dock near the old Lakeshore Inn, he looked for Jacqueline. No one was in sight. Harvey idled slowly towards the dock, and he reached down to pick up a paddle from the forward compartment so that he could hold the boat away from the splintered old wood on the edge of the dock. He felt the boat shift as someone stepped onto the edge of it. He looked up in the rearview mirror on the dash to catch a glimpse of someone standing behind him.

Startled, he whirled around. When he saw that it was Jacqueline, he said, "Judas Priest! You startled me."

In reply, Jacqueline pulled a gun out of her jacket pocket and pointed it at him.

What was happening? Adrenaline rushed through Harvey's veins. He lunged to knock the gun out of Jacqueline's hand. Before he connected with it, though, the gun went off. Harvey felt something sting him in the shoulder, and he looked down to see blood oozing through his jacket sleeve. He looked back up at Jacqueline and asked, "What the hell did you do that for?"

Jacqueline pointed the gun at his head, and said, "Because you never mind your own business."

The boat bumped into the dock, and Harvey lost his balance. He fell back into the open bow. He had to do something, but his mind went blank.

Jacqueline edged closer and aimed the gun at Harvey's forehead.

Harvey tried to think quickly. "You don't want to do this, Jacqueline," he said in a rush.

"Quit calling me Jacqueline. The name's Annabelle." She squeezed the trigger.

Harvey blinked. Surely, he must have misunderstood. His mind was playing tricks on him.

The gun clicked, but it didn't fire.

Harvey scrambled from the floor and then pressed his hand to his sleeve. Blood oozed through his fingers.

Jacqueline advanced towards him.

He lunged forward to wrench the gun from Jacqueline's hand, but a sharp pain shot through his arm. He slumped over into the bow seat and slid downward in it until his head came to rest on the back of it.

Jacqueline aimed to fire at him a third time.

Harvey looked into Jacqueline's eyes. They were filled with hatred, and his blood ran cold. He had to try to distract her so that he could get away. "Did you say you're Annabelle?" he asked.

"Yes," she said with a lift of her chin. "You never would have guessed that in a million years, would you?"

"Annabelle loved me," Harvey said, stalling for time. "She would never do something like this...besides, you don't look anything like her."

Jacqueline smiled and said, "Amazing what plastic surgeons can do, isn't it?"

He held his breath.

She pulled the trigger.

The gun jammed again.

In the next instant, Jacqueline reached into her pocket and pulled out something bright yellow. She leaned over Harvey and whispered in his ear, "You never knew when to shut up, H.T." She shoved something sharp into his lower lip.

The pain searing his lip made Harvey yelp. And in the next instant, he realized that Jacqueline Corbett was, indeed, Annabelle Vernon. No one else but his high school sweetheart ever called him H.T.

Jacqueline turned the boat around, stepped onto the dock, and thrust the throttle forward. The boat lurched forward, and Harvey fell onto the floor. His mind was reeling. Jacqueline Corbett was Annabelle Vernon? Why was she going around killing people? She was the Fishing Lure Killer? The pain in his arm and his lip were making him feel faint. He had to get help. He grabbed a life vest and held it as hard as he could against his shoulder to slow the bleeding. "Come on," he told himself. "You've got to hold on."

He pulled himself back up onto the bow seat and looked ahead. The boat was quickly approaching his father's boat house. There was no way he could get into the driver's seat to stop the engine. He shoved himself up onto the edge of the boat and fell backward into the water. He held onto the life vest and surfaced just in time to see his father's beloved Chris Craft hit the sandy shore, flip, and crash through the side of the boat house. In the next instant, everything burst into flames.

Harvey felt another wave of dizziness, and he knew he had to get out of the water. He turned over on his back and kicked until he felt his head bump something. With supreme effort, he rolled over to find that he was just a few feet from where he had parked his truck. He hauled himself up out of the water and fell face down in the sand.

Oh, he thought, if only I'd bought a cell phone, an ambulance would have been at the boat house before I got there. He rolled over onto his back and looked up at the clouds floating by overhead. The tiny patches of sky between the clouds had never looked bluer. He closed his eyes and thought about how it reminded him of the color in the dress Kit Blume had worn that morning. In the next instant, he knew that he had to get back to town quickly…before Jacqueline…or Annabelle…tried to kill someone else.

17

OONA LOOKED AT THE CLOCK ON THE KITCHEN STOVE. IT read 4:25. If Harvey didn't come back in five minutes, she would have to go out to the lake to find him. She glanced back into the living room at Benny, who was snoring loudly on the sofa. Could she leave him there to sleep, or should she wake him and take him over to Fred and Sophie's? She looked at the clock again. 4:26.

The phone rang, and Oona leaped to answer it. "Harvey?"

A woman on the other end said, "I'm calling from the Golden Acres Nursing Home. Could I speak to Oona Kelly or Harvey Trent, please?"

"This is Oona Kelly," she said.

"I'm sorry to have to make this call. Your father just passed away."

For years, Oona had been expecting this, but she couldn't think straight at the moment. All she could think about was Harvey. She had to get this woman off the phone. "Thank you," she said.

The nurse went on about a funeral home and something else, but Oona wasn't listening. Where was Harvey?

A horn sounded outside, and Oona hung up the phone to run to the front window. Relief flooded through her when she saw that it was Harvey's truck. She hurried out onto the front porch, wondering why he had parked it in the middle of the front lawn. Harvey leaned over sideways in the seat, and she waited. Jacqueline must have given him something that was on the floor. A brisk wind sent the wind chimes on the porch clinking loudly. She shivered and kept her eyes on the truck. That's when she realized that something was wrong. It didn't take that much time or effort to reach down and retrieve something from the floor.

Oona ran down the steps and across the lawn to the truck. She yanked open the driver's door. Harvey had slumped sideways onto the seat, and blood was seeping through a dark hole in his jacket sleeve. "Jesus, Mary and Joseph!" she exclaimed. She reached out to touch Harvey on the arm. He groaned and rolled onto his back. A bright yellow fishing lure hung from his lower lip. She gasped and said, "Harvey! What happened?"

Harvey opened his eyes and lifted his head. "Oona?" he asked.

"I'm going to get help," she said. "Don't move!"

Oona ran back into the house and picked up the phone. She dialed Fred and Sophie's number. When Fred picked up, Oona said, "Fred! Harvey's been shot."

"Is he...dead?" Fred asked.

"No," Oona said, "but I've got to get somebody over here to keep an eye on Benny."

"You'd better call an ambulance."

Oona thought of their town's only ambulance that had left the bakery less than an hour earlier. It was a one-hour drive to the hospital in Bemidji where they had taken Kit. There was no way they would make it back to Moose Creek anytime soon. It would be faster for her to take Harvey to Bemidji in the truck. "The ambulance took Kit to the hospital," she said.

"I'll be right over," Fred said.

Oona ran back outside with a first-aid kit and a stack of clean towels. She crawled up onto the driver's seat and said, "Harvey, I'm going to try to slow down this bleeding. It might hurt."

Harvey didn't respond.

Oona unzipped his tan jacket and gently peeled away the sleeve that was now saturated with blood. "Hang in there, Harvey," she said. "I'm going to take you to the hospital."

With the scissors from the first aid kit, she quickly cut away his shirt sleeve. She discovered what appeared to be a bullet wound in his shoulder. It looked as if the bullet had merely grazed him, but he did have some significant bleeding. She had seen these types of injuries years ago, when the church had sent her to Africa to serve with the Red Cross. Blood loss and falling blood pressure were her biggest concerns.

A voice from behind her asked, "What can I do?"

Oona turned to find Fred standing beside the truck. She said, "Get me the ace bandage from that first aid kit." She swiftly pressed a thick layer of kitchen towels to Harvey's shoulder.

Fred handed her the ace bandage and said, "You want me to drive?"

Oona shook her head and said, "No, I need you to stay here with Benny." She wound the bandage tightly around Harvey's arm. "Help me move him over."

Fred helped Oona slide Harvey over towards the passenger seat. Fred asked, "Any idea who shot him?"

She adjusted the driver's seat so that she could reach the pedals and see over the steering wheel. She looked over at Fred and said, "He went out to the lake to meet Jacqueline."

"Why?"

"She called to say that she knew something about the Lakeshore Inn fire."

"You think Jacqueline shot him?"

Oona didn't know what to think anymore. Nothing was as it should be. It felt to her as if the entire universe had cracked in two. She wasn't sure whom she could trust or what she should believe. She said, "Don't breathe a word of this to Ron Frank or the sheriff. Just get Sophie to do a background check on Jacqueline. I'll call you from the hospital."

Fred touched her on the shoulder and said, "Be careful." He closed the door.

Oona put the truck in reverse and lurched out onto the street. Harvey groaned. "We're on our way to the hospital, Harvey. Stay with me."

On the way out of town, Oona forced herself to creep along at twenty-five miles per hour to avoid being noticed by the cops. She drove slowly past Swenson's Bakery, where a crowd still hovered near the front door. Ron Frank was standing near his cruiser, talking to the mayor and one of the sheriff's deputies. She prayed that God would make the truck invisible. She had to get Harvey to the hospital without drawing their attention. The less Ron Frank knew, the better. When she reached the highway at the far end of Main Street, and no one seemed to be coming after her, Oona stomped the accelerator to the floor.

Forty-five minutes later, she screeched up to the emergency room entrance at the regional hospital in Bemidji. She blasted the horn repeatedly, and a couple of transport men emerged from the building. One of them opened the passenger door and asked, "What have we got here?"

"Gunshot wound," Oona said.

They retrieved a gurney from inside and hurried back to lift Harvey onto it. "Oh, that hurts," he groaned.

Oona trotted along beside the gurney and said, "We're at the hospital, Harvey. You're going to be okay."

Harvey reached out with his good hand and squeezed Oona's arm hard. "Stop!" he said.

Oona held up her hand to the transport men, and they paused.

Harvey motioned to her to lean in closer. She put her head near his mouth, and he whispered, "Jacqueline Corbett is Annabelle Vernon." The lure in his lower lip made the b sounds come out slurred.

Oona felt stunned. "What?"

Harvey took a breath and repeated, "I said, Jacqueline—"

Oona touched her brother's cheek gently and said, "I heard you. Don't talk any more than you have to. That lure must hurt."

Harvey nodded.

Oona put her lips close to Harvey's ear and whispered, "Is she the one who shot you?"

Harvey nodded again.

Oona whispered, "Was anyone else there?"

Harvey shook his head.

Oona's mind was reeling. Jacqueline Corbett was Annabelle Vernon? Like Catherine, Annabelle had obviously survived the fire at the Lakeshore Inn. She had clearly asked Harvey to meet her at the lake so she could shoot him. Why? Was she really the Fishing Lure Killer, or was she just trying to silence him as he uncovered more about the Lakeshore Inn fire?

One of the transport men said, "We better keep moving, miss."

Oona glanced up at him and nodded.

Within minutes, Harvey was whisked away for an x-ray. In a surprisingly short time, a doctor appeared to say, "The bullet just grazed his shoulder. There was no bone involvement, so we won't have to do surgery. There's really nothing we can stitch together."

Oona heaved a sigh of relief. "I'm assuming you'll be running IV antibiotics and a transfusion."

"Yes," he said. "Sounds like you've had experience with this type of injury."

She nodded and said, "Unfortunately. The church sent me to Africa years ago to help the Red Cross."

"Any idea who shot him?"

She knew exactly who had shot him, but she wasn't going to tell him. If she did, the doctor would send the sheriff around to make a report. No one in the state of Minnesota would ever believe that Jacqueline Corbett was the Fishing Lure Killer. At this point, it was just Harvey's word against Jacqueline's. No, they needed more proof, and she had to get Harvey out of the hospital as quickly as possible. She would go straight to the BCA in the morning. To the doctor, she said, "He did."

The doctor looked surprised.

Oona smiled and said, "He was going to clean our dad's old hunting gun, and he thought he had taken out all the bullets."

The doctor shook his head and muttered, "Hunters. I see them in here more often than I'd like to admit."

The doctor cleaned up Harvey's arm, removed the fishing lure from his lip, and ordered an IV and a transfusion. As soon as a nurse finished dressing Harvey's arm and adjusted a sling over his shoulder, Oona asked, "Can we go now?"

The nurse looked at her in surprise. "Why the rush?" she asked.

Oona didn't want to appear nervous, so she simply said, "Harvey hates hospitals. I think he'd be more comfortable at home."

"I'll ask the doctor," the nurse said. She disappeared.

Harvey woke up and asked, "What's happening?"

Oona sat on the side of the bed and said in a low tone, "The bullet grazed your shoulder. It missed the bone. You've had antibiotics and a transfusion. I say we get out of here before the cops come snooping around."

Oona heard the nurse speaking to the doctor outside the curtain. She quickly whispered to Harvey, "If they ask you what happened, tell them that you shot yourself while you were cleaning Dad's gun."

The doctor came into the cubicle and said, "Well, Mr. Trent, how are you feeling?"

"Fine," Harvey said. "Can I go now?"

The doctor held out a clipboard and said, "As soon as you sign these release forms, you're free to leave."

Oona held the clipboard for Harvey and watched him sign them.

The doctor handed Oona prescriptions for antibiotics and pain pills. Then he said, "There is just one more thing."

Harvey and Oona looked up at the doctor. She hoped he wasn't going to detain them.

The doctor said with a grin, "Next time, make sure you take *all* of the bullets out of the gun before you clean it."

Harvey nodded and smiled. "Ow!" he said. He reached up to the place where the lure had been in his lip.

The doctor said, "What I'm not clear on his how you got that lure in your lip."

Harvey looked at Oona and said, "Ask her. It's all her fault."

Oona had to come up with something quickly. She prayed that God would forgive her for lying twice in one week. She said, "We were cleaning out our dad's hunting and fishing stuff from the garage. He's got Alzheimer's, and he can't use them anymore. We thought we'd sell some of it in a yard sale. I was testing out a reel on an old fishing pole, and I accidentally snagged Harvey in the lip."

Harvey added, "And that's when I shot myself in the arm."

The doctor shook his head. "That sounds too ridiculous to be true."

Oona glanced over at Harvey and held her breath.

The doctor laughed and added, "But you wouldn't believe some of the stories I hear. People hurt themselves doing the dumbest things."

Oona slowly released her breath and said, "Thank you for helping us."

"No problem," the doctor said. To Harvey, he added, "Don't go fishing with that arm anytime soon. It's going to be sore."

The doctor left, and Oona asked Harvey, "Do you think you can walk?"

Harvey nodded and said, "I'd better make sure I can do more than walk. With Jacqueline on the loose, I'd better be able to run."

Oona said, "We're going to go to the BCA first thing in the morning. They'll catch her."

"You think we can trust them?" Harvey asked. He leaned heavily on Oona, and they began a slow shuffle towards the exit.

"We have to," she said. "There's no one else."

"You don't think Ron's got friends there, too?"

"Let's hope not," Oona said.

When they got into the truck, Harvey asked, "Are we going home now?"

"No," Oona said. "I'm taking you to a hotel, and then I'm going back over to the hospital."

"Did you forget something?" he asked.

"Apparently you have," she said. She pulled away from the emergency room parking lot and said, "You were supposed to pick up Grant and Kit, remember?"

"Judas Priest!" Harvey muttered. "How could I have forgotten?"

"You've had a lot on your mind for the past couple of hours," Oona said. She pulled into a hotel parking lot down the street from the hospital. "I just hope Jacqueline hasn't called them to offer more answers to our questions about the Lakeshore Inn."

As soon as the truck came to a stop, Harvey said, "I'll get the hotel room."

"You sure you're going to be okay?" Oona asked.

Harvey said, "I'll be fine. I'm related to the toughest little woman in the state."

Oona laughed and said, "I'll be back as soon as I find them."

Several hours later, Oona returned to the hotel room to find Harvey asleep on one of the beds. When she sat down on the edge of it, the movement awakened him.

"Did you find them?" he asked.

"No," Oona said. She sighed deeply and fell back onto the pillow beside Harvey. "I'm too tired to keep looking."

"You get some sleep," Harvey said. "I feel better now. I'll go back over there."

"I think you should rest, too," she said.

He stood up and adjusted his sling. "I've got the rest of my life to catch up on my sleep. Right now, there are two people out there who are in a lot of danger. I've got to find them before Jacqueline does."

Oona watched him walk out the door. She closed her eyes and prayed for his safe return.

CHERYL DENTON

18

KIT LOOKED UP AT THE CLOCK ON THE HOSPITAL CAFETERIA wall. It read 7:03. She muttered, "I hate hospitals."

"I hate being a patient in hospitals," Grant said, "but they do come in handy when you're sick."

Kit snapped a plastic knife in two and tossed it into a half-empty cup of coffee. She felt like snapping Grant Osgood in two. Why did he always have to be so chipper? "Grant Osgood, I hate you," she muttered.

He smiled at her and said, "You can just go on hating me for the rest of time if you want, but it's never going to stop me from taking care of you."

She clenched her teeth and shoved back her chair. "When is Harvey going to get here?"

"Try to relax," Grant said. "I'm sure he'll come to get us as soon as he can."

"We shouldn't have left to go out for dinner," Kit said. "He probably came while we were gone."

"I doubt that he would have given up that easily," Grant said. "We weren't gone all that long."

Kit tried to picture Harvey coming to meet them. An image of Wildred Swenson's severed head in the cake box surfaced in her mind, instead. Fear seized her and made her insides knot. Had the killer caught up with Harvey? "What if the Fishing Lure Killer got him, too?" Kit asked. "We could be waiting here forever."

Grant tilted his chair onto the back legs and said, "If you start thinking about all the what-if possibilities, you'll drive yourself crazy."

Kit rifled through her purse in search of a stick of gum. Sitting in the hospital for hours was making her insane. "What's the alternative?" Kit asked.

Grant said, "Trusting that God will make everything turn out for the good."

She found a pack of gum, but all of the sticks were gone. She tossed the empty pack into the cup of coffee with the broken knife. God doesn't care about what happens to anyone, she thought. He can't even come up with a stick of gum. "Is that why you're always so darned happy?" she asked.

Grant smiled at her and said, "Yes, trusting in God is what makes me so darned happy."

She looked across the table at him smiling that stupid smile. Grant Osgood was a fool. "Don't you ever get mad, or scared, or anything other than happy?" she snapped.

"Sure," he said with a shrug, "but I don't let myself stay there for very long."

Sometimes, Grant reminded her of that guy from Star Trek who didn't have any emotions. She hated the fact that Grant Osgood was always the same. "Where do you go?" she asked. "To the planet where nobody has feelings?"

"No," Grant said. "I pray, or I read the Bible. As soon as I do, I remember that God is in control and that he wants good things for me."

Oh, for Pete's sake! Kit had known Grant for ages, but she had no idea he was such a Jesus freak. "You sound like one of those TV evangelists," Kit said. She got up, walked over to a vending machine, and purchased another pack of gum.

When she returned to the table, Grant said, "Thanks for the compliment."

He wasn't even rattled by the insult she had hurled at him. He just kept sitting there, grinning like an idiot. If she had to endure him much longer, she thought she might scream. She said, "Compliment? I meant it as an insult." She threw herself back into the uncomfortable plastic chair and said, "I don't know how much longer I can stand to sit here looking at you."

Grant asked, "Are you willing to try something to make the time go by while you wait?"

"Anything would be better than sitting here looking at you," Kit said.

Grant leaned forward and said, "Close your eyes."

"Why?" Kit asked. "You're not going to try to kiss me, are you?"

Grant grinned at her and said, "That's not a bad idea…"

He had a two-track mind: religion and sex. What a disgusting combination. She glared at him.

"…but it's not what I had in mind," he said. "Now close your eyes."

At least if she closed her eyes, she wouldn't have to look at his goofy face. She sighed deeply and closed her eyes.

Grant said, "I want you to visualize yourself leaving the hospital and going to someplace safe and comfortable."

Kit thought about her parents' house and how much she wished she could just crawl back into their bed, go to sleep, and wake up from this nightmare. Just thinking about her parents made her want to cry. She swallowed hard.

"Have you found a safe place?" Grant asked.

She was imagining the soft Egyptian cotton sheets that her mother always sprayed with lavender. She wished she could be there with her mother now. "Yes," she said.

"Now," Grant continued, "think about someone you love coming to that place and asking you how you are feeling."

Kit thought of her mother's dark eyes and soft brown hair. She remembered the way her mother's cheek felt when she pressed it to Kit's to give her a hug. Oh, how she missed her mother! She whispered, "I'm scared."

She was waiting for her mother to respond when Grant interrupted with, "Tell me why."

Hearing Grant Osgood's voice, and not her mother's, made her angry. Why wouldn't he just go away and leave her alone? Her eyes flew open, and she said, "Because, you idiot, somebody's been trying to kill me my whole life. They killed my birth parents, my brother, and my real parents. They just about succeeded in killing Harvey and Oona between Cincinnati and here, and they've killed two other people in the meantime."

"So, you're scared," Grant said.

Who wouldn't be? "Aren't you?" she demanded.

"Yes," he said, "but I'm not going to let it make me hysterical."

Rage welled up in her chest. She hated it when people accused her of losing control. "Are you calling me hysterical?"

"No," he said, "but you're getting close to it."

He was really pushing her buttons now. She wished the Fishing Lure Killer would throttle Grant Osgood. Kit stood up abruptly and knocked over the half-empty cup of coffee. "Why do I let you get anywhere near me?" she shouted. "You make me insane!"

A voice from behind her asked, "Excuse me, Catherine?"

She whirled around to say, "No, I'm not Cath—" She stopped and realized that she had been given that name at birth. She said to a stocky man, "I go by Kit now."

The man nodded.

Kit noted that he had thick, hairy arms and enormous hands.

The man said, "Harvey Trent asked me to come and pick you two up."

Relief flooded through Kit. At last, she could put some distance between her and Grant. "Finally!" she said.

Grant stood and asked, "Do you have some kind of ID?"

Kit thought Grant had a lot of nerve. The man looked perfectly nice to her, and he had gone out of his way to pick them up…on a holiday, no less. Kit glared at Grant.

The man pulled out his wallet and handed Grant his driver's license and a business card. He said to Grant, "Name's Eric Larsen. Harvey told me you wanted someone to take you up to the Vernons' old cottage on the south shore of Upper Red Lake."

The last thing she wanted was for Grant to send this guy away. Kit snatched the license and card from Grant's hand. She glanced at them and handed them back to Eric Larsen. "That's right," she said. "How long before you'll be ready to take us there?"

"Right now," Eric Larsen said.

Kit remembered that the only way to get to the old A-frame was to hike through the woods. She looked down at her lightweight dress and sandals. She said, "I'm not exactly dressed for hiking."

Eric Larsen said, "No matter. I've packed plenty of gear for you."

Grant said, "I'd feel better if we heard from Harvey before we left."

Eric said, "Not much chance of that. He doesn't carry a cell phone, and he doesn't believe in answering machines."

Kit recalled a conversation between Cincinnati and Moose Creek about Harvey's disdain for cell phones and answering machines. She glared at Grant and said, "I'm sure that we can trust Mr. Larsen. He's shown us his ID, and Harvey told us all about him on the way here. He's been fishing with the governor, for Pete's sake."

Grant said, "I'm sorry. We've been through a lot for the past couple of days. I guess I'm being overly cautious."

"That's understandable," Eric Larsen said. He stood there looking at them for a moment and then said, "You ready to get out of here?"

If she had to stand there listening to Grant Osgood for another nanosecond, she was going to explode. "Ready?" Kit snatched up her purse and sweater. "I'm going to be wanted for murder if I don't get out of this place."

They traveled for nearly an hour in Eric's red Suburban. It was almost dark when they pulled to a stop beside a small log house.

Eric said, "This is where we pick up our guide. He's Ojibwa and a member of the reservation. You'll be his guests for the next couple of days."

Kit watched Eric walk away from the car and disappear into the log house.

Grant turned to her to say, "From the way Harvey described it, this is going to be a really tough trip. Are you sure you're up to it?"

Why was he always treating her like some breakable china doll? She hated it when people babied her. "I run five miles every morning," Kit said.

"Running is one thing. Hiking through the woods is another," Grant said. He sounded like an old mother hen. "I'll be fine," Kit said.

Eric emerged from the log house with a younger man who had long, black hair. They paused on the path, and she saw Eric Larsen hand the man a roll of bills. When he turned towards the truck, she noticed that Eric was wearing a holster with a pistol in it. It comforted her to know that he could protect her if they came across whoever had killed the fisherman in Doc's boat and Wildred Swenson.

The car door opened, and the Native American man slid into the seat beside Kit. He smiled at her, nodded his head, and said, "Ma'am."

Kit noted that the man wore a wide, maroon print headband. It covered most of his forehead, stopping just short of bushy black eyebrows. He wore thick bracelets and a choker that was strung together from some sort of wooden beads shaped like short segments of drinking straws. What surprised her about him was that he was wearing black jeans, black hiking boots, and a black jacket. He looked more like a Goth or a biker than a Native American wilderness guide.

From the front seat, Eric said, "This is Johnny Red Hawk. He's going to make sure we find our way up to that cottage without any trouble."

Grant stuck out his hand and said to Johnny Red Hawk, "Grant Osgood. Thanks for coming out on such short notice."

Johnny Red Hawk shook Grant's hand and then turned to Kit to offer her his hand. He looked at her expectantly.

She looked down at his long fingers and hesitated. With a deep breath, she finally stuck out her hand and said, "Kit Blume."

When he touched her, Johnny's hand felt warm and calloused. He gave her fingers a gentle squeeze and quickly released them. Kit got the sense that he was a kind person.

Johnny appraised Kit's outfit and said, "This is rough country. Sandals won't protect your feet from poison ivy or sharp rocks."

Eric said, "She's going to change as soon as we get to the boat."

Kit felt surprised. There had been no mention of going anywhere in a boat. She asked, "Boat? I thought we were hiking."

"That's tomorrow," Eric said. He started the engine and pulled away from the little log house. "Tonight, we cross Lower Red Lake by boat. It's a lot easier than trying to muck our way through the marshes."

"We'll have a lot less trouble with the bears that way, too," Johnny Red Hawk said.

Kit's heart beat faster. She'd seen stories about bears mauling people on TV. "Bears?" Kit asked. "There are bears out here?"

"Lots of them," Johnny Red Hawk said. "But as long as you don't bother them, they won't bother you."

"Unless you've got food," Eric said.

Kit could see Johnny's strong profile against a set of headlights coming from the other direction. He had a prominent nose and high cheekbones. A smile played around his lips. Were they joking about the bears?

Johnny said, "Eric loves to tantalize the bears with bacon."

"A man's gotta eat," Eric said.

Johnny said, "And bacon is the only food Eric considers for breakfast."

"Darn right," Eric said. "How else would I have the strength to go wandering around out here in the wilderness like I do?"

Kit didn't like the idea of attracting bears. "I'm partial to coffee for breakfast," she said. "I don't have to eat bacon."

"You'll need a lot more than coffee to keep you going out here," Johnny said.

Kit squeezed her hands together and hoped that she wouldn't become some bear's late night snack. She asked, "What if a bear does come after me?"

"Just play dead," Johnny said.

A short time later, they pulled to a stop. When Kit opened the door, she could hear water. It sounded like waves at the ocean. It was so black outside; she couldn't tell where they were. "Where are we?" she asked.

Eric appeared by the open door with a bright flashlight and said, "Lower Red Lake. This is where we take the boat."

The temperature had dropped considerably, and a sharp wind gusted through the trees. Kit shivered. She might just become a bear's Popsicle if it got any colder.

Grant said, "Do you have something warmer for us to put on?"

"Yep," Eric said. He pulled a backpack out of the Suburban's cargo area and handed it to Grant. To Kit, he said, "You can change back here." He handed her a smaller backpack and a flashlight. He added, "We'll be waiting for you over at the dock. It's right in front of the Suburban."

Eric and Johnny Red Hawk walked away with the big beam of light. Grant stood beside the Suburban in the near-darkness, shining his flashlight at the ground.

He was always lurking nearby. She wished she could shake him off and just go onward with Eric and Johnny. "What are you waiting here for?" she asked.

"I thought you might be scared out here in the dark by yourself."

He was the one who should be scared. If he didn't back off, she might just kill him. "I'm fine," Kit said, climbing up into the back of the Suburban. "Get lost."

"Suit yourself," Grant said.

Kit could hear Grant's footsteps crunching over gravel. As soon as she was alone, she flipped on the flashlight and peered into the pack. It contained a pair of hiking boots, four sets of heavy socks, two pair of khaki pants, a couple of long-sleeve t-shirts, long underwear, and a jacket. She decided to forgo the long underwear and set some clothes out in front of her. She pulled one of the shirts partially over the flashlight. The last thing she wanted to do was give Grant Osgood a show. He was probably standing over there on the dock right now with his binoculars.

As soon as she had finished changing, Kit hopped down out of the back of the Suburban. The boots were a little big, but she could make do. She pointed the flashlight at the ground and began walking towards the front of the Suburban.

"All set?" came a voice from the dark beside her elbow.

Kit gasped and whirled around to find Grant walking behind her. "You scared the snot out of me."

"That's not hard to do," Grant said with a grin.

She didn't know if she could put up with him for the next few days, but she didn't seem to have much choice. Through clenched teeth, she said, "Grant Osgood, I hate you."

"I know," he said. "You ready to have some fun?"

Fun? With Grant Osgood annoying her every step of the way?" "Oh, yeah," she said.

Fifteen minutes into the boat trip, a fine drizzle began to fall. Kit's pants quickly became soaked, and she began to shiver uncontrollably. Grant scooted closer to her and put his arm around her shoulder. Under ordinary circumstances, she would have told him to drop dead. But he was protecting her from both the drizzle and the boat's spray. Through chattering teeth, she asked, "How much longer are we going to be out here?"

"I don't know," he said over the drone of the motor. "But Harvey did tell me that this is one of the biggest freshwater lakes in the United States."

Black, choppy waves licked at the side of the small craft as it made its way slowly north through the murky darkness. Kit imagined endless miles of open water, like the ocean. She groaned and looked at the tiny beacon of light that shone ahead of the boat. "Can't we go any faster?" she asked.

Grant said, "It's pretty rough. If we go too fast, we could take on water."

Kit's entire body felt numb. She pulled her feet up onto the seat and wrapped her arms around her knees. She closed her eyes and tried to imagine that she was curled up in her parents' bed. Suddenly, an image flashed into her head of a boy lying in the bottom of a boat with blood coursing down his face. As quickly as the image came, it disappeared. Kit sat bolt upright.

"What's the matter?" Grant asked.

If she knew, she'd tell him. It was just another nightmare. *You sure?* a voice from inside challenged her. *You're not asleep.* She rubbed her hands over her eyes and said, "Nothing."

"You're really shivering," he said. He unzipped his jacket and pulled it around both of them.

Immediately, Kit felt the warmth of Grant's body, and she allowed him to hold her close. It reminded her of the way she used to feel when her dad comforted her after one of her nightmares. Could it be that she was beginning to feel comfortable with Grant Osgood? The thought of trusting him almost made her pull away. And yet, she didn't want to see any more frightening things that might come bubbling up out of her head. And she couldn't bear the cold. So, while Grant held her tight, she kept her eyes on Eric Larsen's broad back as he steered them expertly over the rough water.

As the motor droned on, Kit reminded herself that she had to focus on whatever memories she could muster up from the old A-frame with the yellow trim. If she could just remember what happened that night, she felt certain that her nightmares and flashbacks would end.

CHERYL DENTON

19

HARVEY HAD BEEN AT THE HOSPITAL FOR OVER AN HOUR, trying to find out if anyone on the staff had seen Kit or Grant. He traced their paths from the treatment room in the emergency department, to the waiting room on the first floor, to the picnic area outside, and finally, to the cafeteria. His shoulder began to throb, and a sense of desperation gripped him. What if Jacqueline had somehow tricked Kit and Grant into going somewhere with her? He had to find them.

A silver-haired woman wearing a navy blue uniform gave Harvey the tip he needed. She said, "I saw them. They were here for a really long time."

Harvey felt relieved. At least they had actually made it to the hospital. But on the heels of that relief came more doubts about their safety. What if Jacqueline Corbett had intercepted them? "Did you see anyone else with them?"

"Yeah," she said. "They left with a big, burly guy."

A big, burly guy could describe lots of people. Who would have picked them up? And then Harvey realized that it had probably been Eric Larsen. He asked, "Did the guy have short hair, a scruffy beard, and really fat hands?"

The woman nodded.

Harvey felt his muscles relaxing. Thank God they hadn't left with Jacqueline. He asked, "Did you hear them say where they were going, by any chance?"

The woman's perfectly penciled brows drew together as she stood there thinking. At last, she looked up to say, "I remember them saying something about going hiking, but I don't remember where."

Harvey knew for certain then that Eric had picked up Kit and Grant. Eric had actually shortened the process of getting to the truth about the Lakeshore Inn. He must have gotten back into town earlier than he had expected from his trip with the governor. Someone in Moose Creek had probably filled him in about what had happened with Wildred. Knowing Eric, he had probably asked around about how he could help. Fred or Sophie must have sent him to the hospital to pick up Kit and Grant. Harvey thanked the woman, and he hurried from the hospital. When he arrived at his hotel room down the street, he let himself in with the security card.

Oona was sitting in the middle of the bed with a bunch of motel stationery fanned out around her. She looked up and asked, "Did you find them?"

His shoulder felt as if he'd been bitten by a bear. The empty bed looked really inviting. "No," Harvey said, closing the door behind him. He turned the deadbolt and attached the chain. "But I do know where they went."

"Where?"

Harvey pushed the security card back into his wallet. "Up to the Vernons' old cottage on Upper Red Lake."

"How do you know that?"

"Some woman in the cafeteria saw them with Eric, and they were talking about going hiking."

Oona said, "Thank God they're safe."

Harvey knew that Eric would take good care of Kit and Grant. But what if the three of them encountered Jacqueline Corbett out there in the woods? Harvey said, "It's a good thing they're with Eric, but have you stopped to consider that Jacqueline might be following all three of them now?"

"Yes," Oona said. She turned to pick up one of the papers from the bed. "But they are on Ojibwa land. Jacqueline wouldn't get very far if she did try to follow them."

Harvey suddenly felt very tired. When was all of this insanity going to end? He sat down beside Oona and peered at her chicken scratching on the papers. "What did you come up with here?" he asked.

Oona said, "Not much. I'm having a really hard time thinking straight. Even when I write something down, it doesn't make sense. But Fred and Sophie are on their way down, and Sophie said she's got a lot to tell us."

Immediately, Harvey thought of Benny stretched out on their sofa. Was he safe? "Who's looking after Benny?"

"Mike is."

Harvey said, "I'm so confused. What happened to Annabelle to make her want to shoot me?"

Oona looked up at him and said, "It's hard to say. But maybe this is a blessing."

"How can you say that?" Harvey asked.

"You've never gotten over her," Oona said. "Maybe now you can move on with your life."

Harvey felt annoyed by Oona's statement. Still, there was some truth in it. His love for Annabelle had never allowed him to date anyone else. "I guess what you're really saying I've been moping around for too long." he said.

Oona shrugged. "The Lakeshore Inn fire was a long time ago."

Harvey felt ashamed of himself. The last thing he ever wanted to be was immature, mooning over the loss of a girl who'd died…or at least so he thought…nearly twenty-five years ago. "Why didn't you ever tell me this before?" he asked.

"Because it's usually better to let people come to their own conclusions."

How was he supposed to conclude that he'd been hung up on grief if he couldn't see that about himself? "How can they, if they don't realize what they're doing?"

Oona shrugged. "Some people take longer than others to look at themselves."

Had he really been that distracted all these years? He looked up at himself in the mirror and thought about how much he had cared for Annabelle when they were younger. So much time had gone by. It was so hard to grasp that she was Jacqueline Corbett, a woman who seemed bent on killing him.

Oona took his hand in hers and said, "I got a phone call from the nursing home while you were out at the lake."

Harvey felt so overwhelmed right now, the last thing he wanted to do was try to figure out how to deal with his dad. "What's wrong now?" he asked.

"Dad's dead," Oona whispered.

Harvey felt as if he'd been hit by a wrecking ball. He glanced over at Oona and watched a tear coursing down her cheek. He put his arm around her shoulder and said, "Too bad he never knew the truth about the Lakeshore Inn. Maybe he wasn't so crazy, after all."

Oona nodded and wiped her eyes on her sleeve. "If it hadn't been for Dad talking about Annabelle Vernon, we never would've gone looking for Kit."

The mention of Kit brought Harvey back to the problem at hand. He had to catch up to her before Jacqueline did.

A knock on the door interrupted his thoughts. He went to the door and peered through the peephole. "It's Fred and Sophie," he said.

He opened the door and motioned them inside. Fred was carrying a suitcase and a large paper sack. Sophie held a cardboard tube in her hand, along with Mike's red backpack, and her purse.

Something smelled delicious…like fresh-baked bread. Harvey suddenly realized that he was starving. "Boy," he said, "one of you two smells good enough to eat."

Sophie smiled and gave him a gentle hug. She asked, "How's your shoulder?"

It was pounding with pain, but he didn't like to whine. "Fine," Harvey said.

Oona said, "He's running around too much." She shoved together her papers and said, "He's going to pay for it later when the pain killers wear off."

Fred closed the door and bolted the locks. He asked, "Where are Kit and Grant?"

Harvey said, "Eric Larsen picked them up from the hospital."

Fred said, "I thought Eric was fishing with the governor."

"You didn't send him to the hospital?" Harvey asked.

"No," Fred said. "I haven't seen Eric since Friday."

Oona said, "Harvey found out from someone at the hospital that Eric's taking Kit and Grant up to the Vernons' old cottage on Upper Red Lake."

"Why?" Sophie asked.

"It's the one place Kit can remember from her childhood," Oona said.

"How did she know where to find it?" Sophie asked. "That's a long way from Moose Creek."

Oona said, "Jacqueline had been there with Eric a long time ago to check out the real estate potential."

Hearing Jacqueline's name made Harvey's heart race. It suddenly dawned on him that Jacqueline knew they would be looking for the old

A-frame house on the lake. What if she went there, too? He asked, "Do you think Jacqueline might be on her way to that old house, too?"

"Let's hope not," Sophie said.

Fred said, "I made up some sandwiches." He carried the paper sack over to the small table in the corner and pulled out several white pastry boxes.

Oona stood up and stretched. "I haven't eaten since yesterday," she said.

Harvey's stomach rumbled. He tried to remember when he had last eaten. It had been the day before. "Come to think of it," Harvey said, "neither have I."

"Sit down and eat," Sophie said. "You've got to keep up your strength."

After polishing off two pastrami sandwiches, a bag of chips, a can of root beer, and three doughnuts, Harvey felt much better. He asked Sophie, "Did you find anything on Jacqueline?"

"It was hard, with all of the commotion at City Hall today," she said. "But I finally got my chance when the chief and the rest of the guys went up to Bemidji to the sheriff's office." She patted her purse and said, "I think I've made some connections, and as soon as the BCA office opens at eight, I'll show them what I've got on Jacqueline."

Harvey thought about his encounter with Jacqueline on his boat. He shivered and hoped that the cops would catch up to her soon. He said, "I don't know what possessed her to tell me that she was really Annabelle Vernon. Maybe it'll help the cops figure out that she was involved somehow in the fire at the Lakeshore Inn."

Oona said, "And it doesn't make Ron Frank look very smart. He definitely either screwed up or covered up something big on the night of that fire."

Fred looked up and asked, "Do you think there's a chance Paul and Mimi might still be alive?"

Harvey had been so focused on the Vernon kids that he hadn't given their parents much thought. He said, "I suppose it's possible."

Sophie said, "I know one thing for sure. We've got enough proof now to convince the BCA to re-open the case."

Harvey wondered how anyone could possibly solve this case. It seemed preposterous that Annabelle Vernon had passed herself off as Jacqueline Corbett for so many years. The fact that Ron Frank was involved muddied the waters even further.

"You really think they can solve this?" Oona asked.

"Yes," Sophie said.

"How?" Oona asked. "We can't figure it out."

Sophie held up her index finger and said, "For one, we've identified at least one perpetrator who was also there on the night of the fire."

Harvey asked, "You mean Annabelle?"

"Right," Sophie said. She held up her second finger and said, "Two, we've got new physical evidence: Wildred's head. Even Peter's missing body may have left behind bone fragments or traces of DNA that the BCA lab can use to try to identify whoever killed him."

Oona said, "But maybe Wildred was killed by someone else...like the Fishing Lure Killer."

"I don't think so," Sophie said. "All of the other Fishing Lure victims were found in their boats. I think Jacqueline used the lure to throw off the cops."

Harvey felt a new wave of dread washing over him. There were two killers on the loose? He asked, "You mean there's someone else out there killing people, besides Jacqueline?"

"It sure looks like it," Sophie said. "The cops in Cincinnati reported that the truck that hit your rental car had been stolen. They're working on identifying the person who took it from their parking lot. Their identity could provide the BCA with another piece of evidence linked to this case."

"It could have just been some random thief with road rage," Harvey said.

"Maybe, maybe not," Sophie said. She held up a third finger and said, "Three, Harvey is a solid witness in this case. He can testify that Jacqueline told him she's really Annabelle, and he can tell the court that she tried to kill him."

Oona said, "We told the staff at the hospital that Harvey accidentally shot himself."

"Why?" Sophie asked.

Harvey thought about the lie Oona had told the deputy and about the ones they had told the doctor. He regretted what he had done, but at the time, it seemed like the safest alternative. He said, "We were afraid that they'd tip off Ron Frank or one of his state trooper buddies about everything. We wanted to get out of there to find Kit and Grant before Jacqueline did."

"Well, we can straighten that out later," Sophie said. "What we don't have at this point is a motive. Eventually, the investigators will figure out why Jacqueline is bent on killing everyone with any connection to that fire."

Harvey remembered the look in Jacqueline Corbett's eyes when she pointed the gun at his head. She seemed so desperate, she looked crazy. He said, "She obviously wants to shut people up."

Oona asked, "Do you think there's any chance that Jacqueline might go after Benny?"

Harvey felt his stomach lurch with that thought. "Surely, not," he said.

Sophie raised an eyebrow and said, "Anything's possible at this point."

"But he wouldn't know anything about what happened," Fred argued.

Oona stood up and said, "That's not necessarily true. Benny may not have the intellectual skills that the rest of us do, but he's always been very intuitive when things aren't right."

Sophie looked at Oona and asked, "You think he knows something?"

"I don't know," Oona said.

Harvey asked Sophie, "Any idea how Doc's involved in all this?"

Sophie said, "It's hard to say. He could be the Fishing Lure Killer, or he could have been kidnapped by whoever ransacked his house, or he might have gone fishing, for all we know."

"I feel terrible," Harvey said. "If I hadn't asked him to help me find the bridge on the Vernon land, maybe he'd still be okay."

Fred said to him, "If he's the Fishing Lure Killer, you're lucky to be alive."

Sophie looked at her watch and said, "We don't have much time if we're going to get some sleep. The Bureau opens up at eight."

Harvey looked at the clock radio. It was after two. "I can't believe it's so late," he said.

Fred said to Harvey, "You and I had better get going. The pilot who volunteered to fly you around Upper Red Lake is going to meet us at six."

Harvey wished he could just lie back on the bed and forget about everything that was happening. But there were so many people counting on him. He couldn't ignore the danger that Kit and Grant faced. Maybe Benny and Mike were in trouble, too. And God only knew what was going on with Doc. He nodded and stood up.

Sophie said to Fred, "I don't like to think about you driving half the night after the day we've had."

Fred put his arm around her and said, "I'm wide awake. On any other day, I'd be heading to work right now."

Sophie kissed her husband and said, "Be careful."

Harvey said to Oona, "Don't forget. No matter what, you stick with Sophie."

"And what about you?" Oona asked Harvey. "Who's going to be watching your back?"

"I am," said Fred, "at least until he takes off with the pilot who's going to fly him over the lake. I'll be waiting to drive straight home as soon as they find Kit and Grant."

Sophie picked up the backpack and cardboard tube she had carried in with her. "I almost forgot!" She handed Harvey both the backpack and the tube. She said, "Mike told me to give these to you. That's the map for the entire Red Lake Reservation." She pulled the top off the tube and said, "He put a compass in there for you, too."

Harvey glanced at the compass inside the tube and then replaced the lid. He said to Sophie, "If it weren't for Mike, we would never have found Peter Vernon's body."

Sophie said, "We're really proud of him."

A short time later, Fred sped onto the highway. While they were driving, Harvey studied the map. He thought about Sophie's optimism regarding the BCA's involvement with the Lakeshore Inn fire. He prayed that somehow, Sophie and Oona could convince the Bureau to re-open the case. Someone had to stop Jacqueline, the Fishing Lure Killer, Ron Frank, and whoever else was involved. He just hoped the law caught up with them before one of the killers caught up with Kit and Grant.

20

KIT WOKE UP TO THE SOUND OF SOMETHING SIZZLING AND the aroma of fresh coffee. She breathed deeply and stretched her arms overhead. She knew it had to be Saturday, because it was the only day Mom made bacon for breakfast. It was the one morning of the week that Dad was home to eat with them. When she opened her eyes, she discovered Grant Osgood sitting beside her with a goofy grin on his face. Kit gasped and asked, "What are you doing here?"

He smiled broadly and said, "Savoring the moment. It's not every day I get to wake up next to you."

"Oh!" Kit cried. She sat up and looked around. They were in a very tiny tent. Grant Osgood was practically on top of her. Was this another one of her nightmares? "Where are we?" she asked.

"Remember, Eric Larsen and Johnny Red Hawk brought us across Lower Red Lake last night."

Kit shivered when she remembered the hours that she had sat huddled in the back of the boat. The rain had sliced into her, and the cold had seeped deep into her bones. The thought of having to go back that way made her feel miserable. She said, "Oh, yeah. I've never been so cold in my life."

"That's because you left your long johns in your backpack."

She had no idea when she was getting dressed in the back of the Suburban that the trip across the lake was going to be so cold or long.

Grant's chiding made her feel defensive. "How was I supposed to know it was going to get so cold?"

"We're in Minnesota," Grant said. "It gets cold up here."

Back in Cincinnati, it was still summer. For the first time in her life, she actually wished she were there to experience the humidity and oppressive heat. "It's the first week of September," Kit grumbled.

"Yeah, and it snows up here in October."

Kit shivered and pulled her sleeping bag up over her shoulders. She heard something clanging outside and remembered the conversation last night about bears. She asked, "Do you think bears will really come after that bacon?"

"If we leave it on a plate for them when we leave," Grant said with a grin.

Kit wished Grant would be serious for once. "Very funny. I've seen shows on TV about bears attacking people," she said.

"If they go after you," he said, "remember to play dead."

Kit wasn't sure she could do that. Running seemed smarter.

"How'd you sleep?" he asked.

Surprisingly, she could barely remember falling asleep, and she hadn't awakened the entire night. She did, however, dream about running from the person with the gun. The woods were so dark in her dreams, and they always frightened her. "Fine," she said.

"You were mumbling something all night long," Grant said. "It sounded like you were saying 'slow and sure.'"

Kit turned away from him and lay back down. She hated that he knew about her nightmares.

His hand came to rest gently on her head, and he began stroking her hair slowly. It reminded her of what her mother had done whenever she was upset by nightmares. He said, "I know you've had a really rough time all your life. I just want you to know that I'm here for you."

Kit wanted to reach up and slap his hand away. But this morning, something wouldn't allow her to. She wished she could talk to her mother or Dr. Irene. But there was no one to talk to, other than Grant Osgood. She turned to face him and said, "I keep wondering when I'm going to wake up. The days are beginning to feel exactly like the nights."

Grant looked down at her and said, "I have a feeling that today is going to be the end of it all."

Kit hoped he didn't mean that it would be the end of her life. She wasn't ready to die. In that instant, she realized why her parents had always tried so hard to talk to her about God. It was impossible to know when your life might end…like Wildred Swenson, who had been planning a big surprise party. Suddenly, the thought of dying scared her. What if God was real? She had never been very receptive to him. She could spend forever in hell…separated permanently from her parents. She blinked back tears and asked, "How do you know it's all going to end today?"

He lay down beside her and slipped his arm under her. Very tenderly, he pulled her in close. Kit should have been beating him off with her fists, but she suddenly felt limp. She buried her face in the front of his shirt and felt the warmth of his body on her cheek. He said gently, "It's what I've been praying for."

Kit had never believed in prayer. It had never gotten her anywhere in the past. But she was beginning to wonder if she ought to try it. She mumbled into his t-shirt, "I've never believed in prayer."

"I know," Grant said, "but I do."

Part of her wished that she could run from him. Another part, though, told her to stay. His arm felt so warm and strong. "And I hate that you've got your arm around me," she said.

"I know," he said, "but there isn't anyone else to do that for you."

Fresh, hot tears spilled from Kit's eyes when she realized again that her parents were gone. They were never coming home to hold her tight and tell her that everything would be okay. All she had was this annoying man who drove her crazy. "Grant Osgood, I hate you," she said.

"I know," Grant said. He put his other arm around her and pulled her closer.

Kit could feel Grant's breath, warm and soft on her ear. Her heart hammered in her chest. Was she reacting like that because of fear…or something else? She whispered, "I don't know why I hate you. I just do." She looked up into his eyes and felt something inside of her heart shifting. Suddenly, she wanted to put her arms around him and hug him back, but something that felt like giant rubber bands held her arms to her sides.

From outside, Eric Larsen called out, "Shake a leg, people! We're wasting daylight."

Grant released her and sat up. He said, "I'll wait outside while you get dressed. I put some dry clothes down inside your sleeping bag last night."

Kit sat up and nodded. She stayed in the sleeping bag to pull on the warm clothes. What Grant had done the night before was very thoughtful. He had always gone out of his way to be kind to her. And how had she repaid him over the years? By telling him constantly that she hated him. How would she feel if someone constantly told her that they hated her? In that instant, she realized how completely mean she had been to him.

She crawled out of the sleeping bag to put on her hiking boots. She couldn't understand it. There were plenty of people in the world to hate… terrorists and dictators and murderers. Why, on earth, had she spent the past twenty-four years hating a guy who had so much love to share? And then it hit her: Dad had been right…Grant *was* in love with her.

Kit froze in the middle of tying one of her boots. She allowed her mind to repeat that thought. Grant *loved* her. What was so terrible about that? She finished tying her boot and thought that there shouldn't be anything wrong with a man loving her. She had a lot to offer. So, why was she so scared?

Kit sat there staring at the sides of the yellow tent, and something dawned on her. Dr. Irene had always told her that when a child experiences something really traumatic, she gets stuck at that age of development. Something really terrible had happened to her when she was four. She was certain of that. She recalled from her child development classes that a four-year-old exists in the latent stage of sexual development. A normal child wouldn't be even remotely interested in sexual advances. And that's what Grant had been doing all these years with his pranks, his constant hovering, and his maddening smile. He was trying to show her that he was interested in her, as men often are interested in women.

Kit thought about the strange new feeling that she had just experienced. When Grant put his arms around her, she had wanted to hug him back for the first time in her life. Could it be that she was finally growing beyond that four-year-old level of development? In spite of all the chaos of the past week, could it be that she was finally learning to trust someone, other than her parents? Kit felt a sense of peace flooding over her, and she sat there hugging her knees to her chest. She felt a smile slowly breaking through the tears, and she thought once again, *Grant loves me.*

And in the next instant, she had to ask herself a question: *Am I falling in love with Grant Osgood?* Immediately, she felt panic welling up in her chest. She buried her face in her knees and muttered to herself, "Keep your head on straight. This is Grant Osgood, remember. Annoying, obnoxious Grant Osgood."

The tent flap opened, and Grant said, "Are you mumbling in your sleep again, or are you talking to me?"

Kit's head whipped up, and she felt her cheeks grow warm. Quickly, she turned away from him and said, "I didn't say anything."

"Must be the bears talking," Grant said.

Kit began rolling up her sleeping bag with her back to him. Ordinarily, a comment like that would have sent her into a panic. Now, she realized that it was just Grant's way of trying to make her laugh…which, she also realized, was Grant's way of quietly saying that he loved her.

After they had eaten breakfast and broken camp, Johnny Red Hawk led them north through the dense forest and marshy ground between Lower Red Lake and Upper Red Lake. Kit walked ahead of Grant, wondering how she would explain to him that she hadn't ever been able to see that he loved her. She wished they were alone so she could tell him she was sorry for all of the times she had said that she hated him. But there was no opportunity for it as they plodded steadily through the woods, with Johnny leading and Eric bringing up the rear.

As the morning wore on, Kit began to feel that today was going to mark the end of her nightmares, too. There was no logic to that thought, because they were headed to a place that would inevitably stir up some terrible memories from her past. But she felt strengthened and ready to face whatever challenge lay ahead of her. With the knowledge that Grant loved her, she felt that she could do anything now.

CHERYL DENTON

21

OONA AWOKE TO THE SOUND OF THE PHONE RINGING ON the hotel room night table. Figuring that it was her wake-up call, she picked up the receiver and set it back on the hook. She sat up and stretched. The phone rang again. That's strange, she thought. She reached over to switch on the light and picked up the phone a second time. "Hello?"

A hoarse voice on the other end asked, "Having a nice stay, Oona?"

Fear gripped her. "Who is this?" Oona demanded.

The voice whispered, "You might as well give up now. You'll never figure it out."

Oona breathed deeply to slow the pounding of her heart. There was something vaguely familiar about the voice, but she couldn't place it. She wasn't even sure if it was a man or a woman. She said, "I'll never give up."

"You will when you're dead," the voice whispered. The line clicked.

The hair on Oona's arms stood on end. Someone was willing to do anything...even kill her to stop her from uncovering the truth about what had happened at the Lakeshore Inn. With a trembling hand, she set the receiver back down.

Sophie sat up in her bed and asked, "Who was that?"

That voice, she thought. Who was that? Was it someone she knew, or did it just sound familiar? "I don't know," she said, "maybe the same guy who tried to stop me at the school. It was hard to understand him."

"What did he say?"

Oona swung her legs over the side of the bed and said, "He said I should give up, because I'd never figure it out."

Sophie asked, "Did he say anything else?"

Just thinking about the words sent a chill through Oona's core. "Yeah," she said, "When I told him I'd never give up, he said that I would when I'm dead."

Sophie threw back the covers and said, "We'd better get over to the BCA office right away."

Oona and Sophie arrived at the Bureau of Criminal Apprehension offices at eight o'clock. They were ushered through metal detectors, and their purses were scanned. Once inside, they were directed down the hall. Oona's fear had been replaced by fury. No one had the right to threaten her. She refused to remain silent. More than ever, she was determined to do whatever it took to uncover the truth about what had happened at the Lakeshore Inn.

Sophie stopped to talk to someone she knew from school, so Oona approached a woman behind a thick glass partition and said, "We need to see the bureau chief."

The woman asked without looking up from some papers on her desk, "Do you have an appointment?"

Oona's heart sank. They needed an appointment? "No," she said.

The woman slid a paper through an opening in the glass and said, "Call one of these numbers for an appointment. Someone will return your call within twenty-four hours."

Twenty-four hours? In that period of time, Jacqueline and whoever else was out there could kill quite a few people. Oona said, "We can't wait that long."

The woman looked up at her and said, "The chief is very busy. You'll have to."

Kit and Grant were out there in the woods with Eric. What if Jacqueline found them before the cops did? What if she killed Harvey? "I'm telling you, we can't wait that long," Oona said, her voice rising. "This is a matter of life and death."

The woman said, "Ma'am, you're going to have to follow procedures."

Frustration mounted in Oona's chest. She wasn't going to take no for an answer. She pounded on the glass with both fists and shouted, "Get the chief out here now!"

The woman behind the glass picked up the phone on her desk and glared at Oona.

Seconds later, a deep voice at Oona's side said, "Ma'am, step away from the window."

Oona whirled around to find herself looking up into the face of an armed guard. Another guard was quickly approaching from the end of the hall. Realizing that she was blowing their odds of getting someone to listen to them, Oona put her hands in the air and said, "Okay, okay. I'm leaving the window."

Sophie grabbed Oona by the elbow and dragged her across the room to a bank of chairs. She pulled her down beside her and hissed, "You can't act like a lunatic in a place like this!"

Oona drew a deep breath and tried to calm down. Sophie was right. They had to make a good impression here, if anyone was going to believe them. "Sorry," Oona said. "I'm getting a little crazy."

Sophie put her arm around Oona and said, "You've been through a lot in the past few days. I understand. But we've got to go about this differently if we're going to help Harvey and Kit and Grant."

The warmth of Sophie's arm on her back helped Oona relax. She needed to trust Sophie right now. Oona nodded and asked, "What have you got in mind?"

Sophie stood up and said, "Follow me and keep your mouth shut."

Oona followed Sophie down the hallway and into the ladies' room. Sophie stopped in front of the mirror and set her purse up on the counter. Oona watched Sophie remove her sweater and unbutton her shirt to reveal her cleavage. Sophie rolled up her calf-length skirt at the waistband until it revealed her knees. Then, she pulled a hair tie out of her purse and twirled her hair up into a loose twist. She pulled a few tendrils free around her face and swiftly added deep red lipstick to her mouth.

Oona was shocked by the transformation. She had never seen this side of Sophie before. She grinned at Sophie's reflection in the mirror and said, "You've got artillery I'll never have."

Sophie grabbed up her purse and turned around. "You ready to go into battle now?"

The look of determination on Sophie's face told Oona that her friend was far better equipped to handle the BCA than she was. "I'm following you," she said.

Sophie sashayed down the hallway, accentuating the movement of her hips as she walked. Oona followed her, glancing around to note that a few of the men standing outside the various offices were nodding at Sophie and smiling. Oona couldn't believe how gullible some men could be. She watched Sophie pause outside of an office and wait while a man held the door for her. Sophie smiled sweetly at him and said, "Thank you, sir. Oh, you're such a gentleman."

The man grinned and stood there holding the door open while he stared after Sophie. Oona glanced at the nameplate on the office door: Gordon Finch. This wasn't the bureau chief's office. The department title under the man's name read Case Review. What were they doing here? Oona slipped under the man's arm and followed Sophie inside.

Sophie walked up to a woman at the desk and said cheerily, "Good morning."

The woman looked up, smiled, and asked, "Can I help you?"

Oona sat down in a chair near the door and watched. She prayed that Sophie would have better luck than she did at getting through to someone.

Sophie said, "I've got an early appointment to see Mr. Finch."

The woman frowned and looked at her appointment book. She said, "Your name?"

"Sophie Ianelli. I'm with the Department of Criminal Justice at Bemidji State College."

The secretary said, "I don't see your name on the book."

Sophie said, "That's because Mr. Finch promised to squeeze me in early. Would you let him know I'm here?"

The woman stood and walked across to a closed door.

When the secretary opened the door, Sophie dropped a file folder on the floor. When the folder hit the floor, Mr. Finch, who was sitting at his desk, looked up. Sophie bent to pick up the folder, and in response, Mr. Finch stood. Sophie dumped a bunch more papers on the floor and turned around to bend over and retrieve them. Oona watched Mr. Finch staring at Sophie's backside. Like a hungry animal approaching a trap, Mr. Finch walked around his desk and came out of his office. Sophie glanced back at Oona and winked.

Oona covered her mouth to keep from busting out laughing.

Sophie scooped up her papers and turned to Mr. Finch with a radiant smile. "Oh, Mr. Finch," she said, extending her hand "It's so nice of you to see me."

"I'm sorry, but I don't recall making an appointment with you. My oversight, I guess," he said. He shook her hand.

Sophie motioned to Oona and said, "My friend and I have some information on a cold case that we think you might find very interesting."

Mr. Finch glanced briefly at Oona, and then looked back at Sophie. "Well, let's have a look," he said, gesturing towards his office.

Oona leaped to her feet, thankful for Sophie's heavy artillery. It had blown the bureau doors wide open.

A short time later, they were sitting with Mr. Finch and one of his associates at a table in a conference room. Sophie gave them a little background about the fire and then began laying out sheets of paper and explaining them, one by one. She said, "I ran a background check on Annabelle Vernon from the day of the Lakeshore Inn fire until today." She pointed to the first paper and said, "I found out that she went to a boarding school in Paris."

Mr. Finch narrowed his hazel eyes at one of the papers and asked, "You sure you've got the right Annabelle Vernon?"

"No," Sophie said, "but I got the right Annabelle LaFollett."

"I'm lost," Mr. Finch's young associate said.

Sophie said, "I started out by looking up Annabelle Vernon's birth certificate. Her mother, Mimi, had been married before, and Annabelle's birth father was Jacques LaFollett, of Paris, France."

"I remember hearing her talk about him when we were in school," Oona said, "but I never thought about her having a different name."

Mr. Finch looked at Oona with mild annoyance. Oona decided she'd better keep her mouth shut if she didn't want to get thrown out on her ear.

Sophie continued. "I looked up school records in Paris for Annabelle LaFollett. It was pretty easy. She finished boarding school and went on to graduate from the Sorbonne with a degree in drama."

"Where did she go after that?" Mr. Finch asked.

"I don't know," Sophie said, "it's like she just vanished into thin air. There were no further newspaper articles, marriage licenses, death certificates, or anything related to Annabelle LaFollett."

"That's impossible," Mr. Finch's associate said. "We know that no one just vanishes."

"Exactly," Sophie said, "but sometimes they resurface as someone else." She pulled out several other papers and said, "When I got to a dead-end with Annabelle LaFollett, I began looking for information on Jacqueline Corbett." She pointed to some dates on two separate papers and said, "In June of one year, Annabelle LaFollett graduated from the Sorbonne with a degree in drama. And in September of the following year, Jacqueline Corbett surfaced here in Minnesota."

Mr. Finch leaned his bald head in his hand and scowled. Deep wrinkles creased his brow. "Did you go back and look at Jacqueline's background?"

"I tried, but she doesn't seem to have one," Sophie said, "unless you consider that Annabelle LaFollett and Jacqueline Corbett are one and the same. When I went back and looked at her birth certificate, I noticed that her mother's maiden name was Corbin. If you put together Corbin and LaFollett, it's easy enough to come up with Corbett."

Mr. Finch ran one hand over his short, greying beard. He looked up at his associate and asked, "Why couldn't somebody have figured this out years ago?"

"Because she was presumed dead," Sophie said. "Most police departments don't waste their time chasing down ghosts."

Mr. Finch raised an eyebrow and asked, "Why was she presumed dead?"

Oona opened her mouth to tell them that Ron Frank was a lousy police chief, but before she could say anything, Sophie gave her a stern look and shook her head slightly. Oona put her hand over her mouth and feigned a yawn.

Sophie said to Mr. Finch, "Our police chief, Ron Frank, claimed that everyone in the Vernon family died the night the Lakeshore Inn burned, including Annabelle."

Mr. Finch asked his associate, "Are you writing all this down?"

The young associate nodded.

Mr. Finch said, "Your chief didn't do a very good job of identifying bodies if one of his victims turned up alive."

Oona felt like leaping to her feet and cheering. Instead, she sat on her hands.

Sophie said, "Annabelle isn't the only one who has turned up. Last week, my friend, Oona, and her brother went to Cincinnati to meet the Vernon's youngest daughter, Catherine."

Gordon Finch asked, "Another one of the kids who was presumed dead?"

"Right," Sophie said. "After Catherine fled the scene of the fire, she showed up buck naked in a laundry basket behind a house in Cincinnati."

Mr. Finch shook his head in disbelief and held out both hands, palms up. "How does a naked kid get from northern Minnesota to southern Ohio?"

Oona's stomach flip-flopped. She was worried that Mr. Finch was beginning to doubt their story. She held her breath and waited for Sophie to respond.

"No one knows," Sophie said. "But we've got pretty solid evidence that she is Catherine Vernon."

"What kind of evidence?" Mr. Finch asked.

Sophie said, "She showed up in Cincinnati wearing nothing but a medallion on a gold chain."

"Lots of parents put those on their kids," Mr. Finch's associate said, "I've worn one my whole life."

"Not like this one," Sophie said. "It has an inscription on the back that is identical to the one that her only surviving brother has worn all his life."

Gordon Finch asked, "What kind of inscription?"

"It reads, *Von Will*," Sophie said.

"What does that mean?" Mr. Finch asked.

"It's short for Von Willebrand's. It's an inherited bleeding disorder that all the Vernon kids had," Sophie explained.

To his associate, Mr. Finch said, "We can verify that with some simple lab tests." He turned to Sophie and said, "How soon can you get Catherine Vernon in here?"

"That's our most pressing problem," Sophie said. "As soon as Eric Larsen got back from taking the governor fishing over the weekend, he took her hiking towards Upper Red Lake to work on identifying an old cottage that she remembers. It could be important to the case."

The associate asked, "Who's Eric Larsen?"

Sophie said, "He's a wilderness guide from Moose Creek."

The associate asked, "Did he tell you that he took the governor fishing over the weekend?"

Oona thought this wet-behind-the-ears kid was barking up the wrong tree. He was focusing on Eric Larsen, when he should really be asking more about Kit. She said, "That's what he told Harvey and me. He took the governor out fishing last year, and they were going again this year."

The associate looked at Gordon Finch and said, "We may have another problem here."

Oona wondered what kind of a problem he was talking about.

The associate said, "The governor couldn't have possibly gone on a fishing trip this weekend."

Gordon Finch asked, "Why not?"

"Because," his associate said, "he had some minor surgery on Friday and spent a quiet weekend at home with his family."

"What rag reported that?" Gordon Finch asked.

"None, that I'm aware of," his associate said.

Gordon Finch asked, "Then how would you know how the governor spent his weekend?"

Yeah, Oona thought, *how would you know?*

The associate said, "He's my mother's cousin's husband."

Oona felt stunned. Why would Eric lie to them like that? She asked, "If Eric didn't take the governor fishing over the weekend, why did he lie about it?"

"And where did he go?" Gordon Finch asked.

Sophie raised an eyebrow and said, "Cincinnati, maybe?"

An image of Kit and Grant in the dense northern woods with a wilderness guide who could also be a killer made Oona even more afraid for them. She couldn't contain herself any longer. She blurted out, "I'll bet he's the one who stole that truck and tried to kill us."

"What truck?" Mr. Finch asked Oona.

"A delivery truck hit us when we went to Cincinnati to meet Kit…I mean, Catherine Vernon."

Mr. Finch's associate said, "Your accident could be coincidental. There's a lot of road rage these days,"

Sophie said, "I don't think so. This particular truck was reported stolen just before the accident, and it was found abandoned at the airport shortly afterward."

Gordon Finch said, "Let me get all of this straight." He held up a finger and said, "Number one: the Lakeshore Inn burns down twenty-four years ago." He held up another finger. "Number two: one of the supposed victims of that fire turns up ten years later, and no one recognizes her." He held up another finger. "Number three: another one of the supposed victims turns up twenty-four years later, after running naked at the age of four from northern Minnesota all the way to Cincinnati." He held up a fourth finger and added, "Number four: that same girl is on her way to

Upper Red Lake with a wilderness guide who's been telling lies and maybe stealing trucks." He looked from Sophie to Oona and asked, "Did I get that right?"

"Yes," said Oona, "but there's a lot more."

Gordon Finch sighed and sat back in his chair. He leaned his head back and rubbed his eyes. Then he looked at his watch.

Oona prayed that Sophie would be able to keep the man's attention. She had to tell him everything before he tossed them out.

Sophie said, "Yesterday, Jacqueline Corbett invited Oona's brother, Harvey Trent, out to Heron Lake. She said she wanted to tell him some things about the Lakeshore Inn fire. When he got there, she shot him."

Mr. Finch glanced at Oona and then asked Sophie, "Is he okay?"

Sophie said, "Luckily, Jacqueline's gun jammed. She only grazed him in the shoulder."

Oona thought of poor Harvey with the hook dangling from his lower lip. She said, "Don't forget about how she snagged him in the lip with a lure."

Mr. Finch's associate said, "She's the Fishing Lure Killer!"

"I don't think so," said Sophie.

Mr. Finch asked, "Why not?"

Sophie said, "Because during this past week, somebody killed a fisherman on Heron Lake, as well as our bakery owner, Wildred Swenson. She's the one, by the way, who found Catherine Vernon through one of those missing and exploited children's groups. Anyway, Wildred had a lure in her lower lip, but she wasn't found in a boat on a lake…which is the typical way the Fishing Lure Killer leaves his victims."

The associate said, "I had heard about the Wildred Swenson case, but not about the guy on Heron Lake. Why haven't they brought us in on that one?"

"Because the sheriff's department is probably still investigating this morning," Sophie said. "There's some question about whether or not our local dentist, Doc Daggert is involved. The body was found in his boat, and he has disappeared."

"Who found the body at Heron Lake?" Mr. Finch asked.

Oona said, "My brother and I did when we went back to look for the rest of Peter Vernon's body."

Mr. Finch looked puzzled and asked, "There's another body?"

Oona could see that their tale was becoming so complex that it was hard to follow. She said, "There *was* another body. Harvey and Doc Daggert found Peter Vernon's remains by accident. They were trying to find an old bridge to help Sophie's son with some orienteering skills."

Sophie added, "But somebody removed the body, and Harvey Trent discovered his maintenance man, Ralph Rivers, building a new bridge in the place where the body had been."

Oona said, "We took Peter's skull to the state police post down in St. Paul."

"The state police don't get involved in criminal investigations," Mr. Finch said, "Why didn't you just take it to your chief?"

Sophie motioned to Oona to be still, and she said, "Because, Mr. Finch, we have reason to believe that our police chief, Ron Frank, was not just negligent in his duties. We believe he may somehow be involved in Peter's murder, or the fire, or both. Oona was afraid that if they brought forth more evidence locally, Ron Frank would simply cover it up, too."

Gordon Finch asked, "What makes you think that?"

Oona was dying to tell Gordon Finch all about Ron Frank, but Sophie looked over at her, gave her a stern look, and then said to Mr. Finch, "Let's just say his skill set isn't exactly professional."

Mr. Finch said to his assistant, "Get a hold of the state police and have them send that skull up to our lab."

Oona thought about the skull and the x-ray in the cardboard box…the one that Doc had put together, and the state police Sergeant had conveniently lost. She said, "That's impossible."

Mr. Finch asked, "Why?"

Oona said, "Because when my brother and I went back to talk to the Sergeant about the evidence, he claimed that we'd never been there."

Mr. Finch scowled. "Did he give you a receipt for the evidence?"

"No," Oona said. "The Sergeant said he'd ask some questions quietly without putting anything in writing so that it wouldn't tip off Ron Frank."

Mr. Finch sighed deeply and then asked, "Have you got this Sergeant's name or badge number?"

Oona was beginning to wonder if Gordon Finch believed anything they were saying. It sounded preposterous to her. But she couldn't let down Kit and Grant and Harvey. She said, "I did, but someone stole my purse from the back seat of my car when we went to Cincinnati. The Sergeant's business card was in my purse."

Sophie said, "We suspect that there are several people involved in this. While someone was stealing Oona's purse and running their car off the road, someone else was in Moose Creek, stealing Doc Daggert's files and maybe killing him. One of them probably killed Wildred Swenson."

"Was he the dentist responsible for the care of the Vernon kids?" Mr. Finch asked.

"Yes," Sophie said.

Gordon Finch rolled back in his chair and folded his arms across his chest. He turned and stared out the window. Oona wondered what he was thinking. Was he even considering the case, or was he trying to figure out a way to shoo them out of his office?

Sophie said, "We really need your help. Harvey Trent, Catherine Vernon, and Grant Osgood are all on their way to that old summer cottage on Upper Red Lake. We've been worried that Jacqueline Corbett might be on her way there to kill all three of them."

Oona said, "I guess now that we should also be worried that Kit and Grant are with Eric Larsen."

Gordon Finch looked at his associate and said, "Are you thinking about where all this is going?"

His associate nodded.

Oona felt completely discouraged. It was all over. Gordon Finch was going to politely ask them to leave. How on earth could they stop Jacqueline without someone's help?

Mr. Finch looked at Oona and said, "I'm afraid we can't do much to help you find your brother or the other two."

Oona couldn't believe it. She opened her mouth, but Sophie turned to glare at her. Oona snapped her mouth shut.

Sophie turned to Gordon Finch and asked, "Why is that?"

"Under ordinary circumstances, we could help you for several reasons," Mr. Finch said. "You've identified a perpetrator, you've come up with new physical evidence, and you've got witnesses."

"That should be enough to get us through the initial case screening process, then," Sophie said.

"Yes, but this is where things get a little muddled," Gordon Finch said. "You see, the state of Minnesota has no jurisdiction over the Red Lake Reservation. We can't go charging in there. They've got their own police force. If a federal crime occurs, then the FBI would be called in."

Oona couldn't bite her tongue any longer. She blurted out, "So, you're just going to sit here until one of them gets murdered on the reservation before you do something?"

Mr. Finch said, "Since the reservation is involved, I'm going straight to their council elders to get their cooperation. If they feel that their police force needs help, they can call in the FBI. And you can count on our office working around the clock to get to the bottom of what's going on."

Oona's jaw dropped. She felt like leaping to her feet and screaming. They did it! They got someone to believe them! She clamped her lips shut and squeezed her hands together tightly in her lap.

Mr. Finch said, "The state of Minnesota owes you both a debt of gratitude."

Sophie reached out to squeeze Oona's hand and said, "Oona and her brother, Harvey, have done the lion's share of the work on this. I just pulled together the paperwork to prove it."

Gordon Finch asked Sophie, "Do you have any photos of any of the people involved?"

Sophie pulled out several large black and white photographs. "You mean like these?" she asked. She spread the photos out on the table one by one.

Oona looked at photos of Paul and Mimi Vernon, the grotesquely overweight Annabelle Vernon, and the slender Jacqueline Corbett. She looked at shots of Catherine Vernon as a child, Kit Blume as an adult, Peter Vernon, and Benny Vernon. Sophie had also included Doc Daggert, Wildred Swenson, Ralph Rivers, Ron Frank, Harvey, Grant Osgood, and Eric Larsen. There were two photos she didn't recognize, but she assumed they were Kit's parents. Oona quickly counted them silently. There were more than a dozen lives that had been negatively affected by someone's actions the night of the Lakeshore Inn fire. She looked up at Mr. Finch and said, "What we haven't been able to figure out is what happened the night the Lakeshore Inn burned down."

"We'll know eventually," he said, "but it may take a good deal of digging."

His associate said, "I think we should start by questioning the Moose Creek chief."

Mr. Finch nodded and said, "Our investigative team will be able to get to the bottom of it." He asked Sophie, "May I keep all of your records? I'd like to forward copies to the reservation council."

"Absolutely," Sophie said. She pushed the papers and photographs across the table.

Oona had a sudden fear that everything might disappear. She leaned over and whispered to Sophie, "Maybe you should just give them copies."

Sophie smiled at her and whispered back, "I just did."

Oona sat back and relaxed. Sophie had done a wonderful job of pulling together a lot of complicated information.

Mr. Finch asked Sophie, "What did you say you do at State?"

"I'm a student in the Criminal Justice Department."

Mr. Finch's brow shot up. "Really?" He chuckled and said, "I figured you must be on staff over there."

"You're good," his associate said.

Gordon Finch smiled at Sophie and said, "Very good."

"Thank you," Sophie said.

Oona felt unbelievably proud of her friend.

"If you're interested in working with us," Mr. Finch said, "I've got a position open in the Case Review Office. I could use someone with your talents."

Sophie stood up and shook Mr. Finch's hand. "Thank you. I'll think about it."

When they stepped outside of the building, Oona leaped up and gave Sophie a high-five. "We did it!" she squealed.

Sophie grinned at her.

"You were really something in there. Fred would've been proud of you."

Sophie giggled and said, "Fred would never have let me walk in there with my skirt hiked up to my hind end."

"Well, it worked," Oona said. "And we needed some kind of an advantage."

They got into Harvey's truck, and Oona said, "This whole experience has taught me something important."

"What's that?" Sophie asked.

Oona said, "I was thinking about moving to Chicago to take a teaching job there. I realize now that I'm a really important part of what goes on in Moose Creek. I'm going to stay and take care of Benny."

Sophie smiled and said, "I'm glad." She added, "This was a big win on our side, but we have to remember that the war's not over yet. Harvey,

Kit and Grant are still out there, Doc's missing, and no one knows where Jacqueline is."

Oona sobered at the thought. She said, "I sure wish Harvey had a cell phone. We could call him and warn him about Eric."

"He probably wouldn't get reception out there in the woods," Sophie said.

"You're right," Oona said.

Sophie said, "Let's just hope that the reservation police or the FBI find them soon."

Oona realized that there were a lot more people in danger besides Harvey, Kit, and Grant. Everyone who knew anything about the case or who was remotely involved was in danger, too. Thoughts of Benny waiting at home with Mike flashed into Oona's head. And concerns about Doc Daggert nagged at the back of her mind. She put the key into the ignition and said, "I want to get back home right away. I need to check on Benny."

22

HEAVY FOG DELAYED THE PILOT WHO WAS SUPPOSED TO pick up Harvey along the eastern shore of Upper Red Lake. Fred had driven through the night to get Harvey to their meeting place by six, but for the past two and a half hours, they had sat waiting by the shore in the Swenson's Bakery van.

While they were waiting, Harvey said, "The nursing home called Oona yesterday while I was at the lake. Dad died."

Fred said, "I'm real sorry. He was a good man."

Harvey swallowed hard past the lump in his throat and said, "Yes, he was." He sat there staring into the mist and wondered what life would have been like if his father had ever decided to leave Moose Creek. He realized that many lives, including his own, would never have been the same without him.

Fred asked, "Now that your Dad's gone, you going to go back to Berkeley?"

Was he? Harvey thought about the old LeClerc mansion and Paul Bunyan's General Store. They had become as much a part of his life now as his childhood home and the store had been a part of his father's. He couldn't possibly leave. So many people were counting on him: Oona, Benny, Mike, his employees, and now, Kit Blume. At length, he said, "No. I'm staying put."

"I'm glad," Fred said. "Moose Creek just wouldn't be the same without you *and* Wildred."

Harvey nodded. Moose Creek would never be the way it was. Maybe that was a good thing.

While Fred sipped coffee in the driver's seat, Harvey carefully studied the map that Mike had given him. From time to time, he looked skyward, hoping to spot the float plane as it came in to land.

Fred said, "We could really use some sunshine to burn off this fog."

Harvey said, "Some days, out at Heron Lake, it never clears." He peered at the legend on the map and tried to calculate the distances. He said, "If Jacqueline was right in telling me that the cottage was just before the reservation boundary line, it should be relatively easy to find."

Fred leaned over and peered at the map. He pointed to some fine print and asked, "What's that landmark?"

Harvey read, "Red Lake Reservation Boundary Marker."

Fred said, "All you have to do to locate the cottage is find that marker and then backtrack away from the reservation."

Harvey looked up and said, "Of course, this is assuming that I can find the marker."

A low rumble from outside made Harvey look up. Out of the fog, a green and white float plane emerged.

"Finally!" Harvey said. He folded up the map and jammed it into Mike's red backpack. He opened the van door and put his right arm through one of the backpack straps.

"Harvey," Fred called to him.

Harvey looked back. Fred was holding out the butt end of a handgun. He said, "Take this."

Harvey looked at the pistol and asked, "Isn't this that new Glock that we saw at the gun show last spring?"

"Yeah," Fred said, "It's supposed to fire, even if it gets wet."

Harvey took the pistol and checked the safety. "Thanks. Let's hope I don't have to fire it." Then, he shoved it into the back of his waistband.

The engine revved as the pilot maneuvered the plane to the edge of the dock. He cut the engine, and everything around them fell silent again. The door swung open, and a tall, slender man with a beard stepped out onto the pontoon. He pulled off his aviator glasses and called out, "Sorry about the delay!"

Fred motioned to Harvey, "Come on," he said. "I'll introduce you."

Harvey followed Fred down the length of the dock.

Fred stuck out his hand and said to the pilot, "It's good to see you again."

The pilot shook Fred's hand and asked, "So, is this Harvey?"

Fred nodded and turned to Harvey to say, "This is Phillip. He's the guy who was in the bakery yesterday morning."

Phillip shook Harvey's hand and said, "I never dreamed that showing up for a free doughnut and cup of coffee would end up like it did."

"You and me both," Harvey said. "Thanks for volunteering your time and plane to help us."

"I just felt like it was something I had to do," Phillip said.

An image of Wildred's eyes bulging at Harvey flashed through his memory. He tried to push the thought aside. He said, "We've got to find Kit and her friend, Grant, as soon as possible. They're in a lot of danger."

"What happened to your arm?" Phillip asked.

Harvey said, "The killer tried to do me in, too."

"No kidding?" Phillip said. "Did you get a look at him?"

"Yes," Harvey said.

"Do the cops have any idea who it is?"

"Not yet," Harvey said, "but I do."

Phillip looked perplexed. He said, "You mean you know who did this to you, but you haven't told the cops yet?"

"That's right," Harvey said.

"Why not?" Phillip asked.

"Because the police chief in Moose Creek has been covering her tracks for the past twenty-four years."

"*Her* tracks?"

Harvey nodded and said, "Jacqueline Corbett is the one who shot me, and we're pretty sure she killed Wildred Swenson."

Phillip whistled. "Man, oh man," he said. "I've flown her all over northern Minnesota to look at lake houses. Who would believe it?"

"I wouldn't have," Harvey said, "unless I'd seen it with my own eyes."

Fred spoke up with, "Hopefully, Harvey's sister and my wife have been able to convince the people at the Bureau for Criminal Apprehension that Jacqueline is dangerous."

"Yeah, buddy," Phillip said. He looked back over the lake and said, "The fog's lifting a little. We'd better get going before it starts raining."

Harvey turned to Fred and said, "We'll be back as soon as we find them."

"I'll wait right here," Fred said.

"Stay in the van," Harvey said, "and keep the doors locked."

Fred nodded, and Harvey stepped onto the pontoon and then up into the small plane. He buckled his seat belt and waited while Phillip prepared to take off. Phillip fired up the engine, and Harvey watched the propeller on the nose begin to spin.

"You ever flown in one of these before?" Phillip asked.

Harvey said, "Never."

"It's not exactly like a commercial flight," Phillip said. "We fly a lot lower and a lot slower, but it's going to feel like we're going at a pretty good clip."

Harvey nodded and said, "I'm ready when you are."

Phillip turned knobs on the instrument panel, adjusted the flaps, and pushed forward on the throttle. The engine revved, and the little plane pulled away from the dock. As soon as they were a short distance from the shore, Phillip pulled up on the controls. The plane bounced over the water for a short time, and then went airborne.

Harvey looked out the window to watch the lake disappearing below. They flew along through a mist that partially obscured his view. He hoped Phillip knew how to fly this thing blind.

Phillip pointed to the foggy shoreline off to their left and said, "I'm going to hang close to the south shore. Fred told me the cottage you're looking for is just before the reservation boundary."

"That's right," Harvey said. He peered at the water's edge below and added, "I don't see much of anything out there but trees."

Phillip said, "It would be a lot easier if the leaves were down, but I think we'll be okay."

Suddenly, Harvey spotted a flat, black roof among the trees. "What's that?" he asked.

Phillip dipped lower and said, "Looks like a school. There's a big parking lot and a bunch of buses."

Harvey peered through the fog at the building and said, "Yeah, I see what you're talking about." He felt a little better, realizing that it was a lot easier to see things from the air like this.

Several other buildings appeared, but Phillip said, "We're not quite that close to the reservation yet."

After a short time, Harvey spotted some white buoys up ahead in the water. "What are those?" he asked.

Phillip said, "Those are the boundary markers for the reservation. Nobody's allowed to go past them." He flew over them and grinned at Harvey, "…at least not by water."

Harvey said, "We must have just passed the house we're looking for."

Phillip said, "I'm going to go a little farther west and then swing around so that you can keep a closer eye on things down there."

Harvey tried to recall the details of the little A-frame with its cedar shingles and yellow trim. Phillip banked, and Harvey felt momentarily disoriented. He closed his eyes and waited for his stomach to catch up to the rest of him. When the plane leveled off, he turned his head to look down to the right. He blinked and stared hard. On a large, grassy finger of land that jutted out into the water, he spotted the house, just as Kit had remembered it in her drawings. It had been far easier to find it than he had imagined. "There it is!" he said.

"That's impossible," Phillip said. "That's Native American land."

Harvey asked, "Can you circle around so we can get a closer look at it?"

"Sure," Phillip said, "but I can't go much lower. The reservation council doesn't appreciate it when we spook the game."

Harvey waited while the plane circled and then leveled off a second time, just slightly closer to the ground. He remembered that Kit had said the intricate trim was yellow. He wished he had a copy of her drawing with him. The plane shot past the little A-frame again, and he peered more closely at it. There was no doubt about it: the trim was painted mustard yellow. "That's the place," he said.

"Are you sure?" Phillip asked.

"Positive," Harvey said. "It looks exactly the way Kit drew it."

"I want to take a closer look along the shoreline here," Phillip said.

Harvey didn't know why he wanted to waste his time looking when they'd already found the house.

Phillip said, "I've seen hundreds of little houses like that. And that particular one is not where it's supposed to be."

Harvey watched the little A-frame disappearing behind them. He craned his neck to watch for similar houses along the shoreline. The only thing he saw was another large public building set a considerable distance back from the water's edge. A curl of smoke rose from the chimney. He didn't see anything else until they came upon the white buoys in the water again. "That was it back there," he said. "I'm sure of it."

Phillip sighed deeply and said, "I'm afraid we've got a problem here."

Harvey felt a little edgy. "What's the problem?" he asked.

Phillip said, "If you're sure that's the place, you're going to have to walk a good distance to get to it."

"Can't you just set me down close to it?"

Phillip banked around again and said, "This is as close as we can get."

Harvey looked out at the white buoys beneath them. The little house had become a small dot on the peninsula in the distance.

"Why can't you go any closer?"

"Because the reservation would be all over me like a pack of coyotes on a wounded rabbit the minute my pontoons touched the water. The last guy who tried to land out here spent six months in jail and had his plane and license confiscated."

"Oh," Harvey said, "I wouldn't want that to happen to you."

"No," Phillip said, "so you're going to have to make up your mind. Do you want me to set you down near the buoys, or do you want to go back where we started?"

Harvey considered his options. "What happens if I walk onto the reservation?"

"If somebody finds you, you'll be arrested or escorted off, depending on the mood they're in today," Phillip said. "I've heard it can go either way."

Harvey watched the trees zipping by underneath them. "How far away will I be when you set me down?" The little house loomed closer.

"At least a couple of miles," Phillip said.

"That's no big deal," Harvey said.

"You ever been hunting in northern Minnesota?"

"Sure," Harvey said. "Plenty of times."

"Then you know that it can be pretty marshy in places, especially around the lakes."

Harvey remembered then a time when he had sloshed through a marsh while hunting pheasant. It had been very slow going, not to mention cold. "I think I can handle it," he said.

Phillip said, "And this time of year, you can count on seeing at least a couple of bears. They're out hunting to get ready for winter."

Harvey said, "Hopefully, they'll be hunting something besides me today."

Phillip flew over the little house and banked one more time. He asked, "You want me to put you down out here or not?"

Harvey thought about it. He had no idea whether Sophie and Oona had convinced the BCA to help them. And at the moment, there wasn't anyone else who was headed this way to help Kit and Grant. He said, "You're not going to get into trouble?"

"No," Phillip said, "I'm going to land outside of the reservation boundary."

"Do it!" Harvey said.

Phillip pulled the throttle back and lowered the flaps. The little plane drifted down towards the surface of the water. With a bump, they landed, and the plane bolted over the water before coming to a stop some distance from the shore.

"Can't you get any closer?" Harvey asked.

"Nope," Phillip said. "I'll get hung up in the sand if I do."

Harvey nodded.

"How long do you expect you'll be?" Phillip asked.

Harvey shrugged and said, "It depends on how far out they are from the house. They're probably coming up from the south across the land between the lakes this morning."

Phillip said, "I'll fly back around in about four hours. As soon as you get to the house, put some sort of a signal out on the dock."

"Got it," Harvey said. He opened the small door and ducked his head to step out onto the pontoon. "I'll see you later."

Harvey jumped from the pontoon into the water. The water felt only slightly warmer than the air, and he was instantly shivering. Relieved that the water only came up to his thighs, he turned to close the door.

Phillip said, "Better stay clear of the shoreline. I saw some fishermen back there who would turn you over to the cops in a heartbeat if they caught you on the reservation."

Harvey nodded and closed the door.

Phillip took off, and Harvey adjusted Mike's backpack over his shoulder. He quickly sloshed through the knee-deep water towards the shore, hoping he'd find Kit and Grant before the reservation council people found him wandering on their land. He prayed for the strength he was going to need to walk all that way through the woods. It wasn't going to be easy, especially with his throbbing arm in a sling. And there was no telling if Jacqueline would be there at the house, waiting for him with a bullet. He shuddered at the idea and then pressed on.

And then a new thought struck him. Could Eric Larsen somehow be involved with Jacqueline? Harvey couldn't figure out why Eric had taken Kit and Grant all that way over the land between the lakes. Eric could have easily flown them in, just as Phillip had just done. Harvey wondered if he could be wrong about the little house he had spotted from the plane. He could miss Kit and Grant completely if the house were someplace deeper inland. He walked faster, determined to think about only a positive outcome to his search. A lot of people were counting on him.

23

GRANT HAD BEEN FOLLOWING KIT FOR HOURS ON THE slow journey through Native American land between Lower Red Lake and Upper Red Lake. From time to time, Johnny Red Hawk paused to point out an interesting plant or an unusual bird. Eric Larsen brought up the rear, saying little.

As the morning wore on, a steady rain began to drip from the leaf canopy overhead. Heavy fog rose up from the steamy bogs. Just before noon, Grant noticed that Kit began to stumble frequently over slippery tree roots and slimy rocks that jutted up out of the sodden ground. He called ahead to Johnny Red Hawk, "I think we need to take a break."

Johnny turned to look back just as Grant saw Kit's right ankle wobble and give out from under her. Grant lunged forward and caught her just before she hit the ground.

Johnny said, "Okay. Better to rest than push too hard."

Grant led Kit over to a fallen log and held her arm while she eased herself down onto the moss-covered wood. Dark rings had formed under her eyes, and her damp hair clung to her forehead. "You all right?" he asked.

Kit nodded.

Grant sat down beside her and asked Johnny Red Hawk, "How much longer is this going to take?"

Johnny said, "Three, four hours."

Eric came to stand near them and adjusted the weight of his pack. He said, "That's if we keep moving. At the rate we're going, we might have to spend the night out here."

Kit shivered and said, "I'd rather not."

"Then you'd better get up and keep walking," Eric said.

Grant looked up at Eric with mild annoyance. He was pushing Kit awfully hard. But, on the other hand, he knew that Eric was accustomed to soft tourists who would spend an eternity getting from one point to another if he didn't push them.

Johnny Red Hawk said, "Let her rest a little here. At noon, we'll stop at the village for a while."

Eric said, "The village is out of the way. It'll take us even longer if we go there."

Johnny said, "If you want to be able to bring people out here, it's important for you to visit with the elders once in a while."

Grant heard Eric mutter something under his breath.

Johnny added, "Stopping at the village will give us all a chance to warm up."

Grant noted that it had gotten considerably colder. Kit shivered beside him, and he put his arm around her shoulder. He asked Johnny, "How long 'til we get to the village?"

Johnny said, "About an hour."

Grant asked Kit, "Can you make it that far?"

She nodded and stood up. "Let's keep moving," she said. "It's warmer that way."

The narrow trail they were following forced them to continue on in single file. Grant wished he could take Kit's hand to keep her from falling, but it would have really slowed them down. After about an hour, Grant could smell smoke. And then, in a clearing, they came upon a long, low building.

Johnny Red Hawk paused and turned back to them to say, "We'll stop here for a while."

"What is this place?" Grant asked.

"It's a meeting lodge for the Ojibwa elders," he said. "They get together here to talk about tribal stuff."

Grant came alongside Kit and slipped his hand into hers. "Your fingers are like ice," he said.

Her fingers curled around his, and he held her hand firmly as they made their way around to the front of the building.

Inside, the low-ceilinged room was dimly lit. At a bar along one end, a number of older men sat drinking beer. A few tables held small groups of men who were eating. On the far wall, an enormous fire crackled. Grant asked Johnny, "Is it okay if we go over and sit by the fire?"

"Sure," Johnny said. "We'll be over in a while. There's somebody we need to talk to."

Grant led Kit over to the fireplace, where they sat on the raised hearth with their backs to the flames.

"Oh," Kit breathed. "This feels so good."

"Take off your jacket," Grant said. "It'll dry out if we hang it here by the fire."

Kit tried to unzip her jacket, but her fingers shook so much, she couldn't.

Grant asked, "You want some help?"

She nodded.

Grant unzipped her jacket for her, and she shrugged her arms out of the sleeves. He took off his own jacket and then hung both of them over the backs of nearby chairs.

Kit leaned her head on his shoulder and sighed deeply.

He thought that she must be extraordinarily tired. Normally, she would not have gotten that close to him. He put his arm around her and gently rubbed her damp sleeve. "This is a lot harder than I expected," he said. "You've been a trooper."

Kit said, "I just want to get to that house. I know something will click for me as soon as we get there."

"It's good to keep yourself focused on that end goal," Grant said. "It keeps your mind off the cold."

"And the blisters," Kit added.

"And the rain," Grant put in.

"Hmm," Kit replied.

He felt her head grow heavy against his arm and realized that she was swiftly falling asleep. He slid away from her a little and eased her over so that her head rested on his leg. He watched her face and noticed that she scowled from time to time. Her arms began to twitch, and he knew that she was dreaming.

He wondered what had happened to Kit all those years ago to make her so frightened. It must have been something really traumatic to have affected her this long. He wished he could scoop her up into his arms and carry her far from her memories, to a place where he could always keep her warm, and safe, and happy.

Across the room, Johnny Red Hawk and Eric Larsen sat with three older men at a table. One of them placed a long, wooden pipe to his lips and struck a match. He puffed smoke through the pipe and handed it to the man on his right. Grant was amazed that the Native Americans still practiced the tradition of smoking a ceremonial pipe.

He watched Eric Larsen as the men talked. Eric frequently looked at his watch. He got up to go to the bathroom and then came back to the table. A few minutes later, he walked out the front door. What was he doing out there? Grant wondered.

The warmth from the fire, combined with the murmur of men's voices, made Grant begin to feel drowsy, too. He closed his eyes and wished he could just stretch out on the hearth and sleep for hours. But he knew that if he did, he'd never be able to make the rest of the journey. He prayed that God would give them the strength they needed to get to the old house with the yellow trim.

Kit began groaning, and the twitching in her arms became jerking. Grant opened his eyes and looked down at her. Her entire body was tense, and he could see that her legs were jerking, too. In the next instant, she sat upright and screamed.

The room fell silent, and everyone turned to stare at her.

Grant held up his hand and called across the room, "It's okay. She's having a nightmare."

A few of the old men nodded and turned back to their beers. One of the old men sitting with Johnny Red Hawk continued to stare. He puffed on the ceremonial pipe and squinted at Grant through the wreath of smoke.

Kit groaned again, and Grant put his arm firmly around her. He said, "Kit, wake up."

Kit whimpered something and slumped against him. She continued to twitch.

He knew that she was still dreaming. "Kit," he repeated a little louder, "you're okay. Wake up."

Kit jolted upright and then crouched on the ground like a sprinter preparing for a race. Every muscle in her body was tensed for action.

Grant stood up and hauled her by her belt back onto the raised hearth. "Let me go!" she cried. She struggled to get away from him.

Grant realized that she was having one of those nightmares where someone was chasing her with a gun. All instincts were telling her to run. "Kit!" he said. "You're safe. You can stop running now."

In the next instant, Kit collapsed in a heap across his lap. She mumbled, "Slow and sure, slow and sure, slow and sure."

Grant stroked her hair, tucking a wisp behind her ear. He wondered how she functioned if all of her time sleeping was also spent running.

Tears began brimming over from Kit's closed eyes, and Grant reached out with his fingers to brush them away. Her eyes fluttered open, and he said, "You were having another one of your nightmares."

Kit sat up abruptly and said, "This one was different."

"In what way?" he asked.

She stared straight ahead and said, "I was in a boat…a rowboat. There was a boy facing me, and he was rowing hard." She paused and swallowed.

"Then, what happened?" Grant asked.

"I heard a shot, and the boy fell over at my feet." Kit pointed to the floor and said, "He had a hole in the back of his head, and…and…there was blood everywhere!" She pressed the back of her hand to her lips and drew in a sharp breath.

Grant put his arm around her and asked, "Did you see who shot him?"

Kit shook her head.

"Did you recognize the boy?"

Again, Kit shook her head. "No," she said, "but I'm thinking it must have been my brother, Peter."

How horrifying it must have been for a four-year-old to witness something like that, Grant thought. It was amazing Kit could even function. "It sounds awful," he said.

She sat there staring at the floor for a moment, and then said, "I'm going to the bathroom."

Grant said, "It's over there," he pointed to an opening in the wall between the fireplace and the bar.

Kit stood up and walked towards the bathroom. The old man with the pipe continued to watch Kit. He stood up and followed her. Suddenly, Grant felt the need to protect Kit more than ever. He hurried to the hallway where the rest rooms were and watched the old man go into the men's room. Grant positioned himself outside of the ladies' room.

The old man emerged from the men's room and stopped. He said something in Ojibwa to Grant.

Grant shrugged and said, "I'm sorry, I don't speak your language."

The old man placed a hand on Grant's shoulder and closed his eyes. He chanted a few words and then looked up at Grant. He dropped his hand, nodded, and walked out the front door.

Grant wondered what that was all about.

Kit emerged from the restroom.

Johnny approached them and said, "Come and eat something."

He and Kit followed Johnny to an empty table. Grant asked, "Where's Eric?"

Johnny said, "Probably checking out the trail."

Grant got the feeling that Johnny was a much more capable guide than Eric would ever be. He was certainly a lot more relaxed about his work than Eric was. "Is that really necessary?" Grant asked.

Johnny grinned and said, "Not really, but he likes to think so."

A man brought plates heaped with fried walleye to their table. A basket of bread followed, and coffee came at the end. Grant had not realized how hungry he was. He wolfed down an entire plate of fillets and several slices of bread before he finally paused. He looked over and noted that Kit was eating a large fillet sandwiched between two slices of bread.

While they were eating, Eric returned and slid into a chair beside Johnny. Eric reached for a piece of bread and said, "The creek's really high. If we don't head out soon, we're not going to be able to cross here."

Johnny said, "It's going to be a long time before the creek gets that high."

Eric scowled at him and said, "I've been out here plenty of times when we couldn't get across. We wasted hours, backtracking to another place where it was lower."

Johnny eyed him from across the table and asked, "What's your hurry?"

Eric shrugged and nodded his head in Kit's direction. "I just don't want her to have to walk any farther than she has to."

Grant noticed that the color had begun to return to Kit's face, and she looked less tired than she had when they arrived at the elders' lodge.

She said, "I can make it."

Grant admired her spunk. He knew she was exhausted, but she never complained. He said, "I can help her if she gets tired."

While they were finishing their coffee, Johnny Red Hawk looked at Kit and asked, "You have those nightmares often?"

Kit nodded.

Johnny said, "You should hang a dream catcher over your bed."

Grant had seen the dream catchers in Native American gift shops as a kid. The wooden rings held feathers and leather strips designed to catch any bad spirits that might enter a person's dreams. He said, "I have a feeling Kit's nightmares are more about memories trying to come to the surface than about bad spirits giving her unpleasant dreams."

"What kind of memories?" Johnny asked.

Grant saw Kit's cheeks redden. He knew that she hated talking about her nightmares, and he wondered how she might react. With him, it had always been a fit of anger. Today, she surprised him.

Kit looked directly at Johnny and said, "I've been dreaming all my life that someone's trying to kill me, and I'm running from them."

Johnny said, "Maybe it's not a dream about memories. Maybe it's more of a premonition of what's ahead."

Grant shuddered. Instinctively, he reached for Kit's hand. For as long as he could remember, he'd been feeling that it was his job to protect her from whatever it was she was running from.

Kit said, "Lately, I've been wondering the same thing. Somebody burned down my house and killed my parents last week."

Johnny frowned and said, "I'm sorry to hear that."

Grant added, "A woman in Moose Creek was murdered this week, and a friend of ours has disappeared. Kit thinks it all has something to do with this house we're heading for."

Johnny asked, "Are you sure you want to go on? Sounds like you're walking right into something dangerous."

Kit said, "I have to. It's the only way I can remember my past and, hopefully, make the nightmares end."

Johnny said, "I think I'd try something safer…like therapy."

Grant was surprised that a Native American who looked like a Harley biker would consider psychotherapy an option.

Kit said, "It hasn't worked."

Johnny nodded and said, "If we're taking this too fast, I don't mind slowing down for you. We could even spend the night with the elder who just gave Grant his blessing."

Eric stood up and said, "She'll be fine. Can we get going now?"

Johnny glared at Eric and said, "Here on the reservation, we learn to take life as it comes along. We're not driven by what a watch tells us to do."

"Well, I don't live on reservation time anymore," Eric said.

"If you had stayed here with the family," Johnny said, "you'd be a lot less uptight."

Grant looked from Johnny to Eric and asked, "You two are related?"

"Unfortunately," Eric said. He walked back outside.

Johnny said, "Eric is my cousin. His father died in a hunting accident when he was ten, and his mother got too sick to look after him. When she died, my family took him in, but he left the reservation when he was sixteen."

Grant said, "He's wound pretty tight."

Johnny said, "We have to be patient with him. He's had a difficult life." He looked across at Kit and said, "But I don't think it's been nearly as difficult as yours."

Kit set down her mug and said, "Thanks for understanding."

Johnny nodded and leaned back in his chair.

Kit said, "I'm ready to go when you are."

"There's no rush," Johnny said.

"I know," Kit said. "But I'd really like to get this over."

Johnny stood up and said, "Just let me know if it gets to be too much for you. We can always turn back and spend the night with the elder and his family."

Grant retrieved their jackets from where they had been hanging in front of the fire. When he slid his arms into the sleeves, they felt toasty.

Kit shrugged on her jacket and said, "Mmm, I wish I could stay inside this jacket forever."

Grant said, "It's going to get colder before it gets warmer out there. But we only have a few more hours left. I'll be right behind you."

Kit looked up at him and smiled. Then, she turned and followed Johnny out the door.

Grant realized suddenly that Kit had not told him to jump in a lake, take a hike, or drop dead. She hadn't even said that she hated him. She had merely given him that adorable smile without a word. He hoped that she was finally figuring out that she could trust him. He followed her outside into the rain, but the chill didn't bother him. His love for Kit kept him warm as they continued north.

24

HARVEY SAT DOWN ON A BOULDER AND PULLED THE MAP out of his jacket pocket. He looked down at his watch. For nearly two hours, he'd been walking towards the A-frame with the bright yellow trim. Surely, he thought, he should've come upon it by now. He unfolded the map and looked at the X he had marked on the place where he thought he had spotted the house earlier. Rain fell steadily on the map, and his fingers broke through it from the underside.

Reaching up, he pulled the red cord from around his neck that held the clear Plexiglas compass Mike had given him. The needle on the compass faced north, and he turned to align his body with it. Then, he laid the compass on the map and pointed it from where he thought he ought to be towards the X. The compass read southwest. "That makes no sense!" he muttered.

He had headed south when he left Phillip's plane. Hoping to remain hidden by the foliage, he had continued south for a while, and then turned west. He didn't want to travel too close to the water, because of the fishermen out on the lake. He definitely did not want to get himself arrested or thrown off the reservation. He had to find Kit and Grant and Eric before Jacqueline did.

Frustration at his inability to read the map correctly drove Harvey to shove it into the backpack. He noticed when he did that there was something in a plastic bag near the bottom. He pulled it out and discovered a sandwich. Feeling discouraged and more than a little hungry, he opened up the pouch and bit into it. "Mmm," he said. Corned beef on rye...his favorite. He closed his eyes and sat there chewing.

The sound of a twig snapping off to his left made him look up. Less than fifty feet away, an enormous black bear lumbered in his direction, sniffing at the air. Harvey stopped chewing. Slowly, he put the sandwich back into the bag. He leaned over and dropped it back into Mike's backpack and then rose quietly to his feet. His heart hammered in his chest as he watched the bear sniffing from side to side.

When the bear made eye contact with him, Harvey began to slowly back away. The bear continued to advance. Harvey reached back to place his hand on the grip of the handgun Fred had given him. In the next instant, he realized that the small bullets in it wouldn't even penetrate the bear's thick fur. He shoved the Glock more firmly into his waistband and continued backing up.

Suddenly, the bear showed his teeth and let out a low growl. Harvey turned his head to see which way he ought to go. Directly behind him, a wide open area covered in what appeared to be moss gave him the idea of making a run for it without having to dodge trees. He turned and sprinted. Within twenty feet, he felt the ground giving way beneath him. He realized then that what had appeared as a moss-covered meadow was actually a peat bog. He sank to his waist in muck.

He turned to look back at the bear. It halted when it came upon Mike's backpack. The bear sniffed it, and then began tearing into it with his enormous teeth. Harvey watched bits of Mike's orienteering map fluttering to the ground around the bear. Harvey shuddered from the cold and from fear. That could be his own flesh the bear was tearing apart.

He quickly side-stepped across the slimy bog until he began to feel the ground rising underfoot. He came upon knee-deep muck, and then ankle-deep water. He stepped out onto solid ground on the other side of the bog and looked back at the bear. It was tearing Mike's backpack to shreds. Harvey looked over at the dense tree growth to his right and hurried away.

After walking for a while, Harvey realized that he had no idea where he was heading. He was, however, glad to be rid of the bear. He sat down on a fallen tree to think, and the Glock pistol in his waistband poked him in the back. He pulled it out and saw that it had bits of peat stuck to it.

He hoped it would actually fire if he needed it. He wiped off the barrel on his pant leg and shoved the gun back into his waistband. He decided he'd better check his position. When he reached for the red cord around his neck, he froze. He realized then that he had been holding the compass when the bear appeared. In his hurry to get away from the menacing beast, he must have dropped it. "Judas Priest!" he muttered. "What am I going to do now?"

With a quick look in all directions, he assessed his situation. Without the compass and map, it was impossible to tell which direction to go to find the old house. He looked up. The rain and heavy cloud cover obscured the sun, so he had no way of knowing which direction was north. Then, he remembered something Mike had told him: if you're lost, check the tree trunks. The sides facing north were generally covered with moss.

Harvey leaped to his feet and circled a couple of trees. Some had moss on one side. He decided to head in the direction with the most moss. He prayed that the mossy trees would lead him back to the south shore of Upper Red Lake. If he didn't get there soon, he'd be spending the night in the woods. He certainly didn't want to do that. He had no tent, no food or water, and no way of making a fire. He'd be bear breakfast if he lay down to sleep.

Harvey felt as if he had been walking forever when he smelled smoke. He stopped and sniffed the air. Where was it coming from? He couldn't tell, so he pressed forward in the direction he had been heading. The smell grew stronger.

Suddenly, the woods gave way, and he heard rushing water. He walked a short distance and found himself standing on the edge of a roaring creek. A large building stood on the opposite side of the water. Its parking lot was full of motorcycles. He realized then that this was the large public building on the reservation that he had seen earlier from the plane. He remembered that it sat south and east from the old house on the lakeshore.

His shoulder throbbed, his legs felt like rubber, and he felt chilled to the bone. The temperature must have dropped by at least twenty degrees. He was hungry and thirsty, and he knew that he couldn't go on much farther without collapsing. Surely, it would be better to cross the creek and tell the Native Americans there that he had gotten lost in the woods. He doubted that they would arrest him or escort him off their land, given the way he must look. Risking the wrath of the Ojibwa people was far safer than dying from exposure in the woods.

He edged closer to the creek and wondered how cold the water might be. In the next instant, he heard a shout. He froze and looked across at the building. A door burst open. Four bikers wearing jeans and lot of black leather appeared. About a dozen men with dark hair and flannel shirts tumbled out of the building, throwing punches at the bikers. Shouting ensued, followed by more fists flying.

As this was going on, two of the flannel-shirted men rushed over to some motorcycles parked beside the building. They pushed them all together and tipped them over in a heap. One of the men ran back to the building and came back with something red in his hand. The smell of gasoline floated on the breeze towards Harvey. The gasoline-toting man shouted something at the swarm of others, and they all rushed back towards the building. In the next instant, the heap of motorcycles erupted into a ball of flames.

One of the motorcyclists broke free from the others and ran towards the pile of burning bikes. Another man pulled him away from the inferno. Harvey felt stunned as he watched a pick-up truck careen to a stop out front. The motorcyclists in their black leather jackets and vests were corralled into the back of the truck by some men who were obviously Native Americans. As the bikes burned, the truck with the Harley riders roared away.

A man in a yellow flannel shirt stood at the open doorway of the building. He swayed slightly, and Harvey thought that he looked like Doc Daggert from a distance. He immediately dismissed the idea. The man was more likely a drunken tavern customer than the old dentist.

Harvey stepped back away from the creek and decided that dying in the woods might be preferable to incurring the wrath of the reservation dwellers. He hurried back to the cover of the trees and stood there, thinking hard. Based on his view of the Native Americans' building earlier, he was pretty certain that if he walked northwest, he would come to the old house on the south shore. He prayed that he had what it took to find the house and the others before Jacqueline did.

25

IT WAS LATE AFTERNOON ON TUESDAY WHEN OONA SAT down at her dining room table with Sophie. She took a sip of the strong coffee she had just made them and said, "Let's take a look at everything you've got so far. I want to have all the facts straight in my head before that investigator from the BCA gets here."

"I'm amazed at how quickly the BCA moved on this," Sophie said. She pulled out the copies of the photos and papers she had given Gordon Finch in the Case Review Office that morning.

"I just hope Fred and Harvey show up here soon with Kit and Grant," Oona said. She glanced at her watch. "They should've been back by now."

Sophie spread the photos out on the table and said, "I still can't get over the fact that Jacqueline Corbett is Annabelle Vernon. How did she fool everybody in Moose Creek all those years?"

"She lost a ton of weight," Oona said. "And it looks as if she had a lot of plastic surgery."

"I guess she had some pretty good acting lessons, too," Sophie put in.

While they were sitting there, Benny walked in from the kitchen and asked, "You hungry?"

Oona pushed back her chair and said, "I'll get you something to eat."

Benny backed up to let her pass by. He asked, "Today raspberry doughnut day?"

Poor Benny, thought Oona. He'd lost everything that was familiar to him. The least she could do was to find him a raspberry doughnut. She opened a large white box that Sophie had brought over from the bakery that morning. It was full of day-old pastries from Monday's party. Oona paused with her hand raised above the box and wondered if their little town's bakery would ever open again. With a kitchen knife, she cut into several doughnuts. When raspberry filling oozed up out of one, she put it on a plate and handed it to Benny. "Here you go, Benny. A raspberry doughnut just for you."

Benny bit into the doughnut. Then, he surprised Oona by patting her on the head. He rarely showed anyone affection. On an impulse, she slipped her arms around his waist and gave him a quick squeeze. Benny just stood there, sucking the filling out of his raspberry doughnut. Oona knew then that Benny was suffering just as much of the rest of them were. He had rarely allowed anyone to get that close to him.

Oona walked back into the dining room and sat down. "Does anything new jump out at you?" she asked Sophie.

Sophie shook her head. "We know that Jacqueline is Annabelle. And we have a pretty good idea that she killed Wildred before shooting Harvey. What we don't know is how any of this ties into the Lakeshore Inn fire, what has happened to Doc Daggert, or how Ron Frank was involved."

Benny suddenly appeared at Oona's elbow and leaned over to pick up a picture of Jacqueline Corbett.

"Put that back!" Sophie said in a sharp tone.

Oona held up a finger at Sophie and turned to Benny to ask, "What do you think about Jacqueline Corbett, Benny?"

Benny said, "If you can't say something nice about someone, don't say anything at all." He shook his head from side to side and began swaying.

Benny's comment reminded Oona that Wildred had always encouraged him to say only kind things about others. She wondered if questioning him about the pictures on the table would reveal anything new. She took the photo of Jacqueline from Benny's grip and held up a picture of Fred. She asked him, "What do you think about Fred?"

"He smells like sugar," Benny said.

Oona looked over at Sophie, who broke into a smile. Sophie said, "It's funny what Benny notices."

Oona raised an eyebrow and said, "Yes, it is. Now, watch this." She held up a picture of Ron Frank and said, "Benny, what do you think about our police chief?"

Benny shook his head from side to side and said, "If you can't say something nice about someone, don't say anything at all."

Oona realized that Benny might just be the best person in Moose Creek to assess the situation. No one had ever expected him to be smart enough to understand what they were talking about. Perhaps he had heard or seen something over the years that might give them some answers. She looked over at Sophie and said, "You pick one for him."

Sophie picked up a photo of Harvey and asked, "What can you tell me about Harvey?"

"He likes Jacqueline," Benny said. He licked the raspberry filling off his fingers and asked Sophie, "You hungry?"

Sophie said to Oona, "I'll get him another doughnut."

While she was in the kitchen, Oona said to Benny, "Now, tell me something about the mayor."

Benny said, "He likes raspberry doughnuts, just like me."

Sophie returned and handed Benny another raspberry doughnut.

One by one, Oona held up photos of the townspeople involved in the case, and Benny gave them some tidbit of trivia about each one. So far, he had only refused to talk about Jacqueline Corbett and Ron Frank. Oona came to the last picture—the one of Eric Larsen—and asked, "What do you know about Eric Larsen?"

Benny walked away and said, "If you can't say something nice about somebody, don't say anything."

Oona's eyes met Sophie's.

Sophie whispered, "I think Eric's been involved from the beginning."

Oona shook her head and said, "It doesn't make any sense. Of all the people in Moose Creek, he's the last guy I'd suspect of hurting people."

Sophie said, "You know, criminals don't all fit the same profile...just like Jacqueline."

"Yeah," Oona said. "Who would've guessed that she'd be running around shooting people?"

"And impaling them with fishing lures?" Sophie added.

The front door burst open, and Fred stepped into the living room, along with a blast of cold air.

Relief flooded through every cell of Oona's body. She ran to the front door and looked out at the driveway. There was no movement around the Swenson's Bakery van, and she turned to Fred to ask, "Where are they?"

Sophie hurried to Fred's side and asked, "Why didn't you bring them back?"

Fred walked over to the sofa and sat down. The two women sat on either side of him. He said, "Phillip picked Harvey up with his float plane at about 8:30 this morning. He was supposed to stay with Harvey until he found the rest of them, and then bring them all back together."

"What happened?" Oona asked. She held her breath, afraid of the answer that was coming.

Fred said, "Phillip came back within half an hour to tell me that he'd dropped Harvey off by himself."

Oona wanted to punch somebody. Why had Harvey done something so foolish? He and the pilot were supposed to stay together. "Why did he do that?" she demanded.

Fred said, "Phillip told me that the Vernon's old lake house wasn't on public land. It was just inside the reservation boundary."

Oona asked, "And Harvey just walked from the public land onto Native American land without permission?"

"Apparently," Fred said.

"Why didn't Phillip take him straight to the house?" Sophie asked.

"He could lose his license and his plane," Fred said. "Worse, he could do jail time."

"So could Harvey," Oona said with a groan.

Fred said, "Phillip went back after four hours to pick them all up, but Harvey never came back to the shoreline. Phillip said he circled overhead for quite a while, but he never saw any sign of them."

Oona's heart sank. She looked up at Fred and said, "We're pretty sure Eric's involved, too."

Fred's face paled. He said, "If that's the case, he could be leading them all straight to Jacqueline."

"That's what we figured," Sophie said.

Fred asked, "Has anyone seen or heard from Jacqueline?"

Oona said, "No."

"What about Ron Frank?" Fred asked. "Has anyone questioned him yet?"

"Not yet," Sophie said. "The last I saw of him, he was sitting out in front of the bakery, chatting up one of the girls from the sheriff's office."

Oona shook her head. If Ron Frank had ever done his job properly, she felt that none of this would have happened. She decided that when this was all over, she was going to see to it that he never held office as a law enforcer again. She asked Sophie, "What do you think we should do now?"

Sophie stood and said, "I'm going to call Gordon Finch. They need to get the reservation council or the FBI to send a Search and Rescue team out right away."

Fred said, "I'll get Phillip on the phone when you're done. He can take the Search and Rescue guys right to the old lake house."

While Sophie made the call, Oona prayed that all of their efforts would not be pointless. She asked God to send help before Jacqueline or Eric hurt Harvey, Kit, and Grant.

26

KIT TRUDGED THROUGH THE HEAVILY WOODED RESERVATION, following close on the heels of Eric Larsen, who had taken the lead after lunch. They had been moving much faster than they had before lunch, and Kit began to feel as if she would drop.

The sound of the rain dripping through the leaves became magnified in her ears. The trees ahead of her blurred, and she saw the ground suddenly slanting up towards her head. She lurched sideways and stumbled onto the trail.

"Wait up!" she heard Grant calling to Eric.

Kit lay there with her cheek resting on the damp ground. It smelled of mold and pine needles. She felt Grant's warm hand on her forehead. His voice sounded far away when he asked, "Are you okay?"

Kit tried to lift her head, but she felt too weak. Instead, she closed her eyes and began drifting to the darkness that was slowly enveloping her.

"Kit!" came Grant's voice from a great distance. "You can't go to sleep now."

Then she heard Johnny Red Hawk saying something that she couldn't understand. His voice was low and soothing, like the darkness.

Eric's voice came to her clearly when he said, "I'm going on ahead to check out the creek. Get her moving as soon as you can, and I'll meet you at the crossing point."

Kit felt herself being lifted up in strong arms. And then, something smooth and warm enveloped her, and she embraced it as she drifted into the dark.

When Kit woke up, the bone-chilling cold was gone. She felt as if her body had been wrapped in warm cotton. Where was she? She opened her eyes to find Grant's face just inches from hers.

He asked, "You feeling warmer now?"

She nodded and tried to move, but her arms were held fast to her sides. "Why can't I move?" she asked.

Grant said, "Because we're zipped together into a sleeping bag like a couple of sardines in a tin can."

Kit looked up. The men must have set up the tent to protect her from the rain. "Are we going to stay here all night?"

"Not if you can make it just a little bit farther," he said. "We're just a short distance from the creek. Once we cross it, the house is on the other side."

She listened for the other men's voices, but she only heard the rain pattering gently on the top of the tent. "Where are Eric and Johnny?"

"After you fell, Eric went ahead to check out the creek," Grant said. "Johnny stayed here to help me set up the tent and get you situated. Then he went off to bring Eric back."

"I'm sorry I've been so much trouble," Kit said.

"You've been stronger than any other woman I've ever met," he said. "I'm glad you keeled over so I could rest."

She smiled at him and tried to stretch a little. That's when she realized what felt so warm and smooth. She felt Grant's skin against her legs, her belly, and her arms. She stiffened and said, "Hey! Where are our clothes?"

Grant said, "Johnny put them in his pack with the rest of our wet clothes from yesterday. He stuffed some dry things down in the sleeping bag before we put you in here."

Kit closed her eyes and said, "Please tell me we're at least wearing underwear."

"Unfortunately," Grant said. "And mine are still damp."

Kit breathed deeply and told herself to relax. Over the past few days, she had begun to realize that the anger she directed at Grant had been like a shield that she held up. She had to admit that she had always been more terrified of him than she had been annoyed by his pranks. But why? She knew now that Grant would never do anything to hurt her. Her reactions to him just didn't make sense anymore.

That's when Kit realized that this was the opportunity she had been hoping for all morning. They were alone, it was quiet, and it was the perfect time to tell Grant that she was sorry about the way she had always treated him. She said, "Grant?"

"Yeah?" he asked. He looked into her eyes.

"I'm sorry about the way I've been acting."

He smiled at her and said, "It's been a rough couple of days."

"I'm not just talking about this trip. I'm sorry for the way I've treated you…well…since I met you."

She looked into Grant's eyes then, and she could see the depth of the love he had for her.

He said, "I forgive you. I'm sorry life's been so hard on you."

She held his gaze, and her heart began thumping wildly.

He leaned over her then, and she could feel his warm breath on her lips.

She felt as if she were floating for a moment, and all of the noises of the forest went silent. She closed her eyes and whispered, "Grant Osgood…I—"

A gunshot exploded nearby. A flock of birds beat furiously at the air overhead and squawked as they flew skyward. Kit's heart leaped into her throat. She began thrashing from side to side and screamed, "Let me out! Let me out!"

Quickly, Grant unzipped the sleeping bag. He said, "Take it easy!"

"Someone just got shot!" Kit hissed. She grabbed a long-sleeve t-shirt from the bottom of the sleeping bag and yanked it over her bra.

"We don't know that," Grant said. "It could be a hunter."

She shoved her legs into the dry hiking pants and said, "It could be whoever killed Wildred and that fisherman."

Grant began pulling on his dry clothes as fast as he could. When he had finished tying up his boots, he said, "Wait here."

"No!" Kit said. "We're staying together."

Grant said, "I really think I should go up the trail and see if I can find Eric and Johnny."

"I'm not staying here by myself," Kit whispered. "I'd be like a sitting duck in this bright yellow tent."

Grant said, "Okay, we'll go together."

Cautiously, Grant unzipped the tent. Kit peered out, but it didn't look as if the other two men were anywhere near. Grant headed up the trail they had been following, and Kit held tightly to his hand. Suddenly, Grant froze.

"What's the matter?" Kit whispered.

Grant hurried forward and bent down. Kit followed him. There, on the side of the trail, lay Johnny Red Hawk on his back. He stared skyward with his mouth in a startled O. Grant laid two fingers on the side of Johnny's neck and said in a low tone, "He's dead."

Kit gasped and put trembling fingers to her lips. Her eyes misted over with tears. She hadn't known Johnny for more than a couple of days, but she could tell that he had a sweet spirit. How many more people would have to die before this ended? A powerful fury began to well up from deep within her. She straightened up and said through clenched teeth, "We've got to stop whoever is doing this."

Grant stood up and started to say something, but in the next instant, he put his index finger to his lips. Quickly, he pulled her off the trail. In the next instant, she was hip-deep in the icy water of a peat bog.

Grant pulled her down beside him until she was neck-deep in mucky water. He whispered, "Silence." Slowly, he pulled a broken pine bough over their heads so that they were obscured from anyone's view who might be walking on the trail.

Kit huddled beside Grant, trusting that he knew what was best when a killer was loose. She just wished it didn't involve getting soaking wet again. And she really wished it weren't in plain sight of Johnny's body up there on the trail.

In the next instant, she heard someone approaching. From beneath the pine bough, she watched boots passing by. The boots stopped beside Johnny Red Hawk's body. A hand reached into Johnny's jacket pocket and withdrew the roll of money that Eric had given him. Then she heard a voice say, "Last time I'll have to pay you."

When Kit recognized that the voice belonged to Eric Larsen, she drew in a sharp breath. Had Eric killed Johnny, or was he simply glad that someone else had?

Grant drew his arm tighter around her, and his eyes met hers. For the first time in her life, she saw a look that made her blood run cold. The twinkling was gone, and in its place had come a look of such sheer determination to survive that she realized how grave the situation had become.

Eric's brown leather hiking boots moved back down the path towards the tent she and Grant had been lying in just moments before. From the distance, they heard Eric shout, "Kit! Grant!"

Kit listened to the slow, steady rhythm of Grant's breath near her ear. Her entire body was quivering, and she was glad for the strength of Grant's arm around her. It made her feel safe, in spite of the fact that they were within firing distance of a killer with a gun.

Eric tramped back past them and then returned to the campsite. Again, he shouted, "Kit! Grant! Johnny's waiting for us at the creek. We've got to go now before the water gets too high to cross."

Kit knew that she and Grant would be Eric's next victims if he found them. Her teeth began to chatter uncontrollably, and Grant reached up slowly to place his thumb between her teeth. She hoped it wasn't hurting him, but she could not seem to stop the rattling of her jaws.

At last, Eric hurried away in the direction of the creek. She breathed deeply and counted to one hundred, two hundred....

After a while, Grant removed his thumb and whispered, "I think we should go back the way we came."

Kit asked, "How will we find our way without a guide?"

"Good point," Grant said.

Kit said, "The old house isn't far from here. We could try to find it."

Grant said, "I don't want you to get hurt in the process. You go back to the tent, and I'll go on ahead. As soon as I find it, I'll follow the south shore of the lake. Somewhere out here, there's got to be some other people who can help us."

"You want me to sit there, waiting for Eric to come back for me?"

"He's given up on us," Grant said.

"No," Kit said firmly. "We go together, or not at all."

"Kit," Grant urged, "be reasonable. You could get shot out there."

Kit didn't like the idea of getting shot, but she really hated the idea of Grant's getting shot and leaving her all alone. "So could you," she said.

Grant squeezed her tighter. "Okay," he said. "We go together. But stay behind me, and keep your head low."

Together, they crawled out of the slimy water and followed Eric's boot prints up the trail. No matter what, Kit became determined to find that old house and get to the truth about what had happened to her as a child. With each quiet step, she grew more and more certain that the old house held the answers. She told herself, *Slow and sure...slow and sure...slow and sure.*

27

AS HARVEY CONTINUED NORTHWEST TOWARDS THE OLD house, he heard a gunshot south of him. He rolled under a dense canopy of ferns growing low to the ground and waited with his pistol drawn. Five minutes…then ten…maybe twenty. Rain dripped off the leaves and onto his face. Every muscle in his body was tensed in preparation for a conflict. He thought about the countless hours he had spent in tree stands, waiting for a deer to amble underneath him. Today, he was hunting a killer. He figured he could wait as long as it took for Jacqueline to wander past.

Finally, a movement to his left caught his attention. He squinted through the dense leaves and saw a figure advancing up the trail towards him. It was hard to make out who it was in the fog. But from the height, he guessed it was a man. He was obviously alone. Harvey breathed evenly and waited.

The man drew closer, and Harvey saw that it was Eric Larsen. His first instinct was to leap from his cover and throw his arms around the man who was the best adventure guide in northern Minnesota. But the gun in Eric's right hand stopped Harvey. Had Eric fired the gun?

He watched Eric hurry northwest, exactly in the direction Harvey had been moving before he heard the shot. Harvey waited a few minutes, considering his options. He was about to get up and follow Eric when he heard another sound. He hunkered back down and looked at the trail where Eric had just emerged. There, he saw Grant and Kit making their way alongside the trail. From time to time, they hurried forward a few steps, and then stepped back in the cover of the brush.

Harvey realized that something wasn't adding up. Eric didn't seem to be leading Kit and Grant…they seemed to be tracking Eric. What was going on? Harvey decided it would be best to just follow all three of them from a distance.

28

KIT GRIPPED GRANT'S HAND TIGHTLY. AFTER A SHORT TIME, the dimly lit forest grew lighter. She glanced up and wondered if the rain was letting up. Then, she realized that the light was growing brighter, because they were nearing a clearing.

Eric side-stepped across a fallen log to cross the creek, and Kit and Grant followed him from a distance. Across the clearing, Eric hurried, and they followed after him, keeping close to the underbrush around the fringes of the woods.

At last, the trees gave way altogether, and the little house with the yellow trim loomed on a small peninsula that jutted out into the lake. Kit could have cried with relief. And at the same time, she was filled with dread. There, at the front door, stood a beautiful woman with long, dark hair. She recognized Jacqueline Corbett, the realtor from Moose Creek. What was she doing at the old house? When Eric approached the A-frame, Jacqueline pulled him inside and closed the door behind them.

Kit and Grant crept closer to the house. Kit whispered, "Maybe if we could hear them talking, we could figure out what this house has to do with my nightmares."

Grant nodded and looked at the house. He said, "The windows have all been boarded up."

It was impossible to see or hear anything from where they crouched near the edge of the woods. They would obviously have to get a lot closer.

That's when Kit spotted the small wooden door in the stone foundation. She pointed at it and asked, "Do you think we could get under the house if we went in that door?"

"Maybe," Grant said, "if it's unlocked."

They scurried across the clearing, and Grant yanked on the handle of the small wooden door in the stone foundation. With another quick jerk, he opened it. A musty smell emanated from under the house.

Kit was scared of dank, dark places. Grant thrust his legs into the opening and eased his broad shoulders through. Reluctantly, Kit crawled in after him. Grant carefully closed the small door behind them. Kit sat there blinking in the murky darkness.

When her eyes had adjusted to the dark, Kit realized that a shaft of light shone through a crack in the crawl space door. She could make out the pipes running along the underside of the house, as well as the foundation of a brick fireplace. A noise overhead made her look up. A procession of mice coming in through a small hole beside the door made their way along the upper edge of one of the I-beams. A second procession was heading back towards the hole in the door, scurrying along the lower lip of the beam. Kit shuddered. She hated mice.

Kit sat there listening, and she heard voices coming from the opposite end of the house. On their hands and knees, she and Grant crawled over sharp gravel. Kit tried to avoid bumping into a lot of old junk that had been stored in the dank space. They stopped in the middle of the house, beside the fireplace foundation. There, the voices grew louder. They paused and listened. It was easy to hear what they were saying, because Jacqueline and Eric were shouting at each other.

Kit heard Jacqueline saying, "I should have gone after them myself."

Eric said, "You couldn't control yourself long enough to get them up here before shooting at them."

Kit shuddered. Jacqueline planned to shoot at them? Why?

"Are you saying I have no self-control?" she snapped.

Eric said, "You've never had any self-control. If you did, you wouldn't let that fat old pig drool all over you the way he does."

Jacqueline shouted, "If it weren't for Ron, we would have spent the last twenty-four years in jail."

Eric said, "If it weren't for Ron blackmailing us for the past twenty-four years, we'd have a lot more money."

Jacqueline said, "I don't care about the money. As long as he keeps covering for us, I'll keep on paying him."

Kit wondered what they had done to warrant such a long jail sentence. And what was Ron covering up?

Their voices dropped. Kit strained her ears to hear them. She leaned against the fireplace, and a hunter's bow clattered onto the gravel. Kit held her breath. She listened hard.

"Did you hear that?" Jacqueline asked Eric.

"Hear what?" Eric asked.

"Something in the crawl space," she said.

Eric said, "Probably a rat in one of the traps."

Kit looked over at Grant. When the two upstairs began talking again, Kit sat motionless. Grant took her hand and held it tightly.

Eric was saying, "You think that paying off that state trooper kept Peter's skull and Doc's x-rays off the radar?"

"Of course," Jacqueline said. "They're all greedy bastards. Pay off the cops, and they'll do anything."

Eric said, "I hate to break it to you, but not every cop is as greedy or as stupid as Ron Frank. Sophie Ianelli's been snooping around for days, right under Ron's nose."

Jacqueline said, "She's an amateur."

Eric said, "Oona's been helping her."

Jacqueline laughed. "Like that's supposed to worry me!"

Eric said, "We've gotten sloppy. I had a chance to kill Oona that night at the school, and I blew it. Stealing her purse and trying to kill her with that truck was just stupid."

Kit felt stunned by what she was hearing.

"We'll deal with her after we kill Catherine and her boyfriend."

Kit's heart lurched, and her mouth went dry.

Eric yelled at Jacqueline, "Are you crazy? You already went too far when you pressured me into killing Wildred. I should never have shot Johnny, either. The reservation cops are going to be after us for sure."

Kit flinched. Eric had killed Wildred Swenson? And he had tried to kill Oona and Harvey with the delivery truck? Her head was swimming.

Jacqueline said, "Ron's got the sheriff thinking the Fishing Lure Killer did in Wildred. And everyone thinks you took the governor fishing. We're covered."

"And what about Harvey Trent?" Eric countered. "You think he won't talk?"

"He's dead," Jacqueline said. "I saw his boat crash and burn after I shot him."

Kit gasped. Jacqueline had killed Harvey, too? Grant squeezed her hand. She looked up at him. He tapped her lips gently with his index finger.

Eric said. "Harvey didn't die. Mike Ianelli told me that Oona took him to the hospital. When Harvey gets out, you can be sure he'll blow off his mouth to anybody who'll listen."

Jacqueline let fly with a string of curses.

Kit breathed a sigh of relief. Harvey was still alive.

Eric said, "You're not making the situation any better for either of us now by trying to bump off everybody who knows something about what happened."

Something shattered overhead, and Jacqueline screamed, "If people would just mind their own business, none of them would be dead!"

"Things don't add up in their minds," Eric said. "Of course, they snoop around when things look a little off. I told you it would come to this someday."

Kit understood now why Wildred was dead. Without realizing it, she had been stirring up evidence about what had happened the night the Lakeshore Inn burned down. But what she hadn't understood was how Jacqueline and Eric were connected to it all.

Jacqueline said, "We're never going to get caught. Ron will cover for us."

Eric shouted at her, "You can't keep them all quiet! If you had just gone to the cops back then to tell them your dad was molesting you and your sister, you could have all gone to a foster home or something."

Kit's mind was reeling. Jacqueline's father had molested her?

"Foster home?" Jacqueline scoffed. "What kid doesn't get molested that way?"

"It would have been better than killing them," Eric shouted.

"My own mother wouldn't believe me!" Jacqueline shouted back at him.

Eric yelled, "Trying to kill them all was a dumb idea! You can't stop everyone who knows."

Jacqueline shrieked, "I stopped Peter when he threatened to tell Wildred about what Dad was doing to us. I'll stop Catherine, too."

Kit's heart thudded in her chest. In that instant, she knew how Jacqueline was connected to her family. This deranged killer was no stranger.

She was her older sister, Annabelle. Kit held her breath, trying to make out every word.

"And what about Catherine's boyfriend?" Eric asked, "Are you going to kill him, too?"

"Yes!" Jacqueline shrieked. "I'll kill every last one of them if I have to, including Benny."

Kit swallowed hard and gripped Grant's hand more tightly.

"It's too late," Eric shouted. "Don't you see? We need to make a break for it before we get caught!"

"Coward!" shouted Jacqueline. "If you can't kill them, I will."

Something clattered overhead, and Kit heard Eric saying, "You'll never find them out there. I know exactly where they are."

"Then get back out there and bring them to me," Jacqueline growled.

Eric said, "If they show up here, don't try shooting at Catherine like you did the last time. If you hadn't missed, none of this would have happened."

Kit gulped. Now, all of her nightmares and flashbacks made sense. Her own sister had fired a shot at her and missed. She had run for her life the night the Lakeshore Inn burned down. All this time, she had been running from her own family…from a father who molested his children, a mother who refused to believe the truth, and a crazed sister who wanted to kill them all. She shuddered.

The voices grew still, and Kit heard heavy footsteps crossing the floor upstairs. A door banged shut, and then all she could hear was the rustling of the mice along the pipes.

"Do you think they're gone?" Kit whispered.

"I don't know," Grant whispered. "Let's sit tight for a couple of minutes to make sure."

Kit held tightly to Grant's hand.

He whispered, "If I hadn't heard all of that myself, I never would have believed it."

Kit asked, "Do you think Eric's the one who burned my house?"

"Maybe," Grant whispered. "How do you feel about all that you know now?"

Kit sat there thinking and finally whispered, "Relieved and sad, all mixed in together."

Grant whispered, "I'm glad you've got some answers about your flashbacks, but we've got to get out of here."

Kit nodded.

"Are you okay?" he asked.

Was she? Kit sat there thinking about how her entire life had been destroyed by the terrible things that her birth family had done to her. She was sick of running scared, and she wasn't going to do it anymore. Now that she knew the truth, she realized that she was not crazy. She also knew that it was time to put an end to the killing. "I'm fine," she said. "Let's get out of here."

The two of them scrambled back to the little crawlspace door and opened it. Kit blinked when the bright light hit her eyes. After a moment, she shoved herself back out through the tiny opening and waited for Grant to emerge.

From behind her, a voice said, "Well, well, well. Those rat traps I put in that crawl space seem to be working."

Kit whirled around to find herself face to face with Jacqueline Corbett, who was really her older sister, Annabelle. Now that Kit knew the truth about what had happened the night the Lakeshore Inn burned down, there was no way she was going to let Jacqueline or Eric kill another human being. She would stop them and go back to town to tell everyone the real story. But first, she had to survive long enough to tell it.

29

MOOSE CREEK WAS CRAWLING WITH BCA AGENTS. OONA watched late Tuesday afternoon from her front window as agents fanned out from Swenson's Bakery to City Hall. A uniformed BCA agent led Ron Frank away from the bakery in handcuffs. Fred climbed into the back of an unmarked car with an agent, and an entire string of black FBI Suburbans roared out of town towards Heron Lake.

Oona presumed they would find poor Jet on Doc's back porch and the mess inside Doc's house. What was still unclear to her was how Doc might be involved. He still had not shown up. And no one knew whether or not the Fishing Lure Killer had anything to do with Doc's disappearance.

The doorbell interrupted Oona's thoughts, and she went to open the front door.

Ralph Rivers stood on the porch with a brown paper bag full of groceries in his sinewy arms. He said, "I brought you a few things for dinner."

Oona was dumbstruck by his kind gesture. She held open the screen door and said, "Thanks so much. Come on in."

Ralph followed her into the kitchen and set the bag on the counter. She began removing the food from it.

Ralph said, "I think I figured out who the Fishing Lure Killer is."

Oona froze with a loaf of bread in her hand. "How?"

Ralph said, "I made a mark on all the lures we had at Paul Bunyan's.

After the store closed at night, I watched the videos that we had of the registers. I showed one of them from last week to a guy from the BCA. He said it looks like it was a fisherman who came through the store all right. They found the marks on the lure that the dead guy was wearing in his lip."

"I can't believe it," Oona said. She really looked at Ralph for the first time. Underneath all that long grey hair and hippie headband was a brilliant mind. She smiled at him and asked, "You want to stay for dinner?"

Ralph looked at her with those far-away blue eyes and said, "Only if I can cook it. You've been through enough lately."

Oona thought that there was more to Ralph than anyone could have imagined. "I'd love that," she said.

From the living room, Oona could hear a newscaster on the TV set announcing, "In a bizarre twist of events, a fire that occurred at the Lakeshore Inn on Heron Lake twenty-four years ago has led to a string of murders in the little town of Moose Creek. A tip-off from a rookie state trooper in St. Paul about evidence that had been covered up by both state and local police sent the BCA…"

So, some young cop at the state police station had done the right thing and turned in the Sergeant. Oona was glad. She walked into the living room just as an image of the Lakeshore Inn flashed onto the screen. The building was engulfed in flames. Benny sat on the sofa, staring at the set with his mouth gaping open. She picked up the remote and turned off the TV. She asked Benny, "You hungry?"

Benny shook his head.

Oona sat down next to him, and Benny laid his head in her lap. He reached up to take her hand, and great sobs racked his enormous frame. She brushed away his tears and said, "Shhh. Everything's going to be okay now. I promise."

30

HARVEY HAD WATCHED ERIC EMERGE FROM THE OLD HOUSE and hurry back down the trail. Why weren't Kit and Grant with him? Where was Eric headed?

Like a three-legged dog, Harvey crawled through the dripping underbrush until he had a better view of the side of the house. Through the light fog, he could see Jacqueline Corbett standing with her back to him. She had Kit in a choke hold. Grant was nowhere in sight.

In that instant, Harvey knew that somebody besides Ron Frank had to take the law into his own hands. And he figured that he was just the guy to do it. He rolled out from under the brush and stood up along the edge of the woods. All he had to do was walk up behind Jacqueline and put Fred's pistol to her head. He watched Jacqueline dragging Kit towards the back of the house. He hurried silently after them, being careful not to step on the flagstone walkway that ran beside the building. He passed an open door that led to the underside of the house. Jacqueline and Kit disappeared behind the house.

With the next step, something hit him hard in the back of the knees. Harvey slammed to the ground. He lost his grip on the Glock, and it clattered against the flagstone walkway. He rolled onto his back.

Eric Larsen stood over him and took aim at Harvey's head with his pistol. He said, "You and Oona should've let sleeping dogs lie."

Harvey couldn't believe that Eric was involved. Harvey said in a rush, "You don't want to do this."

Eric opened his mouth to respond. Suddenly, the outdoorsman's body jerked, and his eyes grew wide. In the next instant, he toppled over onto the ground beside Harvey.

Harvey looked down to discover a hunter's arrow imbedded in Eric's back. He shoved Eric's body aside and stood up. He caught sight of Grant Osgood disappearing into the foundation of the house through the small door.

Harvey jumped to his feet. He turned around and bent down to pry Eric's gun from his fingers. A second later, Harvey felt something hard pressing into the back of his neck.

"Drop the gun," Jacqueline said, "or I'll blow your head off."

Harvey dropped Eric's gun and slowly raised his good arm over his head.

"Now turn around slowly," Jacqueline said.

Harvey slowly turned. He was surprised to find himself staring down the barrel of Fred's Glock.

Jacqueline said, "You should have learned long ago to mind your own business."

Harvey glanced around quickly to assess the situation. Jacqueline had a firm hold on Kit's hair with one hand. She pointed the gun at Harvey's forehead with the other one. Grant was nowhere in sight.

Jacqueline pressed her index finger tightly against the Glock's trigger.

Harvey had to say something to deter Jacqueline. He said, "Maybe now would be a good time to talk about a deal with North Shore Development."

Kit jabbed Jacqueline hard in the ribs.

Jacqueline yanked Kit around in front of her and put the gun to Kit's temple. She said, "You missed your chance."

"No!" Grant roared.

Harvey looked up just in time to see Grant charge around the back of the house. He was holding a boat paddle over his head with both hands. He hurtled towards Jacqueline.

Jacqueline whirled around and fired a shot at Grant.

The bullet splintered the end off of the paddle. Grant rolled across the ground.

Jacqueline fired two more shots in Grant's direction.

Grant tumbled over the tall grass and came to rest beside the back porch.

Kit screamed and pummeled Jacqueline with her fists.

Jacqueline swung the barrel of Fred's pistol at Kit. The butt of the gun caught Kit under the jaw. Kit dropped to her knees.

Harvey lunged for Eric's gun. He stood and aimed it at Jacqueline's head. "Give it up!" he shouted.

In the next instant, Jacqueline bent down and hauled Kit roughly up off the ground. She held Kit in front of her and said to Harvey, "Go ahead, pull the trigger."

Harvey looked across at Grant, who still lay motionless on the ground. There was nothing else he could do as long as Jacqueline was using Kit as a human shield. He lowered Eric's pistol.

Kit's eyes looked wild, and she sobbed, "Grant!"

"Shut up!" Jacqueline told her. She yanked backward on Kit's hair.

Kit clawed at Jacqueline's arm.

Jacqueline yanked harder on Kit's hair.

"Let me go!" Kit screamed.

Jacqueline backed across the grassy, overgrown lawn, dragging Kit with her.

Harvey had to do something. He turned and ran across the side lawn towards the tree line. A bullet whizzed past his head. When he reached a stand of trees, he turned and raised the gun in Jacqueline's direction.

Jacqueline continued backing down the long dock towards a boat that was tied at the end.

Harvey tried to aim at Jacqueline's chest, but he couldn't get a clear shot at her without hitting Kit.

Suddenly, Kit stomped on Jacqueline's instep. Then, she jabbed Jacqueline hard in the ribs. Kit slammed Jacqueline in the face with the back of her head. Jacqueline fell backwards, and the Glock clattered onto the dock.

Kit kicked the Glock into the water and turned to run.

Jacqueline rolled over, leaped to her feet, and dove at Kit. She caught Kit's ankle, and Kit's head slammed down hard on the dock.

Harvey could see that Kit was no longer moving.

Rage propelled Harvey forward.

Jacqueline sat up.

Harvey swiftly spanned the space between them. He halted in front of Jacqueline. Standing over her with his chest heaving, he pointed Eric's gun at her head and said, "Your time's up, Jacqueline."

Jacqueline stared at him.

Harvey pulled the trigger. The gun merely clicked.

Jacqueline blinked.

Harvey fired again. Nothing, but another click.

Jacqueline smiled.

Harvey realized he was out of bullets.

With a roar, Jacqueline lunged at Harvey's knees.

They tumbled onto the dock. The two of them careened over the side, and into the water.

Harvey tried to pin Jacqueline's arms to her sides, but she put a vice grip on his chest with her thighs. He was surprised by how strong she was as she squeezed the breath out of him. The water closed over his head.

Jacqueline lunged forward and bit him in his wounded shoulder.

Pain seared through Harvey's entire body. Air bubbles erupted from his mouth.

Jacqueline continued squeezing Harvey's chest with her powerful legs. At the same time, she shoved his head farther underwater and held him there.

Harvey reached up with his good arm and squeezed Jacqueline's neck with every ounce of strength he had left. He felt his energy draining. His body sagged onto the sandy bottom. In that moment, he realized that his time was up. What a way to go, he thought.

31

KIT OPENED HER EYES AND LOOKED AROUND. GRANT STILL lay motionless on the grass near the house. A noise from the water beside the dock drew her attention. She stood in time to see Jacqueline forcing Harvey's head underwater.

In that instant, the sun broke through the clouds and shone on something shiny on the sandy lake bottom. Without hesitation, she leaped into the water and snatched up the gun.

Shoving the gun into Jacqueline's midsection, Kit shouted, "No more!"

Jacqueline turned to look at her.

Kit pulled the trigger, and Jacqueline's eyes flew wide open.

Jacqueline slowly released her grip on Harvey. Her eyes closed, and she slumped forward in the water.

Kit put her arms around Harvey's waist and lifted his head above the water.

He coughed, and then gasped.

Kit looked down at Jacqueline's body, floating face-down in an ever-widening pool of pink-tinged water.

She hauled Harvey up onto the dock and fell over beside him. She closed her eyes, and in the distance, she heard the chop-chop-chop of an approaching helicopter.

32

A SHADOW FELL OVER KIT. SHE OPENED HER EYES TO FIND an old man in a yellow flannel shirt standing over her. She was too spent to even feel scared.

The man asked, "You okay?"

Was she? Kit sat up and looked around. Grant was lying in the grass near the back porch of the cottage, and Harvey lay motionless on the dock. She felt sad, but relieved to see Jacqueline's body floating in the water beside the dock. In the distance, she could hear something that sounded like an airplane. "I think so," she said.

The old man held out a very shaky hand and said, "It's good to see you again, Catherine."

Kit looked at the extended hand and began to shrink back. But she forced herself to look beyond the hand and into the eyes. From somewhere deep in her memory, something began to stir. She remembered those eyes, twinkling at her. "Doc?"

The old man smiled and asked, "You remember me?"

With a nod, Kit slowly put her hand into his.

Doc Daggert helped her to her feet.

Kit looked over at her sister's body floating face-down beside the dock. She said, "I killed her."

Doc put his arm around her shoulder and said, "No, honey, she did herself in. I saw the whole thing from out there on the water. You were unbelievably brave today."

Kit nodded. Then she looked up at the little lake house with the yellow trim. It had given her all the answers she needed about her past. But it had also taken away everything from her future.

Kit walked over to where Grant lay on the sandy ground beside the back porch. She knelt down beside him and rolled him over onto his back. He looked incredibly peaceful, and she couldn't see any sign of blood from the shots Jacqueline had fired at him.

Tears burned in her throat, but she knew what she had to say. She brushed them away and said, "Grant Osgood, I...I..."

The words got stuck in her throat. She bent down and laid her head on his chest. The steady beat of his heart startled her. She sat up with a gasp and said, "Oh, please God, let him live!"

Grant opened his eyes, lifted his head, and asked, "You believe in prayer now?"

Kit exclaimed, "I thought you were dead!"

He grinned at her and said, "I figured if you can fool a bear into thinking that you're dead, it might work on a crazy woman with a gun."

She slugged Grant hard in the arm. "You just laid there and did nothing to help me? She nearly killed me!"

"No," he said, "I laid there, because I knew that if you thought I was dead, it would make you so mad, you'd do something to defend yourself."

Grant sat up and wrestled Kit down to the ground. Rolling her over onto her back, he leaned over her.

She looked into his sky blue eyes and said, "Grant Osgood, I—"

He lowered his head. His lips were a fraction of an inch from hers. She could feel his breath on her lips. "You what?" he asked.

Warmth radiated through her entire body, and her heart began thumping erratically. Kit had never wanted any man before. Why did Grant Osgood have to be the first? She couldn't stop herself...she reached up to entwine her fingers in his wavy hair. Their lips met, and it took away Kit's breath.

Grant lifted his head and looked into her eyes. "You were saying..."

Kit felt transfixed by those sparkling blue eyes that had always annoyed her. She had to do something. This was Grant Osgood...the pest she had promised herself she would shake off at the first opportunity. She shoved him aside and said, "Grant Osgood, I...I...I want you to take me back to Cincinnati."

Grant stood and held out a hand to help her to her feet. With a smile tugging at the corners of his mouth, he asked, "Your place or mine?"

Kit didn't know whether to slug him or kiss him. She said, "Neither. I want you to take me straight to my psychiatrist's office."

"You want to talk about your family?" he asked.

"No, I want to talk about you," she said. "I must be losing my mind... I'm actually beginning to like you."

33

"HARVEY," A VOICE WAS SAYING, "CAN YOU HEAR ME?"

Harvey opened his eyes to find Grant Osgood kneeling beside him. He lifted his head and looked around. Jacqueline Corbett was floating face-down in the water, and Kit was standing at the end of the dock with Doc Daggert. "What happened?" he asked.

Grant said, "Jacqueline just about did you in. Kit stopped her."

Kit approached and asked, "Are you okay?"

"I think so," he said, sitting up. Now, he felt like he'd been bitten by a bear that had wrestled him underwater. He looked over at Jacqueline Corbett. He was still having trouble believing that she was his sweetheart, Annabelle. How could she have changed so much? He looked up at Kit and said, "You saved my life."

Kit shrugged. "I did what I had to. She was going to kill you."

Harvey said, "I don't understand why she would want to."

Kit said, "She would have killed anybody to keep the secret about what happened at the Lakeshore Inn quiet."

"What happened?"

Kit looked over at Grant, shoved her hands into her jacket pockets, and then said, "She and Eric killed our parents, because our dad was molesting us, and our mother didn't believe it. She killed Peter to keep him quiet and then tried to shoot me. But I ran away. Then they burned down the Lakeshore Inn and paid off Ron Frank to keep it quiet."

Harvey couldn't believe it. So many people had been hurt by Annabelle's decision to take matters into her own hands. He wished she had confided in him all those years ago. He would have helped her. He shook his head and muttered, "Judas Priest. That's terrible." He looked up at Doc and asked, "How'd you end up out here?"

Doc said, "When I found Jet dead and my files missing, I went out on the lake with one of the guys from the reservation to try to find this place. I figured the killer might come here."

Grant asked Harvey, "Can I do anything for you?"

"Yeah," Harvey said, "Get Oona on the phone."

Grant said, "My cell's toast. It got wet out there in the woods."

Doc Daggert stepped forward and held out a cell phone. "Use mine."

Harvey was surprised. "You've got a cell?"

"Who doesn't these days?" Doc asked.

Harvey took the phone from Doc's hand and dialed Oona's cell number. When Oona answered, she said, "Doc?"

"No, it's Harvey," he said, "Kit, Grant, and I are all okay."

"Thank God!" Oona said. "Is Doc with you?"

"Yeah."

"He's not the Fishing Lure Killer," Oona said.

"That's a relief," Harvey said. Then he added, "Can you do me a favor?"

"What?"

"Order me a cell phone. I don't ever want to leave home without one again."

Oona laughed and said, "Done."

EPILOGUE
Five Years Later

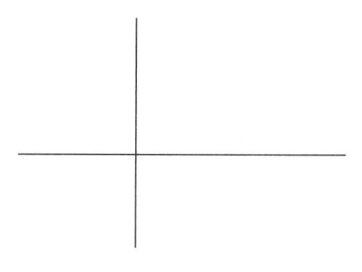

KIT LEANED FORWARD AT THE END OF THE DOCK, EVERY muscle in her body tensed. When she heard the gunshot, she sprang into the water. With broad strokes, she cut through the murky green water of Heron Lake. From behind her, she could hear shouting. She kicked powerfully toward the north end of the lake.

Within a short time, her fingers grazed the sand beneath her, and she realized that she was nearing the shore. With one last hearty stroke, she leaped to her feet and charged up the bank toward the newly rebuilt Lakeshore Inn.

Grant held out her running shoes and shouted, "You're in first place!"

Kit scrambled into her socks and shoes, gave Grant a quick kiss, and sprinted off down the walking trail that now circled the lake.

From behind her came a shrill laugh, followed by, "You'd better keep on running!"

Kit glanced back to see Sophie Ianelli charging after her.

Kit focused on the blacktop path and ran faster.

A well-recognized voice called out from the sidelines, "Run, Mommy!"

Determination seized Kit, and she shot off onto the trail that led into the woods. Her shoes pounded over sharp rocks and broken hickory nuts, but they couldn't hurt her. After a while, her legs grew so weary that all she wanted to do was sit down and rest. Her tongue stuck to the roof of her mouth, but she didn't want to stop. No matter what it took, she would make sure that she finished first.

She never glanced over her shoulder to see whether or not her competitors were catching up. She leaped onto her bicycle at the south end of the lake and pedaled hard toward town. Her legs felt like spaghetti, but with each revolution of the pedals, she said to herself resolutely, "Slow and sure…slow and sure…slow and sure…"

She hurtled around the corner onto Second Street. From the front porch of his refurbished Victorian house, Harvey Trent shouted, "Go, Kit!"

As she whizzed towards the finish line on Main Street in Moose Creek, all of her friends were cheering her on. She flew past Paul Bunyan's General Store, where Benny, Oona and Ralph were chanting, "Kit! Kit!" Fred and Mike Ianelli waved little flags as she sailed past Swenson's Bakery.

She burst through the yellow tape in front of City Hall and braked hard. Leaping from her bike, she gave a triumphant shout. The crowd enveloped her, and Kit hugged everyone within reach.

When the mayor slipped a ribbon around her neck with a gold medallion on it, she felt satisfied that all those years of running had finally paid off. She wasn't running away from her fears anymore. She was running for the future of Moose Creek, which would benefit from the annual Labor Day triathlon that brought swarms of people to town.

Her eyes met Grant's, and she waved to him. He lifted up their daughter in his arms so that she could see Kit. Their happy faces brought a smile to hers.

The crowd applauded, and Kit quietly thanked God for helping her discover all that she had among the ashes that Annabelle created. What her sister had meant for evil, God turned into something incredibly good.

Photo by Spring Olmsted

About the Author

Cheryl Denton is a former book and magazine editor who now writes both fiction and non-fiction to entertain, inspire, and encourage her readers. She lives in a little cottage at a lake with her husband, Chaplain Joe Denton. Register online at **www.cheryldenton.com** for more information about the author, upcoming books, e-books, events, and PTSD.

A portion of the profits from this book will be donated to women who have survived abuse or trauma.